RACE FOR THE GOLDEN TIDE

By the Gordons

RACE FOR THE GOLDEN TIDE
NIGHT AFTER THE WEDDING
ORDEAL
CATNAPPED!
THAT DARN CAT (reissue of UNDERCOVER CAT)
THE INFORMANT
THE TUMULT AND THE JOY
NIGHT BEFORE THE WEDDING
UNDERCOVER CAT PROWLS AGAIN
POWER PLAY
UNDERCOVER CAT
MENACE
OPERATION TERROR
TIGER ON MY BACK
CAPTIVE
THE BIG FRAME
THE CASE OF THE TALKING BUG
CASEFILE: FBI
CAMPAIGN TRAIN
FBI STORY
MAKE HASTE TO LIVE
THE LITTLE MAN WHO WASN'T THERE

FOR THE DORR CLAN

Diana, Ken, Sabrina and Don,
Pauline, Jennifer and John

Strange the world about me lies,
Never yet familiar grown,
Still disturbs me with surprise,
Haunts me like a face half known.

Sir William Watson

ABOUT THE BACKGROUND . . .

Our research happily took us to all the places our people traveled in this book. (We don't like to call our people by that stereotyped literary designation, *characters,* since in the writing they do become friends—and adversaries—who live on in our lives long after the book is forgotten.)

Our research also involved calling up memories, not always pleasant, of spies and intrigue one of us had known firsthand.

Our research took us, too, to one of the most exciting works we've ever read, *Exploring the Deep Frontier: The Adventure of Man in the Sea,* by Sylvia A. Earle and Al Giddings, and published by the National Geographic Society. From it we gleaned much information and more importantly, a feel for one of the last frontiers in the history of man.

We must admit that the people in this book did bend slightly a few facts here and there, a sin that we as writers, of course, would never commit.

RACE FOR THE GOLDEN TIDE

1

TUBAC, ARIZONA

Until that night, Lynne Kennedy had never been caught up in a dangerous situation. Like most women, she had wondered and thought seriously about what she would do if a man tried to mug or rape her or threatened to kill her. Shc couldn't imagine it happening to her. But no woman ever did, did she?

Nevertheless, in recent weeks she had taken certain precautions. She looked inside her 100,000-mile Porsche before getting in, and once in, locked it. She had dead bolts installed on all the doors, inside and out, of her condominium in Tucson. She took a three-hour course in the use of a tear-gas "gun," and at all times carried the weapon. She knew a purse attracted muggers but thought hers was not a likely prospect. It was expandable, with four sections, each jammed with correspondence, reports and other papers relating to her work as an oceanographer. Her boss, Greg Wilson, had once asked if she had it indexed. He called it a lethal weapon.

This night she had shut herself off in Greg's back office of the old, one-story adobe building in Tubac, Arizona, that housed the Carson Mining Company. She had a highly technical report to get out describing her findings in the Truk Lagoon off the Caroline Islands where U.S. air raids during a two-day blitz in February 1944 sank sixty Japanese ships. More importantly, she needed to write up her work on a narrow ocean plateau about 3,000 feet deep between the Mariana Islands and the Mariana Trench. The Trench itself dropped to 36,198 feet, the world's deepest point.

She felt comfortable locked away on this cool April night in this musty cocoon with its brightly colored, floral Mexican tile floor, beamed ceiling, old massive door with a heavy, reassuring bolt, and a hand-rubbed desk of the 1890s that had been shipped from Boston around South America's Cape Horn. An *Ojo de dios* —Eye of God—looked down on her. It was a Mexican Indian talisman of colored yarns woven around sticks. Overhead a piñata floated, a papier-mâché work that children at Christmas time would smash for the assorted goodies stuffed inside. Often it was in the shape of a donkey, but this time, that of Superman. Time changed everything, even the piñatas.

A few minutes before midnight she heard water running. In this office, one could hear the water if it were turned on anywhere in the building.

Yet she was alone. That is, she thought she was.

She switched off the electric typewriter and the lights and sat very still. The night had a dead, strange quiet. It was as if there was no life out there and never would be. The clock began its long, seemingly studied boom announcing midnight. She wanted to scream at it to shut up.

The water ran not more than a minute and was turned off with a twist that rattled the pipes. She stepped to the lone window that was set eight inches deep in an adobe wall. The desert beyond, up to the mountains in the distance, shimmered in nearly full moonlight and was as indistinct and beautiful as a Japanese print. Nothing moved out there. Nothing visible to the human eye.

She chided herself for the first quick surge of fear. It was unlike her. She was made of sturdier material, a logical, reasoning person. There was a simple explanation. On the building side that fronted a sandy road, there was a faucet. Over it Greg had put up a small sign so reminiscent of old Western hospitality, "Help yourself." Roped to the pipe was a battered tin cup, circa 1900. Hikers, tourists and others did help themselves. A few feet away was another sign, the letters burned into a slab of wood by a branding iron: Carson Mining Company, 1883. The sign was flanked by two huge hand-wrought iron lamps. Below the one on the right grew a giant sahuaro cactus pockmarked with holes drilled by woodpeckers setting up condominium units.

Turning the lights back on, she dialed the Emergency number. Tubac, 50 miles south of Tucson, numbered about 350 persons and dated far back. Shortly after Father Francisco Eusebio Kino established a mission at nearby Tumacacori in 1691, Tubac became a mission farm. In 1752 the Spaniards built a fort, the Presidio de San Ygnacio del Tubac. Not so many years later—in 1776—it landed in the history books when one of its presidio captains, Juan Batista de Anza, led a party of 234 on a land trek through hostile Indian country to found San Francisco.

"Thought I'd let you know, Ruth, I'm working late tonight," Lynne told the operator. ". . . about two hours more . . . I don't mind. You don't when you've got a boss like mine."

Hanging up, she regretted the last statement. She must be more careful. It could be misconstrued. For that matter, she must forcibly eject Greg Wilson from her fantasies. Here she was twenty-nine, almost thirty, and a scientist, and she still had the romantic dreams of a teenager. Only now the dreams were X-rated.

Around Greg, for three years now, she had been most discreet. She had been and was overly businesslike, a brilliant, experienced and highly talented expert in mining the ocean floor, sought after by every corporation engaged in this modern-day gold rush.

So she was all of this, a scientist who had worked twelve and fourteen hours a day since high school, foregoing dances and dates and good times to get where she was. While the ocean was her first and true love, she was a woman, too. She wanted a husband at home and a couple of children, a boy and a girl, to worry about her when she dived hundreds of feet down into a dark, unknown world, as much an explorer as any astronaut.

The trouble was, Greg Wilson was married. He had a stunning, vivacious and intelligent wife, Barbara. No one could help but admire her. She had the figure of a model. Lynne was tall and lank. Barb's quick mind could race through a problem. Lynne had the slow, analytical approach of the scientist. Barb could meet people easily, get them to talking, and they would spill out their life stories. Lynne was friendly and outgoing, too, but reserved. Without meaning to, she hid some of herself from others.

She must get off a note to Barb. For two months, Barb had been in University hospital in Tucson recovering from a head-on collision on I-10. She had suffered a broken wrist, a torn knee ligament, many lacerations and internal injuries. Barb's doctor barred visitors. He said she was too weak to see friends.

She resumed her report. Here in Greg's office, she felt close to him. He was all about her. A wall hanging: "If you can't say it in 10 words, don't say it." Ken Dorr's photographic masterpiece, "Grand Canyon." Greg went there every year. It was his Mecca. There was also a small picture of Greg in a T-shirt with printing across his broad chest that read: PADDLE CAPTAIN. It dated from his years running tourists down the Middle Fork of the Salmon River in Idaho.

On the desk top: a baby shoe in bronze, Laura's. Laura was their daughter, now twelve. Alongside it, a bronze shoe, 13D in size. His. One of Barb's little jokes. A paperweight of quartz streaked with gold. A reminder of the day he quit river-running to take over Carson Mining, to rescue it from bankruptcy and turn it into the most successful gold producer in the nation next to Homestake Mining.

Another paperweight, a nodule of manganese from the Pacific Ocean floor south of the Hawaiian Islands. Another milestone. The present one. If he could beat out some of the world's greatest corporations—a few backed with unlimited funds by their governments—if he could start mining the ocean floor first . . . down there were deposits of nodules containing manganese, cobalt, copper, nickel and other industrial metals sufficient to last the Western powers for a thousand years . . . if he could do that, he would go down in the history books.

Thinking about it, she shuddered. It was another Klondike, only this time the stakes were in the billions. The same as before, men would kill over disputed rights and governments fight wars.

Greg was not daunted. She doubted if he knew the gamble he was taking, the risks involved. He considered it one more Mt. Everest, and he was too busy climbing to step to one side and see himself objectively, and the ruthless opposition lying in wait, and the vagaries of nature that often punished man for his trespassing.

The marvelous thing was that she was a part of it, the exacting preparation, the filming of the Pacific's undersea mountains, valleys and plateaus, the excitement of developing new technology, and the adventure that was to come when the Carson ship, the *Marco Polo*, put to sea.

She was Greg's technical brains. She sat in on all the Board meetings. He never made a major decision without a report from her. With underwater movie cameras, she had mapped large areas of the Pacific floor and knew where the Comstock lodes were.

It was all the culmination of long ago back in Long Beach, California, when her father taught her to swim at four. At ten they were scuba diving at Malibu and farther up the coast at Carrillo Beach, named after Leo Carrillo, the actor.

They lived, the two of them, in an old apartment house on Chestnut Avenue. When she was nine, her mother had run off with a man and they never heard from her. Lynne didn't mind. She still thought her father, now dead, was the most remarkable man who ever lived. He fixed boats and it didn't matter what the problem was, he solved it.

Weekends they were in the water. She romanticized that they were the embodiment of the father-daughter team of Scyllias and Cyana who in the fifth century B.C. had swum through a raging Aegean sea to loosen the anchors of Persian ships spearheading the invasion of Greece.

In her freshman year at Polytechnic High School, a gym instructor suggested she try out for the Olympic swim team. Somehow her father scraped up the money for her to study under Dick Jochums, the best swim coach in the world. She cried all night when he told her a few weeks later that she had no chance. Her father then urged her to take up oceanography. At twenty-four she got her doctorate from the University of Hawaii.

When she reported for her first expedition, the other scientists and crew didn't know what to make of her. The second day she told them, "I'm not a female when I'm down there. I'm a sea creature, another kind of dolphin. I think differently, react differently. I have to. It's a different world."

This was the kind of logic they understood, and they accepted her as a sea creature. She dived in Hawaii 300 feet deep for "shocks" of black coral and down to 1,000 feet off Molokai for the pink coral known as angel skin. She explored the Aleutian Trench, descended to the Tuamotu Archipelago and filmed along the Galapagos Rift. She followed in the wet footsteps of Jacques Yves Cousteau and the fabulous Al Giddings, whose camera developments revolutionized deep-sea filming. And her heroine was Dr. Sylvia Earle, who had explored most of the undersea world.

Her reputation was such that when a half score companies plunged into the race to mine the ocean bottoms she was the oceanographer they wanted. Canada's International Nickel and Japan's Mitsubishi in addition to Tenneco and Carson in the United States bid for her. Others in various stages of preparation included Russia, which it was rumored had a ship, the *Kharkov*, about to sail out of Vladivostok, Great Britain's Rio Tinto Zinc, a West German conglomerate, a Dutch one, and in the United States, Kennecott. Their common goal was the Pacific Ocean since its floor was littered with more nodules than other waters.

She was too much of a scientist ever to admit, even to herself, that she went with Carson because of the charisma of Greg Wilson. She had never known any man like him. He had varied strengths: tempered vision and boyish enthusiasm, an openness that held nothing back, an easy way of tackling problems and crises, and yes—to be honest—a tremendous male physical appeal. He was a big man, standing six-foot-three, and broad of shoulder but not of beam. He wore his jeans tight, his boots polished, and his Western shirts open at the collar. On formal occasions he put on a bola tie. He was tanned as an Indian. He had a smile as big as his frame. She was soon to discover, though, that behind the easy-going facade was a hard hitter, determined and driven.

At the second interview, he told her while pacing behind his desk—he seldom sat when talking, "We need an oceanographer and an operations officer combined and we'll pay accordingly. Someone like you who knows the technical end but is also smart enough to function on land and keep it all working when we get it together. Another thing, we're sort of like a family here. Not a happy family by a damn sight, but when the thunderbolt hits we pull together. That's important to me. About as important as knowing what we're doing. We've got wolves out there just waiting—they'll offer you anything . . ."

She was a little angry. "I don't sell out, Mr. Wilson."

"They'll threaten you."

"I don't scare."

He laughed. "I like you. You're my kind of man."

"I'd like it better if you'd said I was your kind of person."

"I'm a male chauvinist and proud of it. I open car doors for women and expect them to get in without bitching about it."

"I'll remember that. I don't like it, but I'll remember."

"Just so we understand each other. One more thing. I run Carson Mining. I *am* Carson Mining. If you want a big company with a lot of people, go with Tenneco or Mitsubishi."

They often collided. Both were outspoken. She was precise, exacting. That bothered him. He detested neatness. His desk resembled a rubbish dump. Every Monday morning he cleared it by opening a drawer and sweeping it all in. "A clean desk is the sign of a sick mind," he would say.

If she had a problem, she broke it down into component parts, studied them and reached a solution. He was impatient, restless. He solved problems on impulse, by what he called "a gut feeling."

Despite her reserve, she loved people. The more the better. He was a loner. His only friends were his wife, daughter and a German police dog named Rambunctious. There were those at Carson Mining who said the dog came first. He accompanied Greg everywhere. He sat beside him in the white Camaro Z28. He spent the day in the office and if anyone idly wandered behind Greg's desk, Rambunctious let out a growl so savage it would instill fear in a Mafian godfather. Once she almost said, "Either that dog goes or I do." Just in time she held back the words. She knew what the answer would be.

As she typed, a faint woodpeckerlike sound crept into her hearing. It was almost inaudible, and she didn't trust her ears until she switched off the typewriter. She sat immobile, her heart quickening, debating what to do.

She turned the typewriter back on, in case anyone was checking on her, then stared a long moment out the window. The desert was too well lighted for anyone to be standing there. She edged her way to the phone and dialed. Midway she stopped. Ruth would immediately notify the Santa Cruz sheriff's office at Nogales on the Mexican border twenty-seven miles to the south. Lynne couldn't have a deputy driving that distance only to find a shutter banging in the breeze or a similar explanation. He would put her down as a hysterical woman. The idea galled her.

She slipped noiselessly to the door. Controlling her breathing, she listened intently and satisfied herself no one was on the other side. Slowly she pulled the bolt without a screech. As she edged the heavy door open, though, it groaned and she stood as still as a hound pointing. She had the door open a crack and could see into the courtyard. The building was laid out Spanish style around it.

A rhythmic click-click, now very pronounced, was coming from the receptionist's office across the way. Without more protests, the door opened wide enough to let her out. Now the full moon, which had been her friend, was her enemy. As she crossed the still-hot caliche of the courtyard, she had the feeling she was on stage, the focal point of a spotlight.

She made her way to a small, octagonal, stained-glass window that Greg had bought from an old church that was being demolished. One tiny section had broken and had been taped up. She pulled off the tape inch by inch until she had the broken pieces in hand. One glance inside the office and she was in shock. Behind the receptionist's desk was a small safe partly sunk in the adobe wall. It bore the date, 1892, and had been freighted, too, by a sailing ship around Cape Horn. A man—it was too dark to make out his age or looks—was chiseling into the adobe, to free the safe.

She shook off the shock, and thinking logically again, started to return to the office and the phone. She had taken no more than a couple of steps when she heard a man's voice. "Lady," he said. In whirling about to locate him, she dropped the pieces of glass. For a moment she couldn't find him, then saw him in the shadows of an overhang made from the skeleton stocks of the ocotillo cactus. He was some twenty feet away.

"Lady," he said quietly, as if to allay her fears, "come over here. We're not going to harm you. We won't even touch you if you do like I say. We've got to take you into safekeeping for an hour or two, and then we'll let you go."

She hadn't seen the gun before. His upper half was blocked out by a shadow. The gun, glistening in the moonlight, was dangling from a limp hand attached to a thin right arm swinging loosely by his side. His voice was not rough. Not cultured, either. An average man's speech. It had a commanding firmness, though, like her Uncle Ben's when she was a child. She heard it, and want to or not, had to obey.

Her mind shattered. For seconds magnified into minutes, she was a stunned animal incapable of response. The click of metal on metal, the hammer on the chisel, continued. Did the man inside know what was happening out here?

"Did you hear me, lady? Come over here. I don't want to rough you up. We're professionals. Burglars, not thugs."

Step by slow step, she walked toward him. She heard the loud crunch of her feet on the gravel, the open-mouthed breathing deep and jerky, the pounding of a heart about to burst its cage.

Waiting, he stood stock still. "Where'd you come from, lady? What're you doing around here this time of night?"

The gun never quivered, pointed still at the ground. A big silver belt buckle bounced moon rays about with every measured breath he took.

His eyes. She searched for them. Above the buckle, though, was only a black swatch.

She was thinking clearly now, and ten or eleven feet away she dragged her feet to a noisy halt. She dared not go on. She had expected him to explode, but there was only silence for her to gnaw on.

Minutes of nothing, it seemed, and then very slowly he emerged, as if he, too, were uncertain. His boots ground loudly as his awkward feet advanced him toward her.

His eyes were hooded, little more than slits, those of a desert breed burned by too much sun. He was an older man with a leathery wrinkled face.

The timing. She had to time it right. She had a sudden, terrifying feeling that the dangling gun was as much a part of him as his hand. One move, not more than one second in its sweep, and it could explode in her face.

Wait, wait, her reasoning screamed at her. Not yet, not yet.

Now, now. The thumb, flat on the top, pressed hard.

One eye, then the other, almost simultaneously. He let out a surprising, agonizing scream and doubled up, a fighter going down with a thud, the gun slipping to the ground. His knuckles worked feverishly to rub the tear gas out of his eyes. He was gasping for breath. "You damn little bitch! You damn bitch!"

She stood paralyzed, totally unbelieving she had done this. She never had before, had never seen the blinding, burning, traumatic effect.

Her thoughts gave her a hard jerk and she ran for the office. She stumbled, almost fell, but righted herself. Midway she heard an ugly shout, whirled about and saw a second man running toward her. She caught only a bare glimpse. In the full splash of the moon he appeared a carbon copy. Only he had a revolver aimed at her. She panicked and as she neared the door she heard the explosion, loud in the quiet night. Next she felt her right shoulder burning in a roaring fire, and there was an animal inside tearing the flesh apart.

Somehow she got through the door and threw the heavy bolt. She fell to the floor then, thinking she was fainting, but crawled, sobbing with pain, to the desk. As if far in the distance, she heard a tremendous force hit the door, a heavy body used as a battering ram. The door shuddered but the bolt held.

Her head was swimming and a blackness slowly dropping a curtain over her. With her left hand, she found the cord, and pulled, and the phone hit the floor with a horrendous bang.

Behind her a gun roared and the door shook as if in earthquake.

She was dropping off. No time at all now. She crawled inches—a mile it seemed—to the receiver. She managed to dial "O," then struggled to speak, her mouth near the phone, but couldn't. She was going out. Only a glimmer now, then the whisper came, "Carson Mining Company. A man—he's trying to kill me."

2

DUBĀ, THE UNITED ARAB EMIRATES

Nothing had gone right this day for Mike McGraw. The first blow came when the air-conditioner in his 1976 Oldsmobile quit.

The heat in Dubā, one of seven sheikdoms on the Arabian Gulf (called the Persian Gulf by the Iranians across the way and diplomatically The Gulf by the big foreign corporations), was one mark short of 120 degrees.

To make matters worse, he was in suit and tie, a combination he wore only under duress. The duress this Thursday was a cable from his employer, a think tank in Santa Monica, California, instructing him to confer immediately on a matter of great urgency with one Mr. Abercrombie of the U.S. State Department. McGraw had no idea why he was to meet this Mr. Abercrombie, and as one who had been in espionage work for eighteen years, fifteen with the CIA, he liked to be prepared. When he wasn't, the worst invariably happened. Like the time he had to swim the Mekong River at night fleeing from Laos under a hail of gunfire.

He had a simplistic view of the world. There were the good people and the evil ones, and a bullet was the quickest way of dispatching evil. He believed American justice was a travesty. He thought it ridiculous that prisons should be overcrowded. He liked the old Arab code. Hang a murderer in the town square for all to see and keep him hanging there until the vultures finished with him. Castrate child molesters and rapists. He remembered a small place in Yemen where they had publicly hacked off a man's penis. That had been ten years ago and not a single crime of a sexual nature had been committed since.

He knew he shocked people. Back home in Abilene, Texas, his wife, Sally, begged him not to talk that way when they were out. He tried not to, but there were times when friends got to discussing the crime situation and he exploded. Later, when they got home, Sally would cry a little. He would beg her forgiveness and later they would make love.

For the children's sake, if no other, he must watch how he talked. Jane, who was fifteen, and Robert, twelve, and Johnny, ten, thought he was greater than Superman. One of the fringe benefits of his job, more important to him than the money even, was their love. He wrote them every week and sent so many gifts the house resembled a museum.

Just thinking about them, he wished he were home. Why was he in this Godforsaken place? Yet when he was home he was restless. He knew this and couldn't completely explain it to himself.

He had to admit he was truly happy only when he was in a killing situation, either stalking someone or being stalked.

He had met Sally in high school in their senior year. He had dated only a few girls. He had been too busy working as a roustabout summers in the oil fields, smoking marijuana and drinking. She had changed all that. He gave up alcohol and marijuana when she threatened to leave him. Once out of high school he had planned on staying in the oil fields since the pay was high. She persuaded him to go with her to Hardin-Simmons University where she tutored him nights when the going got rough. He was highly intelligent, but had never got around to doing much of anything. She organized him and he was graduated tenth in his class.

As he drove, he cursed this Mr. Abercrombie. In his years with the CIA—before he had been fired for his part in upsetting a Chilean government—he had tangled repeatedly with State. If Mr. Abercrombie intended to lecture him on interfering with U.S. foreign policy, he would walk out. He was a private citizen engaged in a private business and Mr. Abercrombie could go to hell.

He had been employed by the think tank to assess the mood and activities of the Palestinian population in the Emirates. In the majority of the sheikdoms, the Palestinians outnumbered the citizens. They were the workers, doing the hard jobs, earning money they sent to families in other Arab nations.

He had thought that Israel was the think tank's client, then discovered the Saudis were. The Saud family, which had ruled Saudi Arabia since 1932, was fearful that outside interests might attempt to engineer a coup of the nature that had befallen the Shah in Iran. The Saudis needed to know what the Palestinian activities were in the Emirates, Kuwait, Bahrain and other nearby states.

As McGraw dug deep with the help of several Arab and Palestinian informants, he discovered a plot by an assortment of interests—pro-Russian Palestinians and other Arabs, a few fanatics who hated various sheikhs, and a few politicians and soldiers of fortune who hoped to seize power. Within a day or two, McGraw would have their names. He was meeting an informant day after tomorrow who would bring a complete roster.

In an effort to escape the heat, he drove at furious speed up Airport Road, a wide, beautiful boulevard lined with fountains and monuments. He was drenched and his clothing plastered to the vinyl. As he neared Deira, the twin city of Dubā, he could see several Arab dhows floating calmly in The Creek. For centuries the scene had been the same. Now, though, the dhows, especially those used in the smuggling trade, were powered with Rolls-Royce diesel engines and armed with M-24 20mm cannons. They ran gold into India, cargoes of ten tola bars worth 20 to 40 million dollars, and carried contraband Sony television sets, Swiss watches and Japanese radios into such Iranian ports as Bandar 'Abbās, Mīnāb and Chāh Bāhar.

McGraw stopped at the Bandar Taleb branch of the First National City Bank where two armed guards outside and two inside, tall giants, looked him over and watched as he approached a teller's window. He offered a check to the teller, a tall, stunning-looking, slender, black-haired woman in her mid-twenties.

He whispered, "Six o'clock?"

"Seven," she whispered back. She didn't look up, counted out the money.

She was Odette, a French citizen who had come to Dubā with her father, a petroleum engineer, and stayed on after his death. Tomorrow, Friday, was the Moslem Sabbath and a day off, and she and McGraw planned to motor seventy-five miles through three Emirates to the village of Ra's al Khaymah. There a fabulous hotel sat on a strand of sand three hundred yards from the Gulf.

Neither had any illusions about their relationship. It was purely physical. Although they enjoyed being together, they were not and never would be lovers. She knew about Sally, and knew that when he left Dubā she would never hear from him. There had been others before him and there would be others after him. That was the way of her world in Dubā.

On his part he felt no guilt. Sally belonged to a world of homes, children, neighbors, churches, civic clubs and Texas. Then there was another world, far off lonely places in distant lands. Back home he would never think of having an affair. That would be infidelity.

On the second floor of the Petroleum building, the sign on the door read: Gulf Enterprises. McGraw smiled. Americans loved the word *Enterprises* when they wanted to conceal the nature of their business.

The receptionist was a blond Arab girl in a light but proper summer dress. She was expecting him and took him to a barren office two doors down the corridor.

She spoke excellent English. "Mr. Abercrombie will be with you in a very few minutes. He is on the telephone. I apologize that you have to wait."

He grinned. "Apology accepted." She laughed and left.

The bastard. He keeps everyone waiting. They do that at State to inflate their importance.

From the window he looked down on a blue-tiled mosque with alabaster white dome, and in the distance a lone camel drifting along a paved highway. At a slight sound he turned quickly. Mr. Abercrombie was what McGraw expected, mod from his styled hair to his Pucci shoes. He offered no greeting, and opening a dossier, spread it across the desk. That was State for you. They invariably carried a dossier. The FBI, a brief case, and the CIA, they acted as if they couldn't possibly belong to the CIA.

He looked up. "Mr. McGraw."

"A remarkable deduction," McGraw said slowly. He knew as many tricks as this Abercrombie when it came to throwing another off base.

Mr. Abercrombie was put out. "The Sheikh would have you deported if he knew the nature of your work."

McGraw took his time lighting a cigarette. "I doubt that."

"We will not debate the issue," Mr. Abercrombie said flatly. "You are a private citizen. You do not represent the United States in any manner."

McGraw waited. He could outwait this character. He had outwaited better men.

Mr. Abercrombie continued, "The Sheikh does not like to have crimes of violence committed in his Emirate. He would be most disturbed if there should be a homicide, especially if either party should be a foreigner. And that includes Americans."

"And the United States would not be disturbed?"

"I did not say or imply that, Mr. McGraw. I want the record clear on that point."

"Let the record show that you did not say or imply anything."

Mr. Abercrombie coughed a very small cough, as if he were ashamed of it. "I should not inject a personal note, but I myself would be most disturbed. We had an American die of natural causes a few weeks back. I cannot tell you how many papers I had to fill out . . . the trouble with moving the body."

He shook his head. The memory was overpowering.

McGraw discovered he was breathing heavily. "You trying to tell me somebody's going to be killed?"

Mr. Abercrombie handed him a passport-size photograph. McGraw studied it, a picture of a dark-skinned, dark-haired, sickly looking man in his early twenties. While he had a small but noticeable scar on his right ear, his well-trimmed beard gave him the look of a scholar.

McGraw's heart speeded up. He had seen that face somewhere. But where? He had been so many places, worked so many cases, met so many thousands.

"You know him?" Mr. Abercrombie asked.

McGraw said slowly, "I'm not sure. I've seen the face, but I can't place it. Who is he?"

"Rashid Jumeira." He read from the dossier. "Born in Damascus. Not far from the Street With No Name. Has worked for the KGB in Eritrea, Somalia, Ethiopia and Egypt. He's more of a hanger-on than an accredited agent. A scruffy individual."

McGraw walked to the window with his thoughts whirling about. "He's here in Dubā?"

Mr. Abercrombie nodded. "According to our intelligence. We don't have all the facts. We know he was sent here to kill you. But we don't know why. Your work would not indicate that anyone, especially the KGB, would put value on it. We at State are quite puzzled. However, I must not digress. I do hope that you leave Dubā as soon as possible. Perhaps tonight? I do not want to cause the Sheikh any undue anxiety and . . ."

". . . you would have all those papers to fill out." McGraw smiled. He had got himself under control, yet he was as puzzled as

Mr. Abercrombie about the reason this paid assassin was stalking him.

"You will leave Dubā?"

McGraw headed for the door. As he opened it, he turned. "I give you my word, Mr. Abercrombie, that I will leave Dubā." He paused a second. "Alive or dead."

The bedlam of evening traffic was horrendous. He pulled behind a Land-Rover and let the Brit driving it inch his way through. Since he had been in like situations many times, he had learned to discipline his thinking. One considered all the alternatives and chose the best. Sometimes there was no best. Sometimes it was a matter of guts and daring and quick movement, of outwitting the enemy. This time he had one serious handicap. He did not know the enemy.

For the moment he had no fear, since it was highly unlikely that this Rashid Jumeira would kill him in traffic on a busy street. Dubā was not the United States. The commission of murder was a far more reprehensible crime in an Arab country than in the Western world. An assassin would be put to death fairly quickly. Rashid Jumeira would know this and bide his time, and wait until he caught McGraw alone.

On his part, McGraw had few escape routes. They would be watching the airport and The Creek, and that left flight by car, which would be difficult. Although ribbons of roads wound off in all directions, to many places on the Gulf and to the other Emirates, they ran over flat sand and were little traveled. A car could be seen for miles. Eventually, too, the roads ran out.

He almost collided with a cart powered by a donkey and loaded with kegs of water; then a woman in stark black except for a white veil dashed in front of him, a wraith out of a ghost story. Overhead a sign loomed: MOTHERCAT, LTD. The Port Said cinema was still playing *Star Wars*.

While he could control his thinking, fear was an undercurrent moving slowly through mind and body. It reminded him subtly that while he had brushed death aside many times in many alien places, he might fail this time. It reminded him, too, of Sally and the children. Surely he wasn't going to die in this Godforsaken place so far from them. If he had to die, he wanted to be at home where he could tell them he loved them. Fear reminded him, also, that he had saved little money and they would be on their own. Sally would have the youngsters to put through college.

He pulled up before the Hotel Carlton. A fourteen-year-old in rags came darting out, screaming he could not leave the car there. He quieted when he saw it was Mr. McGraw, his best customer. McGraw gave him the usual dollar bill to guard the car.

In the entrance he collided with an Italian woman. Apologizing, he stooped to pick up her purse. He hurried on into the lobby where Germans, English, Japanese, French, Italians and Americans were coming and going. In both Western and traditional garb were Saudis, Lebanese, Egyptians, Syrians, Pakistanis and others from the Moslem world. They were principally business men, financiers, technicians and construction experts.

At the desk he asked for messages and mail, but there was nothing. As he turned about, he came to an abrupt stop. Sitting not more than eight feet away was Rashid Jumeira. He glanced up from a paperback he was reading, then without a sign of recognition returned to it. He was in an easy chair, back in the shadows. McGraw's first thought was: In that light he cannot be reading. He was suited, in white shirt and narrow black tie that contained an old-fashioned diamond stick pin. He didn't look sickly. He did look insignificant. Meeting him one would say a pleasantry and then turn to others.

To gain time to think, McGraw bought a copy of the Paris-published *International Herald Tribune.* He fought off his first appraisal, that someone had chosen a weak sister. Rashid could be weak—his pale blue eyes certainly were—but the response of a bullet was the same regardless of who fired it.

McGraw sat only a few minutes, and made no pretense of reading. He considered such ploys the mark of an amateur. Then he went to a phone booth that had a good view of the young Syrian and was protected by the flow of foot traffic to and from the reception desk. Twice during the six or seven minutes he talked, Rashid glanced up. Then McGraw returned to his chair, visibly satisfied with the telephone conversation.

One fact was certain. McGraw dared not go upstairs to his

room. The young Syrian might follow or an accomplice could be waiting. Fact number two was evident, too. As long as McGraw sat in the lobby he was safe. Fact number three: He could not stay here indefinitely.

In the hour that followed, Rashid turned few pages. McGraw could see that it was an old Agatha Christie novel, rather tame fare for a hired assassin. He reminded McGraw of a lizard. He sat absolutely immobile, and seemingly, had no need to breathe.

Glancing at his watch, McGraw straightened. Five minutes more and his plot would begin to unfold. He saw no possibility that it could go wrong, yet he knew from long experience that the unforeseen has a dramatic and sometimes fatal way of injecting itself into the most carefully laid plans. Robert Burns had said something like that, hadn't he?

Before he left, he had to remember where he had seen Rashid Jumeira. Once more, he went over every country in which he had served, and ran the cases down in chronological order. The result was maddening. He couldn't find a clue. The man obviously had not been cast in the role of a killer or McGraw would remember. He had to be an extra somewhere in a cast of hundreds.

Odette, breathing hard and her face sweat streaked, was the first to arrive. He rose, frightened. "I told you not to come."

"I had to."

"Where are they?"

"Outside."

Suddenly the lobby was deserted, and even the desk clerk had his back to them. McGraw put his arm about her, as if he could protect her, and they half ran for the door, stumbling as feet got in each other's way. In one swift last glance, he saw Rashid Jumeira hurrying after them. His long strides were bringing him ever closer.

They were outside then and six huge stevedores closed about them. Three were Senegalese giants, probably the most perfect specimens of physical man on earth; the others, blacks from the Sudan. With the two in the center, they moved in unison down the street toward The Creek. They gained speed until they were half running. They formed a phalanx that brushed people aside, caused cars to swerve out of their way, and brought whistles from traffic officers. Nothing on God's earth could have stopped them.

"I didn't want him to see you," he shouted above the traffic noise.

"I don't care," she answered. "I've got a dhow moving out at midnight for Zanzibar. The captain will see that you get to Dar es Salaam, and I'll make a plane reservation for you to New York. Okay?"

"Okay," he yelled.

At the dhow she grabbed and kissed him hard. The stevedores stared in amazement. A Muslim woman would never do that.

One Senegalese picked him up as if he were a toy and put him on the dhow.

She called up, "If you're this way again, look me up, will you? I'll be around."

She turned before the tears showed and walked swiftly away from The Creek.

3

KĀBUL, AFGHANISTAN

General Dmitri Schepnov, who had arrived only the week before to take over the gathering of intelligence in Afghanistan for the KGB, wandered slowly along the dirty, stinking Kābul river in the heart of the nation's capital. Women were washing, a couple of boys had stripped to bathe and a dead pig, unnoticed, floated by. Somewhere from far off came the Moslem cry, "*Allah-o-Akbai!*" ("God is great!").

He had a date in a half hour to meet a young Afghan who could be setting him up for assassination or could be bringing information, as he had promised, about a plan by the rebels to blow up the Salang highway tunnel. The sixty-six-mile highway ran through the Hindu Kush mountains, connecting the Soviet border with Kābul. If the tunnel were destroyed, the vital flow of troops and supplies by land would be cut off.

The General was sixty-three, tall and gray-haired, with weathered brown skin and the cold eyes of a cellar rat. He was corseted and held his shoulders as erect as if they had been cast in metal. He was tense; he never relaxed, not with friends, his late wife or himself.

He was dressed now as an army captain, his uniform creased and boots polished. For that matter, he never had been a general. In his youth he had played one in a propaganda film that had caught the attention of the Politburo. In thirty-odd years with the KGB, the title had stuck.

In his imagination he was still an actor. He never missed an American Western when he was in a country showing such fare. He reveled in heroes stalking forth at high noon with their guns bursting fire, jumping into saddles from second floors, racing to save the heroine and taking on a bar full of gunslingers or a hundred savage Indians. If only he could have been at Stalingrad and led the breakout from the Nazi encirclement.

He leaned against a concrete wall on the river bank. People hurried uneasily past him. These were a big people, towering giants of brawny, mountain men. Some had long, curved knives fastened to their waist bands. Many were in Western dress but many, too, were in shirt jackets that fell to their knees, baggy trousers and wrap-around turbans with one end dangling down the back.

He knew what the bastards were thinking. He could tell by the quick shift of guilty eyes. They would conquer the Russians the same as they had all the others, all the invaders who had come through here on their way to the Khyber Pass one hundred miles eastward, the gateway to central Asia.

Carefully, he took them all in, the entire street scene. To miss the smallest detail could result in quick death. He had three KGB back-up men whom he had doubts about. They were new to this strange country, as he was. It wasn't the same as when he had headed up Intelligence in Nasser's Egypt where the Russians had been welcomed or in Hanoi during the Vietnam War, or Angola or mainland China during the years of friendship with that nation.

A boy across the street, in a white skull cap, was selling tomatoes from a rickety wooden stand. Another boy passed by walking alongside a donkey with a bell collar. Then he spotted a commotion in a lone tree diagonally across the street. His heart quickened. Three scraggly boys were sitting on limbs watching the scene below.

He gestured slightly to indicate the boys to the nearest KGB agent. He feared children. The first thing native terrorists did was to train the children to throw grenades and plastic bombs. The most lovable child could be more dangerous than a sniper. And while you lay there dying, she would be jumping about clapping her hands and laughing and calling to her friends to come and see what she had done.

He had killed many times. He could not remember how many because the years and faces tended to blur, but he never had taught a child to kill—and never would. That would be the ultimate sin.

For many months now, the Soviets had been in Afghanistan, a primitive, mountainous country the size of Texas with no railroads, no navigable rivers and a population of about 21 million. At first they had maintained a low profile, staying in compounds they hastily constructed. They had sent in paratroopers to support a coup, which resulted in the execution of the president, Hafizullah Amin, and his family. They had named a Communist to take over the government, one Babrak Karmal.

Karmal quickly found himself in serious trouble—so serious that Moscow had to funnel in upwards of 100,000 soldiers who could not be hidden. With their T-62 tanks, armored vehicles and helicopters belching gunfire, they had spread over the countryside. Soon they realized that the most they could hope for in the immediate future was the control of the capital, a few other towns and the very few roads the nation had. Unlike in other countries the Soviets had "visited," the Afghans were fighters.

Often this past week the General had thought to himself that the military should have read the history books better. Others had come this way to discover the going rough: Alexander the Great,

Genghis Khan and Baber "The Tiger," a descendant of Tamerlane.

But then the army had probably never heard of Baber, an excellent writer and military strategist. The military was stupid and arrogant, and so was the KGB. Their egos defeated them. They thought they could conquer Afghanistan in a few weeks. They consistently underestimated the enemy. Not that the General was not a patriot. He loved the Motherland dearly and would die for it. He did his job, did it well, and had never failed.

He might this time. He had arrived to find Intelligence in complete disarray, although he could scarcely blame his predecessor. The guerrilla movement consisted of splinter groups, motivated by strong spiritual fervor, which operated independently of each other. Like the Indians of America's Old West, they would sally forth from their mountain retreats and strike at a small contingent of Russians, perhaps try to knock out a tank or bring down a helicopter gunship with a World War I Lee-Enfield rifle.

The General's problems were many. He couldn't plant a spy in every little group, even if he had that many agents. As it was, he had no more than six. He knew he would have a difficult time recruiting more since the Afghan people overwhelmingly opposed the occupation.

So the General welcomed what might be a stroke of luck—or a trap. He had risen the third day at his usual time, about four, and taken his exercise. No matter where he went, he took along gymnastic equipment. He placed his feet on a flat piece of plywood imbedded with two large hooks. To these hooks he fastened springs which he pulled up with each hand simultaneously.

Although he had been warned against venturing forth alone, he set out for a brisk walk. He climbed the rounded hill that Fort Jabakhana sits upon, found the tomb of Baber, and passed the University of Kābul. He noted signs in English as well as Pushto: SINGH STORE—CLOTH MERCHANT, SOLIGOR—FINE LENSES, and NATIONAL CLINIC. These would have to come down and be replaced by ones in Pushto and Russian.

He was returning to his quarters in the Soviet Embassy when he was accosted by a young Afghan who was clean shaven, with bushy hair, and wearing a good dark blue Western suit with the coat buttoned.

He said quickly, "My friend, please to stop. You busy but I help you." Although his vocabulary was limited, he spoke Oxford English. The General himself spoke fluent English, as he did French, German, Spanish and Italian, together with a smattering of Chinese, Egyptian and Vietnamese. He prided himself on never having lived in a country without learning the language. He had set himself the goal now of getting to know conversational Pushto, spoken by the Duranis who numbered more than 70 percent of all Afghans. The Duranis were a strange people. They boasted they were descendants of Jews who in 557 B.C. had been captured by the Chaldean king, Nebuchadnezzar II of Babylon. Yet they were Moslems of the Sunni sect. While calling themselves "the Sons of Israel," they worshiped Allah.

The General's right hand slid furtively inside his jacket to a revolver anchored in the belt. His forefinger slipped lightly about the trigger. He was an excellent marksman. In recent years he had twice outdrawn killers who thought a man around sixty would be no match.

The young man continued, "My name Knox. Fort Knox." He smiled. "American gave me name. I sell money."

He opened his coat to disclose all kinds of bills pinned inside: U.S. dollars, Indian rupees, Burma kyats, Nepalese rupees, German marks, Swiss francs, Russian rubles, Iranian rials and Sri Lanka rupees. "You want Russian money? Much cheaper. You go Nepal on holiday . . ."

The General shrugged and started on. These kids . . . every country he went into, they had some kind of petty racket.

The youth continued. "Also, I have information. Good information."

The General took note of the restaurant across the way where an old man was standing at the door ladling soup out of a large tin bowl to customers with paper cups. It was a fast-food place, Afghan style.

He studied the Afghan carefully. "If you have grain to sell or textiles, I would be interested. Also, antiques. Information, no."

Knox took his time counting out Indian rupees, pretending he had made a sale. The General continued, "I am the consular officer at the Embassy in charge of trade."

Knox put a rubber band around the bills. "I give you small information. No charge. You know Salang road?"

The General nodded. "I know Salang road."

"The tunnel—how you say—explodes. Soon. Night."

The General stared, debating. "As a good Afghan citizen, loyal to his country, you must tell me about this. When?"

"Five hundred United States dollars."

The General faked anger. "You are a traitor."

"I am business man."

"I should call the police and have you shot."

Knox smiled, completely unfazed. "Five hundred dollars. No counterfeit. I know counterfeit."

"Two hundred."

"Four."

"Three."

The young man nodded. "When?" the General asked.

"I meet you two mornings . . ."

"Day after tomorrow. Here. Same time."

"Take rupees, please. Must look like sale made."

Accepting the packet, the General said slowly, accenting each word, "I will have you shot if this is a trap."

The young man smiled. "I kill you if you bring counterfeit money."

So now he waited, as he had waited many times, in other lands, in other situations where the possibility of death iced the blood. Thirty-three years and each one an eternity. He had seen comrades grow disillusioned and bitter. One could take only so much of the sordid, of double crosses and men killing for no more than Judas got, of weasels in powerful positions who used that power with no regard to life or suffering.

On his sixtieth birthday he had resigned from the KGB to fulfill a dream of many years. His wife was dead and also his two brothers and three sisters, but his daughter was alive as was her nine-year-old son whom he had seen only in snapshots. He went to live with them in their third-floor rooms at 32 Peace To All Mankind Street in Minsk. A walk-up, the front left corner.

When he entered the small, airless room, he knew he had made a grave mistake. The building smelled of too many people living in cramped quarters. His grandson was boisterous and unruly, and the rapport that might have been there if they had seen each other through the years was only in his mind. Too many years had passed, too, since he had last seen his daughter at her wedding before the civil magistrate. All these years he had kept her picture, that of a happy, laughing girl of innocence with black, silken hair falling down her back. Now she had grown old and suffered from the malaise that all Russia did, the knowledge that tomorrow would not be better, tomorrow would be more of the same, a gray, dark life growing a little grayer with time. She tolerated him only because he was her father.

He asked for his old job back and got it. Master Control needed him badly, if for no other reason than to set him up as a fall guy for the Intelligence failure Master Control anticipated in Afghanistan. He knew what Master Control was doing, the same as Master Control knew he knew. He extracted a promise he could choose his next assignment after Afghanistan and that they would send one Rashid Jumeira to Kābul. He needed a Moslem, one he could trust. He had worked with Rashid in Egypt those years when the Soviets were constructing the Aswan dam. Rashid had lied for him, protected him and killed for him.

Rashid, Master Control said, was on a case in Dubā. When his assignment was completed—and it should be soon—Master Control would order Rashid Jumeira to Kābul.

4

TUCSON, ARIZONA

As he hung up the phone, Greg Wilson heard the soft tap and call, "Daddy."

"Come in, Laura." He prayed the phone hadn't awakened her

grandmother. Night or day she could talk anyone into a critical case of heebie-jeebies. But he shouldn't think like that. The day of the accident, Barb's mother had come up from Arivaca and stayed on. He didn't know what he would have done without her.

Laura was in pink-trimmed pajamas with a big Snoopy sprawled across the front. She sat on one corner of the bed and Rambunctious, who bounded in after her, took the other.

"I heard the phone." She was slender with a pixie face, blue eyes and her mother's dark, abundant hair.

"You hear too much." He smiled and faked a punch. He pushed the covers back and swung his feet to the floor. "There's some trouble down at Tubac. A couple of guys tried to steal the safe."

He thought it better not to mention Lynne. His gaze rested on Barbara's twin bed, neatly made up as she had left it two months ago. A stuffed panda sat atop a lacy pillowcase. At the side was the end table with her gear: a little radio she took everywhere, sleeping tablets, cough drops, a small, well-thumbed Bible, a folded Swiss handkerchief, a diary she wrote in every night, a tiny flashlight, a snapshot of Laura at age six . . .

"I've got to run." He tousled her hair and went to the bathroom to dress.

She called out, "Daddy . . ."

"Yes."

"When I was at the hospital after school yesterday, I talked to Mom and I'm sure she knew I was there."

He wiped the residue of shaving cream off, washed the razor and put it back on the shelf. His massive hands were trembling and that in itself shocked him. He had never known unsteady hands. He straightened and took tight control of himself. He dared not break.

As he came out, she was saying, "I want to be there when she wakes up. Some day I know she'll wake up."

He took her in his arms. "Hon . . ."

She pulled away from him. "I'm not giving up. You can if you want to. But I'm not."

"But Dr. Randall said—"

She interrupted. "I don't care what he says. I don't care what anyone says. I don't see how you can . . ."

She broke then and clung to him. "I know, Daddy, I know."

At 3 A.M. he and Rambunctious were at the Arva airstrip near Tucson. As Greg warmed up the Cessna 182, he took deep, labored breaths to still his nerves.

Barb. He could scarcely concentrate on what he was doing.

He revved the engine until the little craft went into spasm. The two men would be back. Perhaps not the same two but others bent on theft, terror, destruction and possibly death.

Rambunctious sensed his mood and licked him. The dog sat in the co-pilot's seat, erect and proud. He liked flying.

As Greg took off in the blue dark, he suffered guilt feelings. He never should have permitted Lynne to work alone. But in Tubac where nothing ever happened? That was the trouble. There was no longer a place where nothing ever happened.

At St. Joseph's Hospital in Nogales, he talked briefly with her. She had been patched up without complications and would need only a few days to recuperate.

"Did they get anything?" She spoke in a whisper.

He shook his head. Both knew what the men had been after, but skirted the subject. There were too many ears on all frequencies.

"I'll be back on the job tomorrow." She could scarcely talk.

Her doctor, just entering the room, overheard. "We'll see."

"Tomorrow." Her eyes dared him to keep her.

"I can't make any promises," the doctor said brusquely.

"I'm not asking for promises. I'm leaving."

Damn, she had the spirit of a wild mare.

He had breakfast at Denny's and outside the restaurant, fed Rambunctious the sausages he had saved for him. Afterward he ordered a dozen roses sent to Lynne.

He flew directly north and put down at the Tubac Country Club airstrip. He hoped he wouldn't have a rough time with the Carson Mining Board about the night's events, although likely he would. Even when there was little to squabble about, they came loaded for bear. They were mostly desert people—a gnarled, weather-beaten, hard-drinking lot. During rough times they had put up the money to keep Carson afloat.

Carefully he examined the safe that had been partially chipped out of the adobe, then parried questions with a Santa Cruz County deputy sheriff who was young, sharp and inquisitive, especially about the safe. What was in it?

"Just some petty cash," Greg said. "Papers. You know, the usual for a little company."

"What kind of papers?"

Greg didn't care for his inquisitorial tone. "Sales contracts. Old agreements signed when we bought mines. That kind of thing."

"How about taking a look?"

Greg shook his head. "I'd have to get an okay from Washington."

"A government contract?"

"Not exactly but—it's classified."

"I think you're giving me the shaft and I resent the hell out of it. You've got something in the safe that two guys were willing to commit murder over."

Greg shrugged. "I'm trying to be helpful—but you can see how it is."

"I sure can, pardner. I sure can."

The deputy left and Greg paced about. He disliked the double-talk of the big cities, the big corporations. He wanted people to say what they meant in so many good Anglo-Saxon words without hedging, equivocations or euphemisms—and here he was guilty of doing exactly that.

He sat at the big, old 1890s desk to make some last minute notes. He would feel strange going before the Board without Barb and Lynne. For three years Lynne had sat beside them passing notes, cueing them in on names, dates, facts. She possessed a tremendous fund of knowledge and was efficient—and at the same time, feminine. Without her he doubted if he could have got Carson this far in the mining business.

He straightened a small picture of his mother alongside one of Barbara and another of Laura, the only three women he had ever loved.

His mother. So long ago, back in Anderson, Indiana. He could see her still, a tall, handsome woman who lived for him and his younger brother. She had been a schoolteacher who loved the classics, and Greg had never understood how she had fallen in love with his father who had only gone to the third grade and read with effort. Yet they seemed to work well together although they were never demonstrative.

His father was from a farm family over at Summitville. He had been a barber, had done well, saved his money and bought an eight-chair barbershop. Greg could still see the line-up of the chrome-plated Kokomo chairs and the barbers. After school he would rush home, drop off his books and hurry to the shop where he worked as cashier. On the side he sold cigars, cigarettes and American Beauty hair oil.

Summers, during his high school years, he was employed as watchman in a deserted tire factory where he was supposed to keep the plant free of hitchhikers. He couldn't bring himself to do that. Most were young and on their way, hopefully, to jobs out West. He would take them scraps from home.

He started hanging out around the airport, and for doing odd jobs for a little air school, the owner taught him to fly, and by sixteen he had his license. He suffered a crushing blow, though, when he tried out for the high school football and basketball teams. While he had the height and physique, he wasn't properly coordinated and failed to make even the third platoon.

When he was seventeen his parents died within a few months of each other. To escape a domineering aunt, he fled west to Tucson, got a job waiting tables in a student hash house, and worked his way through the University of Arizona. Summers he earned money flying supplies to the Yaqui Indians of Mexico who paid off in gold dust and nuggets. In doing so he violated federal statutes since at that time no U.S. citizen could own gold. He thought the law ridiculous. It was his first major rebellion against authority.

Yet in many ways he was a part of the establishment. That was the era marked by student protests against the Vietnam War. He refused to join them. He thought the Vietnam War a mistake, but he also believed that to refuse to support one's country was an even greater one and came close to treason. John Wayne was his hero, or rather the image of John Wayne projected on the screen. He told no one since that was the era of the anti-hero. He thought then and still did that heroes were needed, especially Superman, whether he took the form of James Bond, Douglas MacArthur, Clint Eastwood, Lawrence of Arabia or Moses.

The work force at the Tubac headquarters of Carson Mining numbered twenty-three, of whom Janet Stowe was one.

At five minutes to eleven she brought in two files Greg would need at the Board meeting. She was his executive secretary and knew where every piece of paper was that came into Carson Mining. She typed letter-perfect, was charming over the phone and seldom erred in her suggestions for handling people and problems. She went hungry to keep her five-feet, seven-inch frame down to 120, and the result was that her face was haggard and her breasts resembled door knobs. Greg could forgive her the face and knobs but not her neat desk, and he made a point on passing the desk to put one paper clip in dead center. He wanted to like her, but there was something indefinable about her that brooked no camaraderie.

"Everyone's here, Mr. Wilson. They're waiting for you."

Waiting to scalp me, he thought, although they were all friends of many years. But they said and did so many things "for his own good."

Rambunctious, stretched prone on the floor, opened one eye a slit and thumped his tail. He liked Janet who brought him meat scraps. He numbered his friends by his stomach response. Usually he nosed her by way of greeting, but at this moment he was in dire need of sleep.

Greg got up and stretched.

"I've got Lynne on my prayer list along with Mrs. Wilson," she continued.

Well, that's good, he thought. Everyone could do with one more prayer.

He should go out of his way to do little things for her, the way he did for Lynne. After all she was Meg Stanley's protégé. Meg was a Board member and had been since his river-running days.

She had supported him all the way, contributing thousands when the ventures seemed hopeless. She was well into her fifties, stately but very outgoing and with an ingratiating smile. That was her image except when she sat down at a Board meeting or engaged in a business deal. Then she turned serious, outspoken, hard and quick to attack.

She said her money had come from "my dear Joe," her late husband. Greg knew better. It had come from twenty-three years of operating a bordello outside Boise, Idaho. She had asked him to hire Janet as a "special favor to me." She said Janet's mother had befriended her. He wondered if Janet could be the daughter of one of Meg's "girls."

Meg had only one hangover left from her bordello days. She looked men over from head to foot, especially young ones in tight jeans.

"Okay, let's go," he said, taking a deep breath and throwing his shoulders back. He was ready for them.

In the courtyard where the Board members were milling about, Powder River Ike Levy cornered him. He was an enormous man, well into his sixties, with bushy white hair falling from under a black sombrero. He had a craggy face made up of mesas and valleys, and bright, intense eyes. He was from the Powder River Basin in Wyoming. His grandfather had sold pots and pans in the mining camps, traveling in a rickety old wagon pulled by mules. Unlike many, Powder River was proud of his heritage. "He was a great man," he liked to say about his grandfather. "Used to carry a Torah with him, and every Friday evening he'd read it to his mules."

"How's Barb?" he asked.

"She's coming along."

"I want to see her."

"Give her a few more days." Powder River should know. Above all people, Barb would want him to.

"You told me that last week. You think I want to move in on you? Hell, if I was twenty years younger, I'd take her away from you . . . I'm a better man than you'll ever be—and don't forget it."

He had known Powder River since his sophomore year at the

university. Powder River had hired him to run the cargoes to the Yaquis and in time cut him in on half the profits. When Greg on graduation wanted to start up a river-running company, Powder River handed over $5,000, and then another $5,000, and another. "You're like me, boy," Powder River had said. "We're not the smartest fellows around, but we know how to work hard and go without a meal if we have to, to make it and stay in there."

Greg got a permit from the Forest Service to run the Middle Fork of the Salmon River, a trip of 105–120 miles of swift currents, wild rapids and mirrored pools, through some of the most primitive country left in North America where bighorns, cougars, bears and bald eagles lived, and at night bats flew out of caves in formations. He hired a bush pilot to fly the parties out of Stanley, Idaho, to the Middle Fork, and at the end, he trucked the people from the river to Salmon, Idaho. He bought neoprene survival boats of World War II design. They were inflatable ones that had to be blown up. He developed muscles and a quick mind for charting rapids, and learned survival. He browned up under the sun and grew a beard. He came to look like a mountain man.

With him through all of this was Barb. They had met as freshmen and married in their senior year. She was Arizona born, from Arivaca, a ranch settlement south of Tucson. She thought of it as a secret place, far off any highway, buried back in rolling hills and desert country, known only to God and those few who lived there. She was certain God did look kindly upon Arivaca since the first sign of habitation on entering the outpost was St. Ferdinand's chapel. Then came the post office and A. Mercantile Company where she was a checker summers. Farther up the road was the Silver Belle Bar, the sign-off.

She grew up with a father too busy managing a cattle ranch to bother with her, and a mother who sat outside most days staring at the mountains and dreaming of a better life. Barb had her books and records and a tiny bedroom that was all her own where she retreated after finishing the dinner dishes.

Greg was her first and only date. He asked her to the February rodeo, a major event in Tucson. She remembered she was joyously happy but trembling, and too excited to recall much of the day. Their next date was a movie which was followed by a cloudburst.

Since neither had a car, they walked and were drenched, but thought it great fun. She didn't push herself on him the way other girls had, and he, the loner, found himself in love with this quiet, easy-going girl with a quick, perceptive mind. She responded to his gentle, thoughtful ways, and his compassion for others. He was an escape hatch, too, from a loneliness that had become a growing ache as she had matured.

They became engaged the summer before they started their sophomore year. She was to remember walks far into the night with her scrawny, black cat following them, "bean holes" on the desert as dusk settled about them, long horseback rides into mysterious canyons weekends, scraping dimes together to buy movie tickets, the pungent odor of the desert after rainstorms, and sitting far into the night on her doorstep talking and dreaming of their future.

She was to remember, too, the night they crawled into sleeping bags dead tired after a hard day running the Middle Fork. The river had changed course since they last had made the run. They had been caught up in a whirlpool in a back eddy and had spun about wildly for almost an hour. Working like a madman, he had brought them out of it.

Now, though, he had his mind on a business other than river-running. Hesitantly, he told her about a plan he had been chewing over for several days, a high-risk venture that would take them off their beloved Middle Fork. He had learned about a mining company down in Arizona that was about to go bankrupt. At $35 an ounce for gold, it could not break even. The owner would sell to Greg for $12,000, and Greg was certain Powder River would advance the money.

Greg said, "The company's not worth much of anything right now, but I think we can make a fortune. Gold isn't going to remain at thirty-five dollars. Why, in time I bet gold will be worth a hundred dollars an ounce. But it'll mean scraping along . . . sticking it out."

She was all for the idea. "I've got all the clothes I need." Her wardrobe consisted of one dress, one pair of jeans, a couple of T-shirts and a pants suit.

She continued, "We don't spend much money on food, and we can get a camper and sleep out."

"What about Laura?"

"She'll love it. Don't worry about her." Laura was then little more than a year old.

Barb was confident God was in His heaven looking after them. Her faith was a simple one. She believed in the teachings of Jesus and tried to live by them. She was a happy person, "born happy." She was even happy mornings before she had her coffee. "You're disgusting," he would tell her. "Everyone's supposed to be grumpy."

By return mail Powder River sent a cashier's check for $12,000. He didn't ask for details. He wasn't interested. He invested in people, not projects.

With Barb alongside, Greg worked twelve hours a day and sometimes sixteen. Carson had mostly dry placers, one near the Esterly at Grant's Pass, Oregon, and two along the Hassayampa in Yavapai County, Arizona. Carson also owned a small Nevada copper mine with ore that contained both gold and silver—and a slag heap that could be picked over for gem-quality turquoise. South of Phoenix was a quartz vein property with gold content. None was in operation when Greg took over. He slaved away to put them into working condition. He replaced rotten timbers, built new sluices, and bought new retorts, flotation machines, shaking tables and other equipment.

He got more money from Powder River and scouted about for new funds. Meg Stanley put in $5,000 and then followed Al Nakya, a Papago Indian friend from university days; Dr. Ron Jordan, a black professor in the College of Mining at the University of Arizona; Carlos Lopez, who patrolled his 10,000-acre ranch along the Mexican border by helicopter; Jim McAdoo, a film star cowboy known as Utah Jones; and John J. Passos, whose grandfather, an Apache Indian fighter, had brought the Southern Pacific railroad to Tucson.

A year after Greg bought Carson, President Richard Nixon revalued gold to $38 a troy ounce. That was in 1972. One year later the official U.S. price was set at $42.22. The quotation on the London market climbed steadily, passing 100 in 1973, reaching almost 200 by the end of 1974, and in 1980 blasting off to more than 800 before dropping to the 300s.

During those years, Carson showed a fantastic profit.

As Carson expanded, Greg recalled a university class about fabulous fortunes on the ocean floor that could be mined. The professor said they were ready for the taking if technological means could be found for scooping or vacuuming them up. There were nodules of manganese, used to toughen steel. The United States had no reserves. There was cobalt, vital for certain electronic equipment and alloys. The United States depended upon Zaire for 80 percent. Moreover, the United States imported 20 percent of its copper and had only one plant producing nickel. The professor predicted a world war over such resources. The United States should not and could not depend on nations that might cut off the supply of essential metals.

Greg put Barb to work researching the subject, and she learned that scientists had known about the beds of nodules for more than a century. They had been discovered during a historic expedition of the H.M.S. *Challenger* in the 1870s. Subsequent research established that a nodule consisted of minerals that attached themselves to bits of rock, shark's teeth and the like. Eventually the minerals encased the hard center forming layers, like those of an onion.

The process had taken millions of years. A nodule the size of a walnut could be ten million years old. They "grew" at the rate of three to six millimeters each million years, and yet the beds were extensive. Estimates of the tons lying on the ocean floor varied from 100 billion to one-and-a-half trillion. They contained ten times all the manganese known in the world today and thirteen times the nickel. The most amazing fact was that the beds lay in plain sight. For some reason not yet definitely determined, Father Time had not buried them under mountains of sediment.

"Imagine all that wealth down there," Greg said. "Why that's more than the California gold rush, the Klondike and all the other gold discoveries put together."

Barbara tempered his excitement by pointing out the obstacles to be overcome in mining these Comstock lodes:

The cost of developing the technology for bringing the nodules to the surface would be enormous. Engineers would have to invent machinery to suck or rake them up. Pinpoint navigation would be necessary, and even in rough seas, the ship's stabilizers would have to hold the vessel to one spot. Refineries would have to be built on land at tremendous cost to remove the minerals from the hard core and separate them.

Even after all of this had been done, the backers would have no legal assurance they could proceed. Several United Nations conferences to determine the Law of the Sea had failed because the nations could not agree on who owned the ocean floor. The Third World demanded a share even though the smaller countries lacked the money and scientists to participate in the development and actual mining. They based their claims on the premise that the oceans were the heritage of all mankind.

Several multinational companies and a few countries would fight all sea mining. They feared that if vast supplies of minerals, especially copper, were dumped on the market, they would be ruined.

Environmentalists would want to control the extent of the mining. If all the nodules were vacuumed or swept up, then there would be no more for several million years. Mining the nodules in itself might disturb and possibly destroy the marine life at the bottom of the seas. Direct pollution might come when the plants refining the nodules emptied the tailings and chemicals directly into the ocean, thus threatening marine life near the surface.

Greg's interest was further fired when he learned that the Soviets were close to developing the technology for getting the nodules to the surface. The next day he urged the Carson Board to put the company in the sea-mining business at a cost of about $800 million, which with overruns could climb to one billion. Except for Powder River and Meg Stanley, the Board termed the plan unfeasible. Where would they get that kind of money? Greg had no idea but thought he could. A billion dollars? Forget it, the Board members said. They hooted at the idea. Greg Wilson was off his rocker. In the previous quarter, Carson had shown a profit of $25 million. Why risk it on a mad adventure?

"We're all desert rats," said one. "What do we know about the ocean? Let's stick to country we know something about."

Nevertheless, Greg scouted through the financial world and found an interesting conglomerate, Massachusetts Diversified of Boston, headed by one Karl Neustadt of German origin. Neustadt took an instant liking to Greg. They were two of a kind, daring and innovative and ready to assume high risks.

Greg was ecstatic. He had $30,000 in personal assets and an $800-million-dollar fund to draw upon. He would head a company that for the first time in history would mine the ocean floor. He would earn Carson and himself millions and become a hero for providing resources the United States needed to survive.

Such had been the dream until a short time ago when the realization hit him with frightening impact that there were forces out there seeking to destroy Carson.

5

Eighteen months after General Dmitri Schepnov arrived in Afghanistan, he had put together an espionage network of twenty-seven major agents plus two minor ones. The twenty-seven were a rabble aggregation, all except two on salary. They were constantly groaning, complaining and begging, and he was sick of the lot. Yet just when he thought he would rid himself of them, one would come up with information that would save a Russian column or result in the ambush of a guerrilla band. He owed his Afghan successes largely to Rashid Jumeira, the Syrian Moslem, for Rashid had a way with the Afghans that the General did not. Rashid knew how to approach them in the name of Allah, and convince them that the Soviets were on Allah's side and the guerrillas were the minions of Satan.

The General had had a good year and a half. He had defied KGB regulations to make friends inside the 27th Tank Brigade. They had taught him to drive and fire the cannons. The last time out he had been caught unawares in a guerrilla attack. He had killed nine Afghans and run over two. The skirmish finished, he had climbed out with a Sioux war cry he remembered from an American film, and with a wave and flourish jumped to the ground. Never had he acted out a role better. By the next day, though, he was back in his shell, once again the master spy, feeling both guilt and jubilation.

It was Rashid who brought the General the first rumor about Mr. Fort Knox. He was allegedly selling information to both sides, but the General had trouble believing that. A year-and-a-half ago Mr. Knox had provided information that led to the slaughter of a guerrilla force of Mujahiddin (holy warriors) intent on blowing up the Salang tunnel under the Hindu Kush mountains. The General had considered him his best spy. Rashid checked his people and discovered that Mr. Knox indeed had been selling military information and moreover, had offered to set the General up for assassination for $10,000 U.S. The General never had been one for cool deliberation. He had stayed alive by quick thinking and quicker action. He confronted Mr. Knox with his knowledge and before Mr. Knox could react, he shot him. In the brain.

Only a few days later, the KGB summoned the General to its headquarters on Dzerzhinsky Square in Moscow. He was flattered when Vitaly Fedorchuk, KGB's chief, sent a plain black car to his hotel.

At KGB's headquarters, an escort silently ushered him into a first-floor office where he saw Fedorchuk for all of sixty seconds. However, they were sixty seconds he would remember forever. Fedorchuk was a graying, distinguished but severe-looking man in a dark suit, white shirt and black tie.

He looked up from a sheaf of papers he was scanning and said, "You have done good work in Afghanistan and I commend you. You are a credit to our organization." He returned to the papers, the General said, "Thank you," and was escorted out.

To be received was an honor in itself. Fedorchuk headed some 50,000 agents and allied people, such as technicians, crime scientists, code experts, photographers, assassins, etc., of whom half worked inside Russia. The others included 6,700 spies assigned to overseas duties. Roughly 3,000 were posted to the United States.

In the crowded corridor, the General met an old friend. While the escort waited, listening, they talked about the changing nature of the KGB. The Politburo had upgraded it. The ruffian types had been replaced by lawyers, scholars, army men and others with education and varied skills.

Shortly the General found himself on the floor of the First Chief Directorate and in the 'T' section of the First Department, which handled North American "technology." The KGB setup included three other chief directorates and numerous independent departments. Most were concerned with internal security.

In a spartan office that reminded the General of a hospital room, he waited only a few minutes before the secretary, a broad-hipped, big-bosomed woman in a dark suit, took him into Master Control's quarters. It was austere, too: white walls with no pictures, as if the occupant expected to move any day, a dirty window only big enough for a child to crawl through, ragged, dark carpeting, a fair-sized desk and steel files that lined two walls.

Master Control wasted no time. The General was being reassigned, this time to Washington, D.C., for an off-beat mission. It was espionage of a kind never before undertaken by the KGB, or as far as Master Control knew, by any other intelligence agency. It would call for great ingenuity and might be hazardous.

"We want you to murder a ship," Master Control told him.

Master Control was a small man, wizened by his work and the years. He was very precise, both in his thinking and language, and at one time or another had headed most of the departments. He had become a legend. There was nothing, seemingly, he could not work out on paper. His men said he was the greatest spy strategist of our time.

Now he repeated, "We want you to murder a ship called the *Marco Polo*. Kill it as if it were a human. Destroy its vital parts. I have some suggestions you will want to read tonight. So come back tomorrow and we will talk."

The "suggestions" began with background information concerning the mining of the sea. Master Control had set the facts forth succinctly but with sufficient details to paint a broad picture. The General read the papers with growing fascination. His heart beat hard when he read about the possibilities of men fighting over underwater claims and nations battling, perhaps another world war. At sixty-three he had resigned himself to serving in far-off places such as Afghanistan. And here Master Control was offering him the choice assignment of years.

The next morning Master Control filled him in on other aspects. "We know our ship the *Kharkov* is having serious problems. Its equipment for raking up the nodules has proven defective. We don't know how long it will be before the *Kharkov* can begin actual mining operations. And there is another problem. We do not have the film footage that this Carson Mining Company has. We must get all their information."

Master Control paced about. "We have very little on the *Marco Polo*. We have failed there because certain parties did not take the assignment seriously. So it's up to you, Dmitri, to save our good name, to gain us time until the *Kharkov* can sail. Your total mission will be to destroy the *Marco Polo* and see to it that under no circumstances does it ever put to sea. The Politburo will not tolerate it. I believe you grasp my meaning.

"What can we do for you that we've missed?" Master Control asked.

Now was the time to come up with requests. Later, they would forget you. "I have an agent I want assigned to me."

Master Control was instantly wary. Master Control did not like others choosing assignments. "Who?"

"Rashid Jumeira. A Syrian. He worked with me in Afghanistan."

"We'll see."

"It's most important. I must have him."

Master Control shrugged. "If possible."

"I ask for nothing else. Surely . . ."

"Very well." Master Control acted as if he were humoring a child.

He handed the General a thick, bound booklet. "I have been instructed to give you this policy paper drawn up by the Foreign Ministry which states the Soviet position on the subject at hand. It is lengthy and verbose as are all of these papers."

He was disgusted. "I will summarize it for you. Our experts advise there are five principal mining sites in the Pacific. The *Kharkov* will mine at each for two or three days or more, and stake out each in accordance with historical precedent dating to the conquest of the New World. That is, the first power to explore a new territory may lay claim to it.

"The United States will react violently, but we know from the Cuban situation we need only to stand firm. As you know, Dmitri, we have everything in Cuba we want, including missiles. The unofficial Washington policy has been to pretend they do not know this and to minimize the extent of the Soviet supply centers and control of the island. To reveal the facts, Washington might be pressed by American public opinion into a confrontation.

"This position paper, hence, assumes that Washington will take a strong stance but will not actually confront the Soviet move, which will be backed up with full naval support. U.S. public opinion will never tolerate risking a war over sea-mining operations that the Americans know nothing about. Washington, of course, will bring charges in the United Nations, but by then we will have established a plan to share a small portion of the profits with the Third World and, hence, will have the votes to negate such a move."

Master Control spread out a dossier. Some pages were new and clean but others were torn and yellowed with age.

"Our principal agent on this case," Master Control said, talking rapidly, "is Nataya Fussen." He looked up. "It may surprise you to know she is seventy-two, maybe older. She gives seventy-two as her age, but you know women. Too old, you may think, but she will amaze you.

"She's an American citizen although her father was German and her mother, Russian. They went to the United States from Düsseldorf shortly before she was born and she has spent most of her life there."

He paused for effect. "She is the only member of the Frederick Duquesne Nazi spy ring the FBI didn't capture when that organization rounded them up in 1939."

The General looked up in puzzled astonishment.

"That is correct," Master Control said. "She worked for the Abwehr until the Germans invaded our country, and then disappeared and sat out the rest of the war in the Hudson Bay region of Canada by posing as a Jewish refugee who had fled the Nazis. She is not Jewish, but quite an actor, like you, Dmitri.

"To get along with it, she has been working for us since World War II and mostly in the English-speaking countries—England, Canada and the United States.

"We will proceed briefly now to what she has to report on the people around the *Marco Polo*. First, let us consider the financial arrangement. The small company called Carson Mining owns the *Marco Polo* . . ."

After sketching out the details, he continued, "The overall direction rests with a comparatively young man named Gregory Wilson who is married, but the woman we are interested in is a brilliant scientist who handles the technical end. She and Wilson work very closely together."

"She is his mistress?"

"No, nothing like that. Miss Fussen has come up with some recommendations, however, for handling the two. She thinks if something should happen to this Gregory Wilson, the *Marco Polo* would be delayed in sailing by weeks, perhaps months. She thinks we should eliminate him. But I will leave that up to you, Dmitri. I know from your record you will not hesitate to remove him if you think it best.

"About the scientist—her name's Dr. Lynne Kennedy—Miss Fussen believes she could prove to be an excellent source of information. Miss Fussen would like to have another agent, preferably a young man, win her over and supply us with information at low cost. She has several plans outlined that you will want to think about. If Kennedy will not cooperate for a small fee—I would consider a far bigger one than Miss Fussen suggests since we have so much at stake—if Kennedy won't cooperate at all, then Miss Fussen suggests we have an agent threaten to rape her, and if that does not work, he then rapes her and continues to rape her until she breaks.

"I have no recommendations. We will leave the decisions to you. You are the general in the field."

By the next night the General was on a train bound for Leningrad. For two weeks he studied at the Institute of Oceanography and tried to absorb this strange knowledge, but it was pumped into him too fast. When he left he was confused. He told himself that only a thorough grasp of espionage and sabotage were essential, and he had that. Far from being a great spy, he considered himself a talented craftsman who could delve into years of fabulous experience for the answer to virtually any problem. When he finished, the *Marco Polo* would be down there with all of those nodules.

On his arrival in Washington, D.C., he settled into an office in the Soviet Union Embassy's annex. Nataya Fussen flew in to brief him. He was totally impressed. She looked not more than sixty—it was evident she had a tightly knit, freshly done face lift—and was smartly coiffed and dressed. Her Russian, learned from her mother, was archaic.

The second day they met with a Libyan agent who offered them a "pool"—like a stenographic pool—of 7,000 graduate terrorists who had trained in twenty camps. The agent advised that Libya's thirty-nine-year-old strongman, Colonel Muammar el-Kaddafi, would back the destruction of the *Marco Polo* with men and money.

The General suggested, and Fussen readily agreed, that Rashid Jumeira would handle such personnel if needed. Rashid would arrive in Honolulu shortly from Tokyo. He would be traveling on a forged Canadian passport.

The General reported that he himself would have access to experts of every kind from several terrorist training centers.

By the third day the General was making his first setup.

The young woman's name was Rona Hale, twenty-five, and she was described by Embassy employees as outgoing, pleasant and efficient.

She walked in hesitantly, a cub not knowing how the bear would treat her. He looked evil, she thought, but I shouldn't judge. Then he smiled and the evil disappeared. She smiled back. She was again herself. She was comfortable around people only when they were smiling.

"Thank you for seeing me, General Schepnov." She pronounced the name correctly. Few Americans did.

He nodded. "Please sit."

His office, which looked out on a small garden abloom with tulips, violets and pansies, was luxuriously furnished. He would have had it no other way. The carpeting, soft to the step, was burnished gold as were the draperies. The furniture was ultramodern and handcrafted, including the gold-edged desk which extended almost the width of the room. On the wall behind the desk stretched a map of the world, flanked on one side by a picture of Karl Marx and the other, Andropov. The portraits, framed in heavy dark wood, had the look of old masters. Behind the swivel chair he had dumped his gymnastic equipment.

Only the wall decorations argued with the modern motif. They were memoirs of his assignments: a small, mother-of-pearl inlaid tray from Damascus, a large copper one from Beirut, candle holders from a Vietnamese temple, a curved sword from Afghanistan, and a Chinese gold-leafed wood carving. The office reflected his expensive tastes. Even in Afghanistan he had ordered his underwear from Robbins, Ltd., of London, jewelry from Cartier's of New York, and gold pens from Cross.

Now he fussed with a pipe. In all his life he had never smoked one, but a pipe gained him time in a difficult situation. Not that this one should prove difficult. Still, he could size up the woman. She had a nice face, blue flashing eyes, lips on the full side, just right, breasts the same, hips spread enough to interest the most demanding male, and long slender legs. She was sexually stimulating in the most innocent way.

He wondered if she would give him—what was it the Americans called it—yes, he remembered, a matinee. He had been told that some of the highest-paid secretaries in Washington took two hours off at noon, one for lunch and one for a matinee.

He was conscious his stare had flustered her. "I ask your pardon, Miss Hale. I was back in Russia . . . a long time ago . . . with a beautiful woman like you . . . my wife. She died five years ago."

"I'm sorry."

Scarcely moving, he bustled his body about. "My comrades at

the Embassy . . ." He stopped to correct himself. The word, *comrades,* had a bad connotation in this country. "The people at the Embassy have spoken well about you. You were the receptionist here?"

"Two years, then my mother fell ill with cancer and needed me, and I was with her a year until she died."

"My people tell me you are a student of my country."

"I read everything I can get on Russia. I have ever since I was a little girl."

"My people tell me you speak Russian."

"Not very well."

"Not necessary. Did my people tell you I head a trade mission . . . to buy grain . . . when American politics will permit?"

"Just that. Nothing about the job."

He pretended to light the pipe. "I need a secretary who knows this big United States. Where these strange names are. I cannot pronounce them." He indicated a small map on his desk. "Dubuki. Dis Moanes. Where they grow corn and wheat. I see by your paper"—he pointed to her resumé—"you lived in Chicago—"

"I was born there and lived there until I finished university."

"That is good. You know the—"

"Midwest."

He nodded. "I would want you to be my secretary and also to do some research for me."

She stiffened. "Research?"

"Nothing secret. I wouldn't ask you to do anything secret."

"What kind of research, General?"

"The weather . . . what it is like . . . whether it hurts or helps the crops. How big the crops will be. You check with your government and they will tell you it is all right to do this."

"Are you offering me the job?"

"What about starting Monday?"

She nodded, rose and offered a hand. "Thank you, General."

As she left, he admired the rear end triangle with the lovely hypotenuse moving sinuously from hip to hip. He walked from behind the desk to the center of the room to take sitting up exercises. He felt elated. The Federal Bureau of Investigation probably knew she had been here. Possibly she had called the FBI when she learned the Embassy was interested in employing her again. If not, the FBI would talk with her shortly—as soon as the two agents running surveillances on the Embassy and this annex reported a U.S. citizen was entering and leaving on a schedule.

Either way, he had what the Americans would call a pipeline into the FBI. He would feed Miss Hale misinformation with bits of truths scrabbled in, to make it all sound credible. He had used the same ploy in London. He had deceived M-5 for eight months and regrettably it had ended on a sad note. When his London secretary found out he had used her, she gave him trouble and he had had to advance the date of her death, which with her state of good health might not have come for a good many years.

He had finished counting twenty-five squats when a young man from the Technical Staff knocked. He brought a letter in a cellophane bag and an envelope in another. These he placed on the desk with the care of one handling eggs.

"If you are busy, sir, I could return." He spoke in Russian with a heavy Ukrainian accent. He was dark complexioned, tall and bony. The General watched him as he would a mongoose. One could not trust a Ukrainian.

"Make it short," the General said.

"I examined the letter and the envelope for fingerprints and found none. The party either used gloves in preparing them or wiped them clean afterward. You will note the typing."

"What about it?"

"The party used a very old typewriter, and you probably know, sir—"

"Get on with it." The General was curt.

The young man was upset. He was not accustomed to being treated like Polish swine. "The paper is a type commonly found in variety stores and the postmark shows it was mailed from Woodland Hills, California, a suburb of Los Angeles."

"Man or woman?"

"There is no way of determining that. As you will note, the party did not sign but typed in the initials, MJ."

Leaning back in the swivel chair, the General studied the letter. It set forth no date, no place. It read:

> Dear Comrades—I have a complete report on the Carson Mining Company—copies of undersea films, both still and motion pictures, studies in the areas the company plans mining operations, including underseas maps. I will get the date the *Marco Polo* will leave and its destination. My price is $25,000. I will not bargain. I will phone the pay box at K and 14th at 7 P.M. this coming Sunday. If I get no answer, I will phone again at 8 P.M. the same night. I will make only two calls.
>
> Very truly yours,
> MJ

The General looked up and said matter-of-factly, "Very well, I will keep this."

"If there's anything else, sir—?"

"No, no."

Damn, fawning Ukrainian! He was bidding for more information. By the blood of the Czars, he would get none.

He paced about. For minutes he stared out of the rain-streaked window at the budding firs, then returning to his desk, he arranged the papers in neat stacks. The phone rang interminably, but he failed to hear it.

The message could be a clever ruse designed to elicit information later or to plant misinformation the General would forward to Moscow—or the message could have been sent by an employee embittered over his treatment by Carson Mining.

And of course, the message could be what it purported to be: an honest offer of honest information for a price.

The General leaned back in the creaking swivel chair and closed his eyes. He recalled a highly unlikely case handled by KGB agents in the Soviet Embassy in Mexico City. A boyish-looking chunky young American by the name of Andrew Daulton Lee had walked up to the Embassy guardhouse on Calzada De Tacubaya and offered the receptionist a stack of computer programming cards. The receptionist had summoned the General's old friend, Vasily Ivanovich Okana.

Lee refused to discuss where the cards came from. Later Okana was to tell the General he surmised at the outset he was dealing with a psycho. What American, obviously well educated and well-to-do and without any pro-Soviet feelings—as Okana's questioning brought out—would peddle secrets in such a naïve way?

That was back in April 1975, and in the months to follow, the twenty-five-year-old Lee delivered for a total of $70,000 the plans and results of the manufacture and use by TRW Industries of spy satellites for the CIA.

Eventually—the General learned from Okana—Lee revealed that his information came from his close friend, Christopher John Boyce, a TRW employee who had access to the "Black Vault" where the CIA satellite data and other U.S. espionage material were stored. Boyce had top secret clearance.

What a coup, the General thought, if this note led to another fantastic espionage break. Yet he remained skeptical. Suspicion was an ingrained part of his business. He would move cautiously and probe slowly.

At 7:10 A.M. the following decoded message from the U.S. Embassy in Moscow to the State Department in Washington, D.C., was delivered to parties on the red alert list:

> ATT: DEPUTY SECRETARY BROWNELL. SOVIET FOREIGN MINISTER PUSHKIN HAS PERSONALLY REQUESTED ON BEHALF OF ANDROPOV A CONFERENCE TO DIVIDE THE PACIFIC OCEAN FLOOR BY THE UNITED STATES AND RUSSIA TO AVOID WHAT HE TERMED SERIOUS MISUNDERSTANDINGS LEADING TO POSSIBLE CONFRONTATIONS. HE REQUESTED, MOREOVER, AN EXCHANGE OF UNDERSEA MINING TECHNOLOGY BY SCIENTISTS OF THE TWO NATIONS VISITING EACH OTHER'S PROJECTS. HE ADVISED HE THOUGHT SUCH AN EXCHANGE WOULD SAVE COSTLY AND TIME-CONSUMING RESEARCH. HE ADDED THAT IN HIS ESTIMATION IT WOULD COOL DOWN WHAT MIGHT GROW INTO AN OVERHEATED SITUATION THAT COULD DO IRREPARABLE HARM TO RELATIONSHIPS BETWEEN THE TWO NATIONS. HE WISHED TO POINT OUT THAT THERE WERE SUFFICIENT METALS ON THE OCEAN FLOOR TO TAKE CARE OF THE NEEDS OF THE UNITED STATES AND RUSSIA FOR CENTURIES TO COME AND COMPETITION TO GAIN CONTROL OF THE SEABEDS WOULD PROVE A COSTLY DISASTER FOR EACH COUNTRY. ADVISE SOONEST.
>
> BLAKISTON

6

The long adobe room at Carson Mining headquarters in Tubac was cool and dark compared to the smelterlike heat and brilliance outside. As Greg called the meeting to order, there was much scraping of huge, old Spanish-type chairs on the tile floors. Dr. Jordan, the mining professor, and John J. Passos, the financier, were in conservative business suits. The others wore Western garb, shirts open at the collar, Levi's or jeans, boots and cowhide belts with enormous silver buckles. Meg was fashionably attired in a Navajo squaw dress complemented with a costly squash-blossom necklace of silver and turquoise.

Greg called for reading of the minutes. "Forget it," said Carlos Lopez, a giant of a man, tanned a deep Indian brown, and with shoulders like oxen yokes. He had no hips or waistline, and his legs, wide set from years astride lean range horses, appeared to be attached to the far-out corners of his torso. Even when he walked, he seemed to be sitting a saddle. These days, though, he did little riding and considerable flying. He bossed and patrolled a ranch of several thousand acres from a small Cessna. The ranch was contiguous with the Mexican border.

"Minutes approved," said Al Nakya, the Papago Indian secretary who never kept minutes or other paper work.

"So be it recorded," Greg announced. For the first time he was conscious Janet Stowe sat alongside him at the head of the table. That was Lynne's spot. She was moving in on Lynne every chance she got.

He averted his eyes from the chair Barbara customarily used. During her long absence no one had sat there. It was as if she were dead and the chair a memorial.

He narrated in detail the events of the previous night. "Lynne will be back in a couple of days. As for the investigation, the deputies don't have much. Four tire prints, very clear, on the sandy ground where they parked. No fingerprints, though, but they figure it was a pickup."

Jim McAdoo interrupted. "Why is it no one's ever passing by when there's a burglary?"

Years ago, Jim McAdoo had made thirty-two Westerns at Republic Studios for $3,000 a picture. He had used some of the money to buy land in San Fernando Valley, which was then far out of Los Angeles. He only wanted a place where he could ride his horses, and then much to his amazement, communities grew up about him, towns that Los Angeles eventually confiscated. A ten-story bank building now stood where the stables had been. A millionaire many times over, he could buy out half the big names in the film colony.

Greg said slowly, "We've used the safe all along to store the movie footage we took of the potential mining sites on the ocean floor. Also, the still films, the maps, the oceanographic reports . . ."

"My God, whose crazy idea was that?" John J. asked. He was short, stocky and balding, with the inventory eyes of a detective.

"Mine," Greg said defiantly.

Dr. Jordan broke in. "Do you mean to say the burglars could have got away with a million dollars' worth of exploratory material?"

Powder River corrected him. "Three million one hundred and fifty-three thousand, counting all the expenses of the expeditions."

"We couldn't put the film and papers in a bank vault," Greg said. "We had to have ready access to them. I thought we were protected by the low profile we've been keeping so that no one would dream—"

"Could it be the three Ws?" Al Nakya asked.

W.W.W. Enterprises, a conglomerate based in New York City, was Carson's principal American competitor. It had a deep-sea-mining ship docked in Seattle. According to rumor, though, the company had failed to develop the necessary technology.

"How would anyone know about the safe?" Dr. Jordan asked. "Unless someone here at Carson talked too much—"

Carlos interrupted. "Or sold us out."

"Not at Carson," Greg said firmly.

"Well, what do we do now?" Carlos asked. "Where do we put the stuff?"

John J. coughed. "We'd better talk about getting some security in here."

Carlos continued, "What about the *Marco Polo?* Do we have any security there except for old Bill Madden? Hell, I could drop him with a pop gun."

Known affectionately as "the old man," Bill Madden at seventy was a formidable, robust figure with a detective's bland, expressionless face. He had been with Carson since Greg and the others bought the company.

Greg was quick to defend him. "He's got tight control over the situation out there."

He was covering for Bill who needed to hire additional guards.

John J. coughed again, to get attention. "Before we go further, gentlemen, we should know the date we have set for the *Marco Polo* to sail and which mine field we will work. Those facts will have considerable bearing on our decisions in regard to security and where to place our exploration material."

He looked pointedly at Greg who said, "I've got a plan I was discussing with Meg."

Meg broke in. "I don't think you should talk about it." She rose and stood tall and straight. Greg thought, she's still a handsome woman.

She continued, "Our thinking is still back in the days when Carson was a small company. We don't quite realize that we will be spending close to a billion dollars by the time the *Marco Polo* sails—and we're going for a potential profit of several billions if we get there first."

John J. cut in. "I'd like some specific facts."

"Let her finish," Powder River said gruffly.

"Thank you, Mr. Levy." She shot John J. a withering glance. "Naturally, with that much money at stake, our competitors are going to do everything they can to find out what we know, and try to stop us and destroy us. Some of you have been through this on your ranches. I know a couple of you have been in gun battles."

Carlos nodded. "It's kill or be killed. You either get him first or he gets you."

"I don't like the sound of any of this," John J. said.

Meg stared him down. "We need tight security—tough security—but we also need counterespionage, just as in war time—because this is war. Somebody to spend full time probing around to find out what the competition is trying to get out of us by theft or bribing or wiretapping or other means. And most important of all, just how far they'll go to stop or destroy us. Are they going to resort to arson or murder . . . ?"

Not a foot moved, not a body.

She took a deep breath. "I recommend that we set up an espionage unit. We need to know—it's absolutely vital—what our competitors are doing, how close they are to staking out claims, and any new technologies they have developed. I know espionage is a dirty word, but we're in a dirty game."

She sat down to utter silence. Powder River broke it drumming on the table.

"I can understand your emotional state, Mrs. Stanley," said John J., stuffing a pipe, "but our fears are all predicated on a simple burglary. We have no reason to believe they knew the contents of the safe."

Powder River looked at Greg. "How much would Meg's program cost?"

"About $50,000, add or subtract ten."

"Will Massachusetts Diversified go for it?"

Carlos jumped in. "Set it up and then tell them."

Dr. Jordan said, "I can't vote for a plan that would authorize murder."

Al Nakya groaned. "We're not going out to kill anyone."

Greg had to put an end to this turn in the discussion before it got out of hand. "I assure you, Dr. Jordan, that we will not employ anyone who would use a weapon in other than self-defense. I consider that espionage in our case means the gathering of information quietly through normal channels. It would be the same as the investigative reporting of a newspaperman."

Purposely he avoided looking at Meg. She would have given the word, espionage, a stronger definition.

John J. raised his voice. "I have not had an answer to my pertinent question about how soon our ship will sail and its destination."

"It's none of our business," Meg said flatly. John J. irked her. He was a hornet constantly buzzing around.

Greg said quietly, "I can't tell you."

The target date was May 25, a month away. Greg was working desperately to shorten the schedule. He had little information about the Russian ship, the *Kharkov,* in Vladivostok, or the W.W.W. one in Seattle. Even a day could mean a difference of a billion dollars or more. The first ship to begin mining could stake out the best beds and by maneuvering might conceivably lay claim to a good part of the Pacific.

"You don't know or you don't trust me?" John J. was angry. He puffed vigorously on the pipe.

"Oh, what the hell," Carlos said. "Let's get on with deciding whether we want to hire some gunmen. I got this banker friend. Ran a bank back in Ohio that was being hit every week. He bought .38s for all the tellers and had the guns right out in plain sight on the counter. The bank was never hit again."

"You think I'm a spy?" John J. pounded the table. "Answer me!"

Powder River stepped into the breach. "Let's cool it. We've all worked together for years. We know each other. But if you tell two people something, one's going to blab innocently. I move that Greg keep all information about the *Marco Polo* strictly confidential except for Lynne and Barbara and those actually engaged in the operation."

Meg seconded, John J. protested, Greg called for a vote and the motion carried.

McAdoo asked, "Do we need an espionage unit? Aren't we getting reports now from the State Department?"

"Some," Greg answered. "Mostly about what other countries are doing. Not about private corporations. Nothing, of course, on our competitors in the United States."

John J. coughed. "I don't mind telling you, gentlemen, I'm disturbed about all of this."

"Put that down in the minutes." Greg had reached the point of no return with John J.

Al looked startled. He reached for a sheet of notepaper. "Yes, sir."

Carlos said, "Let's hurry it up. I'm going to be late for my golf game. I move we authorize Greg to hire a gunman—"

"Carlos!" Powder River stopped him cold. "I'll word the motion. I move we authorize Greg to employ someone to head up security and espionage and authorize him to spend whatever it takes to get the job done."

"Second," Meg said.

"Now hold on," John J. said.

Greg ignored him. "All in favor signify by raising their right hands." He looked about. "Motion passed."

John J. protested. "You didn't give me a chance to vote."

"I counted you," Greg said. "Seven to one."

Carlos leaned over to Powder River. "I don't know what's against coming right out and saying we're hiring a gunman."

Meg got up to open a window since John J. had laid down a heavy smoke barrage with his pipe. She covered by saying, "Hope no one minds. I'm a fresh-air fiend."

Greg stood up. "You're right, Carlos. We need gunslingers. And before anyone says anything"—he looked toward Dr. Jordan—"we're not out to do any killing. But more than two men may hit us tonight."

"Your imagination's running away with you," John J. said caustically.

Greg ignored him. "We've got to move the contents out of the safe and do it fast. How about it, Carlos? You're handy with a gun."

"And give up my golf game? No way." He grinned. "Okay, señor, I'm with you."

Meg held up a hand. "I'm not Belle Starr, but I'm not a bad shot. My late dear husband insisted on it."

Maybe he had, Greg thought, but her training preceded him. Her place outside Boise had been an armed compound. She had been arrested twice on disorderly charges involving gunplay.

Greg said, "Thank you, Meg. Jim?"

Jim McAdoo laughed. "I've never fired a gun in my life outside of blanks on movie sets."

Dr. Ron Jordan put in, "Same here. I must tell you, Greg, in all good conscience and not meaning to be overly critical, that I cannot approve of this course of action. I'm a pacifist. I don't believe killing is warranted under any circumstances."

Carlos said, "You've just never met anyone who needed killing."

"Hold it, Carlos." Greg took a deep breath. "I respect your beliefs, Ron. I think every man should stand up for what he thinks is right."

John J. took a final puff before tapping the pipe bowl. "I'm no pacifist. Not by a damn sight. But I'm not out gunning for a fight. Count me out."

"I've never owned a gun," Al said.

Powder River spoke up. "I'm in, of course. What've you got in mind?"

Greg glanced at his watch. "Two ten. I figure on four hours to box it. Ten to Los Angeles. We'll charter a plane there."

"You're putting the stuff on the *Marco Polo*?"

Greg nodded. "For two reasons. We're using the film footage and maps all the time, and we've got to have them accessible. So we can't store them in a vault. And two, we'll turn the ship into an armed fort and it'll be as safe as a vault. Any other ideas . . . suggestions?"

"You telling me," said Carlos, "I'm going to Hawaii?"

Meg tittered. "Don't worry, Carlos. They play golf there, too."

"How much will it cost us?" John J. asked.

Greg referred to notes. "I've reserved a Grumman Gulfstream II—"

"You did what! Without Board approval?"

Greg continued quietly, "—at a cost of $3,350 an hour. We figure five hours to Honolulu from Los Angeles which will run to $16,750. And then there will be a deadhead return of the plane to Los Angeles at $6,700. Call it $24,000."

John J. hit the table hard. "I've backed you up for years, Greg!" He hesitated, sputtering. "But this is the final straw. We've got to crack down on costs around here. You've gone too far without . . . without . . . a vote of this Board."

Carlos came to his feet. "There's only one vote I want to take—and that's to vote you off this Board."

Meg had difficulty restraining herself. "As a banker, John, you've got to admit that $24,000 isn't too high an insurance policy to cover an investment of more than three million."

"We'll take a vote," Greg put in.

"I've taken it," Al said. "Seven to one. Measure passed."

Carlos spoke up. "I move we give John J. two-weeks' notice and severance pay of one dollar."

John J. advanced on him, shouting, "You spics and niggers are all alike! Can't take criticism."

Greg blocked him. "Sit down!" He waited until John J. sat. "I didn't hear that. But if I ever do in the future, I'm going to knock the guy who said it straight out the window."

He paused, then turned to Powder River. "Can you get us armed in four hours?"

"No problem."

Carlos left for his ranch near Wilcox to pack and Meg for Tucson. Powder River said he would buy whatever he needed in Honolulu. The others drifted away in stunned silence.

By 6:30 they had completed the packing. They loaded eight sizable cartons into a Purolator armored truck rented by phone from Tucson. An identical eight cartons were stacked in Powder River's Chevrolet pickup. Another identical eight were carted to Greg's Cessna on the airstrip.

It was the old shell game. Only one set contained the exploratory material. The other two sets were dummies.

Greg had a caller that afternoon. The receptionist said she had been in several times. She had a mining claim to sell him. He was desperate for time. In Los Angeles he would have refused to see her but here among desert people one didn't do that. One always had time.

She was in her early seventies, he would guess. She was stoop shouldered and walked with a shuffle. She wore a drab, monotone-gray dress that looked threadbare. Her hair was dirty white, stringy and long, and bunched into a bun. Her low black shoes were badly cracked. Her only decorative feature was an old-fashioned cameo on a rattan chain. He felt immediately protective of her. He always did around old people.

He told her Carson was not in the market to buy mining claims, but he would take her name and address. Her name was Nancy Fickett and she lived at 101 Slag Alley in Bisbee.

Afterward Greg placed several phone calls. The first was to Bill Madden in Honolulu.

Bill cnjoyed rambling. He never used ten words when fifty would do. Greg asked how many security men he had working for him.

"Three. Two at night and me and another feller days. I figured—"

"Double the number—and buy all the weapons you need. And figure on a sneak attack. We've had trouble here. Two guys tried to make off with the safe. Lynne got shot."

"Shot!"

"She's okay. She'll be up and around in a couple of days."

"Nothin' like that's goin' to happen here. You know me. I can handle 'em. I don't need any more—"

"Dammit, will you listen? I said double the guards. I know what I'm doing."

Bill was hurt. "Well, if you say so . . ."

"I want revolvers, shotguns, rifles . . . and put an M3 submachine gun on the bow and another on the stern . . . and get some M2 carbines. I want people to think we'll blow anyone sky high who comes messing around. You got that, Bill?"

Hanging up, Greg sat disturbed. It wasn't that Bill was seventy but that Bill thought of himself as an invincible army.

The second call was to Laura. Before Greg could start, she said sadly, "You're not coming home."

"Something's come up, hon, and I've got to get to Honolulu tonight. I'll call you from there."

"I miss Mom."

He swallowed hard. "Of course you do. I do, too, hon. I'll be back in a couple of days and we'll go see her together, okay?"

"Sure. Tomorrow's her birthday. We ought to take her something . . ."

"No rabbits."

When Laura was seven, she had taken her savings and bought her mother a live, white, pink-nosed rabbit.

"Right, Daddy." Her voice brightened. "No more rabbits."

Powder River pulled out first. He had a citizen's band radio. Meg sat beside him, taut as a cat in alien territory. Her hands rested on a .45.

The armored truck followed by a hundred yards. A quarter mile behind, two Santa Cruz Sheriff's Deputies trailed in an unmarked car. To their rear, in another unmarked car, were two Arizona Highway patrolmen. Overhead, Greg hovered in the Cessna, Carlos in the co-pilot's seat. Rambunctious had been left behind, to be looked after by Janet Stowe.

7

As far as Greg could see, the land stretched up into great mountain ranges. They were old and tired, their wrinkles furrowed deep, their shadows heavy. Barely moving overhead were small white clouds, daubs of whipped cream from an aerosol can.

Below was a harsh desert of scrub growth, pockmarked by green oases and scattered settlements and schools. The Apaches had swept this land, led by the great warriors, Cochise and Geronimo, and now in the twentieth century others prowled the land: muggers, rapists, killers, the Mafian brotherhood and all the personified ingredients of the criminal wave that had splashed across a terrified world. The Apaches had fought for their homeland. Those below murdered and tortured because they had no regard for life. Everyone died sometime, didn't he? What did it matter if he died now? So what?

Greg flew far behind the caravan. He scanned the Nogales-Tucson highway for evidence of a surveillance. Then he shot ahead. The traffic appeared normal. Cars roared past the armored truck and officers at 65, 70 and 75 miles an hour. The caravan maintained a steady 55, the speed limit. In the west, the sunset took on the look of theater banners unfurled across the sky. They were red with a spectacular overlay of black from the smoke of a nearby forest fire.

The glistening whiteness below of the old Spanish mission, San Xavier del Bac, "the white dove of the desert," indicated Tucson was near. Built by Father Eusebio Kino in 1700, the mission still tended the spiritual needs of the Papagos, the only major Indian tribe that never fought a war with the white man. Its wings spread a considerable distance and its wide body rose tall. Two Moorish towers reached toward the heavens, one never finished—and no one knew why. He thought it must be the most beautiful expression man had ever conceived in the telling of his love for God.

Though they were not Catholics, they had come every Christmas for midnight mass and crowded in with the Papagos. In the starry, wide eyes of the Indian children they discovered anew the joy of Christ's birth.

Tucson, a desert town that had mushroomed to a half million, looked far bigger from the air. Looking down, he experienced a shadow of guilt creeping over him. He should be with Laura. Yet he knew Barb would want him to keep their plans moving, this dream they had worked so hard to bring to maturity.

He remembered their wedding, the gift she bought him, a cuckoo clock. She had lacked sixty cents of having enough but the old clockmaker had shrugged and wrapped it for her. Greg prized that clock. It still ticked away in the hallway. If it ever stopped . . . there had been another cuckoo, back in his boyhood. He had been brought up with it. It died when he was seventeen and its death had marked the end of his youth.

On the dashboard Powder River's .38 Colt jolted with every movement. Anchored firmly between him and Meg was his old .30-.30 rifle, and easily within reach behind the seat was a .357 Magnum. If ambushed, he intended to come out firing.

He glanced at Meg who was a quiet woman, seldom engaging in idle talk. Actually, he didn't know much about her. She had come out of nowhere to buy up a hunk of stock, and Greg had put in a good word for her.

He had liked the boy, as he called Greg, from the night they first met at a football game. He was straightforward, honest, hard-working, yet quick to laugh. It was obvious he was going somewhere.

Gradually Powder River came to think of him as the son he had never had. He had never married, and looking back, couldn't figure out why. Too busy making money? Never a girl he wanted so badly it hurt? Maybe. Anyway, the years went by and here he was. He was ambivalent toward the subject. He saw Greg and Barbara and wished he had known the love they had. He saw other couples who fought and screamed, and he thanked the Lord he was single.

Although Greg was like a son, Powder River would never have invested a dime in him on the basis of sentiment. He was tough minded when it came to putting out money. Along with the hundred thousand he had inherited from his father, a dry goods merchant in Pocatello, Idaho, had come a mind steeled against emotion, a mind that could appraise a man as if he were on a slave block. In his twenties he had worked out his financial strategy. Invest in people, not things. Invest in ten persons at a time. One would lose you money, five would get your money back without a profit, three would show a small return, and one would prove a bonanza. Greg was the bonanza.

Powder River considered himself fortunate. Not only did he have a money-making machine but a son who was appreciative. Any time he did anything for Greg and Barbara, they let him know they loved him for it. Some of his friends hung the moon for their kids and never got a thank you.

"Meg," he said, "what're you so quiet about?"

"Didn't want to be a bother when you're counting your money."

He laughed, a big, roisterous roar in the night. "Mind if I smoke?"

"Keep the window down."

He lit up, then picked up the radio phone. "Boy?"

"Yeah," Greg answered.

"What's holding us up? I've never driven fifty-five in my life."

Greg talked with the highway patrol. "We could be sitting ducks. Can't we get special dispensation to move at seventy?"

"We'll ask Phoenix," was the answer.

They rendezvoused in Gila Bend, a collection of motels and gas stations searching for a town. By now it was 9:30 and Greg was nervous. The big rigs that carted America's freight had come out of hiding. They were a thundering, smelly herd and their spotlights pierced the dark like something out of science fiction. It would be easy for one to block the armored car, roll out an arsenal of high-powered weapons, and hijack it.

Greg hurried in refueling the Cessna at the little airstrip outside of town. At the Phillips' station, the cars loaded up on gasoline. At the same time a waitress from the Space Age restaurant across the street brought packaged dinners.

Before Greg took off, all parties held a final check of plans. Once they reached the main highway, 10 West, not far beyond Buckeye, they had many miles to cross of lonesome, sparse and eerie desert. There would be no signs of human habitation, no service stations even, only a few mines up in the canyons of the far mountains. It was another galaxy.

It would be an ideal area for a shoot-out. Armed with the proper cannon, the enemy could blast the officers and Powder River and Meg off the highway before they knew they had been attacked. The armored-car guards would have no choice but to surrender. The attackers could drive the car up into one of the canyons and rifle it before the news reached Blythe in one direction or Phoenix in the other.

Greg might thwart them. Powder River had armed him with hand grenades, a submachine gun, flares and several small firearms. Still, the enemy might have the fire power to bring him down.

Fleecy white clouds, back lighted by a nearly full moon, floated gracefully across the sky ahead. The night was so bright that Greg could spot tire carcasses along the road below.

Shortly after the Buckeye turnoff, a sign loomed up: BEGIN FREEWAY-2 MILES-LOS ANGELES, 382. A long way to go.

"I think," Greg said to Carlos, "I know how the pioneers felt when they came through here in their wagon trains and knew Indian war parties were up ahead."

Carlos yawned. "Yeah."

Over the radio, a highway officer said, "Phoenix advises we must hold to fifty-five. Sorry but it's a hot issue in Arizona. The state legislature voted down a proposal to raise it."

"Thanks for asking," Greg said.

Chalk one up for the killers. Give them every break.

His cheeks hot with resentment, he turned to Carlos. "How's Rosita?" Anything to get his emotions subdued. Besides, he liked Rosita. Carlos' wife was as beautiful as any Spanish woman Goya ever painted.

"Worried sick about my shooting the rustler. So are the boys, even if they are only ten and twelve. Kids grow up fast these days. They're scared I'll be charged with murder—and my lawyer says I could be."

He took a deep breath. "They got away with thirty-six cows off my spread in the last two months."

The cars below sketched a circle to enter the freeway. On the right, shimmering in the moonlight, rose-gray, scarred mountains, rock monoliths out of the Ice Age. Greg moved toward them, away from the highway, to scan the ground for movement.

Carlos' voice trembled. "So help me, God, I'm not going to let the scoundrels run me off the land. It's been in my family since 1792. A land grant from the Spanish crown."

He was quiet a moment but had to talk. "Did I tell you about the Mexican wetbacks who have been stealing me blind? They come across at night and take anything not nailed down. Hell, I fired a few shots over the heads of three or four one night last week and a couple of days later a smart-ass county attorney, a deputy, comes around and says if I threaten human life again, he'll haul me in. I tell him they didn't have any right being on my land much less being in the United States. He wouldn't listen. They never do."

Greg pointed to a pack of animals running below. "Coyotes."

He added, "If I can do anything . . . anything at all. You'd think the criminals have all the rights . . . look down there."

A Seville was following the caravan, maintaining identical speed. "Could be on automatic cruise," Carlos said.

A few miles later, the Seville zoomed ahead and passed the unmarked police cars and the armored vehicle. After several more miles, it pulled over and stopped; then after the caravan passed, resumed its trail position. It was the classic surveillance pattern.

"A woman's driving," an officer reported. "Sacramento advises license belongs to Budget Rent-A-Car agency at the Los Angeles International Airport. We're asking airport police to run a check. We could use a pretext to stop and question her, but if she is tailing us, I don't like to show our hand. Okay with you?"

Greg agreed. "Any chance she's talking with someone up ahead?"

"We took a fix on her. Negative. We're passing her. She's an older woman. At least fifty. Could be sixty. We couldn't make out coloring or features. What about up there? Everything clear ahead?"

"You're approaching a big rig. About a mile away. Nothing coming at us from any crossroads or trails. About three miles behind, another rig but he's well loaded and moving slowly."

Carlos said, "We need security."

"I'll get security lined up before the week's out."

"What if we get slammed up ahead?"

"I'll make a sweep over them, drop a few grenades, and you let them have it with the .30-.30. I'll pull up fast and pray they don't hit us. Then I'll bank and come back in for another sweep."

"You know what? For a quiet guy who seems so damn relaxed, you've got an awful lot of guts."

Below on the ground, the cars passed a sign: REST AREA, 22 MILES. NEXT SERVICES, 64 MILES.

Greg tensed. Under them was a small craft barely skirting the brush, flying dangerously low. It was obvious the pilot was staying under the radar screen.

Carlos said, "He's got a load of coke or heroin."

"Probably—but he could be spotting us. He could be loaded with firepower."

Greg reported the plane to the Arizona Highway officers. In turn, they notified the Border Patrol. Shortly afterward the craft headed north and out of sight. It was still hedge-hopping. Perhaps, Greg thought, it would return; perhaps, though, it had completed its mission of informing someone somewhere of the location of the caravan.

The miles droned by. The monotony told on nerves and strength. A weariness set in. Each one fought it. Each one knew he had to keep alert, tense. The Seville disappeared far into the distance and was not seen again.

Off to the left a line of steel girders stretched for miles. They once had carried power lines but now belonged in *Star Wars*. A playful desert twister spun out of nowhere, skirted across the road and vanished.

For the most part, the freeway ran straight. As clouds filtered the moonlight and the hours grew longer, they struggled against drowsiness. Bodies shifted and moved and lungs drew more and deeper breaths. Powder River turned the wheel over to Meg, the guards exchanged positions, and so did the highway officers. Only Greg remained at the controls. To keep awake, he dipped the little aircraft, flew at different altitudes, and would race far ahead, scouring the countryside.

They passed EXIT 19, QUARTZSITE, and finally reached the Colorado River, the border line between Arizona and California. As they bade farewell to the Arizona Highway Patrol, the California one took over. Across the river was the Blythe Marina, an oasis of palm trees. Beyond the Marina was Blythe proper where they would refuel and have a quick snack.

The time was 12:44. Los Angeles was five hours distant.

General Schepnov was sleeping when the call came through. He leaped in a moment's fright to his feet, then remembered where he was, in a beautifully decorated apartment far out on Massachusetts Avenue. He had taken it over from a military attaché who was being recalled to Moscow.

The woman on the phone was breathless and happy. "I just arrived, darling, and thought you might be worried, so I called you right away."

She was Nataya Fussen. He knew from the hour that she was calling from Blythe, California.

"I'm glad you did, my dear. I've been worried about you."

Decoded: Did everything go according to schedule?

"You shouldn't've been, darling. It was a beautiful trip."

Decoded: Everything's okay.

"Will you be staying very long? I thought your mother—"

Decoded: Will the party proceed to Los Angeles or spend the night in Blythe?

"Mother's so anxious to see me. I just talked with her and I'll be going to her place soon as I can get away from Uncle Bert without hurting his feelings."

Decoded: The party will leave Blythe shortly.

"Good night, darling."

Decoded: She must go.

"Good night, my dear."

Decoded: Message understood.

Elated, General Schepnov started to pour himself a scotch and soda. He preferred it to vodka. He pushed the bottle back. That morning he had weighed six pounds more than he should have.

There would be no more bungling such as last night with the safe. Nataya was in charge at this end and Rashid Jumeira had taken control in Honolulu. This first step would delay the sailing of the *Marco Polo* by months. What was equally important, the *Kharkov* would have the film footage, the maps, all of the scientific data the Russian oceanographers needed. With the right break, Gregory Wilson might be killed.

"I've passed his picture out to our men," Nataya Fussen had said. "If they decide to shoot it out . . ."

8

Freshly bathed, the Gulfstream II sat at one far end of the commuter terminal at Los Angeles International Airport. Two airline transport captains were fussing over it, and inside, a steward, who was also a certified mechanic, was stocking the bar and checking the food for a catered breakfast and dinner. The twelve seats were leather trimmed and the lavatory the size of a dressing room. There was an air-to-ground phone. With such appointments, 2,400 charter companies in the United States were flying nine million passengers a year.

Greg was busy supervising the loading of the twenty-four cartons. Powder River and Carlos were wandering about looking the ship over. Meg was not in sight. The trip from Blythe had been uneventful.

The airport police had cordoned off the area. The officer in charge reported to Greg that the Budget Rent-A-Car agency records showed that one Mrs. Odessa Sampson, 418 South Grimaldi, Oakland, California, had signed for the Seville. She had shown a California driver's license, Y0137613. A check of the Department of Motor Vehicles, Sacramento, revealed that that particular license had been issued to a party in Encino, California. The clerk on duty at the time recalled little about Mrs. Sampson, other than that she was an older woman, well dressed and with a pleasant voice. She had turned the car in an hour ago and paid cash.

Powder River took Greg aside. "Before the police got here, a woman in her fifties was noseying around. The pilot found her inside the plane and asked her to leave."

"Get me the pilot." Greg turned to the charter company man. "I want the plane checked for possible sabotage."

The man was taken aback. "Our mechanics—"

"I demand that the plane be gone over very carefully."

"Very well, sir, but it'll delay us several hours."

Greg nodded and turned to Carlos. "Where's Meg?"

"She went to get coffee."

The steward spoke up. "I told her we had coffee aboard."

"You wanted to see me, sir?" The pilot was Greg's own height.

"This woman—was she poorly dressed? With stringy hair?"

"On the contrary, sir. Very attractive, well dressed, hair done. She was curious, that's all. Not many people get to see the inside of a luxury craft."

"May I interrupt?" A nicely suited airport detective with a bold nose and the eyes of a Weimaraner strode toward Greg. "Do you have reason, Mr. Wilson, to suspect sabotage?"

Greg shrugged. "Let's just say I'm paranoid."

The detective stared in disbelief, then turned away. He met all kinds.

When he had the boxes loaded, Greg looked them over one last time. No one knew which set of eight contained the film footage, maps and other documents. Not Meg or Carlos or Powder River. And to his relief, no one had asked.

The detective reappeared. "I have instructions to ask if any of the passengers will be carrying firearms aboard?"

Greg smiled. "We're too tired to hijack a plane tonight." He had warned the others to conceal their weapons. He had no idea where Carlos and Powder River had hidden their rifles and didn't want to know.

"Is that yes or no?"

The officer was getting on Greg's nerves. "Don't hassle me."

The charter company man spoke up. "He said no."

The detective asked if he might inspect the boxes. Greg couldn't keep the anger from surfacing. "Those boxes are classified. Top secret."

"By whom, sir?"

Greg said contemptuously, "Washington. Who else?"

The detective hung on. Greg had seen a Gila Monster once with jaws clamped about a wrist. "Do you have a document, sir, some kind of paper I could mention in my report?"

Greg raised his voice. "The Pentagon's going to hear about this."

The detective moistened his lips. "I guess everything's in order. I'm just trying to do my job, sir. Hope you understand?"

Greg relaxed. "You did one hell of a job. Next time I'm at the Pentagon, I'll tell them."

The waters of the Pacific should have been as turbulent as his thoughts. But the waters were calm, though dark.

"Well, so far, so good," Powder River said. Carlos was seated alone, and Meg, too. Scarcely had the plane left the ground than they dropped off to sleep.

When he didn't answer, Powder River said, "I'm not going to give you a blasted penny for your thoughts, but if you want to tell me without charge . . ."

Greg said slowly, "It's got to be an inside job. How else can you figure anyone would know we kept the film and papers in an old safe in a crumbling adobe building in a little settlement in Arizona?"

"John J.?"

Greg shook his head. "He's a stuffed shirt and a bigot, but he's no rat fink."

"Who else?"

"I don't know, but I'm going to get a guy to find out. We're going to out-think them and out-gun them."

A few minutes later the steward handed Greg the phone. "Radio call for you, sir."

"Karl here, Greg." Karl Neustadt of Massachusetts Diversified never needed to identify himself. His gruff, old, St. Bernard voice was as distinctive as his signature.

He continued, "We need you for the Board meeting Tuesday. We've got a ruckus going on back here. About half the Board wants to call off the venture and take our loss. It's going to be close."

Greg was incredulous. "You mean—"

"That's right. They're scared of what Washington may do to us. You'd better run by on your way here and straighten things out with the State Department."

That was impossible. There were people at State who would call out the Pacific fleet, if they could, to stop the *Marco Polo*.

"Trouble?" Powder River asked when Greg hung up.

"A little, back in Boston. Nothing I can't handle."

"Nothing you can't handle anywhere."

The captain's voice came over. Estimated arrival time in Honolulu would be 7:25 P.M.

Now they were encompassed in a soft, white cloud world. They seemed to stand still. Only the faint roar of the jets assured them they were in flight.

He had never been so exhausted. He hadn't slept in nights and couldn't now. He kept replaying a scene from two months ago that he couldn't get out of his mind, and never would.

He had sat by Barb a few minutes. She was sleeping peacefully and had a wisp of a smile. He bent over and kissed her on the forehead and thought she stirred. She was so beautiful. Her dark hair framed perfectly her pixie face. He whispered a prayer.

At the door he almost collided with Dr. Emory Randall. He had been their physician since their university days. He had brought Laura into the world. By now he was an old friend.

"I'm glad I found you, Greg. I want to talk with you." He was in his early sixties, a little stooped, hair graying, matching his gray suit, his glasses slipping down his nose. He was a blunt man who scorned the bedside manner, yet had tremendous compassion for his patients.

He led the way into the corridor. "Should be a vacant office around here this time of night."

Greg was panicked. Physicians did not take one aside unless the situation was critical.

Emory Randall found a dark administrator's office, switched on a fluorescent light, and seated himself on a sofa. Greg took the opposite end. He had not said a word.

"You know how fond I am of you and Barbara." He looked directly at Greg. "But I have to give it to you straight. The two specialists we brought in will send you a report filled with medical terms. They will tell you that the electroencephalogram definitely establishes that she has cerebral atrophy and cerebral dysfunction. This means that the electroencephalogram runs in a straight line. To put it simply in layman's terms, Barbara's brain has died and she will never come out of the coma. I can't tell you how long she will live. It could be years—if we keep her on the machines and continue feeding her intravenously."

Greg had a hand over his eyes. His breathing was spasmodic. "She'll come out of it," he said quietly. "I know she will. She believes in miracles."

Emory Randall felt the heartbreak himself as he told Greg, "In this situation there can be no miracle."

He shifted his position on the sofa and leaned forward. "Now that I've talked to you as a physician, I want to as a friend. You've got to steel yourself, Greg. You've got to go about your work. I know the pressures and responsibilities you have—and I'm glad you have them. Barbara would want you to continue as if she were with you. Remember, if you fail because you bury yourself in grief, you will be failing her. And the project meant a lot to her.

"As for Laura, tell her after school some afternoon. Just the two of you. Let her sit by her mother's bedside if she wants to. For hours if she feels better about it. In time she'll come out of the shock. She's young and strong and adaptable. The main thing is, you've got to set an example.

"Now I'm going to leave you. You sit here as long as you want to."

Greg sat a long time. He would ask Emory Randall to bring in another specialist. He would ask God to heal her. He would have faith. He might not even tell Laura.

He walked to the door. His legs seemed about to buckle. He turned off the light. He stood moments in the dark. Another specialist could do nothing more. God, for whatever reason, had already taken Barb. Now he must sort out his life, start over. He must think of Laura.

Barb would want it that way.

9

That morning General Schepnov arrived at the office a little after nine. He dragged in a collection of aches and pains that increased with each year. They diminished at the sight of Rona Hale. She was busy typing up condensations she did each day of stories in the Midwestern newspapers about the grain crops. Dutifully he initialed them to indicate he had read them, which he had not. The next time he swore he was going to get a "cover" that did not involve such ridiculous procedure.

"Good morning, General," she said brightly. She was better for his aches than aspirin. She wore simple, modest dresses that were never revealing, and yet somehow they were. She had casually dropped into the conversation the first day the fact that she was engaged. Decoded, that meant no sex. Still, in time . . . one never knew.

He had formed a liaison with a young Russian woman at the Embassy who could quote Karl Marx verbatim and unfortunately did so in bed at the most inopportune times. Nothing could deflate a man's interest as much as Marx. For that matter, he didn't care for Marx in bed or out. It was one of those tragic mishaps of history that someone as tedious and boring as Marx had founded the Socialist movement.

"We got the mail early," she said. "It's on your desk."

He nodded. "I'll take the phone calls today." He offered no explanation. He handed her a Garfinkel department store advertisement torn from the Washington *Post*. "Please, will you buy this 'Star Wars' machine and wrap it and tell the mail room to put it in the diplomatic pouch. It's for my grandson."

In the inner office he found the desk dusted as usual, pencils sharpened, the carafe filled with ice water, a new supply of paper clips and one fresh rose in a slender vase. As per instructions, the mail had not been opened. Not that he could determine. Daily he examined it carefully. It was a little game he played to see if he could catch her.

He was scarcely started on the mail when Nataya phoned. She said, "Darling, I shouldn't be putting in all of these calls. I know how expensive they are, but I had to let you know I'll be on my way to Mother's soon."

Decoded: They will take off shortly for Honolulu.

He asked, "Uncle Bert didn't mind?"

Decoded: Any problems?

"Not at all. He's so understanding. I'll call you when I get to Mother's."

Decoded: She will call from Honolulu.

They engaged in brief chitchat. After she said good-bye, he waited before hanging up until he heard a second click which indicated Miss Hale had returned the receiver to its receptacle.

He smiled and continued with the correspondence. A half hour later he called a friend at an import-export business. They asked about each other's health and that of several mutual acquaintances.

The General brushed into the conversation a quick question. "Have you talked with Meg out in Arizona?"

"No, I haven't. Have you?"

"Yes, she calls me occasionally. Still the same old Meg. She's been very helpful."

They set up a date to go to a concert. Once again when the General said good-bye, he waited for the ensuing click before hanging up.

Afterward he took a transcript from his inside coat pocket. He had recorded the phone conversation he had had in the sidewalk booth at 7 P.M. last Sunday, at K and 14th streets. Each morning when he was fresh, he studied it. It was amazing how much information an unknown party could reveal about himself in conversation.

He had arrived at the booth at 6:55. It was on the northeast corner in front of the Golden Skillet, a coffee shop on the ground floor of the Hamilton Mall. Like most Washington phone booths, it covered only the top part of the body. His gaze skirted nervously about. An older man, certainly in his sixties, appeared to be watching him from in front of McDonald's across the street. He picked his teeth a few moments, then took off down K, passing the Robinhood Restaurant.

The General felt other eyes on him. On the other side of McDonald's, a tall, stooped figure in his thirties, in a rumpled dark suit and with shirt collar open, stared brazenly. He raised a hand as if in signal to someone, then sauntered in the direction two blocks away of the honky-tonks, the adult movies and Doc Johnson's Marital Aids.

The General felt conspicuous and insecure. He feared he might have been lured into a death trap by an assassin. Even a terrorist from his own country or one of the satellites. Comrade Andropov and the Politburo had done much for all the ethnic groups, yet there were those mentally unbalanced dissidents who in the name of independence killed without reason.

He could have sent another to take the phone call. The Embassy had any number of bright young men and women who were expendable. But if the note had come from a legitimate party—legitimate in the sense that the writer sincerely wished to be of service to the Soviets—then the job required one of experience and diplomatic finesse. Such a phone call could be ruined by a wrong word or intonation.

Under his coat he held a tiny recorder. He would tape the phone call by pressing a small rubber suction disc at the end of a wire running from the recorder to the phone receiver.

Within a few feet of him passed an expensively dressed couple. They strolled hand in hand, too enveloped in their own orbit to notice him. A streetwalker sauntered by, caught sight of him, and stopped. She switched on a tired smile and waited. When he shook his head, she shrugged and walked on. A couple of boys shot by on a skateboard. As they did, a Caprice crawled along slowly. The driver and his companion, both young men, looked him over. A prickly sweat crawled over the General's body. Possibly they were homosexuals searching for a pickup. Not only did an agent have to shrug off the women prostitutes these days but also the men. He hated the lot of them.

On the dot of seven, the phone rang. He picked up the receiver and said, "Hello."

A man's strong voice said, "I'm calling for MJ. Do I have the right party?" He spoke with authority.

"Yes." The General's voice was low, inviting confidences.

"Do we have a deal?"

"You are not MJ?"

"I speak for MJ."

"We cannot talk with MJ?"

"Later."

"A man or woman?"

"I'm not at liberty to say."

The General deliberately hesitated. "This is awkward. We like to deal with the principal."

"If you have the $25,000 ready . . ." The man was pressing. He was obviously harried.

"Does she work for the *Marco Polo* people?" The General had concluded from the note that the writer was a woman.

"I did not identify the sex of MJ." The man wanted that on the record. "I cannot tell you where MJ works."

The General took another approach. "We need to see what you have to sell. I hope you understand. Could I meet you somewhere?"

"Why talk? I have 5,000 feet of the Pacific Ocean floor, the best mining sites, 24 maps, several score pages of notes vital to any mining expedition, the date the *Marco Polo* will sail, and the exact mining date. I think MJ's charge of $25,000 is very reasonable."

"Too reasonable. My people know it is worth much more if it is what you say, and this bothers my people. They cannot understand—"

The man broke in. "MJ knows this. MJ is asking only for expenses. MJ believes in what the Soviets are doing for the working people of the world and wants to help. MJ is a party member."

"In the United States?"

"I cannot say."

The General was sweating. He had to be careful. He could blow the deal. KGB would authorize payment of at least $100,000 if the merchandise were as described. The asking price of $25,000 reinforced the possibility that MJ was acting out of belief in the Soviets. He said slowly, "If we could meet, I would bring the money and hand it over to you after I see the material."

"I can't meet you or let MJ. It's too dangerous. But if you'll leave the money, I'll leave the product."

The General dared not pay sight unseen the $25,000. This could be a rip-off. There had been others, and the agents involved were no longer with the KGB. "We need assurance that we are dealing with the right party. You have not told me where MJ works or how MJ came into possession of this merchandise or what part you play in these arrangements."

The man reacted violently. "Okay, the deal's off! MJ told me to forget it if you were difficult."

"Now just a minute," the General said patiently. "We are never difficult. We are easy to deal with. We are known throughout the world for our generosity when it comes to buying merchandise. But I have superiors to account to, and they require that I know whom I am talking with. I must meet MJ."

"Then it's off!" the man said sharply. "Good-bye!"

"Wait!" the General called out. He was squirming. He knew the man knew he and the KGB were hooked. Hundreds of millions of rubles were at stake, perhaps billions.

"Be reasonable," the General continued. "Why don't we do this? You send me what you think is worth a thousand, and I will leave $1,000 at a place you choose. My superiors then will be assured they are dealing with the right parties."

The man calmed. "Do you have someone in Hawaii who can drop the money?"

"Where?"

"You have someone?"

"I asked where?"

10

That same morning, Hotel Street in Honolulu, not far from the docks, belied its reputation as one of the world's most sinful districts. It had the feel of a ghost town. Only a few persons were about. A Chinese hurried along with an attaché case. A couple of Japanese girls, chattering like teenagers everywhere, passed him on their way to school. A little old Portuguese, his furrowed face a photographer's dream, toted a fishing pole and a can for bait.

Only the signs in English and occasionally Japanese indicated Hotel Street's business: Risque Theater, Open Upstairs 24 Hours; China Sea Tattoo; Hubba Hubba, Topless and Bottomless; All-American Theater—Films for Males—Films for Females; and the Original Bath House.

Shortly after dusk the place would come alive but not until

about ten would the streetwalkers come out in droves. They sold straight sex. On the side streets off Hotel, the male homosexuals had taken over two blocks where they paraded, and the lesbians an adjoining two. Agreement was unanimous that the men were more beautiful than the women.

Hotel Street may look much the same as it did to the GIs of World War II, but beneath the hedonistic search for thrills there has grown a fear that respectability may accomplish what the authorities never have. That part of Hotel Street closest to the city has been taken over by stores and banks, and smart new buildings have climbed skyward. Gradually the hated Establishment has been creeping in and money has been ruthlessly routing the playgrounds.

These thoughts were furthermost from the mind of Rashid Jumeira as he walked Hotel Street under a hot sun tempered by the well-advertised balmy ocean breeze. He wore a cheap, splashy-colored Hawaiian shirt that fell over dark seersucker trousers. The shirt concealed a .22 automatic stashed under his belt. He had removed his watch and had no wallet. He had the greatest respect for pickpockets.

Near the corner of Hotel and Nuuanu he entered a saloon, and stopped just inside the door to reconnoiter. A swarthy bartender was checking his liquor supply behind a long, highly polished bar that would have been at home in an old Western town. Two billiard tables overwhelmed the remainder of the place. A couple in their thirties were quietly playing.

At the bar he ordered a beer. "Coors," he said. The bartender took a second look. Jumeira had studied at Oxford and had diligently cultivated the accent acquired there. The barman would take another look when Jumeira failed to drink the beer. He was a strict adherent to the tenets of Islam, not only in regard to abstaining from alcohol but in other pursuits as well, such as homicide. He never used a gun except when he was convinced the party was an infidel and it would be to the glory of Allah to eliminate him from the current scene. Since the strict, historic definition of infidel included all Christians and Jews, he never had to debate the issue at much length with himself.

"I'm looking for the Welder." He pushed the beer back and slipped a dollar bill under the glass.

The bartender said crustily, "If you don't drink, don't order. You're welcome here whether you buy or don't. You know the Welder?"

"I've got work for her."

"Where you from, mister? I can't place the accent, and we got nothing but accents around here. We're all minorities. The Fed Government comes in and says we got to take care of the minorities. Hell, that's all of us."

"Oxford. A long time ago."

"You're like them New Zealanders who come in here. They don't even understand them in England. They work at it."

He shot Jumeira another sharp glance and decided he was a right guy. "She doesn't come in until one. Brings her own sandwich. Has a couple of beers. Wants to talk mainly. Lonesome. Lives by herself. Never married."

He picked up the dollar. "You get a lot for your money here. Turn right, go two blocks, turn right again, half block, and you're there. Check the mailboxes. Tell her Jimmy sent you, and she's to bake me a pie as my share of the deal."

Jumeira had no difficulty finding her. Before he could knock, she opened the door. She was short, in her fifties, easily weighed 200, and her bright, shifty eyes set in a crab-apple face were recessed in fat. She was in a muumuu which did little to conceal her poundage.

"Come on in. Sit down. What kinda work you got in mind? Jimmy phoned. I don't do nothing illegal. I'm not into drugs, bank holdups, muggin's, con jobs. I'm legit."

She led him into a dark room. The shades were pulled. The room was so small he watched where he placed his feet.

"Sit down," she repeated. "Right here. I only got two chairs. One for me, one for the customer. I'm not into no Mafia racket, no gang work. I'm legitimate. Where ya from?"

"I studied in England."

"God help 'em. Well, look, I like to get right down to it. Whatcha got?"

"I need four strong men to do some moving."

"Like a safe? I'm not in that neither, mister. Whatcha puttin' out?"

"Four hundred for the four. You pay them, keep what you can for yourself."

"Well, why didn't ya say so? For that I could do something a little illegal. Just a teeny bit."

"If you'd turn on a light, I'd show you."

She lit a candle. "Didn't pay my bill. They're screwin' me and I'm screwin' 'em right back."

He unrolled a crude map drawn with a black nylon pen. "You know the airport?"

"Not very well. Figure why should I leave God's country. From what I hear tell they're all goin' straight to hell on the mainland. God'll wreak his vengeance. The Lord says—"

"I'm sure he will." He took a deep breath. He had to get her under control. A friend had told him the Welder could round up as many big muscle guys as he needed. The friend had not told him that once she had the ball she ran with it. The nickname, Welder, had stuck with her since her World War II days at the Lockheed plant in Los Angeles.

He continued quickly, "When you come out of the airport, you take Nimitz. Right here." He indicated with a pencil. "Down at this point, maybe a half mile, Nimitz splits. If you go left, you're on Kam Highway—"

She broke in, irritated. "Kamehameha. It's disrespectful to call it Kam Highway. We had several Kamehamehas. They were our kings before the American bastards took over, and I don't like it when—"

"I understand. I'd feel the same way if I was a Hawaiian." He took another look. "But you're not. You're an Anglo—"

"Don't insult me, you son-of-a-bitch. I'm a hundred percent Hawaiian. My mother—"

"I didn't mean—"

"Well, be careful how you treat a lady."

He got the pencil busy again. "If you take Kamehameha it becomes Dillingham Boulevard. They're building a freeway right over there. But we're not interested in this area. I just wanted to orient you—"

"Do what? Don't talk dirty to me."

"The word means—oh the hell with it. Could you find another candle?"

She rummaged around in a chest drawer and came up with one sadly bent from the heat. She managed to light it. "There. How's that?"

"Fine. Let's go back to Nimitz. At the split, it goes to the right, toward Waikiki. At this point here where the highway splits, there's a triangle, a little plot of ground marked by a string of red iron posts that force the cars to go left or right. Inside the triangle are two white timber barricades with orange stripes. They're the second line of defense in case someone knocks down an iron post."

"Do I have to know all this to do the job? Why don't you run me out there and show me?"

"I'm getting around to that."

"Okay, so you want four men out there doing what?"

"I should tell you there are no shrubs or trees on the triangle. Only weeds. Now this is what I want you to do . . ."

Once he had the muscle men, he would have his staff all set. Already in Honolulu on tourist visas were two military experts from Libya, one from the PLO in Tyre, Lebanon, and a fourth from Havana.

11

On the other side of the field, directly opposite the passenger terminal of Honolulu's International Airport, the Gulfstream II came in for a smooth landing. The pilot pulled it up close to the Air Service Corporation Building. Air Service handled all needs of the charter companies, including fuel, food, permits and bonds when needed. The time was 7:18 P.M. Daylight was beginning to fade.

Meg, freshly made up, looked rested. Powder River had slept fitfully and the dark circles under his pouchy eyes revealed as much. Greg's rugged, youthful looks never deserted him, no matter how worried or harassed he was.

"Hey, Carlos, you old gunslinger, wake up." Greg pushed him hard and Carlos barely opened his eyes.

"Get away from me," Carlos said gruffly.

"Let him sleep," Meg said.

Outside an armored car backed up to the plane's cargo bay. Other cars pulled alongside. Greg shouted at the armored car guards to hold where they were. He had to wait for the stair ramp to be wheeled up. The night was warm and balmy. He breathed deeply and smelled a faint mixture of fragrances. There was nothing like a Hawaiian night.

Greg hurried to the plane's underbelly. Already two loaders were working the boxes. "I'll do that," he said forcibly.

"We handle all freight," one guy muttered.

"Not mine, you don't."

"Who says so?"

Greg gave him a hard push. "Get out of here before you get busted!" The loader took a swing, Greg ducked, and landed a haymaker. The guy hit the ground hard. Carlos, sleepy-eyed, came out of nowhere. He swung a foot to kick the man in the crotch. Greg blocked the blow.

A police officer appeared. Greg explained he had classified material, and the officer told the two loaders to stand off. Furious, they moved a few feet away and stood glowering.

"Trouble?" Meg asked. Greg noted her hand inside her skirt waist and a telltale bulge as it held a small weapon.

He said quickly, "No, no trouble."

Box by box, he personally loaded eight into the armored car, and handed eight to Powder River to place in the station wagon, and eight to Carlos for the 1977 Lincoln.

"Watch the boxes," he told Meg. "Don't let anybody tamper with them."

As he headed for the building, he smiled to himself. Meg looked harmless but was as lethal as Bonnie Parker.

Inside he noted for future reference that Burns International

Security had offices on the second floor. The immediate security, however, took shape in the robust, heavy figure of a brusque, no-nonsense Honolulu police captain, head of a detail of seven officers. His tightly folded lips were only a slash on a melon head. He motioned Greg into a cubbyhole office.

"We're going to hug you tight." He talked in a deadly monotone and sized Greg up as he spoke. "I've got two unmarked cars. One to lead and one to tail, but very tight. Very tight. The Lincoln will come second, then the armored car, then you in the station wagon, and our tail. I'm putting two officers in the lead, two in the tail, and one each in the other vehicles. I was told you were carrying paper. To me that means securities."

Greg nodded. "Negotiable?" the Captain asked.

"Yes."

"How much?"

"Three million, seven hundred thousand."

The Captain got up. "Any of you got firearms?"

"Yeah."

"Don't get in our way if there's trouble. Tell the others. You got that? My officers will do the shooting if any's to be done."

"I'll tell them." A lot of good that will do, he thought.

"We'll run at about 55 when we can. One final check. Dock 14-A. Right?"

"Right."

"About 10 minutes—unless we run into traffic. Nimitz is always busy. Let's go."

The Captain climbed behind the wheel of the lead car. Carlos and Meg sat next to each other in the second. Meg took the driver's seat before Carlos could. When Carlos protested, Meg said, "Come off it, Carlos. You're no driver and never will be."

"Dammit, Meg, I wouldn't take that from anybody but you—and I don't know why I take it from you."

Greg, Powder River and the officer followed the armored vehicle. Greg drove. Behind them, two officers staffed the tail car.

The Captain signaled with a hand and the caravan pulled out. Leaving the airport, he turned left on Lagoon Drive. Beyond the drive was the farthermost stretch of Keehi Lagoon. At this point it had dwindled to a swamp. They passed an old bridge that spanned it.

They proceeded to Nimitz where a red light stopped them. There was an incessant steady roar of traffic moving to and from the airport passenger terminal. The noise, Greg thought, could blot out gunfire.

"I've got a gut feeling I don't like." Greg unholstered the .38 and placed it on his lap. Powder River pulled the .30-.30 closer. Overhead the nervous throbbing of a helicopter sounded. Not too far distant the blinking lights of a 747 signified it was swinging low for a landing. The sound mixture of cars, rigs, planes and copters was overwhelming and distracting. The swelling roar defied concentration. Then the animal scream of an ambulance cut through and Greg shuddered. For some the wail signified men of mercy and medicine on their way to alleviate suffering. Since his teens, though, Greg had associated the cry with unbearable pain and ultimate death.

"What's taking so helldamn long?" Powder River had little patience.

As if to please him, the signal changed. They turned right on Nimitz and soon came to a split in the highway. To the left, the traffic flowed into Kam. Nimitz itself continued on the right to the harbor and docks. The first two cars passed the split-off, taking the road to the right. Then as the armored truck approached, two quick shots were heard and the overhead lights over the triangle went out. At the same moment, the roar of a copter indicated to Greg that the craft was dead overhead.

"Watch it!" Powder River shouted. "Something's up."

The armored car speeded up and passed the split-off. Greg's foot went down heavily on the brakes as a cement mixer suddenly loomed in front of him. Beyond the mixer, he spotted men in the faint night light rushing about carrying white barricades from the triangle and placing them across Nimitz, blocking traffic down that highway and forcing it to move on Kam. Overhead a short distance the whirlybird was dropping ever lower, its lights blinking in the dark. He recognized it as a Sikorsky Sky Crane, designed in the 1960s for the Vietnam War.

"Hold on!" Greg yelled. "I'm going through!" Greg gunned the car and zoomed in front of the cement mixer. The monster suddenly lumbered ahead to attempt a collision. Greg missed it by inches, put more pressure on the gas and crashed the barricades. Hitting one, the car lurched and he almost lost control.

He raced to catch up. An explosion burst in his eardrums. The copter had dropped a mine directly in front of the armored car which shook and jerked convulsively as the driver brought it to a halt a few feet from the gaping hole dug by the exploding shell.

Greg grabbed the emergency brake. An officer jumped out, and hugging the ground, fired shot after shot from his .30-.30 at the big copter. Greg yelled at Powder River who stood in the open, erect and tall, his rifle steady against his shoulder. Again, Greg shouted at him to take cover, then tackled him, throwing him to the ground. Greg grabbed the rifle and for protection squirmed along the ground to the far side of the car. A rifle was no weapon to use on a whirlybird unless the craft descended within range, and it was doing just that. He waited seconds, then aimed for the fuel tank. He figured the others would be gunning for the two men at the controls. He could see only the co-pilot who was a vague shadow until the craft was caught up in the flash of an explosion. The pilot was leaning far out, gripping a tommy submachine gun. He let go with a burst of fire aimed at the armored truck. He had a triumphant smile that somehow was evil.

A second earthquake explosion dug a pit ahead of their station wagon, cutting them off from the armored car. The smoke lay down a thick screen and the smell of gunpowder was heavy in the air.

They were under fire now. Greg could hear the ping of bullets hitting the hood. He heard the officers in the car behind shouting and their gunfire erupting. He was aware Powder River was squatting alongside him.

The copter dropped a smoke shell both in front of and behind the armored car, then descended into the smoke and was lost. He heard the scream of someone wounded or dying. He heard men shouting angrily. He held his fire but kept his finger on the trigger. Up ahead there was incessant gunfire.

He couldn't stay grounded. Everything inside him cried out for action. He got to his feet, and crouching and hugging the ground, stumbled through the blinding acrid smoke. He was coughing hard and gasping for breath. His eyes were streaming and he kept rubbing them with his free hand. He had the terrifying sensation he was alone in a deafening world of explosions and any second would be blown to bits.

He came to the shell hole and barely caught himself in time. One step more and he would have catapulted in. He heard the thrashing close by of rotor blades. He brought the rifle up and fired in the direction of the roar. He visualized it as a target and aimed for the vortex.

Then the copter was rising. Through the smoke he saw, as if looking through a dirty window, the armored car being lifted. It was a baby elephant cradled in a cable pendant about fifty feet long. He fired more rounds but they were wasted. The smoke lay in layers which distorted the copter's position. It moved under full throttle steadily upward until it had gained elevation. Then with its double rotors roaring the copter moved north toward Diamond Head. Soon it was lost in the dark.

Back at the car, Greg ripped asunder Powder River's right shirt sleeve. "What're you doing, boy?" Powder River shouted. Below his elbow was a light crease where a bullet had cut the flesh as neat as if a knife had been used. Powder River stared in amazement. The wound was bleeding profusely. Greg tied a tourniquet above it. He glanced back. The officers in the tail car were coming their way. They had survived the gunfire unscathed.

With Powder River, he struggled through scrub growth at the side of the highway. They skirted around the two great holes dug up by the shells. Ahead were the two cars. He saw men looking down at someone prone on the ground. His heart pounded. Someone had been shot.

It was Meg. And she was dead.

12

For the next few hours Greg moved in a stupor, his mind numbed, his thinking clogged. He was to remember little. He had prepared for an attack, yet like most people had not projected the possible consequences.

At Dock 14-A, the bay doors of the *Marco Polo* opened and they drove straight into the cargo section. He watched the unloading of the boxes from the Lincoln and the station wagon. He said nothing. He was conscious that nearby Powder River and Carlos stood silent.

Bill Madden came lumbering up, his face ashen, his lips trembling. "I'll look after the boxes. I'll put them in the captain's quarters and post a guard."

"Two guards," Greg said. "Heavily armed."

"Nothing'll happen to 'em." He patted his .45. "I'll kill anybody who touches 'em. The dock's crawling with detectives and reporters and TV camera crews and curiosity seekers and a funeral director. I gave instructions to keep 'em off the ship."

"You want I should talk with them?" Powder River asked.

"Tell the funeral director to ship Meg's body to Boise. She had a plot there alongside her husband. And phone Hilo-Aloha Lei Greeters—I got friends there—and ask them to send some anthuriums. Ask them to write something on the card. I guess, we love you and our names."

How could he be talking like this? How could Meg be dead?

He looked down at the dock from the deck. There were thirty or forty people down there, and they were belligerent, demanding to board the ship. He took the landing stairway slowly. Everyone yelled at him at once. At the bottom, two FBI agents showed their credentials and asked to board. He stalled them and the Honolulu detectives, then faced the reporters.

They fired their questions fast. Microphones were shoved into his face. Several brilliant spots flooded him as the TV cameras zoomed in. He wanted to yell at them, to tell them to get the hell out. A friend had died. A loyal, devoted friend who had loved him, as he had her. He clenched his fists to tighten control of himself.

"Who attacked you?"

"I don't know."

"You must have some idea. We heard you had an armored car and one in California. What'd you have in it?"

"Valuable papers."

"Securities?"

"Valuable papers."

"When are you starting to mine the sea?"

He was jolted. "We're engaged in a scientific exploration of the ocean."

"Why can't we come aboard?"

"Because I say so."

"You've got something to hide?"

"Our backers don't want our findings revealed until we finish the expedition."

"What about the Russians?"

"Well, what about them?"

"Aren't you in a race to dig up the ocean?"

"I repeat, we're on a scientific expedition. We have had no contact with the Russians and don't expect any."

"We're coming aboard. As members of the press—"

"You have no right. This is private property."

A few surged toward him. He backed up a couple of steps and pulled his .38. "You want to know what rights you have? I'll let this Colt explain your rights to you."

An older, white-haired newsman turned to the others. "Come off it, guys. Why bait him, since we're going back and write up a lot of speculation anyway." He laughed. "If he tells us too much, it may kill our stories."

Greg left to confront the two FBI agents and police detectives. They hammered away with questions about the contents of the boxes.

"We want to see them," the police Captain said.

"You'll have to get a court order."

"We've had a woman killed, a highway blown up, five minutes of outright war when others could have been killed—and you stand there and obstruct us. Why?"

"I'm willing to cooperate in every way except when it comes to the exact contents of the boxes."

"In other words, the motive? Okay, we'll let that go for the time being. What've you got down in the hold?" Bill Madden had blocked them from going below deck.

"The usual. Some cargo—machinery—nothing illegal, if that's what you're hinting at."

"I wasn't—but we'd like to see it."

Greg hesitated. All the engineering—the machinery—for scooping up the nodules was in the cargo section. They would see it, and wouldn't mean to, but would talk, the same as they would if he opened the boxes to reveal the film footage, stills and maps.

"If it had anything to do with the attack—" Greg began.

"The answer is no?"

"I don't think Washington would permit it."

"You mean it's classified—the entire hold?"

"I didn't say that."

When the Captain left, tight-lipped and face flushed, the FBI agents hung back. One said, "I want to ask about the woman who was killed."

Greg was instantly apprehensive.

"How long had you known her?"

"Several years. Why?"

"Did you ever have reason to suspect her of doing anything disloyal?"

Through tight lips he said evenly, "Get out of here and stay out!"

The agents stood momentarily stunned.

Greg shouted, "Well, what're you waiting for? You want me to help you?"

An hour later Greg was still walking the deck. He was torn physically and emotionally. He had acted in anger, out of grief and rebellion, when he should have masked his feelings. If Barb had been here, she would have calmed him.

He descended the landing stairs and wandered aimlessly up and down the walkway in front of the warehouse. Across the water a few weak lights indicated Sand Island. High above rose the Aloha Tower with its enormous old-fashioned clock that read 1:14. Along Nimitz the street lights shone bright from their high supports.

He glanced up at the ship and remembered what Carlos Lopez had said on seeing it, "It's weird. Looks like something you found at Disneyland."

It did look like a floating observatory. Amidship was an enormous dome known technically as a weathertight geodesic housing. It covered a gimbaled derrick, the word "gimbaled" meaning that the derrick pivoted freely. It remained constantly vertical regardless of the sea's rolling and pitching. Otherwise it would have torn up the pipe and thick, heavy hose that would lead down from the ship to the massive dredge head (vacuum) on the ocean bottom. Under the dome, too, far down in the ship's hull, was the "moon pool," a well through which the derrick lowered the vacuum, hose, pipe and other equipment.

Originally the vessel, 560 feet in length and 28,000 tons in weight, had been used offshore in oil drilling. Greg had revamped it for ocean mining. The derrick and pipe had been replaced and the dome built. Ocean mining called for pipes nine and five-eighths inches in diameter, larger than those used in drilling for oil.

The bridge was toward the bow. A superstructure in the stern, behind the dome, housed the computers, offices and laboratories as well as the living quarters. A cargo hold was under the fore deck, a pump room next, then came the "moon pool," and another cargo hold.

Greg was still on the walkway when the police Captain materialized out of the dark.

"I think you're a bastard," he said bluntly and with feeling, "but I guess I ought to tell you that the copter dropped the armored car on a narrow, rocky stretch along Keehi Lagoon where a party or parties blasted the back door open and ransacked eight boxes. The copter was subsequently located deserted on Sand Island. In case you don't know, it's right in the harbor. There's an access road to Nimitz Highway, but from markings in the sand, our officers think the pilot escaped in a motorboat.

"That's about it, except you were right about it being a Sikorsky Sky Crane. Not many of them around. Only about ten on the mainland where they use them for big jobs such as in Oregon during the logging season, and none on the islands except at Pearl Harbor Naval Base. It was stolen and the Navy is mad as hell. You guys really tore up their whirlybird. They counted twenty-three bullet holes."

He walked about. "They had two men hidden in the shrubs. They shot over the heads of the guards as they spilled out of the armored car, and disarmed them in seconds, then fastened the cable basket around and under the car. We figure they did all of this in about three minutes."

13

General Schepnov kept his voice low but permitted his fury to come through. He had risen at 4:30, taken his exercises, and driven miles to a pay phone at River and Falls roads, just over the D.C. line in Chevy Chase. A block away was a Roy Rogers Coffee Shop, where he would have breakfast.

"You told me you had a gopher working for you. What happened?"

Nataya Fussen came over clearly from Honolulu, but brittle and hard. "The boxes were in the armored car when it left Tubac and were switched at the Honolulu airport. They were identical with other boxes. I can't hold the gopher responsible."

"You'd better—or it's your neck. The Company's going to be furious and I'm the one who gets it. Not you. I didn't have as much trouble in Afghanistan working with idiots."

"Don't talk to me like that or I'll walk out on you."

"You wouldn't dare. You know what happens—"

"I'm an American citizen. Don't ever forget that. How'd it look if anything happened to me? I've got it all down in my safe-deposit box, and it'd be on the front page of every newspaper in the world."

"Why, you conniving, scheming old bitch! I should report you. You're not safe to have around."

"I'm hanging up. Go get yourself another bitch."

"Wait!" He raised his voice and regretted it. Outside a young man waited for the phone. He could have heard. "We're getting unduly excited and I apologize. We always have a few negatives on every assignment. I have the greatest admiration for your record. It was just that—"

"I've had a rough night. I hope you understand."

He glanced at his watch. He allotted himself only six minutes a call. If the FBI somehow had followed him and requested a tracer, he figured all parties involved would need nine to eleven minutes. He had broken the time schedule down this way: Two minutes for the FBI agents shadowing him to call the Washington Field Office by radio and for Washington Field to request a liaison person at the Washington phone company to run the tracer. One minute for the Washington phone people to ascertain the pay booth number at River and Falls roads. Three minutes for the Washington and Honolulu phone companies to track the call to the Honolulu phone booth. One minute to report the location to the Honolulu FBI. Two to four minutes for the FBI agents to reach the pay station and begin a surveillance.

"Does your gopher know when the ship will sail?"

"Soon. No exact date yet."

"We need more time. I think we should remove Mr. Gregory Wilson."

"Is that an order?"

"It is."

"I'll tell our friend."

"No, no, I want you to take care of Mr. Wilson."

Her voice reflected panic. "I can't. I haven't the experience. I've never done—"

"That is exactly why I am choosing you. I will inform the Company you will handle it within the next forty-eight hours."

He hung up. That would teach the old bitch a lesson. She had deliberately informed him about the safe-deposit box. She had let him know that she had the upper hand. He would be violating a cardinal rule if he did not advise Moscow immediately, and yet he needed her. Rashid was excellent but had to have on-the-ground direction. Then, too, there was the matter of the gopher. Repeatedly the General had insisted Nataya give him the gopher's name and position inside Carson Mining, and she had refused. She thought she was a clever one. Well, we'll see about that. Once the case was wound up, he would have Rashid remove all identification and dump her body in a rubbish bin of some remote town.

There was a tap on the glass. The young man wanted the phone. As he left the booth, the General took note of him. He wore a dark suit, a white shirt, a conservative tie and his shoes were polished. The FBI type.

At the office, the General's dark thoughts vanished when Rona Hale surprised him with a 1976 Jackson Five album. He was collecting the Jackson Five, and this one completed the set.

He was elated. "I owe you a bottle of bourbon."

"Make it perfume," she said. He had forgotten that she didn't drink.

He ignored the mail, put the record on a stereo player, turned it up loud, and sat back to enjoy himself. Midway through, she tiptoed in, closing the door behind her.

"Lieutenant Jaroslav of the Cultural Section is outside," she whispered.

The General was irked. Lieutenant Jaroslav was not from the Cultural Section. He was from the Wet Section of the Thirteenth Chief Directorate. The Wet Section was in charge of assassinations and plotting targets for sabotage in case of war. The Lieutenant had come in repeatedly to solicit business, and the General just as often had turned him down.

"Ask the Lieutenant to wait. Tell him I'm on the phone on an important conference call."

"He can hear the record," she said.

The General smiled. "I hope so."

He was happy with the album. The sound was clear and crisp and, of course, the Jackson Five superb. The United States did have a few attractions Moscow could not offer.

Once again the Lieutenant offered the services of his section. He should have looked like a hangman or a funeral director, but instead he was a big, friendly bear. "Keep me in mind," he said. "Everyone needs us at some time."

The General informed him once again that he, the General, had complete autonomy over the case and that included assassinations.

The Lieutenant frowned. "Amateurs. You must never trust amateurs."

No sooner was he gone than Miss Maria Kaluga appeared. She was tall, broad of hip and had a pretty face puffed up with too much wine. She kept her full black hair cut short. She had been in Washington for years with Tass, the Soviet news agency. A few months ago the KGB had lured her away with the promise of a good apartment when she returned to Moscow.

She had continued to represent herself as a Tass correspondent, and her work, for that matter, was still along journalistic lines. She headed the Dezinformatsiya (Disinformation) Section, more properly known as Service A of the First Chief Directorate. Specifically her job was to work up stories, both true and false, that would create mistrust between countries; and stories that would promote street warfare and revolutions.

"I'm leaving for San Francisco tomorrow," she said, sitting on a corner of his desk. The San Francisco Consulate, which numbered about a hundred with fifty assigned to missions for the KGB, had requested her services for two weeks. She would report directly to the Consul General, who at one time had served as chairman of the Soviet Committee on Science and Technology.

The Consulate's work was possibly more important even than the Embassy's in Washington. The Consulate sniffed out with the dedication of a bloodhound new research projects among the six hundred companies in the Silicon Valley south of San Francisco that were working on advanced technology and the 350 in the Los Angeles area. Through a complex legal web of business fronts, the Consulate bought and exported—under various names—computer chips, laser components and all kinds of research. If the KGB purchasing agents reached an impasse, then they would burglarize plants, bribe technicians and secretaries, or blackmail key plant people who had pasts they dared not have exposed. As one researcher put it, "We can't keep up with ourselves. As fast as we develop new technology, they steal it—and then we have to push harder to develop something better."

"They've got problems out there," she continued, "and the Consulate General thinks I might help. But after that assignment I'm free, and I thought since I would be so close to Hawaii . . ."

"Could you first run a background check on all the principals in the Carson company? I believe most of them are from states close to San Francisco."

"I'd be happy to. Just give me the names."

The General had not the faintest idea how she might fit into the Hawaiian operation. But she was not bad looking, and his current girl friend was a cold fish who reacted to sex with all the enjoyment of cleansing her face at night . . . well, if this very outgoing young woman wanted a week's vacation in Hawaii, he would arrange it.

14

After tossing for an hour, Greg took an aspirin. He needed only one to put him to sleep. The next he knew Bill Madden tapped on the door. The stateroom was afire with the usual hot morning Hawaiian sun. As was true around every harbor, men on the pier shouted, metal clanked against metal, and the ocean beat against the ship.

Bill brought black coffee and a Danish roll. "You told me to get you up before ten."

Greg sat up, pounded the pillows and shook his hair in place. "You ran a tight ship last night, Bill. I was proud of you."

Bill swept a big hairy paw over his face to hide the beam. Greg remembered when the Board had wanted to conduct a security check on Bill Madden. Greg had blocked it. He wasn't about to have Bill humiliated by anyone questioning his competence or integrity. Bill had said, "Not much they would have found out. Prospected ten, eleven years up around Durango. Worked a time as a cook over at Aztec, and put in a spell as a security guard in Coconino county. Nobody woulda learned much seeing as how I wasn't much."

Now Bill said, "You've got company." He called, "Come on in, Miss Lynne."

Lynne entered, struggling to muster a smile. "What in the name of . . ." Greg said in astonishment. He pulled the sheet up above his navel. He slept in the nude.

Her right arm was in a white sling that contrasted sharply with a simple red dress. "I thought I might be of some help . . . about Meg . . . do something. Do I get fired for coming?"

He laughed. "I'll think about it. How are you?" He indicated the sling.

"Fine. I just wear this to get sympathy." She pulled her eyes away from his hairy, primitive chest with the half-hidden dark nipples which strangely stirred her.

"Meg died quickly," he told her. "She didn't suffer."

They explored the night's events and speculated about the identity of the enemy.

"We can't let this hold us up," Greg continued. "If we only had some idea when the *Kharkov* will sail . . . we're getting right down to the wire."

They fell silent, then she asked about arrangements for Meg and he told her. "Would you go through her cases? See what we should forward to her relatives."

Lynne nodded. "I never cared much for her. I know you don't say things like that when someone dies—but I didn't."

He was quick to defend Meg. "She was a good friend. Helped us out when we were about to go under."

"If it hadn't been for Barbara, she would have got you in bed. Or tried. She told me so."

He stared in disbelief. "She was old enough to be my mother."

"What's that got to do with sex? I'm sorry she was killed. I honestly am, Greg. I'm not as heartless as I sound."

"I know."

"When you get time I've got some slides and footage to show you."

He interrupted. "Before we get into that, I want to tell you something." He took a deep breath. "About Barbara."

She gasped. "She's not going to make it?"

He repeated what Dr. Emory Randall had told him.

"I don't believe it," she said. "She's a fighter. She'll come out of it, I know."

"No, Lynne. No. I've had specialists in. They say she'll never come out of the coma." He squeezed his eyes to hold back the tears.

You need a woman, she thought. *A woman to get you through these days. A woman who would be loyal to Barbara but would look after you. God forgive me, Meg was not the only one who wanted to get you into bed.*

The day was busy, hectic and frustrating. He called Powder River and Carlos in to discuss security with Bill Madden. They instructed him to employ five more guards and gave him strict instructions. No one could board the ship at any time without clearance from Greg or Lynne. The rule included police officers, city and state inspectors, and harbor authorities. He was to refuse admittance to the hold, and this included the guards. The only exceptions were to be Greg, Lynne and Bill himself.

Afterward, Powder River took Greg aside. "I know you like old Bill and I do, too, but this is way beyond him. We need an antiaircraft gun in case they come over to bomb us out, and then, too, boy, we ought to get some of them magnetic sensors to let us know if frogmen plaster explosive sandwiches to the hull. Bill wouldn't know about either one. I'm not suggesting you fire him. Keep him on, but let's get somebody who knows his way around."

Carlos agreed and Greg experienced a sinking feeling. They were right, but old Bill would never understand.

They called a meeting of the ship's officers and briefed them. Captain A. W. Parker was on leave on the mainland. He was in his late forties, cold, haughty and arbitrary but highly efficient. A thorough security report indicated he could be trusted implicitly. His relations with Greg bordered on the formal, and as a result, Greg avoided him.

At Lynne's suggestion, the two checked over the physical equipment. In the Tech room they took inventory of computers, depth recorders, slow-scan television (for relaying pictures from the ocean floor), still-camera screens (for the same purpose), seismic profilers and sonars.

She stopped before one computer. It controlled the *Marco Polo's* thrusters, which a landlubber might term stabilizers, that would keep a ship at one exact spot, directly over the mining operation, regardless of storms and other turbulence. The hose/pipe, or "leash," would permit the vacuum to work one hundred feet in all directions before the ship had to move.

The computer would pick up messages sent electronically by underwater acoustic transponders. As fast as the messages were received, the computer would "translate" them and "issue" directions to the thrusters. In calm waters, the computer did little. In high seas, it responded in split seconds to each change in the velocity of the wind, the height of the waves and any shift that would push the *Marco Polo* off location.

She said, "I want to ask IBM to come in before we sail to make sure these are in working order."

With his handkerchief, he brushed dust off one instrument. "We've got to get someone aboard to keep this room dust free. About IBM, they ran a complete test when they installed them. I don't like to breach security—"

"That was months ago. We can't have a foul-up."

She indicated a second computer. It controlled the dredge heads on the ocean bottom that would crawl along, pick up the nodules, crush them and transfer the resultant slurry by pipe to the ship. If a dredge head ran into an outcropping or got off course, the computer would correct it. If the head's lights went out or its massive Archimedes' screws failed to work, it would report the trouble.

"If this baby went out, we'd have to call off the operation."

He shook his head. "I don't know."

She did what an intelligent woman invariably did with a stubborn man. She turned feminine. She touched his hand, lowered her voice. "We've got to compare the risk as opposed to an operational breakdown. We're going to take many security risks before we move this ship. We've got highly technical machinery and equipment—and it's like sending up the astronauts or a space shuttle, everything must be fail proof."

"We'll see," he said.

They took the elevator to the *Marco Polo*'s nether regions. He held the door for her as they exited, and she walked ahead, taking long, graceful strides. Her waist was nicely tapered and her hips barely outlined.

He thought of Barbara whose hip line was more pronounced. It seemed ages since they last had made love. After thirteen years of marriage, he still felt the thrill each time their bodies melded. Love-making had been something joyous and theirs alone, with the world shut out for those moments and hours . . . an expression of their deep love that rose to the sublime . . . a soaring happiness and afterglow that had to be divinely created.

Lynne talked rapidly. "We must get technicians in to go over the Monster and then diving experts to do the same after we put it in the water, before we drop it to the ocean floor. We need to check out all the cables and hoses, the television cameras and the sonar system after the Monster has been in the water for a time. The water may reveal flaws we didn't catch in the hold."

Greg pushed a button to open a massive hydraulic door. Powerful fluorescent lights came on instantly to reveal a dinosaur in steel 183 feet long, 40 feet high, weighing 274 tons. Enormous steel beams formed a rectangle at the base that supported all kinds of equipment. Two dredge heads for scooping up the nodules sat on the front, one in the center, and two at the back. If all went according to plans, they would gobble up 17,000 tons of nodules a day.

"I never see it," he said, "but what I don't get excited all over again."

She smiled up at him. "I don't believe it—and I helped design it. I can't get over the fact that in the last century we've discovered more about the oceans than in all the thousands of years before."

The advancement of oceanographic technology had brought a flood of knowledge. New gas mixes, masks, helmets, chambers and submarines with diving compartments had made it possible for man to explore deeper than ever before. New rebreather systems, free of bubbles, allowed man to spend hours cruising underseas. And there were propulsion devices that would send divers into the depths.

They walked about. Desert trained, he knew nothing about the Monster. She knew every screw, every hose connection. "The amazing thing," she said, "is that we've got space-age technology working along with ancient methods. See these hydraulic screws here? They were invented around two hundred years before Christ by an old Greek named Archimedes."

"What do they do?"

"Raise water from a lower to a higher level. They're called Archimedes' screws. We couldn't move the Monster without them. As they turn, they propel the dredge."

He laughed low. "You lost me somewhere."

"You keep the money coming and I'll keep feeding it to the Monster. Come over here." She led him to one of the front dredge heads, which looked like an overgrown lawn mower.

He asked, "Are you still worried about the mud?"

She nodded. "The samples we've taken indicate it's worse than desert caliche, if that's possible."

The dredge head would pick up mud along with the nodules. Heavy jets of water would spray the nodules before they were passed to a crusher which would grind them into particles.

"We've got a serious problem," she continued, "if the mud is too thick or cohesive, like glue. If it clogs the dredge head, we'll be stopped cold."

She and other divers had experimented with a single head at three hundred feet. They had fed it caliche from Arizona and red clay from Georgia. The jets had done their job effectively.

"So now," she said, "we've got to determine if the jets will clean the nodules at 15,000 feet from mud that may be more viscous than either the caliche or clay."

She continued scanning the Monster. He, in turn, couldn't take his eyes from her. When she was intent, she squinted a little and her lips pursed questioningly. Even her body tightened.

She caught him smiling. "What's funny?"

He shrugged. "Nothing. Problems?"

"Not with the Monster, but look here." She went to an engineer's plan tacked on a wall. "As you know, the nodule particles will be pumped from the crusher in a slurry to conduits." She traced with a long forefinger what she was describing. "From the conduit it goes into this flexible hose to a buffer where the slurry is transferred to this rigid pipe that runs up to the ship."

He broke in. "Hold it. I know the lesson by heart." He continued in a monotone, "The slurry is propelled up the pipe by air from a compressor aboard ship."

She was repentant. "I didn't mean to act like . . . but sometimes, Greg, in these engineering matters you're so . . ."

"Stupid."

"I didn't say it. Anyway, it's the pipe that concerns me. No one needs to destroy the ship to stop us, or all the hardware we're putting on the ocean floor, but if one frogman cuts this pipe, we're dead."

"He'd have to come from a submarine or ship. We'd know."

"So what if we did? We're not at war. You couldn't blow up a ship or submarine."

"No, but we could finish off a frogman without international repercussions—if we caught him in the act."

"How?"

"What about one of those little . . . I call them compact subs."

"Submersibles?"

He nodded. "We could drop one down with a man in it . . . sort of to ride shotgun on the pipe."

Her eyes lit up. "Greg, you're positively brilliant. I know just the right submersible. The Navy developed it some years ago. It's called NEMO, which stands for Naval Experimental Manned Observatory. It's like a fishbowl. Made out of acrylic plastic. You can sit in it, look up, down, all around. It has a small base for batteries, motor, all of that—and the line down from the ship provides communications and the right mixture of air."

He interrupted. "We can't ask the Navy."

She thought she could locate a rental one at a Maui maritime firm. She added that because of the water pressure on the bowl, they would be limited in how far they could take the submersible down. The depth, however, would be no problem, probably, since a frogman would choose to work as close to the surface as he possibly could and still escape detection. He would swim under the survey field of the sensors attached to the hull.

He fell quiet, obviously bothered, and she prodded him until he opened up. "We talk about killing a frogman as though human life was nothing. I never dreamed when I got into this . . . I thought it would be a straight mining operation."

She had too, she said, and in talking they discovered how much they thought alike. They condemned the hypocrisy and cruelty of nations and their statesmen and politicians who worked on one level, who pretended all was peaceful and were very gentlemanly in the use of language. Aided and abetted by television, the diplomats came and went while millions watched. They were beautiful people, even the ones in disfavor. They talked glibly, although they never said anything. They dressed immaculately, although they only went in and out of offices. They rode in luxury cars, although some were supposed to represent the downtrodden workers of the world.

They pretended they didn't know what was transpiring in the subterranean regions. They closed their eyes and ears to bombings and assassinations, to death squads and terrorists, and to guinea pig experiments more horrible than any horror movie ever filmed. By mutual consent governments had established rules for this secret world. The killings had to be confined to only one or two at a time, the bombings could destroy only limited property, and the horror experiments, too, had to be restricted. Any operation in this nether region on a large scale would be considered ungentlemanly and in violation of Robert's Rules of Order. However, the commission of a slit throat now and then was not only tolerated but encouraged.

In the Plotting room, she took the 35mm slide camera out of its case and placed it on a table in the center of the room, toward the back. He sat beside her, conscious of her scent, Chanel 22, the same as Barbara used.

"I want to show you," she said, "why we must get the sled out and reshoot some of the nodule beds."

The sled was just that but adapted for undersea photography. It held battery-powered strobe lights and two cameras that took color pictures every ten seconds. It was operated by remote control from a surface ship which towed it. In minutes the cameras could photograph sections of the ocean floor that a few years ago would have taken divers weeks. Carson Mining had rented the sled from the parties who had filmed the Cayman Trench in 1976.

"The shots here are too foggy to know for certain the contour of the ocean floor."

She ran a succession of pictures which usually would have been of remarkable clarity. They were of the sea floor at the western edge of the so-called Golden Tide, considered the most valuable area of the Pacific, although there were other smaller ones of equal potential. The Tide stretched roughly 2,500 miles long and 800 miles wide from a point about 600 miles west of Mexico to another point at the Line Islands, 600 miles southwest of Hawaii. Mining experts had estimated the value in nodules at $10 million a square mile.

Lynne had filmed much of the region and marked out twenty-three major sites. She figured the *Marco Polo*, by working each site for only two or three days, could lay claim to the most valuable. Each day's delay of the ship's departure could mean a loss of hundreds of millions—if someone else got there first.

After she ran the last slide through, Greg said, "They're not good, but I'm sure if there were any scarps we'd see them."

"We can't gamble. We've got to have sharp pictures."

Turning the light back on, she stood very straight a few feet from him. She moistened her lips and flounced her dark hair.

He thought: *She should not do this to me. I'm vulnerable.*

She continued, "We could get a hang-up that would take hours or days to clear up, or we could break up the hardware."

"For heaven's sake, Lynne, I can't tell Mass. we need another $50,000 for more pictures."

"For $50,000 they may be saving millions."

"We'll see."

She sat down across the table from him. Again he caught her scent. "When you say 'we'll see,' you're saying 'no.' I think I know you about as well as Barbara does."

Back on deck, Bill Madden advised him that one Miss Teresa Birkett from the State Department was at the landing and wished to speak with him about a matter of considerable importance. "She's a knockout," Bill said.

"I'll see her in the Captain's quarters," Greg told him.

She looked like a model, a stunning, tall, thin blonde. She floated, rather than walked.

She offered a firm hand. "Teresa Birkett. The State Department, Honolulu office. Thank you for seeing me."

She was all business. "I'm here on a highly confidential mission and would like your promise that you will hold our conversation in strict secrecy."

"Sure, if revealing it would prove injurious to the best interests of our country."

Her skirt billowed as she crossed her legs. She said brusquely, "I must have a flat promise, no qualifications."

"You'll not get a flat promise." He softened his tone. "I can't make such a promise when I don't have any idea what I'm promising."

"It's a question of national security."

"If it is, I give you my word."

"Very well. I don't know you, but I guess I can trust you."

"I don't know you, either."

Her cheeks colored. "Very well," she said again. "The State Department wanted me to report to you that our embassy in Moscow has been informed by the Soviet Foreign Office, presumably on behalf of Mr. Andropov himself, that the Soviets would like to enter into an arrangement whereby Russia and the United States would exchange information about deep-sea mining and permit oceanographers from each country to visit the ongoing projects in the other nation—"

He stopped her. "Never."

"I haven't finished." She kept her cool, but let him know she was unhappy with him.

"You don't need to finish." He quieted, then said, "Let me explain. It's not that we don't cooperate. We have with the Japanese and the Germans. We've traded information with them, as they have with us, and when we don't have anything to trade, we buy and sell technology. It's the same as in Silicon Valley, south of San Francisco, where little companies often sell what they have to big ones like IBM, and the other way around."

He paused. "Do you know what the Russians did in Silicon Valley? They came in and with a German front bought up what they could, and what they couldn't buy, they stole. Bribed scientists and secretaries and broke into plants."

He raised his voice. "So they want to come on the *Marco Polo* and prowl around? And like nice kids, we'll turn over everything we have to them? I'm telling you, Miss Birkett, that the first Russian who steps aboard this ship will get a bullet through him—and I'll personally see to it."

She rose slowly and very quietly said, "I did not say that State approved. State only wanted me to get your thoughts—"

"You've got them."

"I most certainly have." She offered her hand. "I cannot say that it has been pleasant meeting you, Mr. Wilson, but some other time, under other circumstances . . ."

He smiled. "I hope so."

The next day the State Department sent a coded message to the U.S. Embassy in Moscow:

> RE SOVIET PROPOSAL TO ESTABLISH WORKING RELATIONSHIP BETWEEN AMERICAN AND SOVIET OCEANOGRAPHERS ENGAGED IN MINING THE OCEAN FLOOR, ADVISE THE SOVIET FOREIGN MINISTRY THAT THE STATE DEPARTMENT WILL COOPERATE FULLY AND DESIRES TO ENTER INTO NEGOTIATIONS TO THAT EFFECT. ADVISE FURTHER THAT WE WILL MAKE AVAILABLE ALL CURRENT, OPERABLE PROJECTS IN THIS COUNTRY ONE AT A TIME WITH THE SOVIETS MAKING ONE OF THEIRS AVAILABLE ON AN EXCHANGE BASIS OF ONE AT A TIME.

15

General Schepnov was sweating. Once again he was standing outside the telephone booth at 14th and K. He had no choice but to violate his cardinal rule: Never use the same phone. MJ had sent a note through to the nonexistent Anatoli Ratoff, the name the General had given MJ's spokesman in case he wished to establish contact. The note read: "Will call you at phone we used before, 10 A.M. your time Tuesday." There was no signature.

Schepnov paced about. He kept close to the booth. Foot traffic was heavy and the street ran solid with cars. Yet this could not be a setup. He had received in the mail twenty-three sharp eight-by-ten glossies of an ocean floor somewhere. There had been no identification. The package brought another brief note: "Please remit immediately $1,000 in $100 bills if this merchandise meets your approval to Miss Pearl Punaluu, Pali Highway, Honolulu." He had sent the money by return mail and had instructed Nataya Fussen to check out the address and learn what she could about the mail drop.

At exactly 10 A.M. the phone rang. He pressed the receiver tightly to his ear and turned facing the sidewalk and street.

"Hello," he said.

"I'm speaking for MJ. Do I have the right party?"

The General recognized the voice. "You do."

"I assume the merchandise was satisfactory."

"It would be if I knew what the pictures were of."

"Yes, of course. MJ asked me to call you about that. It was an oversight. MJ will be sending you a technical report and a map. The pictures are of a plateau only about 3,000 feet deep west of the Mariana Trench and east of the Mariana Islands."

"The Marianas?"

"They are south of Tokyo more than a thousand miles. You will get a full report."

"What have they got to do with—"

"The pictures are of the seabeds that Carson will be mining."

"I thought they were going to mine near the Hawaiian Islands."

"That is what they want everyone to believe, but MJ learned that they will mine an area east of the Mariana Islands. They will use Saipan as a base."

"Saipan? Is that American territory?"

"Yes, a trust territory. MJ has learned, too, that Mr. Gregory Wilson will be flying shortly to Saipan to set up arrangements for the final operation. One thing more, we agreed on $1,000 to show good faith. MJ believes that this new information should be worth $5,000."

The General mulled over the figure. The pictures were all that the *Kharkov* would need, and the ship could move into the region probably well ahead of the *Marco Polo.*

"The same person, same address?"

"Yes."

"I'll put the money in the mail today."

"Thank you. Oh, yes, it may be none of MJ's business, but it was obvious to MJ that you have another source. Obvious because of the disaster you suffered a few nights ago. If you had asked MJ, MJ could have averted that. MJ can get all of the merchandise you wish without engaging in open warfare. If you would care to reveal the identity of the other source, MJ might work with the other party."

"I would have to consult the other source."

"Very well, why don't you do that? MJ may be hesitant in certain situations if MJ thinks we might be working at cross-purposes or endangering the other one. You know, it could be a very dangerous setup with MJ and your source working independently. Is the other source motivated by a very real desire to help the Soviets and the working people of the world?"

"I think so." He would have to pin Nataya down. He would force her to identify her gopher and the gopher's background.

"One more thing."

"Yes?"

"MJ sends a salute to the workers of the world and the Soviets and their friends."

He hung up. The General left the booth elated. By habit, he scanned the people about him and the car traffic, then walked briskly toward his office. A taxi was too much of a hassle to flag down. Besides, he liked walking. He did his best thinking on the march.

The General was very much in the thoughts of Nataya Fussen. She would not take abuse from anyone, especially from a phony, self-appointed general. She kept in direct touch with Moscow, and one negative report from her and he would be back in Afghanistan.

She had no idea what his connections were, if any, with the higher echelon of the KGB, nor did she care. She had never married but had a son fathered by an English journalist. Both were dead and her only living relative was a grandson she adored. Through friendships in the KGB she had set him and his young, charming wife up in one of the best apartments in Odessa. She had established a $50,000 trust for the couple with a New York bank. Hence, she now had no responsibilities due anyone in this world, and it was amazing the courage that gave one.

She had failed, it was true, with the ambush. That, however, was only Step One, and Rashid shared the blame. She had yet to meet him in person. She had studiously avoided him. If the authorities were running a surveillance on him, then if she met him, she would draw attention to herself.

She was still horrified that the General should order her to remove Gregory Wilson. She had never actually pulled a trigger on any man or woman, though she had consigned many to their deaths.

She recalled Paris vividly. In those early months of World War II when Hitler and Stalin had signed a peace pact, she had worked in Paris for the Nazis. She remembered the wild parties with French officers, the nights at the Bal Tabarin. She was a whelp in heat the year round. Now in recalling, she wondered how a body could be so consumed and yet a brain work objectively and efficiently. How could she have slept with a man and been deliriously happy with what his body was doing to hers, and yet the next day report to the Abwehr with information that would destroy him? She never had thought of herself as a cold person. Never had she refused anyone help, whether it was a distant cousin in Kalinin or a girl friend in Paris or a hungry child she chanced across.

Now she sat sketching in detail on an architect's big drawing board what she saw from her office a short distance from the *Marco Polo*. The ship had dropped anchor alongside a three-story warehouse painted green. On the far side a dozen or so fishing boats were tied up. In front of the vessel was a parking lot and then a causeway. The parking was illuminated by four lights on each of two tall poles. The lights could easily be shot out. The entire area of parking and the causeway was enclosed by a chain-link fence. At one side a manually operated gate permitted auto and pedestrian traffic to pass through.

Her office was on the other side of Nimitz. At this point traffic roared by at sixty-five miles or better. The office was one of several that sat over businesses on the ground floor: a garment factory, produce business and an import-export firm. She had furnished her quarters with a desk and chairs bought from the Goodwill. For appearances, she had a telephone put in. She had posed to the rental agent as a writer in need of privacy.

As she drew the scene in detail, she would pause to jot down random thoughts. The chain-link gate could be forced open in a matter of seconds with a heavy crowbar or perhaps snapped open with a car bumper. If anyone left the ship whom she wished to follow, she could reach her car in four minutes. She had timed several parties departing the vessel, and they had taken five to nine minutes to reach the gate, open it and enter Nimitz.

She pondered the possibility of using a long-range rifle with a silencer to target Mr. Wilson when he arrived or left the ship. She discarded the idea. Her aim was not that good. If she missed, he would be warned and would take precautions.

She would follow him. She would be patient and wait for a time when he was alone or with Dr. Kennedy and she had a clear shot. She would wait, too, for a time when the chances of fleeing the scene were in her favor. She believed strongly in odds. She wanted them 80–20. She had survived to the age of seventy-two on those odds.

A few days later her gopher advised her that Mr. Wilson and Dr. Kennedy would leave for Los Angeles two days hence by United Airlines at 12:35 P.M. After much thought, Nataya decided to use a Saturday Night Special, though she despised the weapon. However, in Hawaii alone there were thousands that changed hands frequently, and hence, one would be difficult to trace.

The next day she went to the beach behind the Hilton Hotel complex and rented a pedal boat from the C and K kiosk. As usual, the beach was crowded with sun worshipers. Most were stretched prone, a layer of brown bodies with an occasional stark white one.

On the water she passed an outrigger canoe with boisterous tourists aboard, a yellow-and-white sailboat, and several little ones called sabats. On her left was a long catwalk leading to the big catamarans, those double-hulled boats the Polynesians used long before the coming of the English explorers. On her right was a breakwater of volcanic stone.

When she passed the end of the breakwater, Rashid appeared, swimming toward her. His head was barely above water when he steadied himself on the pedal boat.

"I am happy to meet the famous Nataya Fussen," he said. He handed over a waterproof pouch containing the Saturday Night Special, which he had bought on Hotel Street for an outrageous $80.

For a half hour they talked about Project L that Rashid was putting together. They arranged a meeting a week hence in a hideout on the Pali, that dark, often brooding summit violated by a highway from Honolulu to the other side of the island.

She had been up around the Pali the day before to check out MJ's mail drop, one Miss Pearl Punaluu. A heavy fog was settling and the air was gorged with moisture. She walked past gaunt scrub trees hungering for the sun. Well back from the highway, she found a tiny but well-tended cottage that looked as if Mother Goose's children might live there. It was weathered clapboard capped by a tin roof that rattled in the breeze. A macaw announced her approach in a voice like two boards being scraped together. As she retreated, she heard a lock noisily being undone.

In her usual quiet way, she asked around and learned that Miss Punaluu was in close touch with the Aumakuas, the guardian spirits. She conversed often, too, with Pele, the goddess of volcanoes. She had many islanders, from fieldworkers to attorneys and merchants, coming to her to contact their ancestors. She used none of the stagecraft of the mainland spiritualists. She would listen to the ones who came and then retire to a back room to close her eyes and call out in a whisper a name that had been given her. If she had difficulty in arousing the party, she would ask for Pele's help.

Nataya would assign two of Castro's agents to stake out the cottage. In time, Miss Punaluu would either deliver the payments to MJ, or MJ or MJ's man would come to collect.

Nataya hurried to escape from the fog and the dark, cloud-shrouded Pali which conjured up fearsome visions from out of *Götterdämmerung.*

Nataya put on her old clothes, smeared her face with dark makeup to give it a dirty look, tied a frayed black ribbon around her hair at the back, and picked up a fishing pole and bait can. She invariably felt filthy after one of these masquerades and purposely had arranged appointments for the next day with the hair stylist and the masseuse. Also, as a reward for suffering through this kind of makeup, she might buy herself the high boots she coveted.

Crossing Nimitz at a stop sign, she limped slowly toward the side gate. She could loiter there without attracting attention—since she was an old, bedraggled woman—until Mr. Wilson and Dr. Kennedy arrived at the gate. One would have to leave the car to open the gate. She was gambling that it would be Mr. Wilson. It really didn't matter. She would pull the trigger on the one who came to the gate. Inevitably, the other would leave the car and come running to learn what had happened.

16

Lynne picked up Greg in her taxi at the *Marco Polo*. She had been to the Sheraton shopping. Entering the taxi, he stopped suddenly. She had bought an Alfred Shaheen hand-painted blue dress and had her dark hair set. Cascading to her shoulders, it beautifully framed her face. "You're a dream walking," he said softly, and slid in beside her.

Their thighs touched and she got high on his nearness. His bushy chest hair tufted above a blue Western sport shirt. His Levi's were well broken but still tight and shoved into polished boots.

The taxi moved out across the parking area toward the gate. A passenger in a car coming in from the other side was opening it. The cabbie waved thanks as he gunned the taxi out.

At Honolulu International Airport, the driver shot the taxi to the entrance to United Airlines. Passengers were leaving a taxi directly ahead and another cab pulled in behind them. Suddenly, a dozen persons were heaving bags, paying fares and struggling to get their overweight baggage and tired bodies inside.

They went through Agricultural Inspection, which the natives called Customs since everything, including hand bags, was examined meticulously, and afterward through Security. "You'd think we were in a foreign country," Greg said.

In the main concourse Lynne did more shopping: plumeria leis, shell necklaces, macadamia-nut chocolates and a T-shirt for a teenage friend. He purchased orchid leis for Laura and Barbara.

She thought: *At some time, Greg, you've got to admit to yourself that life has ended for Barbara.*

Everywhere signs were in Japanese as well as English. No longer was Hawaii a paradise that lured only U.S. mainlanders. Now the Japanese tourists swarmed in by the thousands—groups of factory workers on holidays paid for by their plants, and groups from business and trade associations. All dutifully followed guides holding little flags aloft.

Greg decided to go for a shoe shine and she waited. A Hawaiian ran the concession. Three chairs: $1.25 regular, $1.75 super shine. When Greg returned he saw a woman seated behind Lynne whom he thought he remembered from somewhere. He was unable, though, to place the face and forgot about her.

A shuttle ran the half mile to the plane but they decided to walk the concourse. Lynne said she needed the exercise.

Nataya clutched to her waist an old battered purse with a torn handle. Her right hand fitted snugly about the Saturday Night Special inside. The metal was cold, but how could it be since the day was so hot? It was her hand that was cold. Very cold but not trembling.

She wanted to get the job finished. If the people coming and going would only move out of the way for just a few moments. She had no doubt she could escape. She would simply fade into one of the tourist groups, preferably a foreign language one, and go along with them during the hue and cry. For that matter, no one would suspect an old, forlorn woman. She would add a few years to her age. She would totter a little, breathe as if she had an asthmatic condition and feign poor eyesight.

Now . . . now . . . Kennedy and Wilson were alone. But no, three hurrying flight attendants pulling those silly little carts with their luggage blotted Kennedy and Wilson from view. Wait a moment. Be patient. They will be gone. They're passing the two. But in the background a mother in jeans and a Hawaiian shirt and two little girls, about eight and ten, were within possible range. If Nataya missed, the bullet might strike the mother or children. She held her fire.

But she shouldn't have since the corridor would dwindle shortly, and become a narrower passageway leading directly to the waiting rooms for the various flights. She had only a little time. She might not have another chance for days or ever.

Now . . . now . . . Kennedy and Wilson were in the open. But she missed her chance. She wasn't quick enough. Three chattering teenagers with their parents lagging behind came into view. They weren't in a direct line. Still, if they happened to move over a few feet . . .

What was wrong with her? What did it matter if she killed a teenager along with the couple? It would be only an accident. And so much was at stake. Several billion rubles, a historic breakthrough. The *Marco Polo* would be delayed months if she got rid of Kennedy and Wilson.

Her hand was trembling. She was certain it was the frustration and wait, and nothing more. Once the two were lined up, her hand would obey her orders. Still, the metal was so cold and the mere touching of it sent a revulsion through her, as if she held a cobra.

Greg looked back. He didn't know why, except he had an inexplicable feeling eyes were upon him. He recognized the woman instantly—and where he had seen her. The remembrance sent a shock through him. She had approached him in Tubac to sell a mining claim. Her hair had been stringy, her clothes old, and her demeanor whipped. She looked the same now.

He grabbed Lynne's arm. "We've got a woman following us."

They quickened their pace. Lynne's heels clicked sharply on the concrete. His breath came a little faster.

Then Lynne sagged against him. "I've got to slow down. My shoulder, it's killing me. You go on."

"Not on your life."

She paused to look back.

"Don't look back."

"Who is she?"

"I'll tell you later. Just keep going."

The teenagers sped past. Nataya thought the parents would never clear out of view.

Now . . . now . . . Kennedy and Wilson were each perfect targets, right out in the open. But they were half-running. It was as if they had discovered her.

She dropped her pose as a shuffling, old woman. She had to keep up with them, even if it meant attracting attention. She had had little experience with firearms and knew her aim might be off at a distance. She ran; she had to close in on them.

Her hand gripped the Saturday Night Special. There was no tremble, only complete obeyance.

Now she had shortened the gap. She came to a complete stop. She had them lined up. One shot, then another, and she alone, all by herself, would have saved the Pacific seabeds for the Soviets.

Then it happened. She never knew what struck her. One moment she was holding the weapon, her finger tight about the trigger, beginning the squeeze, aiming for Kennedy first since she was the most valuable.

Her finger suddenly went limp, then her body. She staggered over to a bench by the ocean side where cargo was being loaded into a big ship. She sagged and crumpled into a heap. Her thoughts had shattered, her mind blacked out. For the first time in her long, distinguished career she had failed an assignment.

She was a judge who could sentence a man to death but could not execute that sentence.

17

In Tucson, Laura and Janet Stowe met them. Laura ran into Greg's arms, fighting back the tears, and then hugged Lynne. Janet had brought the car. He and Lynne had only five hours until their plane left for Washington.

As he drove, Janet went over papers that called for decisions. She expected immediate ones. She was so blasted efficient, too efficient for him. She was intolerant of people who didn't have their lives well organized. He knew he was a cross she bore. He was too casual about correspondence, returning phone calls, and in general, playing the executive. While she was usually pleasant about it, at times she was abrupt and curt.

Barbara knew her better than anyone. Janet had confided in Barbara up to a point. She mentioned once that she was born in Boise and when she was ten her mother sent her to a private school in San Francisco. She was evasive about her mother, and Barbara speculated that her mother had worked as a prostitute in Meg's bordello. About her father, Janet said he deserted them when Janet was a baby and Janet had never heard from him.

When she was nineteen her mother died and she went to live with an aunt in Fresno, California, who put her through the University of California at Berkeley. She was graduated cum laude in Business Administration, but the economy was depressed and when she couldn't find a job, Meg had persuaded Greg to take her on as a secretary with Carson Mining.

She was overly ambitious. "I'm going to make something of myself," she told Barbara once. "You just watch." It was as if she had to prove to herself that she could rise above her background.

She spent most of her salary on clothes and a Corvette. She bought herself costly jewelry and was constantly in debt. "She doesn't have many dates," Barbara told Greg, "and I think I know why. When she starts talking about all the expensive things and trips she wants, she scares the boyfriends away."

Still, despite the fact she nettled him, Greg needed her. She never took a day off, never was late, and never complained no matter how much work was piled on her.

By the time they reached her apartment on East Broadway, she had prodded Greg into reaching a decision on every letter in the file folder. Afterward he let Lynne off at her condominium on Oracle Road, and then he and Laura went to the hospital. Tenderly, he lifted Barbara and placed the orchid lei about her, then kissed her forehead and held her hand. Again, Laura struggled to hold back the tears.

How am I going to tell Laura she shouldn't come so often? Or should she? Would it be worse for her to stay away? God, I need someone to help me with Laura.

In the corridor, they encountered Dr. Randall at the nurses' station. "Greg, I need to see you." He led Greg out of earshot of Laura.

"We've got to move Barbara to a medical facility specializing in her type of case."

"No," Greg said and started away.

"Greg! You have no choice. The hospital needs the room. They won't keep her."

"Wait until I get back from Washington."

"Okay—but Greg, you've got to face up to it."

At home Rambunctious landed a tackle worthy of a fullback.

"Good old Rambunctious." Greg got down on the floor to wrestle him. "How's he been?"

"Fine," Laura answered. "Except when I'm sad he's sad. So I have to keep a bright face for him. Mom used to say you loved him more than you did us. Is that true?"

"Sure, your mom's number two and you're number three."

"Thanks."

"Where's your grandmother?"

"It's her Bingo day."

"When will she be home?"

"I don't know. This is her bowling night."

He had to do something about Laura. Her grandmother was too ineffectual, and besides she couldn't stay indefinitely. She had a husband and a home.

In Washington, D.C., he and Lynne took adjoining rooms at the Sheraton Washington. He had two interviews scheduled: the first, a luncheon one with a party named Mike McGraw, a possibility for Security Chief, and the second, Jonathan Switzer, head of the Underwater Development Section, Department of State.

Lynne begged off on the luncheon. She had paper work to catch up with. "But I want you with me when we see Switzer," Greg said. "He's a tough one."

Shortly afterward Greg left for the Jockey Club at the Fairfax Hotel. He was studying the menu when Mike McGraw came up on his left. He was in his mid-thirties, about six feet, stocky but mostly muscle, light hair and features, perhaps of Nordic heritage. His face was nondescript except for the washed-out blue eyes. They were a hunter's eyes, constricted and very distant.

Rising, Greg offered a tight grip. "Good to know you. Sit down. What'll you have to drink?"

"Iced tea."

"Nothing stronger?"

"Thanks. Iced tea."

Greg learned he had been an alcoholic. "My wife talked me out of it. Sally. You've got to meet her. She and the kids, Jane, Robert and Johnny. They're living down in Abilene, Texas. They're disgusting, same as all Texans. Think God made Texas. If it's not in Texas, it can't amount to much."

He talked of them with love and tenderness, and Greg stared in surprise. Later he was to learn that there were two worlds inside Mike McGraw, and McGraw moved comfortably from one to the other without conflict or guilt.

Greg broke off the chitchat. "I don't know how much you know about the *Marco Polo*—"

McGraw interrupted. "You're in a deep-sea mining venture and competition with a dozen other companies and they'll stop at nothing, even to blowing the *Marco Polo* and you to hell and gone." He smiled. "When I heard about the job I talked with friends over at State. I read, too, about the ambush the other night. It got a big play here."

They ordered small dinner salads. McGraw dumped several packets of sugar into his tea. Greg took his coffee black.

To sound him out, Greg asked, "What would you suggest we do? On a broad scale?"

McGraw lit a cigarette. "I've got several close friends who fought in Biafra and Angola, and sure, they're mercenaries, but don't hold that against them. I'd bring several in and post a few around the *Marco Polo* and hold a few in reserve. I'd give them plenty of firepower. Get a couple of antiaircraft guns on the ship and some big guns aft and fore. Big enough to blast anything out that might come in by sea."

He finished the salad. He was a rapid, compulsive eater. "Then —and this is where I come in—I'd plant a spy inside every company so that we'd know what they're trying to do to us."

"What if it's a nation?"

"Russia?"

"Possibly."

"The same."

"You could do that? Get someone inside an embassy?"

"No problem. Takes a little time."

"One more thing. I've got a conservative Board, and I'm not the kind, either, who could accept gunplay that wasn't warranted —that is, that wasn't in self-defense."

McGraw stubbed out his cigarette. "Depends upon what you mean by self-defense. If a bastard's coming to kill me, I'm going to get him first."

Greg's lips tightened. "I couldn't go along with killing for the sport of it just because someone *thinks* he has an excuse."

McGraw struggled to hold his voice down. "You're a business man, Wilson, and you don't know about all the bloody, murderous, sadistic people out there. They'd rather torture you than kill you. They'll rape your wife and run a knife up her, and cut up your children, and put an electric gadget about your genitals until you scream yourself to death."

He thought a moment. "I'm killing them, every damn one of them, when they come my way."

Greg sat stunned. "That makes you the judge, prosecutor, jury and executioner."

McGraw shrugged. "So what? We clean up the world. Somebody had better do it—and do it fast. I think you'd better get yourself another boy."

Greg thought of Meg. Once again he saw her crumpled up on the asphalt, a hand frozen in death to her bleeding head. It could have been Lynne, and another time, Barb.

"How much?"

"Ten thousand a month with a three months' guarantee."

When Greg hesitated, McGraw continued, "It's high, but I'm putting my ass on the line. At some time they'll come gunning for me, and I've got to think of Sally and the kids."

"When can you start?"

"Today. Now." He glanced at a Patek Philippe gold wristwatch. "At one thirty-five I went on salary."

Greg nodded. "Just be sure. I don't want any innocent victims."

"On my oath I promise you, Wilson, I'll be sure."

As they left, a well-dressed young man took a picture of them and disappeared before either could get a sharp focus on him.

Greg instructed the taxi driver to let him out at the University Club on Sixteenth Street. Next door was the Russian Embassy. He paid the cabman but instead of entering the Club, crossed the street. Oblivious to the curious stares of passersby, he stood on the curb and craned his neck to take in the Embassy building, a mansion patterned after the Louis XVI era. It had been built originally as a residence. All it needed were a few patches of fog drifting by to give it the foreboding look of something out of a Gothic novel.

Morbid curiosity had brought him here. He had to see the enemy's headquarters. He knew someone in there behind the shutters was plotting to do away with Carson Mining and the *Marco Polo* and perhaps all of them individually. The building was tall and gaunt, of dirty gray granite with dormers and a slanting copper roof turned green with the years. Above the roof was a forest of antennae and other transmitting and receiving equipment. He had heard it said that in addition to the diplomats and trade delegations, the building housed the largest aggregation of espionage agents anywhere in the Western world. And one or more—possibly more—had a working dossier on him.

His gaze dropped back to the street level. A high iron fence, six feet or more, topped with pointed spikes, guarded the short approach to the french doors. A tiny red guard post, like something out of the *Wizard of Oz*, sat near the gate. A sentry exited when a long, black Lincoln Continental driven by a handsome, dark-featured young man pulled up. The sentry nodded in recognition. Next, the front doors opened and eight women in dark, thick wools emerged. They were heavyset, stone faced and masculine in their walk, stereotypes out of a Hollywood film.

He experienced that strange, unexplainable feeling one has when he is being covertly watched. A District of Columbia police officer, who sat on a motorcycle parked on the sidewalk just outside the gate, had him under surveillance. His duty was to protect the Embassy, to turn away psychos or possible assassins or just garden variety troublemakers.

Greg moved on.

When Greg stopped at the hotel reception desk for mail, he heard a voice boom out behind him. "Greg Wilson!" He turned to find Bill Brockton approaching. Greg detested the man. Brockton was vice-president of W.W.W. Enterprises, one of Carson's foremost competitors in the ocean-mining business. He was a typical con artist, glib, persuasive, outgoing, and a liar, a cheat and a behind-the-back knife stabber.

He offered a hand and a tight grip. "Old buddy, what a surprise to bump into you."

"Hello, Bill," Greg said quietly.

"I guess the good Lord arranges these chance meetings. Here I've been wanting to talk with you for months. Can we get together for dinner?"

"Sorry, I'm only in for a day and booked solid."

"How about now? Wouldn't take more than five minutes. Come on, buddy boy, you wouldn't brush your old friend off, would you?"

He led the way to the cocktail lounge, talking all the while. "I've got something for you, you wouldn't believe. I've been working on it for weeks. Just came through."

Once seated, he ordered a straight gin. "We've got nothing but problems. Absolutely nothing. And that's where you come in. I'm authorized to offer you twice your salary and all the fringe benefits you want, and what's more, you take over. You have full authority. Now how's that for an offer? Big money and you're the big man on campus. I told them weeks ago they had to get you . . ."

Greg smiled. "I wouldn't go with W.W.W. if you offered me a million dollars a year."

Brockton dropped his hail-well-met approach. "Wait a minute there, buddy. You can't just throw this away without giving it some thought. I've sweated like a hog on ice for this. You're my friend. I want you with us. Take a little time. Talk it over with Barbara. Carson's only paying you peanuts. Peanuts. An offer like this doesn't come along once in a lifetime."

He polished off the gin in one swallow. Greg said, "The answer's still no. A flat no."

Brockton turned hostile. "Look, with you or without you the *Marco Polo* will never put to sea. I don't like what some of our people do. I keep telling them to cut out the rough stuff, but I can't get through to them. They're going to stop you one way or another."

He lowered his voice. "One way or another. So grab the money. Grab it while you can."

Greg rose. "Nice seeing you, Bill."

Brockton grabbed him by the lapel. "I want to talk with Barbara about this."

"She's in the hospital. She was in a bad accident."

"In the hospital! Look, Greg, I know she would go for this. She knows business. You don't. You told me so once. Remember? Talk with her, will you? That's all I ask. Just talk it over with her."

18

Jonathan Switzer failed to rise when Lynne and Greg were ushered in. He was overweight, florid and balding. His eyes looked past you as if you were positioned three feet behind yourself. He was the State Department's section head for Underwater Development.

He was pawing through a litter of papers and muttering angrily. Greg stood a moment looking down at him. He had a great urge to crack him on the head. He had seldom known a man so rude. In addition, he was certain Switzer had strong ties with W.W.W. Enterprises and was determined to block Carson.

Greg broke the silence. "I brought Dr. Lynne Kennedy with me today. She's our second in command and as you know one of the world's foremost oceanographers."

Switzer failed to respond. "I thought you'd like to meet her," Greg continued.

Switzer grunted. Greg waited a second, then knocked over a vase of flowers. Switzer swore and Greg said, "How clumsy of me." The water seeped through the papers. Greg made no offer to help Switzer mop it up.

"Every time you come in here . . ." Switzer said.

Greg interrupted. "I feel the same way. Now that we've got that settled, can we talk for a few minutes?"

"What about?"

"You sent word you wanted to see me."

"Yes, yes." Switzer put the wet papers in the sunlight. He turned about, eyes flashing. "State has had disturbing reports about you. We've learned that you contemplate starting up mining operations any day."

"I haven't heard anything about that."

Switzer raised his voice. "I've warned you about this. I told you before that you cannot begin until we get this Law of the Sea business settled. State will not tolerate it. Absolutely not."

Lynne sat speechless. She could not believe the man. A government official behaving in such fashion?

Greg said quietly, "That could be years."

Switzer nodded, pleased with the fact.

For more than a decade, the countries of the world had struggled to set up laws regulating the mining of the ocean floor. A recent treaty called for the creation of an International Seabed Authority which would be under United Nations control. It would grant claims to governments and private mining companies. They would pay royalties to the United Nations, which would then divide them among all countries.

Greg could accept the draft up to this point. However, the treaty provided that: (1) the United Nations would set up its own company, called The Enterprise, which also would mine; (2) the private corporations must make available their technology to The Enterprise in return for being given mining sites; (3) no company would know what its production quota would be until after it had submitted a request for a mining site—and spent hundreds of thousands in exploration necessary for submitting a claim; (4) production could be halted after the work was underway if the output should threaten prices in a nation mining the same mineral on land, such as copper; (5) Russia and its allies would be given three seats on the authority and the United States and its allies, two; (6) the possibility that the United Nations in future years might interpret the royalties as taxes, and on that basis levy taxes in other fields, and hence, set itself up as a sovereign superpower.

There was no precedent for dividing the ocean floor except possibly what the great powers had done centuries ago in laying claim to sections of the New World and Africa. They had operated on the principle that the first explorer on the scene could plant a flag and stake out the territory for his country. The claim, of course, had to be backed up with gun powder.

In the Gold Rush days of the last century, the miners followed the same principle. In the beginning, a miner would merely stake out a claim and the others would respect it. In time, especially in the bigger camps, the miner would register the claim with the "district recorder" who might be the general store owner, a saloonkeeper or the town marshal. In all instances, one cardinal rule was observed: the miner had to work his claim. Usually the law of consensus required him to show up one day out of three. If he neglected digging or panning for one to two weeks, he lost the claim. The claims varied in size. If the gold strike were large, the community might restrict it to ten feet. If small, perhaps a hundred.

Even dividing up the surface land between individuals had once been a controversial issue. In the seventeenth and eighteenth centuries the dispute over how to adjudge rights reached fever heat. John Locke, the English philosopher, argued, in 1690, that the land belonged to mankind in general, no individuals could own a piece of it, and only those who used it had a right to settle on it. The idea was not new. Many African tribes, the Aztecs and others in the pre-Columbus era held that a family could hold a parcel only as long as they cultivated it.

Later, feudal lords and countries decided their sovereignty extended three miles out from land, the range of an eighteenth-century cannonball. In that era privateers and men-of-war defended the sea claims. No one ever thought about who owned the ocean bottom. No one knew there was anything of value down there. Eventually a few countries extended the three-mile claim to two hundred miles, to grab more fishing territory.

"So we don't have any historical precedent to go by," Greg had once told the Carson directors. They had wanted to know what would happen if Russian and American ships attempted to mine the same territory. Would a little country like Peru send out a gunboat? Would the United Nations advise the powers that they were trespassing on international property? Would a company like Carson, if threatened by Washington, dump its nodules and return to port? Would the superpowers engage in a naval battle?

No one knew.

Greg said, "With all due respect to the State Department, we're not waiting, Mr. Switzer. We're not going to let the Russians get there first—or W.W.W."

Switzer again raised his voice. He believed the louder he talked the more he got his point across. "The United States and Russia are in complete agreement on this matter. As for W.W.W., State has given them and the other countries the same ultimatum. State will not permit any deviation from this policy. We must have unanimous agreement. If we don't have one, we could have piracy on the high seas. We could have a great war between nations determined to mine the whole ocean floor."

"There's no law against the *Marco Polo* sailing," Greg said flatly.

Switzer was outraged. He shouted, "If the *Marco Polo* puts to sea, we'll use every power at State's disposal to stop you. Do I make myself clear? We'll stop you, Mr. Wilson. We'll stop you!"

Greg struggled to hold his own voice down. "Are you speaking for the White House?"

"I said State, didn't I? What's the matter with you? Can't you cretins get anything right? The White House supports State, of course. It stands behind State on this."

"Who in State promulgated this policy?"

"Who promulgated it? I did. I have full authority to set all policies regarding the underwater development of the oceans. I did—and State backs me entirely. If the *Marco Polo* puts to sea . . . I've already warned Massachusetts Diversified . . ."

So you are the one, the cause for the unrest. The old fear technique. The directors fear their income tax returns might be audited if they oppose a government agency as powerful as the State

Department. They fear government regulators may swoop down on them in their businesses, the whole body politic of bureaucracy. They fear their bank accounts might be blocked.

Switzer could wield enormous power. Greg conceded that. More directly he could persuade port authorities and Honolulu to refuse permits for the *Marco Polo* to sail, stop essential supplies for the ship and its crew, and begin investigations of the staff and crew on the grounds there were fugitives and spies aboard.

And, of course, the killing one—cutting off all funds from Massachusetts Diversified if the Board could be convinced that Carson Mining and one Gregory Wilson in particular were about to start World War III, and the directors would be held to blame forever in the history books.

Greg said, "Have you made a deal with Russia yet?"

"What deal? What are you talking about?"

"Exchanging information."

"Oh, that. I don't know anything about it. A lot of talk goes on."

"I told the young woman I'd kill any Russian who boarded the *Marco Polo*. I want you to know that."

"You're gun happy. You don't have any sense of responsibility. You'd start a world war—"

Lynne interrupted. "May I say something, please." She sat very straight. She looked Switzer straight in the eye.

He sank back into his big leather office chair. His attitude was that she was a woman and he had to let her talk, but he didn't have to listen.

"I'd like to discuss this without emotion and find a common ground." She spoke firmly, with authority. "We have countries that are desperate for food, such as Bangladesh and Chad and Somalia where hundreds of thousands die each year. And I don't know of a single mining company that wouldn't pay royalties into an international fund—if they could operate with some chance of realizing a profit.

"But no firm, Mr. Switzer, will ever invest hundreds of millions in a project that might be canceled at any time by a sea authority that may be controlled by unfriendly nations."

She hesitated a second, then continued softly, "We could save all of these lives and help the undeveloped countries immeasurably—and at the same time work for the best interests of the United States. As you know, we're terribly vulnerable. We depend on Zaire for eighty percent of our cobalt and South Africa for more than ninety percent of our manganese. I'm told that if Russia and Zimbabwe worked together to impose an embargo on chrome, they could bring the industrial world to its knees within six months.

"I don't want to run on about all of this, but we consider thirty-six minerals absolutely essential to our welfare, and out of the thirty-six, we're dependent on foreign sources for twenty, and all twenty and more can be found on the ocean floor—minerals used in such things as jet engines and steel and telecommunications, and I could go on and on.

"So what I'm suggesting is this. Couldn't State work out some kind of an agreement with the Western nations and Russia, perhaps a temporary one if there are insurmountable problems, that would make it possible for the advanced countries and their private corporations to mine under leases, or something of that nature, with the provision that they must pay royalties to the lands that do not have the resources or technology? I think every country in the world should share in the profits, perhaps on a population basis. I would like to say on the basis of need, but who would determine that? It would be impractical.

"So, Mr. Switzer, if we don't do something like this, the ocean floor will never be mined. And millions will die of starvation and the United States and the industrial nations could find themselves in a far worse situation than when OPEC raised prices. This country could become one more page in history, a great power that in its prime made a wrong and fatal decision."

Switzer sat slumped, staring at the ceiling. She was another one of these women libbers. She should have been at home raising kids, cooking and keeping her man happy in bed. An oceanographer? Had civilization come to the point where females were actually walking around on the ocean floor?

He roused himself slightly. "You don't understand the political situation, Miss—"

"Dr. Kennedy." Greg supplied the name.

"Yes, yes, Kennedy. You scientists are way up there in another galaxy while we down here have to face up to the real world. The real world, Dr. Kennedy. A tough world. But you're a nice lady."

As they rose, she knew how a dog felt when petted.

Switzer followed them to the door. He was breathing heavily, his cheeks ruddy. "Don't you try anything, Wilson. You'll sail when State gives you permission—and not an hour before. If you try anything, we'll stop you, Wilson. We'll stop you."

"I'll keep that in mind," Greg said quietly.

Outside, on the corner of 22nd and C, they held a postmortem. "I was proud of you, Lynne."

She looked up at him. A warm sun bathed her face, highlighting eyes bright with the adrenalin flowing through her. *It's a beautiful face,* he thought, *marked with character. How could one know another for years and still make discoveries?*

He continued, "He's stalling for W.W.W. He doesn't care about a treaty. It's an excuse. The day W.W.W. makes a breakthrough, he'll quit talking treaty."

He hesitated. He was bothered. "We'll know shortly about the *Kharkov.* I hired the guy I told you about, but he's no knight on a white horse. Instead, he's a period piece right out of the Old West. A hanging judge. Fifteen minutes for the trial, fifteen for the hanging."

"I don't like that."

"We're desperate, Lynne. See that man down there looking in the shop. He's been looking in the window ever since we came out."

Lynne took a tight hold on his arm.

"I don't want you alone, ever." Greg stressed the words slowly.

He had thought of himself as the target. Now with a sharp thrust in his left side he realized that Lynne might very well be the prospective victim. He could be removed without too much loss to Carson Mining. She could not. The very success of the venture depended on her.

He held his hand high for a taxi. One after another the cabs passed them by. He swore under his breath. At last one stopped. As they slid in, he discovered he had a hand gripped tightly about her arm.

He looked back. The man was hurrying to the corner. He could not follow them. Not with the taxi problem in Washington.

About ten that night Greg walked down Woodley Road to the street corner at Connecticut for an early edition of the Washington *Post*. The day had taken a toll. His nerves were about shot. In the morning he would rise early and jog. Jogging relaxed him, and after a mile the problems diminished like a car moving into the distance. Besides which, he reveled in roaming about the city. In Washington there was constant excitement in the air, the thrill of knowing that in the buildings he passed was being wielded the far-flung influence of the world's most powerful nation. And the excitement of walking past some of the country's most historic moments, frozen in steel and concrete, in the plaques and monuments and buildings. A feeling emanated auralike about them, a feeling that we must not let these heroic men and women down, or the greatness they achieved in times of sacrifice and despair.

Suddenly he was conscious of a car bearing down very slowly and hugging the curb behind him. In that instant he realized how foolish he had been leaving the hotel. He had sauntered forth without thinking, or rather thinking about something far afield. His mind ran on a single-gauge track.

Only a short time ago Lynne had taken him to task for his failure to plan for his personal safety. "I like to think of myself as a surrogate for Barbara. Someone has to look after you . . ."

He wanted to inform her he didn't need a surrogate, that he could manage very well.

The car was barely moving when it passed him. He slowed his walk, thinking to fall flat if the man alongside the driver opened the window. He saw only the one man and at that a vague outline. To see the driver he would have to stoop.

The car came to a stop a few feet ahead. He pulled back into the doorway of the People's Drug store. For a reason he could not later explain he was calm, his thinking orderly. He would have felt safer, though, with his .38 Colt. He had left it on the *Marco Polo*.

The car door swung open and for a few seconds stayed open. Then the man got out awkwardly. He had a time getting his muscles to propel his feet properly.

The man shut the door as if he held a personal animosity toward it, then lumbered down the sidewalk away from Greg. The car shot off with a screech of tires. The driver had to be under twenty-five.

Greg took a deep breath and as he emerged from the dark, stretched his muscles. There was no exhilaration that peaked as high as when fear had passed and one was still alive. The ambush in Honolulu had keyed his responses to the point that ordinary happenings caused him to react.

He decided to forget the newspaper and return to the hotel. He had gone only a few feet when a young woman in her late teens crossed the street swiftly toward him. Again, he brought his feet to a halt.

She was coming straight for him. There was no question about that. She wore a light-colored coat and both hands were in the pockets. Her lustrous, dark hair fell to her shoulders and was low on her forehead. When she neared, he saw by the street light a nice smile on a pretty, wholesome face.

"Do you have the time, mister?" She had a happy, upbeat voice. She stood only a few feet from him and he was reassured. If she had a weapon concealed in a pocket, he could grab her before it exploded.

He moved a step closer and glanced at his wristwatch. He could not see the time but was not about to hold the watch up to the street light and take his eyes from her.

"Five after ten."

"Thank you." And then quickly, "I've got a neat apartment near here where we could have a good time."

He stood staring at her. She couldn't be more than eighteen. Nineteen at the most. There was a vibrancy about her and a freshness. Suddenly he wanted her. He had awakened that morning with a strong sexual desire. The day with its hassles had diminished it. But now it came coursing back.

She continued hurriedly, "I don't like asking, mister, but I need the money. I'm going to Georgetown University and I'm an A student. Honest, I'm not giving you a line. I don't ask every man. Only the ones who look . . . gentle and decent."

She talked rapidly but was at ease. She had the confidence of one who knows her business and has a good sales record.

She said softly, "No one needs to know. I'm sure we could have a lot of fun. I've got a waterbed."

She held eye contact. They were sparkling blue eyes in the reflection of the street light. They were dancing, inviting eyes.

For a long moment he stood there. Then he broke eye contact. "Sorry," he said, and started on.

"Don't be. I'll find someone." She wanted him to know she was a success.

She hurried after him. "You married?"

He nodded. "I hope I find a husband like you," she said. "I'm not giving you a line. I really do."

Back in his hotel room, he undressed slowly. His thoughts pounded in a vortex. *A streetwalker? How could he have considered her even for a moment? And Lynne, what had she meant by a surrogate for Barbara? Had she used the word in its complete definition . . . a substitute figure . . . in every way?*

Perhaps he had only to tap on the connecting door.

He thought of Laura. *Laura could be that university girl six or seven years from now. Not likely, but she could be. I've got to look after her. I can't go wandering off to all parts of the world and leave her.*

Then he heard a stealthy sound in Lynne's room. Someone slipping quietly over the rug. Sitting up, now wide awake, he listened intently. It was only a wisp of a sound. Bare feet perhaps.

He knocked softly on the connecting door. "Lynne?"

There was no answer. He called again, louder. "Lynne, are you all right?"

She answered, but it was unintelligible. He heard her leaving the bed and then unlocking the door. She was in a white, lacy negligee which she pulled together above the rise of her breasts. Her hair was tousled, her eyes dull with sleep. Yet later he was to think he had never seen a woman quite so appealing. Except for Barbara.

She looked at him quizzically. "Yes, Greg?"

"I heard someone moving about . . ." He was embarrassed. "I'm sorry I got you up. But I was so sure. I guess it was someone out in the hall. But I'd feel better if we left the door open." He added hurriedly, "Don't worry, I'm not coming in."

She wanted to tell him she wouldn't mind. But, of course, she would. There was Barbara . . . and then there was love. She was a romanticist. She wanted a wedding with a huge bouquet of red roses. It could be a small wedding with only a few friends. She wanted a ring. It could be a small diamond. She wanted a new dress and to look glamorous, which with her lanky frame was an impossibility. She wanted a minister to say something more than recite a ritual. Maybe he would read that passage Paul wrote in Corinthians about "faith, hope and love—and the greatest of these is love."

19

If one took Wisconsin Avenue all the way he would come to the placid waters of the Potomac's Georgetown Channel. If he turned left and walked a short distance, he would encounter the Potomac Ferry, a saloon that dated, according to legend, to Civil War days. It did have a historic look, no paint having been applied in years. It had a board front like the film people build, and various colors were beginning to show through the last paint coat which had been a dirty gray.

A customer was announced by a groaning door whose joints had been repeatedly nailed together. Inside, the establishment was even more disreputable appearing than outside. A long, hacked-up bar covered the entire left wall. Behind the bar was a mirror, also the length of the room. A bullet had shattered the far left side and fly specks had hardened with the years over the rest. Intricate wood carving had been built around the mirror but chunks had fallen out.

A handsome young Swede with the muscles of a bouncer owned the Ferry and was its sole barkeeper. He enforced certain rules which he said had been in effect since the Civil War. If a couple of women came in for drinking purposes, they took one of the booths to the right. If a strange man tried to strike up a conversation, the Swede hustled over and explained that no woman in a booth was to be accosted, and if the man pursued his course he would be ushered out. If a woman came in to have a drink and pick up a man, she sat at the bar. The booths were off limits. She could smile and say "hello" to a male customer, but if he failed to respond she could go no further. If she did, she was shown to the door.

Mike McGraw drifted in at 1 A.M., sat at the bar and ordered a Pepsi. A woman at the far end smiled tentatively and her friend more boldly. He pretended he did not see them. When the Swede brought the drink, he said, "Enjoy yourself, sir."

Those were code words. McGraw made his way to the far end, and turned at a small door with a sign that read, PRIVATE. The office was a dark cubbyhole with an old-fashioned ice cream table for a desk.

Behind the table slouched Nicholai Kazan who had a patch over his right eye, black unruly hair, and a scar on his left cheek. He did not need the patch, the hair was a wig, and the scar could be removed with cleansing cream. He had darting, bright eyes that were real. He was in his mid-sixties but had the voice of a teenager.

"Hello, Mike. How's my good friend?" His tone reflected deep fondness.

They shook hands, McGraw saying, "You know me. I'm always okay. How about the arthritis?"

"Got me in the hip. I don't get around so well."

Kazan had been a courier at the Soviet Embassy for more than thirty years. McGraw knew little about his background or personal life. He had inherited Kazan when he had been assigned the Soviet desk at the Central Intelligence Agency. About all that he knew was that Kazan had fought at Stalingrad and emerged a hero. He had been decorated by Stalin in person. He had had a few government jobs in Moscow, then in the 1950s had arrived at the Embassy in Washington to serve as courier. Why he had turned informant for the CIA, McGraw could never determine.

He had pried as much as he dared, but Kazan had only smiled and kept the reason to himself. For a long time McGraw had feared that he was a double agent. The information he had given, though, was accurate and had cracked several espionage cases.

"Thought you were over there with the Arabs."

McGraw lit a cigarette, offered him one which he refused. "Just got back. Your wolves put out a hit on me in Dubā. Almost got me. I've got a job for you."

"I told you before you went overseas, Mike, I don't take jobs anymore."

"You will this one."

"They've probably got this place bugged." He cast around to locate evidence of a bugging. "They've got everything bugged. It's not like the old days. They know everything that goes on. Ever since Congress scared the FBI about investigating American citizens."

"How many agents they running these days?"

He shrugged. "More than the FBI's got."

McGraw continued, "It's cash. Lots of it. And the nice part, it's not the usual. No risk."

"Sorry, Mike. I like you. Always have since the first day. We had some great times, didn't we? I retire in October. Can't take a chance."

"Where to? Siberia? With this kind of money . . ."

The Swede brought a beer and a Pepsi. "All's quiet," he said and left.

"Listen me out, huh?" McGraw stubbed out the cigarette. "For old time's sake?"

Kazan sipped at the beer. "You talk and I'll drink." He raised the frosted glass. "Here's to old times . . ."

"To old times." Mike swigged down a third of the glass. "I'm working for a company called Carson Mining. They've got a ship called the *Marco Polo* that'll put out from Honolulu soon to mine the ocean floor. They'll rake up rocks the size of potatoes that contain minerals. They think there are billions in it."

He stared at Kazan. "You know about this, huh? I can tell."

"A little."

McGraw took out ten new crisp hundred dollar bills. "This much?"

"Whatever you say. I don't push. You know that."

"What've you got?"

"Not too much." He finished the beer. "There's a woman named Nataya Fussen. She's in Honolulu now. Maybe you read in the papers about the hijacking—"

"She set it up?"

Kazan nodded. "She has a gopher working for her."

"How about a name?"

"She refuses to identify the gopher and her control is furious."

"Who's that?"

"General Dmitri Schepnov. Just came in from Afghanistan to run the job."

"What's the agenda?"

"To eliminate the top man—"

"Gregory Wilson?"

"That's the party. And to destroy the ship."

"Anyone working with the woman? Nataya . . ."

". . . Fussen. Yes, the General brought a rat from Afghanistan. Name of Rashid . . . I don't remember his last name."

"Rashid Jumeira?"

"That's it."

McGraw found himself standing bolt upright. A vivid picture flashed into his mind of Rashid Jumeira sitting there that afternoon at the Hotel Carlton in Dubā . . . suited, white shirt, narrow black tie with a diamond stick pin . . . glancing up, evil-looking, gloating over the prospects of a kill.

"You know him?" Kazan asked.

"I'd like to know him better." He had trouble breathing, but at the same time he experienced an exuberance. He'd nail the bastard this time.

Kazan was quick to read thoughts. "He was the hit man in Dubā? No?"

"Yes." He unloosened his fists and took a deep breath.

He said slowly, "There's ten grand in it for you if you get me the complete setup in this country—times, names, everything—and if you get me the *Kharkov* situation, dates for sailing, all of that. The whole, damned schmeer. Ten grand."

20

In Boston, Lynne and Greg checked in at the Sheraton the following evening. A stack of mail awaited them and Lynne offered to take care of it. More and more Lynne was volunteering to look after the little duties that Barbara had. He, too, found himself turning to her. Did this shirt look all right with this suit and did the tie match?

Before retiring he called Laura to let her know when he would return. Her grandmother had arranged to stay on another few weeks.

When the alarm went off at six the next morning, he bunched the pillow to raise his head and lay thinking. As if from afar came the muffled roar of traffic, and worked into the sound pattern was the buoyant ringing of a carillon. Outside dawn was overwhelming the dark. Stretched out, he found Lynne appearing ever more on his mind's video set. She was fond of him. He was certain of that. Very possibly she loved him. Not that she had ever said anything or ever made a move. She had acted as she had before Barbara was injured, efficient and circumspect, concerned for him but only as a friend would be. They had worked closely together these last few days, taken their meals together, talked nights, and slept in adjoining rooms. Without the slightest friction, their lives had meshed beautifully. There had developed a warm feeling, a glow held back by each's discipline from burning into an intimacy.

At this very moment he wanted to walk into her room and take her into his arms. It was a fleeting compulsive urge, followed by overwhelming guilt for even momentarily desiring her.

He remembered that traumatic night when Dr. Emory Randall had told him Barbara would never recover. The kindly, old doctor had said gently, "In time the shock will pass and some of the grief, and you will discover that you are a very virile young man."

Greg had only half listened. He didn't care. He was too swept up by the tragedy, his world that would be forever shattered without Barbara.

Now the words came back. "You will have some choices. You can take care of your own sex needs. Many single people do and I think it's good therapy. Not every doctor agrees, but most would admit it's better than some of the alternatives. You could establish a liaison with a single woman. However, you might start out with both of you thinking of it as only a physical relationship and then find it developing emotionally, and then one of you gets badly hurt. And then, of course, you could pick up a prostitute or some other man's wife in a bar. You might try to abstain, but that doesn't work out with very many men or women. And then, you could remarry. Of all these choices, I think that's the one Barbara would pick for you."

He never would.

Karl Neustadt ushered them into his office with a kiss on the cheek for Lynne and an arm about Greg. He was a bear of a man, tall and ruggedly built, with deep crevices in his tanned, time-sculptured face.

"It'll be close," he was saying. "Damn close. I tell you we're in for one hell of a fight. Seven to six is how I count it. Against us. Please sit down. Take this chair by my desk, Lynne. Greg can sit over there in the corner. I don't get many handsome women in here. You should see some of the secretaries they hire for me. Round them up at Halloween time, I think."

He dropped his weight into an enormous red-leather chair behind a glistening desk the size of a billiard table. He had it staked out with small stacks of papers. On the wall behind the desk hung the famous photograph of Marilyn Monroe with her skirt billowing up to her hips. He had started his career with a small movie house in a decrepit neighborhood, parlayed it into a theater chain, and then parlayed the chain into the nation's third largest conglomerate.

He saw Lynne's gaze go to the picture. "Marilyn Monroe," he said fondly. He sank back into the chair. "She built this conglomerate. That girl right up there. God, we couldn't cart the money fast enough to the bank when we played her. All thirty-three theaters. Standing in line. In the rain and snow. I don't like what they're doing to her today. Making her out to be a tramp. They wait until somebody dies and then jump on them. John Kennedy, J. Edgar Hoover, Joan Crawford. Hell, none of us are angels, but we're not junkies, either."

He was in a reminiscing mood. "Do you know how much I had when I came to this country? Ten dollars and forty-two cents. Walked all the way from Munich to Hamburg. But don't tell my daughter. She likes people to think we've always had money. Kids. They get strange ideas. Not only about that but about this country. Nobody's going to tell me this isn't a great country. Not with the chance it gave me. A youngster who didn't know where his next meal was coming from or what he was going to do. They took me in, people did, and helped me get started. Strangers I'd never seen. Don't tell me this isn't a great country."

He swung about and straightened. "That's the soap-box lecture for today. Elsa—my wife—keeps telling me either to get into politics or shut up." He drummed on the desk. "Like I said, I count it seven to six unless we come up with something awfully convincing."

Lynne flounced her hair in a defiant gesture. "I don't see how they can do this. We're on the eve of a great historic event."

Karl nodded. "It hasn't sunk in with them. Let me break this down for you. First, you've got to keep in mind that these are old-frat boys who've made their millions. Sure, they're interested in the bottom line for old Mass., but personal things come first. Take old J. M. Radcliffe. Remember him?"

He looked at Greg. "White-haired, pompous son-of-a-bitch. Was an Air Force General. A paper man during World War II. Never saw action. But he has clout in New England and the Air Force wines and dines him when he goes down to Washington and takes him on junkets. All ego trips. He's not going to do anything to wreck that setup, and if he thinks the government's against it . . .

"Then there's Bob McLean. Nice chap, very polite and quite ordinary. You'd never know he inherited fifty million. He's a big supporter of the Administration. Gets invited to the White House several times a year. Like Radcliffe, he's not going to jeopardize that. It's the biggest thing in his life. Bigger than his wedding day when he goes down there.

"And then there's Tony McAufliffe. He's got extensive copper holdings and been against us from the start. He's scared that if we haul up too much copper, we're going to ruin the world market price.

"And so it goes. The point I'm trying to make is this: Don't talk much about the millions we're going to lose if we cancel out. Talk about the Russian threat, and wave the flag, and what it'll mean to the American people, and the Government, and the Administration. Throw some politics in. About how this will help their friends get reelected."

Karl rose from the chair in sections. His legs were losing the propulsion power they had in former years. "Well, it's time we went in and bearded the lions. They're going to tell you everything you propose is wrong. But be respectful. The older we get the more respect we demand. Listen to everything they say and agree with them, and then if by chance we win the vote, go out and do what you've got to do. This country wasn't built on old men sitting around seeing goblins everywhere."

He led the way to a massive door. On the other side was the conference room. They could hear low voices.

With a hand on the door knob, Karl stopped them. "May I be very blunt? I've never done this before."

They nodded, puzzled. He continued. "You answer the questions put directly to you, Greg, but you, Lynne, you do most of the talking."

Lynne looked up in surprise. "I'm not good at—"

Karl interrupted. "You're a striking-looking woman and that's what we're going to have to sell. You've got a damn good face with a lot of character in it, and poise, intelligence, all the attributes that these fellows look for in a successful woman. These men are all in their sixties and their wives are mostly old bags who've let themselves go. They're going to be sitting there looking at you and thinking to themselves . . . well, you know what they're going to be thinking. All right, let's go and let's all say a Hail Mary. We need all the help we can get."

21

The rich rosewood walls of the conference room, the tasteful New England scenes, the long, highly polished table, even the draped window at the far end overlooking the river—all bespoke subtly of wealth. But not nearly as much so as the patricians in their expensive conservative suits and subdued ties. They quieted as Karl Neustadt stepped to the carved tall-backed chair at the head of the table. Lynne and Greg sat to his right. Lynne acted as if she had been born to this world. Greg was uncomfortable. These were not his people. They had cold eyes and severe lips in contrast to the tanned, easy-going men of the canyons and desert. Like Barbara, he thought, Lynne would fit in anywhere. They were chameleons.

"Gentlemen," Karl said, "I've asked Dr. Lynne Kennedy to come here today with Mr. Wilson to give us an assessment of the current situation. As you may know, Dr. Kennedy is one of the foremost oceanographers in the world, but she comes to us today in her dual role of operations director for Carson's sea-mining venture. Dr. Kennedy."

She rose slowly with a faint smile about her lips. She stood very straight and there was a sense of regality about her lanky frame. She said she would be brief, that she knew how valuable their time was. As she talked, her eyes traveled from one to the next, lingering for a few seconds on each, as if he were the most important person in that room. Greg thought, how could she be so confident, so assured? The directors were not exactly hostile, but they were hard-nosed, sharp-eyed, old New England traders going down to sea.

She set the scene in Washington, the talks with Jonathan Switzer, the Senate and House majority and minority leaders, and the chairmen of several influential committees.

No one smiled, no one offered an expression of encouragement. The combination of massive wealth and age tended to render them immobile.

She said, "Mr. Switzer has formulated a policy that you know about. To our knowledge he has not obtained the official approval of the State Department or talked with congressional leaders. So at this point it is his personal opinion. We believe he is deliberately delaying the sailing of the *Marco Polo* until a competitor has time to perfect its technology. The danger in this is that the Soviets may stake out the best seabeds and begin mining."

She tossed her hair back, then continued, "We have no objection to a valid, workable agreement that would be fair to the mining companies, the industrial nations and the Third World. We would welcome it most enthusiastically since it would provide us with a legal base that we need badly. However, we cannot wait any longer—if we are to be first."

They listened intently and sat more comfortably. They liked her straightforward manner.

She ended by saying, "Mr. Wilson and I would be most happy to answer questions if we can."

The questions came fast. J. M. Radcliffe was the first. "What you say, Dr. Kennedy, is all well and good, but Mr. Switzer—I've known him for years, a fine gentleman and diplomat—has informed me that this is a brink-of-war situation and Carson Mining, by some reckless and unforeseen act, could precipitate World War III. What've you got to say to that, Mr. Wilson?"

Lynne spoke up. "May I answer, please? Mr. Radcliffe, I was reared a Quaker. I was brought up a pacifist. I would never be a party to any venture that might precipitate a war. I assure you we are not reckless people. We are as cautious as any of you."

A melon-head director with pumpkin eyes, who was in his midfifties, the youngest present, raised a hand as if he needed permission. She nodded. "I say get out. It's costing too much. A billion dollars! It's outrageous. Let's take our loss and forget it."

"I know a lot has been made in the press about the cost," she answered, "but it's not as much as some land projects come to. May I point out that we don't have to bulldoze any mountains or sink shafts. We don't have to build a railroad to get the ore out or put up homes for hundreds or thousands of miners. We don't have any cartels like OPEC manipulating prices—no governments that may be overthrown tomorrow. We have a lot working for us."

The director on Karl's right spoke up in a thin, squeaky voice. "Can't we sell out to W.W.W.? I don't want to put my money into something political. Never have, never will."

Lynne's eyes held his. "The only political part of this is that we're doing this for our country, our people, for an Administration that will be remembered for centuries to come. Let me give you some figures I've just come across. I think they're frightening."

She referred to notes. "The United States imports 97 percent of the manganese we use, 98 of cobalt and 73 of nickel. If we were cut off, we couldn't build a plane. A jet engine takes more than 900 pounds of cobalt and 5,000 of nickel."

Another wanted to know how soon the Russians would begin mining.

"We'll have that information shortly," Lynne told him.

"I hope so." The director took a newspaper clipping from an ostrich billfold. "I have here something a friend sent me from the Honolulu *Advertiser*. It says a Russian schooner, the *Vitiaz,* put into port at Honolulu as far back as 1968 and a year later another Soviet ship, the *Dimitri Mendellev,* called at Honolulu and they both worked some seabeds. Do we know the whereabouts today of either the *Vitiaz* or the *Mendellev?*"

"We know about both ships," Lynne said, "and the two seabeds they worked briefly on an experimental basis. But no, we do not know their whereabouts."

"I think we should."

Directly across from Greg a director raised his hand. "What

happens if you meet a Russian ship at the mining site? An armed ship?"

Greg nodded to Lynne to take the question. She said quietly, "We would leave that decision to Washington. We would hope that this Administration with its deep concern for the security of this nation would give us permission to proceed and provide us with air cover and sea support. We think it would since it would be such a great achievement for this and the other industrial nations—our allies through the years—to be freed from dependence upon often highly unstable countries for our essential minerals."

She raised her voice slightly. Once again she looked from one to the next. "This is a giant step, the same as opening up outer space, putting an astronaut on the moon. And all of you who sit here and make this possible—I can see it now—you will be there on a flattop somewhere in the Pacific being honored at a ceremony. Men of vision who opened up a new world. I'm sure the President would want you in the Rose Garden with television and other media recording this historic event. It would be a tremendous thing for the Administration when it goes before the voters next fall."

The director next to Karl broke the ensuing quiet. "I don't know why we had this meeting. We've known all of this all along. I guess we needed to have someone as articulate as you, Dr. Kennedy, put it into words. Do we need to vote? I think we're all in agreement."

"One minute!" Radcliffe rose. "I don't believe we should be carried away by the excitement that Dr. Kennedy has engendered. I am still worried—very worried—about the prospect that at this very moment we may be planting the seeds of war."

"Sit down, J.M.," someone said. "You're too old. You won't be drafted."

Radcliffe ignored him. "When do you plan to start mining operations, Wilson?"

"We don't have a definite date." He hated to lie but had no choice. Radcliffe would pass the information directly to Switzer.

May 25. May 25. Only eighteen days now. And the fear grew. Every morning he woke up shaken by the possibility the Kharkov *had sailed.*

Radcliffe continued, "You're being evasive, Wilson. Is it a month . . . three months . . . six?"

Karl Neustadt spoke up. "Any time he gives us, J.M., would be a wild guess. We've got a couple of problems to work out."

Radcliffe snorted in disbelief. "I move, Mr. Chairman, that we continue to finance Carson Mining up to the day the *Marco Polo* is prepared to sail, but at that time we cut off all finances until such time as we can study and reassess the situation."

Lynne said softly, "We might not have time, Mr. Radcliffe. The Russians might be there long before we leave the dock if we have to return to Boston for another conference."

"She's right!" It was a loud voice.

Karl took over. "Do I hear a second to the motion?" There was a second. "Any objection to a show of hands? All right, all in favor of Mr. Radcliffe's motion so indicate."

Four hands went up. Against, nine hands.

Karl continued, "Do I hear a motion and second to continue our financing in accord with the schedule voted originally?"

There was such a motion and second. The vote was nine to four in favor.

She rose again to request $50,000 for additional filming of the site Carson would mine. It was readily granted. She could have got $100,000. Except for J. M. Radcliffe, they had fallen for her. Each would have given half his fortune to have her as his wife.

Back in his office, Karl turned to Greg. "If you weren't such a good friend, I'd steal this lady from you. I could certainly use her."

He switched to Lynne. "Don't tell me you've always been an oceanographer. I know a used-car salesman when I hear one."

She laughed but was concerned that Greg might have taken offense. Through no doing of her own, she had pushed him into the background. At dinner that night she apologized.

"For what? I should send you roses. From here on, I'm putting you on center stage any time we've got a crucial meeting."

She said thoughtfully, "You know, I think you're a fake. You're not as much a male chauvinist as you make out to be."

"I try hard, but sometimes I slip."

She couldn't sleep. The adrenalin from the triumph of the day still had her on a high. *I could go dancing all night,* she thought.

I wish I could go in and tell Greg how much I love him. We would make a happy couple. We would fit in every way, mentally, physically and spiritually. It was like being married these last few days, all except for the telling and the touching.

And Laura, we get along so well. She needs me and I do her. I need someone to mother and a man like Greg to hold in my arms, to spend long winter nights with before a fireplace, to come out of excursions into cold, dark seas far below and find him aboard ship to watch over me in a decompression chamber, to work hard together and play hard and go to all the oceans of the world, and best of all, to laugh together, to grow old together.

What in heaven's name do I do? Go on loving him but never showing it, waiting for Barbara to die? That might be years away. Growing into my thirties, then my forties, and waiting, waiting.

What a horrible thought, waiting for a dear friend to die. Wanting her to die. How can I even think like that. It's cruel. I'm cruel. But can I help it that I'm desperately in love, that I want him in bed with me this very moment, now?

The next morning Greg awakened with a bursting headache. These nights he slept less and less, tossed more and more. He had awakened frequently thinking about the Board meeting. While the directors once again had voted the full budget, men like J. M. Radcliffe would never surrender. He would keep working on this and that director. He knew their eccentricities and prejudices, their thinking. Next week or next month the Board might reverse itself.

Thinking about the matter further, he decided to confer with a close friend, Mark Finley, a Hearst newspaper executive in Boston. Finley had a quick, brilliant mind and might come up with suggestions for coping with this situation.

Outside the sky was still murky although the combined city's lights threw a moonlight-cast across the room. He rose and dressed quickly. He would shower and shave later. He had to escape this room and these problems. He would walk the streets, jog a little, and breathe deeply the morning air that the night had put through its purifier.

The air was not as good as he had expected. These days it was never good in any great city. The streets were not as deserted as he had anticipated. Auto traffic was mounting and the people on the sidewalks were growing in number.

He was faintly aware of the rapid click of a woman's heels behind him. Then the sharp sound grew in his consciousness. He turned and not far behind a woman was hurrying toward him. As she passed a well-lighted dress shop, she took shape as Lynne.

He hurried to meet her. "What in the world are you doing?"

She struggled for breath. "Following you."

"Why?"

"Because you're being followed—and I had to tell you, and I was afraid . . ." She had been sitting in the hotel lobby when she happened to glance up and saw Greg leaving—and a man following.

They drew to one side. A hundred feet behind them a short, squat character took the classic surveillance stance of staring into a store window. It was a woman's shoe shop. Every few seconds he glanced around, as if looking for a friend. He was in a dark suit and crushed hat and had his jacket collar turned up. He blatantly looked the part he was playing.

Greg recalled a detective friend once telling him that the quickest way to shake a tail was to turn suddenly and confront the party.

Greg said, "I'm going to end this once and for all. You stand in that store entrance—that one there." He indicated. "And stay there until I come for you."

"I'm coming with you."

"Don't worry. He won't pull a gun on me. Too many people about. And if he starts anything, I can handle a dozen his size."

"We'd better call the police."

His tone was sharp. "Get over there and stay until I come for you. Do you hear?"

"But, Greg . . ."

His tone grew blistering. "Go on."

Hurt and shocked, she walked slowly to the shop's entrance.

He sauntered toward the shadow who continued to stare in the window. When Greg was even with him, Greg quickly moved in close—so close he was breathing in his face. The man could not possibly draw a weapon.

Greg asked, "Did you want to see me?"

The man glanced at him quizzically. His look said, "Are you nuts?" He took his time answering. "Why'd I want to see you?" he asked gruffly.

Greg was belligerent. "You're running a tail job—and don't deny it."

"Sure, sure I am. Look, take it easy. I don't know what the game is—but didn't Mike McGraw tell you? Said he would."

"Tell me what?"

"I'm to keep an eye on you and the dame."

"Why?"

"To make sure you don't end up in the morgue. It's my job. I get a bonus if you don't."

Greg sagged against the windowpane. Damn McGraw, damn them all.

"I hope you get the bonus." In a mental fog that hadn't cleared, he retraced his steps. Seeing him coming, Lynne emerged and he told her who the shadow was.

She couldn't talk. She was near tears.

He said angrily, "How dare McGraw put a tail on us? I'd like to fire the guy. I'm not going to have any tail on me. I can take care of the bastards if they come for me."

She had difficulty speaking, "Didn't you tell me that the trouble with Bill Madden was that he thought he was invincible?"

He heard the tears. He took her in his arms and held her ever so tightly. "I shouldn't've spoken to you like that. I never will again."

It was good feeling the softness of her body, her head on his shoulder, her hair in his face, her breasts rising and falling against him, the quick pounding of her heart.

And it didn't matter that there were early risers walking past and around them. It was still dark, and they all had their heads pointed straight ahead, too numb with drowsiness to look or care.

The two of them were on an island six feet by six and they heard no sound except their breathing.

22

At 5 A.M. the General dragged his aching body out of bed. He had slept only intermittently. He cursed the slow, steady rain that had started shortly after midnight. He could take blizzards and storms but not the deadly monotony of nasty, bone-chilling drizzles.

He had set up two telephone calls, one for six and the second for 6:30 A.M. The phone booths were a short distance apart. He wondered if the rain would delay him. He had half a notion to return to bed and report in ill. He was getting too old for this nonsense. He was annoyed, too, that for the last week two FBI agents had shadowed him from the apartment to his destinations. He wished he had the nerve to walk up and hand them a list of his appointments for the day. That way, they all could relax.

When he took the Metro subway, one agent crowded in ahead of him while the other boarded the car behind. Washingtonians called the Metro the most luxurious in the world, and he conceded it rivaled Moscow's. Each car was carpeted and color coordinated. Gentle two-tone bells signaled the arrival and departure of the trains. Blinking lights at the platform's edge alerted the waiting commuters. The art decor at the stations, which were immaculate and without graffiti, was modern and softly pleasing.

He left the Metro at the Connecticut and M station. One agent walked briskly by him as if on his way to work. The other disappeared. The General's car had stopped alongside lighted advertising signs on uprights. They were out a few feet from the wall and behind them were three phone stands. He was a little early and took his time reading the advertisements. Both agents reappeared. As if in a rush, they walked swiftly past him. He smiled. They had nowhere to go. Once the commuters had disappeared they were most conspicuous. He liked them about. They were his security. As long as they had him under surveillance, no one would dare take a shot at him. He chuckled inwardly. The American taxpayer paid for them. What more could a Soviet agent want?

At straight up six, the phone rang. Rashid Jumeira was calling from Honolulu. The General could never quite peg the kind of relationship he had with Rashid. Whatever the General suggested, Rashid did willingly and gladly and well. Yet he was not a man the General felt comfortable around. He was a watch too tightly wound, and there was something indefinably evil about him, an aura he threw off.

He said his usual, "Good morning, General. How are you today?"

"Fine. And you?"

"Good. Very good."

"My people want a report on Project L."

"We are all set. I don't foresee any problems."

"I don't want to mislead my people."

"Tell them to read the newspapers."

"What about Nataya? How did she take being removed from the project?"

"She gave no indication that it mattered, and I don't think it did. She has all that she can carry."

"As an old friend, Rashid, I tell you that we must be careful in dealing with Nataya. I have reason to believe that she might be disloyal."

"You mean—"

"Oh, no, she would never betray us. But she has said—I will tell you when we talk. Just a warning."

"When do I get my woman?"

"Yes, well, I was going to discuss that. My people thought if we generously increased your check, you could find a woman in Hawaii—"

"I want Anya."

"Well, you see, Rashid—"

"What do I see, General?"

"Don't worry. Takes a little time. Problem of getting an American visa."

"Why can't she enter as a tourist? Same as I did."

"We are working on it. Just take it easy and she'll be with you in no time. Still, if you want a Hawaiian woman . . ."

"I want Anya."

"I know. Of course you do. Well, thank you, Rashid. I'm glad everything is going well."

When he hung up, the General stood in momentary shock. Anya was dead. The KGB had arrested her on a charge of treason. A few hours after she was executed the KGB discovered they had erred. It was a case of mistaken identity. That happened, of course, during war times, and especially in Kābul where there was turmoil and everyone was suspect.

The next time the General talked with Rashid, he would inform him Anya had died of pneumonia. The day of her death she had asked a nurse to give Rashid a message. It would have to be a message of great love. The General wished he had someone to write it for him. He might copy something. Yes, that was it. He would paraphrase a beautiful death passage from a novel. Perhaps there was something in Tolstoy.

With only a minute to spare, he made the next phone booth. The FBI agents had switched roles. The one across the street now walked hurriedly by him. The other stood on the far corner, going through the motions of hailing a taxi.

This call was from Nataya, also in Honolulu, and the General had a sour taste in his mouth. He had liked Nataya, and still admired her incredible work. But like many of these females she was too aggressive, too ambitious.

The General took a cold, impersonal attitude. "My people want to know why you have not completed your assignment? You were given forty-eight hours."

"The party left for the mainland—as you well know."

"You had plenty of time before he left. What was the difficulty?"

"I am going to state a fact or two and then I will hang up. Do you understand, General? I will hang up."

"If you do—"

"Don't threaten me. You know perfectly well that it is very difficult to find an opportunity in a crowded metropolitan area. There are people all about. You have to wait for an opening, for a chance to get him alone."

"He sleeps, doesn't he?"

"On the ship. I can't get on the ship and expect to escape."

"So that is it. You won't take a risk for your country. You're thinking of yourself."

The sound in the receiver was like it had been struck with a baseball bat. The General slammed down the receiver himself. How dare she? Perhaps he should dispense with her now. What was there to be gained waiting?

By the time he reached the office, he had reversed himself. She was too valuable to waste at this point. He hated the thought, but he needed her.

At the office he hung up his raincoat and took off his soaked shoes and socks. He felt miserable. The room added to his gloom with its musty, damp odor. On his desk, neatly typed, were more of those nonsensical reports about grain conditions, etc.

At 8:55 Rona arrived and shortly afterward walked businesslike into his office with a cheerful good morning. They discussed the rain. She liked it since it gave her a cozy feeling. That was youth for you, he thought. He had given up all hopes that they might have a "matinee." Skillfully she had blocked that idea with occasional references to her fiancé. She couldn't help but note his constant appraisal of her to know he would like to turn fantasies into reality.

When she returned to her outer office, he placed a phone call to a friend at a Russian import-export company. He talked in Russian. "I've had some news about the *Kharkov*, and I'm sorry to tell you, Vladimir, that it will be in dock for many months."

"What's the trouble?"

"I don't know. The message didn't say."

He had the decoded message from Moscow before him. It reported that the *Kharkov* would leave port within fourteen days. It reported further that the Politburo had met and decided at least one gunboat should accompany the *Kharkov* for "defense purposes," to repel any attack that should be made on the vessel.

The General continued, "Can we meet somewhere for lunch? I want to discuss that project I mentioned to you."

"The project?"

"Code name, Janet."

"Oh, yes, yes, of course. We must discuss that."

When Vladimir hung up, the General waited a few seconds, long enough to hear Rona put the receiver down. He was glad she knew Russian. It was more logical to confer with a Russian friend in their own language than in English.

The General rearranged papers on his desk. He felt immensely better. He had forgotten the drizzle outside. A little intrigue was good for a man.

The day was a busy one. The Embassy head for Service T, First Chief Directorate, came by. He was in his fifties, distinguished looking, with dusty gray hair and gogglelike glasses. He was a scientist of world repute. Service T handled all technology. He asked permission to assign three of his agents to Honolulu to learn technical details of the vacuum system developed by Carson Mining.

The agents would work independently as a unit and would stay completely out of the General's domain. They would get what information they could by: (1) sending a writer for a scientific journal to interview Dr. Lynne Kennedy; (2) setting up a European scientific front organization, probably in England or Germany, that would request specific information from Gregory Wilson; (3) offering fantastic sums to susceptible employees for research documents; (4) digging up criminal records and threatening employees with disclosure; and (5) hiring sophisticated call girls to wring information out of their clients.

The General was unhappy about yielding any of his territory, but had no choice. Only yesterday Master Control had instructed him to cooperate.

Service T himself was apologetic. "Sometimes we get a big breakthrough, but usually it's not worth the money. We get more by far out of the 78,000 publications we get from the Information Center."

The U.S. National Technical Information Center packaged most of the scientific papers and magazines published each year. It served U.S. research laboratories, libraries, scientific groups and the like.

"I don't understand the Americans," Service T continued. "They have to rush into print with everything they've done. It comes from the ridiculous idea that a scientist or educator must publish if he is to have any recognition. Publish or perish."

A few moments after he left, the Ukrainian code clerk placed two messages on the General's desk. With growing interest the General read the first. His heartbeat quickened. Master Control reported that as of this day the Kremlin had assigned Satellite 95 to spy on the *Marco Polo*. It had other missions, but this would be top priority.

The General knew of Satellite 95's capabilities. It was the type commonly known as a "ferret spy." It had such sensitive equipment aboard that it could pick up conversations on the ground, even of people conversing in cars. That meant it would record for the time it was over that part of the world everything said aboard the *Marco Polo*. As a routine matter, it would photograph the ship and surrounding area. Its infrared cameras might possibly penetrate to the hold. It would intercept radio and radar signals. To date, the 95 had photographed and listened in on every military installation in the United States and all of that country's bases abroad. It had mapped the radar stations that would have to be knocked out in case of war.

The General knew there was one drawback. A satellite followed a route. The *Marco Polo* might sail while 95 was orbiting elsewhere.

His adrenalin continued to flow when he read the second message. Master Control advised that the Kremlin, moreover, had ordered a spy submarine on duty off the coast of California—that ran surveillance on the missile testing at Vandenberg Air Force Base—to sail for Hawaii to photograph and keep watch over the *Marco Polo*. It was one of sixty-two spy submarines the Soviets operated worldwide. They maneuvered outside most U.S. bases, in the English Channel, in the straits between Denmark and Sweden (including one that ran aground 10 miles off a Swedish naval base), in the Strait of Hormuz at the entrance to the Persian Gulf, and in Japanese waters.

The submarine would photograph the *Marco Polo* through its periscope and also take underwater pictures. If the *Marco Polo* managed to put to sea (the fates forbid, the General thought), the sub would follow and keep Moscow informed. The sub had underwater receivers that could detect the presence of U.S. and other submarines and ships.

The *Marco Polo,* of course, would never sail.

23

Janet met Lynne and Greg at the Tucson airport with a car. He said, though, he would see them later and took a taxi to the University Hospital. In the lobby he stopped to buy a dozen roses. Barbara lay in almost the same position as last time. With her eyes closed, she looked at peace. Her skin tone was unnaturally pallid, not like the outdoors tan she had had winters as well as summers. He stooped and kissed her lightly on a cheek, then busied himself arranging the flowers on a nightstand.

At the nurses' station he asked to use the phone. When Dr. Randall came on, Greg said, "I know we need to move Barb. Will one of your nurses find a medical facility where they care? I want to see it, though, before you move her."

At home he got his usual rousing and flying-leap reception from Rambunctious. A few minutes later Laura returned from school to rush into his arms. "You've been gone years and years and years," she said. Her grandmother was not about. She was at a movie.

He took Laura out for a hamburger, then left for Tubac where there were the usual people waiting, quick decisions to make, correspondence to answer, telephones ringing, pandemonium. He took it all in stride. He was geared for this kind of life.

Before anyone else could get in, Janet cornered him in the

office. "I've got bad news. The President can't see you. The senator phoned an hour ago."

She referred to notes. "The President will see you at some future time and sends his deepest regrets. He has too many crisis situations at present and must concentrate on them. He told the senator that he had not had time to study the State Department policy paper prepared by Mr. Switzer, but from what aides had told him he agreed with it subject to certain reservations. He is most deeply appreciative to you, as is the nation, for what you, Carson Mining and Massachusetts Diversified have achieved thus far with this project."

"*. . . agrees with it subject to certain reservations.*" That was Washingtonese for saying yes and no in the same breath.

The blow hit Greg hard. He was certain he could have persuaded the President to his way of thinking. He needed support desperately from some quarter, to give at least a quasi-legal basis to the project.

Janet said Mike McGraw and an FBI agent were among those waiting. Jonathan Switzer had called from Washington. Greg opted to take Switzer, McGraw and the FBI in that order.

As usual Switzer was formal and cold. "I have an interesting report from one of our sources. The *Kharkov* has serious problems that will keep it in port at Vladivostok for months. I think that helps the situation greatly. Relieves the pressure. Gives the United Nations time to come up with a treaty satisfactory to everyone. I must repeat again, Mr. Wilson, State's position. We will not permit any American ship to put to sea until a unanimously supported agreement has been reached. Do I make myself clear?"

Greg thanked him, hoped he would have a good day, and hung up.

Mike McGraw reported he had "an informant right in the kitchen where the cooking's being done."

Greg was astounded. "You don't mean—?"

"Yeah, smack inside the Soviet Embassy. I ought to have a bonus. He hasn't had much time, but he did corroborate the fact that the KGB set up the ambush that night in Honolulu. Just like you said."

"What else?"

"The *Kharkov* will sail within fourteen days."

Greg straightened. "Fourteen days!"

"Yeah."

"I just got the rundown from Switzer that the *Kharkov* can't sail for months."

McGraw was floored. "Somebody's selling him bad pot."

"He's been right so far. What about your man?"

"I've worked with him for years and he's never steered me wrong."

Greg paced about, lost in thought, talking more to himself than to McGraw. "We can shave a couple days off the schedule, and it'll take the *Kharkov* several days to reach the mining site."

McGraw continued, "That's it from the man in the kitchen. But I scouted around and came up with some dope on W.W.W. Enterprises."

He was pleased with himself. "They've brought in new people and are working on a chain-line bucket system."

He took out a dirty, crumpled bank check on which he had scrawled notes. "They drop a steel cable to the bottom. Hooked onto the cable are several hundred buckets. They use a pulley on the ship to rotate the cable and as the cable moves, the buckets scoop up the nodules from the ocean floor. Then the buckets travel to the vessel or to a companion ore ship and are upended. You know about this system, huh?"

Greg nodded. "Costs only a third or less what ours does, but Lynne tells me there's too much chance the cable will break at 15,000 feet or could get tangled up, and the buckets will only scoop on fairly flat sea bottom. How far along are they?"

"They've run one successful test and they're debating now whether to run more or put to sea. They figure we're ready to go any day."

Greg was stunned. "They've got a pipeline in here?"

"Not inside but someone in Honolulu picking up bits and pieces from the crew."

McGraw referred to notes. "I've got reports of what other companies have been doing in recent years. The Hughes Tool Company in collaboration with Global Marine put a ship, *Sea Scope*, into Honolulu some time ago. The lowdown is that Hughes' outfit, Summa, plans a ship carrying a hundred with a sea-going capacity for up to one year. Another American concern is Deepsea Ventures, a one-time subsidiary of Tenneco, which is operating a pilot ship, *Deepsea Miner II*, for Ocean Mining Associates, based in Gloucester Point, Virginia. They have an extraction process they're excited about."

Greg sat staring at McGraw. He couldn't help but admire the man. McGraw had already earned his salary.

Briefly, McGraw discussed four other U.S. corporations in addition to W.W.W. that had spent hundreds of millions on technology and explorations: the Kennecott Group (Kennecott Copper); Ocean Minerals Company of Mountain View, California, in cooperation with Lockheed, Shell and Standard Oil of Indiana; Ocean Management of Bellevue, Washington, a consortia that included German and Japanese firms, Inco of Canada, and Sedco, a Dallas-based off-shore oil concern; and Ocean Resources, San Diego.

McGraw continued, "Now for foreign ships. The Germans have the *Valdivia* that has been exchanging information with the University of Hawaii and the Hawaii Institute of Geophysics. As for the Russians, the *Vitiaz* from the Institute of Oceanology in Moscow worked out of Honolulu several years ago and also the *Dimitri Mendellev*. I'll have more on the *Kharkov* soon."

McGraw rose. "I've got Colonel Jean Montand on board the *Marco Polo*. He performed brilliantly with the Biafran forces during that war and will take command of the mercenaries. He's a soldier's soldier and we're lucky to get him."

The FBI agent, Marvin Stone, was in his thirties and good looking except for a De Gaulle nose. He had the appearance of a harried young business man.

After the pleasantries, he asked, "Do you have a Janet working here?"

Greg nodded. "Janet Stowe. She brought you in."

"How long has she been with you?"

"Why do you want to know?"

"It concerns national security. However, I must add that our inquiries by no means indicate that we have Miss Stowe under investigation or suspect her of anything."

"If I refuse to answer your questions," Greg said, "it looks like I'm covering for her on something incriminating, doesn't it?" He took a moment considering. "She has been with us three years. She's a fine young woman, very capable, and I might add, she is not a political animal. I'm not sure she even votes. I've never heard her talk politics."

"Thank you. Did you get a security clearance when you employed her?"

"Hell, no. At that time we were just a little mining company."

"Do you intend to?"

"I know her and work with her every day I'm here and trust her. You don't go around investigating your friends."

"She's a friend?"

"Everybody at Carson's my friend. That's the kind of an outfit we've got here. And I'm not going to run a security clearance on my friends. I think that about completes our conversation. It's been a pleasure to meet you, Mr. Stone."

Stone picked up his briefcase. "You think a lot of your friends, but do you know—"

"Let me put it this way, Mr. Stone. There was an Egyptian by the name of Anwar Sadat. When the deposed Shah of Iran was dying, and just about every country in the world had refused to accept him, including the United States, Sadat said he could live in Egypt the rest of his life. And when someone asked Sadat why he had done it, and drawn such criticism, he looked surprised and said simply, 'He was my friend.' And I hope to God that I can be a man like Sadat."

Late in the afternoon he flew back to Tucson. As usual, Rambunctious, who had accompanied him to Tubac, was co-pilot. Greg had promised Laura he would attend her PTA school bazaar. In past years he and Barb had gone together.

At the affair that night—with the air warm with the pungent desert scents of spring—Laura proudly showed him off. She introduced him to students, teachers and parents. She was overly vivacious and he knew she was concealing the deep hurt they both suffered.

He strolled about, bought doilies, ragged paperbacks, an old shoehorn, a bead necklace made of piñon nuts that he thought Lynne might like, and a pound of fudge. He talked with everyone. He knew Laura wanted them to like him.

At the food booth, he collided with Celia Knott, the neighbor from two doors down. While she apologized, he apologized.

"Have you tried the pizza?" she asked, and when he said no, she bought a piece for each. Talking, they walked away from the crowd. She was a stunning-looking brunette in her late twenties, the mother of two daughters, seven and eight, for whom Laura had baby-sat. Along with Barbara, Greg admired her. She was a divorcée getting little child support who had managed to keep her home and take good care of the children.

"I cried when I heard," she was saying. "I loved Barbara. We were such good friends, like when I needed a friend so badly at the time Tom and I broke up, she was there. If I can do anything, Greg—well, like—maybe I shouldn't even mention it."

"No, tell me."

"I know Barbara would want it. I know I would if I were in her shoes." She cleared a nervous throat. "I thought if we could get together once a week or something like that. It's been awfully hard for me since the divorce, and I know it must be for you."

She hurried as if her courage might give out. "It would be just being practical. Wouldn't mean anything. No ties, no emotions. I wouldn't be taking Barbara's place. We'd just be being practical. Just taking care of each other, and I know you need it. I sure do. I guess I shouldn't have said anything—but I've been thinking about this for the past week, and I had to get it out."

Greg stood stunned.

She broke the silence. "I have shocked you, haven't I?"

"I guess you did, a little." His voice was suddenly husky. "You're good to offer to help . . . to help . . . I don't know. I'm leaving in the morning for Hawaii."

"Barbara would want it," she said softly. "Especially with me since I loved Barbara and she loved me."

He had trouble getting to sleep. He had escaped from Celia on the flimsy pretext he had to take Laura home.

He guessed he was getting old. He had been shocked. Yet women talked like that. He had heard them. Barbara's friends. And he could understand Celia. Why shouldn't she look after her needs? Wasn't it the intelligent, rational thing to do?

Not in his world, it wasn't, and thinking about it he grew angry. How could she when Barbara was very much alive? What a horrible thing to do.

At the first ring, he reached for the phone on the nightstand. The clock read fourteen minutes after three. It couldn't be. He had slept more than he realized.

Bill Madden was on the line. He was so shaken he wasn't coherent.

"Bill!" Greg said sharply. "Bill! Get hold of yourself."

Finally Bill did. The *Marco Polo*'s computerized guidance system had been sabotaged. Damaged beyond repair.

24

The General had been up for an hour waiting for the call. When it came he was on the exercycle he had purchased a few days before from Sears. The big department stores in Washington fascinated him. They were jam-packed with every materialistic comfort a human being could desire. He had to keep reminding himself that they were a part of the capitalistic system for keeping the masses under control. Sell them expensive playthings they don't need. Turn them into slaves struggling to make the next payment. Don't give them time to think or the strength to revolt.

He had to admit that at times he had heretical thoughts. He would like to settle down in Virginia and become a country squire. To do that, however, he would have to renounce the Motherland he loved. His roots were there, his friends, and most of all, his memories. The memories never let one go. The smell of spring in Virginia was different from that back home. The people were alien, their thinking strange.

Rashid's voice over the phone from Honolulu was the usual monotone. He said nothing about Project L. "Call me at this number," he said.

The General put on warm clothing since the spring days were more like fall and jogged to a pay phone off Dupont Circle. He liked jogging. He liked the thought of the FBI agents puffing along behind him.

Rashid answered on the first ring. "General," he said, "you will be happy to know that Project L went off very well. A complete success. The ship will be in dock for six to eight weeks."

The General let out a deep breath. "I congratulate you, Rashid. You never let me down."

"What about Anya, General?"

The General hesitated. This moment of elation was not the right time to deliver the fictional story about Anya's death. "You know how it is, so difficult to get information out of Kābul. I will be talking again today with them. I know the Company is doing everything possible."

"I need her. I must have her soon."

"I understand—and you shall, Rashid."

"One more matter," Rashid said. "I know the man they have hired as security head. I was assigned to him in Dubā and I want to be assigned to him again."

The General thought fast. Would there be any reason to kill McGraw? What purpose would be served? Carson Mining would sign another immediately. McGraw, of course, had a remarkable reputation. Another might not be nearly as effective. Still . . .

"Do you have a special reason for wanting this assignment?"

"I never leave a mission without completing it. I must complete this one."

The General continued to probe. "But that was Dubā. There is no connection. This is another matter."

"I want my record clean. I ask it as a favor."

That did it. Rashid had performed too well to be denied a favor. "Very well," the General said. "I will inform the Company that he is a key part of the Carson organization and his discharge would deal Carson a blow."

On his return to the office, the General called Rona in and handed her a check for $12,000 drawn on the Embassy. He asked if she would stop by the bank at noon and get cash in that amount. Her eyes went to the slip of paper on the desk which read: Lynne Kennedy—$12,000. She was reading it upside down. He idly pushed it under other papers.

She stood a second, thinking. "The bank must by law report to a government agency all cash withdrawn over $10,000. I could get $8,000 today and $4,000 tomorrow."

He got out his pipe. He needed time. Why was she telling him this? He had assumed she was an FBI plant, and the fact she listened to his telephone conversations tended to corroborate the conjecture. Yet now she was protecting him, or appeared to be. Could she be a plant for someone else?

He nodded. "Very well."

For minutes he sat frozen in position. She had a sharp, analytical mind and would have a reason for volunteering this information. He felt badly. He preferred only a figure and face, nothing more. The girl in London had had a mind, too, the girl he had had to dispose of.

Rashid left the booth near Woolworth's on Kalakaua Avenue. It was Waikiki's main shopping street and crowded with American and Japanese tourists. Signs in Japanese were everywhere and across the street Deak-Perera had a large one with the latest quote on the yen. The yen was accomplishing what the Japanese military machine had failed to do during World War II, take over Honolulu. The bright, young Americans manning the hotel reception desks were only camouflage. Many hotels as well as office buildings and shops were Tokyo owned.

He stepped a few feet from the curb, flagged down a taxi, and asked to be taken to the Aloha Observation Tower where he followed a few tourists into an elevator and rode to the tenth floor. He found a rather large lookout with two cubicle offices that interested him. One was marked, Marine Traffic Controller, and the other, Harbor Police Dispatcher. He made notes in a legal-size, leather-covered notebook, and sketched the surrounding area, including Sand Island which squatted at the entrance to the harbor. Two Coast Guard cutters were anchored on this side, painted white with red slashes across the bows. He described the paint job carefully. It might mean something on a dark night.

In prowling through the neighborhood, he discovered what he had hoped to find but feared he wouldn't—acres of parking on River Street at the Nuuanu bridge.

He would draw up a full report on the harbor layout this night. Once he had it in the mail, he could turn to the more interesting prospect of tracking down Mike McGraw and quietly removing the infidel from the passing scene.

Praise be to Allah.

25

For a few minutes they stood quietly as if gathered at a cemetery for the interment of a good friend. They were crowded body to body into the glassed-in instrument room on the foredeck of the *Marco Polo*. Present were Greg and Lynne, Bill Madden, Powder River, Mike McGraw, Captain A. W. Parker and Colonel Jean Montand. In the doorway hovered Janet Stowe.

They stared down at a new computer sitting partly inside a sizable, metal-framed upright. Both the computer and the support looked normal except for several long, deep incisions. They were no more conspicuous than surgical ones on a body. The edges were distinctly clean as if a cutting torch had been used.

When programmed by the Executive Officer, the computer had controlled the knots covered, compass setting, radar functioning, oil feeds, gyrations of the vessel such as might be caused by tidal waves or underwater storms, weather readings and two score other factors. These included monitoring the performance of the diesel engines, propellers, rudder, thrusters, dynamos, pumps, and the electrical, plumbing and fire-warning systems.

"Not only did they destroy the computer," Captain Parker said, "but also the sensors up above and the radar deflector."

He showed no emotion. He could have been reading a phone book.

Greg couldn't remember when he himself had been more shaken. "The same way?"

The Captain nodded. "I'll take you up when we finish here."

The sensors were positioned on top of the bridge. They were encased in weather covers and set to face a radar disk.

Bill Madden cut in, his voice trembling. He was taking this personally. "Nobody could've gotten in here. I've had four of my men on deck every night and the Colonel had four—"

"Six," Colonel Montand said. He was short, about five seven, with cropped graying hair and dark brown almost black eyes. He had a hard-lined, sculptured face. On the lower right of his neck was a large purple blotch. On the same side, the lobe of the ear had been shot off. He wore a faded blue uniform with a cluster of moldy medals pinned to a pocket flap. He had a wide, black leather belt reined about the jacket as tight as a cinch on a horse. From the belt hung a holster with a gun bulging out.

"Six," repeated Bill. "We had a guard at the landing and—"

"Someone did get in," the Captain said accusingly. "It didn't just happen. I want a committee of inquiry to sit on this. You bring these mercenaries aboard—"

Colonel Montand said in a chilling voice, "I've spoken to you before about this, Captain, and I will not do so again. These men may not look like much to you—"

Greg could agree to that. When he and Lynne had come aboard, the sight of them had stopped him dead still. They were slouched about here and there, all over the deck. Several wore only shorts with their navels and bare hairy chests prominent. Others had on torn and patched jeans or dirty, ragged uniforms from some war or other. They sported mostly heavy, black beards they had not trimmed in months. To the man they had scars that attested to the savage lives they led. Proudly they displayed enough hardware to arm a regiment. All in all they looked like pirates left over from an old Errol Flynn movie.

Colonel Montand continued, "—but they are the best soldiers in the world, and before this is over you may be damn glad they're aboard." His English was good, though overlaid with a pleasing French accent.

Greg took over. "No accusations. Not until we learn what caused this. We'll take it step by step—"

The Captain interrupted. "For your information, Mr. Wilson, I am the captain and the final authority on this ship. My word is law. I'll decide what we do and how we do it."

"You go right on being the final authority to your heart's content," Greg said heatedly, "but while you're being so almighty some of the rest of us are going to be using a little common sense."

Powder River spoke up. "Don't you think, boy, we should call the FBI in?"

Greg hesitated. His aversion to anyone snooping around surfaced.

"I'll call them," the Captain said flatly.

Greg cut in. "Powder River will take care of it."

The Captain bristled. "This is a crime committed on the high seas and a ship's captain has full authority."

"I don't see any high seas," Greg said.

"I'll handle it." Powder River's voice brooked no dissension.

As they broke up, McGraw turned to Greg. "Can we talk? I've got decisions to make."

At the same time Janet was at Greg's side. "I've got to see you. Right away." There was urgency bordering on hysteria in her voice.

"Can Lynne take care of it?" he asked. "Soon as I've talked with her."

He took Lynne by the arm and guided her out on deck. The sun beat down hot, but a gentle breeze caressed them, playing lightly with her hair. They stood at the railing staring down on waters frolicking against the ship, waters that until a few hours ago had held such promise.

"Will you get replacements in here right away?"

She nodded. "I'll get on the phone. But it's going to take time. Maybe several weeks."

"Weeks!" he shouted. His anger was a geyser going off. "We've got to have it tomorrow, the next day. We've only got a week or so to go—or the *Kharkov* will stake out claims."

She brushed the hair out of her eyes. "I'll do my best."

In her first months with Carson Mining, she had kept out of his way when he exploded. In her scientific world she had known tempers to flare in personality clashes but not to blow sky high on meeting immovable objects, absolute truths or irrefutable facts.

He quieted as quickly as he had erupted. He put a hand on hers by way of apology. "You always do. It's just that we can't wait. We won't wait. I'm not going to let any saboteur stop us."

Long after he was gone, she felt his warmth on her hand.

In McGraw's cabin, Greg tried sinking into a straight chair. He was beaten. The night flight and the shock of knowing the enemy could penetrate the tightest security to commit an act of sabotage had sapped him.

"How did the saboteurs get aboard?" he asked.

McGraw shrugged. "Beats me. Before you get involved with too many people I want to bring you up-to-date."

He had placed outdated antiaircraft guns aft and fore and posted mercenaries who had used such weapons in the Rhodesian (Zimbabwe) guerrilla war. Spotted about were light field artillery 75mm pieces, a howitzer, two mortars and several mounted recoilless rifles firing small-caliber artillery shells. He had positioned responders underwater on the hull that would record the presence of submersible craft or frogmen.

He had a heavily armed helicopter based five minutes away on the charter end of International Airport. If an enemy attacked the *Marco Polo*, one of three pilots, each working eight-hour shifts, would airborne the craft. They were veterans of the Angolan civil war.

McGraw's Washington informant had reported that the Soviets had ordered a submarine that had been stationed outside the missile-testing site at Vandenberg Air Force Base in California to take up temporary duty outside Honolulu harbor to keep watch over the *Marco Polo.*

"So I've ordered our copter to patrol the area a few hours every day," McGraw said.

"What then?" Greg asked. "How does that help us?"

McGraw smiled. Greg was quick to interpret it. "Don't you dare. That's an order. Do you know what it would mean if you dropped a depth bomb? We'd be at war with Russia."

McGraw took his time lighting a cigarette. "I didn't say we were going to do anything. But it is an interesting thought."

He paced about the small room. "We've got a more pressing problem. We've got forty-three people on this ship. Fourteen mercenaries Montand will vouch for—and your people, whom you say are okay. That leaves the crew, the men in the engine room whom we never see, the cooks and stewards and all the rest. One or several could be working for the enemy. I want your permission to run security checks."

Greg straightened up. "I don't like it."

"You trust everyone. If you were in my work you'd know that most people are nothing but a stinking, rotten, lying, murderous lot. They'd turn themselves in for a buck. What're you going to do? Wait for them to blow up the ship?"

Greg got up and stretched. "I trust people because most are trying to live good, decent lives against awful odds. But you've got a point. Go ahead and check them out. But take it easy. Don't go in like the Gestapo."

McGraw smiled. "I don't know why you think I'm a tough son-of-a-bitch. I go to church Sundays—"

Lynne and Janet were waiting in Lynne's office. Both were obviously distraught. Janet had flown in with them that morning, and since there were no cabins available aboard the *Marco Polo* she had checked into the Ilikai Hotel.

"You'd better come in, too, Mr. McGraw," Lynne said, "and I'd like Bill if he's around."

She didn't wait for them to find chairs. "I think you'd better tell them about it, Janet. I could, but the facts never get spelled out right when it's second hand."

Janet took a viselike grip on the chair arms. She could scarcely be heard. "I'd been in the hotel room maybe a half hour, I don't really know, I'd finished hanging up my clothes, and the phone rang. A man—he had an accent, I don't know what kind—he asked if I was Miss Janet Stowe and I said yes, and he said I didn't know him but he had a business proposition to make me, and it would mean a lot of money to me. I started to say he must have the wrong party, but he talked louder and said he could offer me a lot of money if I would get the film and maps. He didn't say of what, just the film and maps. Maybe he was going to say more, I don't know, because I broke in and said I didn't know what he was talking about. I was going to hang up, I was shaking so I didn't know what I was doing, when he said . . . when he said . . ."

Lynne put a hand on her arm. "Go on."

". . . when he said if I didn't want to take the money he was going to rape me, and he went into horrible details about how he was going to do it, and it would be tonight . . . tonight . . ."

She straightened. "I shouldn't be acting like this. I never have before. I don't know what's wrong with me. He said after he attacked me he would strangle me, and no one would ever know what happened. He said it was up to me. He repeated that two or three times—and I hung up. The phone rang again but by then I was going out the door and there was this couple walking down the corridor, a nice-looking young couple, and I asked if I could walk to a taxi with them, and would they stay with me until I got a taxi . . ."

For a moment the others sat with their thoughts spinning. McGraw uncrossed his legs. "I thought they'd start with you, Dr. Kennedy. You're the logical victim."

He turned back to Janet. "They figure they'll keep working on you until you're so paralyzed with fear you'll do anything they say."

"Never."

Greg looked up in admiration at a woman he had not known before. She had guts. He realized he had let his annoyance with her at times obscure the fact she had shown courage in handling numerous major responsibilities.

He said, "We'll get somebody else on the phones."

"No! I'm not going to let anybody scare me off my job. I'll hang up next time he calls."

After some discussion, they decided she would use a ship's cabin as her office and bedroom. They would temporarily close the Tubac headquarters. McGraw would post two men to keep watch over her, and similar precautions would be taken with Lynne.

Greg conferred the next morning with Colonel Montand. The Colonel showed him where he had stashed the firearms—grenades in tote bags off the galley, folding AK-47 assault rifles in a lifeboat, tommy guns next to the radio room, and ammunition in a cabin off the foredeck.

"I have a jock in charge of each." He nodded toward the bridge where a squat, bulky mercenary in his mid-forties had torn down a .30-.30 rifle.

"Crazy Charlie's looking after the submachine guns. He was one of the wild geese in the Belgian Congo back in the sixties and got shot up. What a campaign that was, monsieur."

Greg found himself liking this ramrod-backed French officer who was sensible and briskly efficient. He was no killer like McGraw. He discussed ways to limit the casualties on both sides if the *Marco Polo* were attacked. He had given instructions to his troops, as he called them, to hold all fire until he so ordered.

"They are due their first money Saturday."

"They'll have it," Greg said. He made a mental note to instruct Janet Stowe to bring the cash from the bank Friday. The deal called for payment of two thousand dollars plus expenses to each soldier for one month's duty plus a bonus of four thousand when and if the *Marco Polo* left the pier.

The two had finished checking out the antiaircraft guns when Powder River and Captain Parker brought up a handsome, tall, clean-shaven black man in white trousers, white shoes and white open-necked shirt. He was lean as a hunting dog. The Colonel drifted away.

Powder River said, "This is Special Agent Jim Manley of the Honolulu FBI office." And to Manley he said, "This is Gregory Wilson, president of Carson Mining Company."

After the two shook hands, Manley looked about. "I assume, Mr. Wilson, that you have the proper papers for all of this hardware?" He indicated the antiaircraft guns.

Powder River moved in quickly. "We'll have to discuss that with Colonel Montand. He's in charge of security."

Manley continued glancing around. "I assume that this Colonel is in charge, too, of this army?"

"Not an army," Greg put in.

"I'm glad to know that." Manley studied a mercenary hugging a Thompson submachine gun. "There is a statute that prohibits the recruiting and support of a private army."

"We'll talk with Colonel Montand," Powder River said.

Manley nodded. "I have informed Captain Parker that the guidance system was destroyed by a laser beam."

"A laser beam?" Greg was incredulous.

"A laser beam," Manley repeated. "Our subjects—there were two of them—took over a second-floor office in that building across Nimitz."

He indicated a low-slung building across the street. "An older woman in her early sixties rented the space and then disappeared. A young man took over whom the other tenants described as in his mid-twenties, medium height, with a slight, wispy beard, and dark complected—but not black. They said he looked Arab or Iranian but had an English accent.

"We know the subject used a laser beam for two reasons. One, there was evidence that stabilizing jacks had been locked into position on the floor."

He explained that the electronic gear for a laser of this type usually had to be mounted on a platform set in stabilizer jacks. The gear itself would call for a container about the size of a four-drawer file cabinet.

"The second reason," he continued, "is that we have a witness who looked up from the sidewalk across Nimitz and saw the laser, but he was some distance away and thought it was a telescope."

The laser, Manley said, was gunlike in appearance and probably mounted on a swivel. He speculated that for this type of operation it was possibly three to four feet long and six to eight inches in diameter. For the precision-sighting required, it had to have a telescopic sight.

"This operation needed a lot of power and took hours. The subject brought up a generator loaded on a truck. The tenants remember seeing it but thought nothing about it.

"In regard to the time required, we think they started shortly after dusk and worked to dawn. They may have taken more than one night since they wanted to be certain to destroy the circuit boards stored in the cabinet of the computer, and the memory chips."

Greg was incredulous. "I can't believe it. I thought we had the tightest security . . ."

Manley continued, "One tenant saw the truck bearing the generator pull out shortly after he came to work yesterday, about eight o'clock. They probably finished the job the night before."

Manley wiped the sweat from his forehead with a large red handkerchief. "The humidity gets to me. I'm from Nevada."

"Arizona," Greg said, and they became fellow sufferers.

Manley remembered a point. "I should add that the subject had one decided advantage when it came to the computer. As a precautionary measure, your security people kept the place well lighted. No one would commit an act of sabotage under floodlights. But for the subject across the street, it was a plus. He could easily see the computer and target it with the beam. No one came aboard, Mr. Wilson. No one at all."

Manley maneuvered Greg out of earshot of the others. "I must talk with you about Dr. Kennedy."

Greg was instantly hostile. "What about her?"

"The Bureau is conducting a routine inquiry, nothing more—"

Greg broke in. "I've heard this dialogue before. The FBI came to me about Meg and then Janet Stowe, and now you about Lynne. I don't like it."

Manley surprised him. "I don't either, Mr. Wilson. And neither does the Bureau. But we have to investigate. We can't take a chance."

"Just what're you telling me?" Greg asked.

Manley looked around the deck. "I could be sacked for telling you."

"You've got my word."

Manley continued, "We have an informant—the FBI has—who saw a slip of paper on a desk that read 'Lynne Kennedy—$12,000,' and then the informant was asked to get the $12,000 from a bank, which the informant did, getting $8,000 one day and $4,000 another. The informant reported all of this to the FBI, and if you were the FBI what would you do?"

Greg shrugged. "What you're doing."

"Right, man, right. But as you pointed out, this is the third person who has been fingered and it doesn't stand to reason . . . well, to get along with it, the Bureau figures it is being fed misinformation. Not by the informant who is trustworthy but by another party who is using the informant."

Greg shook his head. "Why? What's the purpose? So you investigate and clear them."

Manley smiled. "You have to know the world of espionage, Mr. Wilson. The party thought you might possibly fire Miss Stowe and now Dr. Kennedy. But if not that, then you would become suspicious and there could be a lot of trouble. That's what the party thought, even though the party should have known that by now his misinformation was getting nowhere. But in espionage the players continue the game long after there's no purpose. It's like a football team losing by a 28 to 14 score with a minute to play and they're still knocking themselves out, risking injury, because the unwritten rule says they should."

"I hadn't thought of it in that way," Greg said. "I guess you know I'm a loner, always have been, but I'll keep you posted from now on, and on your part, how about letting me know who the rat fink is in our organization?"

"I couldn't tell you that—if we knew—which we don't."

Greg was angered. "I would swear we don't have a single traitor in our organization."

Manley nodded. "I'm sure no one who is Communist or even pro-Russian."

He took a deep breath. "The time was when a spy did it out of loyalty to his country or a cause, was willing to die, but no more.

They do it now for only one reason, money. I don't know of a single espionage case in our country in recent years where the motivation was anything but quick cash."

He glanced at his wristwatch. "I've got to be going. There are contributing causes, of course. Big gambling debts, keeping girl friends, living too high. And emotions . . . mad at the boss or the system, wanting to be big man on campus . . . trying to escape from punching a time clock. But it all gets back to dollars."

Greg said flatly, "We don't have anybody like that."

Manley shrugged. "You may be surprised. There's something else. In war time we think of espionage as high treason, betraying our country . . . but in peace times . . . well, we have so many spy novels and films and they depict it as an exciting game of matching wits, a lot of glamour and adventure . . . so we get to the point where we're sated, and espionage is not nearly as serious a crime as burglarizing a home. Yet it's during peace times that a spy has tremendous freedom of movement, and if an enemy country knows when it engages in war everything that we know, then we're in serious trouble."

Jam-packed on the *Marco Polo* bridge, they held a council on strategy: Lynne and Greg, McGraw, Carlos, Bill and Colonel Montand.

McGraw took the lead. "The Soviets will be working this on several levels at the same time. I've seen it so often. The Politburo makes a decision and sends the word along and then all the people down below get busy."

He lit a cigarette. "The diplomats will square off on the top level. They'll jab and feint, a ritual that may take weeks.

"Then one step under them come the strictly Intelligence people. I can see a couple of their men now sitting in the Library of Congress reading everything ever printed about mining the ocean floor. They'll use pretexts to talk with every company engaged in mining and try to get their hands on research reports.

"Then come the scientists who will want to exchange information. It's not that the Soviets can't do this on their own. But it's cheaper to steal our stuff. And quicker. Russia was years away from developing the atomic bomb until they stole the plans from us.

"While all of these efforts are going on, the sabotage people move in, just the way they have here, and then if all else fails they bring up the murder squad which some call the Wet Section."

Wet for blood.

26

The beach at Waikiki was ablaze with sun, and the searing sand burned through Nataya's thonged sandals. She took long strides but slipped a half foot back for every foot gained. The beach was ablaze, too, with youth sporting splashes of color. Shouting surfers crested waves and seemed engulfed only to rise like magic. The catamarans added their own picture-postcard effect.

Usually she felt safe among the young. They seldom noticed an old woman. It was as if she did not exist. But today she was being followed. A black man in his late twenties wearing blue-and-white shorts was trailing her. He was using a metal detector as a prop, but his pace was the same as hers. Anyone searching for coins would work the sand slowly.

Her heartbeat picked up tempo. Most probably he was an FBI agent, although he could be with the CIA or the local police. But what could she possibly have done to attract attention?

She stopped before the Royal Hawaiian Hotel, the "Pink Lady" of another era that was still one of the world's great luxury hostelries. It sat on what had been the Royal Palm Grove, a playground for Hawaiian kings.

She joined a small group on the beach watching a young, sunbrowned artist in dark bathing trunks constructing a sand castle. Every day he built one, every night destroyed it. He had put out a battered cooking-oil container for donations. She dropped in a five-dollar bill. He noticed and nodded in thanks. She asked a question and he answered politely. She would come tomorrow and cultivate him. He might turn into a good "mail drop." She could then leave messages for Rashid to pick up.

She turned about quickly and walking very fast, entered the Royal Hawaiian grounds. She passed the pool where those who did not want the gritty life of the beach could swim in the same comfort provided by their expensive rooms.

Unexpectedly she did a complete reverse and sat under a turquoise umbrella table near the pool. No one had followed her. She had not expected anyone to. The man with the metal detector had probably signaled a compatriot who would be waiting inside the hotel. It was standard surveillance practice.

She ordered a Mai Tai which came with orchid, mint leaves and a tab for $4.75. She was forever feuding with Moscow about expense accounts. Of course, Moscow probably had no idea what a Mai Tai was. She would put the name of the drink down as that of a Chinese informant she had entertained. She had other such informants: Mr. Harvey Wall Banger, Mr. Screw Driver, Miss G. Fizz, Mr. Rusty Nail, Miss Green Lizard, Mr. Greyhound and Mrs. Velvet Hammer.

She would have enjoyed basking in the sun but was growing increasingly apprehensive. She paid the bill, entered a side wing of the hotel, and casting quick glances about, walked swiftly down a long, wide, red-carpeted corridor flanked with white pillars. She swept every face but concentrated on movements: a hand going into a pocket or purse, a hand holding magazines or papers that might conceal a weapon, an attaché case being opened.

At the bellman's work quarters in the lobby, she turned right, passed the elevators, and exited onto an immense, tiled porch overlooking a garden festive with pink-balloon lanterns. A Japanese camera crew was working there and she turned quickly to avoid being caught on film. In a corner of the porch, secreted behind a wall outset, were two pay phones, hidden away as if the management frowned on something that plebian.

She placed a call to a Washington, D.C., pay phone. She had coins neatly stacked before her and dropped them in the slot.

The General answered immediately. His voice was acid cold. He asked sharply, "Have you taken care of him?"

She remembered to talk into the receiver. Even at that, a sound cone some distance away could pick up her voice.

She feigned anger. "How dare you come on me like that? If you persist, I'll hang up, even though I've got something vital to report."

He quieted. "What've you got?"

"Our friend left for Hong Kong on Pan American at 8:27 this morning. He will gain a day when he crosses the International Dateline en route to Tokyo and will be in Tokyo only about an hour before he flies Pan American into Hong Kong where he'll check into the Peninsula Hotel on Kowloon."

The General was surprised. "What's he going there for?"

"I don't know."

"Where'd you get this?"

"You know perfectly well."

"I've got to have the name. I'm getting it heavy from our people. It's the rule. I've got to have a name. I've been protecting you, and you don't give a damn."

She turned on the repentance. "Sorry I've given you problems. You got a pencil handy?"

She glanced at a newspaper she was carrying, the *Advertiser*. Her eyes caught a name. "She's Terrie—that's spelled t-e-r-r-i-e. The last name's Kapiolani. K-a-p-i-o-l-a-n-i. She's a close friend of Lynne Kennedy—"

"What does she do? Her address . . ."

"She gets in touch with me when she has something. She doesn't trust me."

"Haven't you run a tail job on her?"

"Don't be a fool. If she discovers me shadowing her, we lose a pigeon."

He didn't pursue the matter. He was too elated. He had a name. The rest would come.

At the office he called the code clerk in and instructed him to relay the name by Code O, the code reserved for KGB's top priority matters.

The clerk brought three sealed messages that had come in during the night. The first contained a synopsized report of two conversations picked up from the *Marco Polo* by Satellite 95. An unidentified man and woman (see picture) talked on the deck about obtaining a replacement for the guidance system. In the second conversation, also from the deck top, a man informed another (see picture) that a laser beam had been used to destroy the computer.

When the General shook the envelope, twelve small photos fell out that the Embassy had received from the satellite. They showed antiaircraft guns on fore and aft and half-naked soldiers who looked more like barbarians than Americans.

The General was puzzled. These had to be hired thugs. The U.S. Army would never permit such attire.

In the second envelope he found more pictures, these taken from the submarine. The sub's commander called attention to one underwater photograph that revealed responders had been attached to the hull. The commander noted that only a frogman could put them in place.

The General found his hands in a tight grip. In the last two days the *Marco Polo* had changed from a peacetime ship into one preparing for open warfare.

He was relieved somewhat when he opened the third document. It contained a brief memo from the Soviet Foreign Ministry stating that Mr. Andropov's request to the United States for an exchange of information had entered into the negotiating stage and looked promising. The Ministry expected to place a scientist within days on the *Marco Polo*.

There was a fourth envelope. Hastily he read a transcript of the conversation he had recorded the evening before with MJ's spokesman who had called from Honolulu. The salient points were:

Gregory Wilson had recognized a woman following him at the Honolulu Airport as the same who had called at the Tubac headquarters the day after the attempted theft of the safe. Mr. Wilson was convinced the woman had been assigned to kill him.

MJ's representative advised that MJ wanted to work with the woman. MJ thought a team effort would prove highly effective. The General had stalled. He would never bring two agents together when he did not know one. MJ's spokesman said MJ would be glad to meet the General in Washington. The General said he would have to consult his superiors. MJ's man charged testily that even with all the films, maps and information MJ had furnished, the General still had misgivings.

"This may be my last call," the spokesman said bluntly. "I cannot advise MJ to continue in this kind of an atmosphere. We must have complete trust."

The man had then dropped the bombshell. "They've got fifty more mercenaries coming. It's going to be an armed fortress. If you don't act soon, and get MJ with your agent, it'll be too late. They've got depth bombs on order and a whole arsenal of the latest weapons."

The General flinched. Depth bombs? Were they mad enough to try to sink the submarine cruising off Honolulu? How could they possibly know about it?

MJ's spokesman continued, "MJ has just received information about the project at Saipan. They will slip a mining ship into hiding somewhere off Saipan within the next week. Like the *Marco Polo,* it's a converted oil-drilling ship. Named *Tai Peng,* out of Hong Kong. The site they've chosen is between the Mariana Islands and the Mariana Trench and is only about 3,000 feet deep."

He hung up without his usual pleasant good-bye. The General stood stunned by his anger and the developments.

By an hour later he had regrouped his thoughts. First, he must get the information about the Saipan operation to Master Control. He must ask Master Control for guidance in regard to bringing MJ and Nataya together.

Most important, he must launch an attack quickly on the *Marco Polo.* He had thought it a sitting duck to be knocked off slowly. It was becoming a war vessel. He must instruct Rashid and Nataya to sink it. He must insist on the immediate execution of Gregory Wilson and Lynne Kennedy. He used the word, *execution,* in the strict military sense since each was the enemy as much as any Afghan traitor.

Nataya hung up the receiver and waited. The phone rang almost immediately. She owed $5.85. Slowly she dropped a raft of quarters into the slot and added a dime. Long after the operator said thank you, she stood motionless. She was scanning the word processor in her mind. She concluded she had said exactly the right thing, including lying about the informant. There was little chance she would be caught up.

She put another quarter in the slot and dialed her hairdresser. She set up a date for the next day. She was glad she had remembered. At the same time she would get a pedicure and manicure.

She turned to step out on the porch and then remembered to reconnoiter. On the lawn, the Japanese camera crew was packing the equipment. A young couple exited laughing from the hotel, an older man entered, and then there was no one about.

She had taken no more than two steps when she heard the faint snap of gunfire. The bullet cut so near her cheek that it seared the flesh. A second followed. Automatically she dropped and lay perfectly still, her body curled on her left side. Years ago she had programmed herself for such an attack.

Her right hand sneaked out over the floor and found her purse. Slowly she brought it within eyesight. With one hand she unsnapped it and felt of the contents. Her mind screamed at her to hurry. She had to force herself to inch out the .22.

She had a good view of the porch. In sweeping it, her eyes stopped when they reached the big, broad-leafed, rusty-colored crotons that formed a border about fifteen feet distant. They were moving ever so slightly and there was no breeze. Someone was watching her. Someone was waiting for her to get back on her feet. If she did, his aim might be better this time. If she didn't, he might conclude he had found his target.

Minutes passed and they seemed hours. She would outwait him. She had the grit and determination to control an almost overwhelming compulsion to get up and run, to cry out. That was what he expected. That was what every killer counted upon in this situation. She knew from the case histories she had studied that this was what most victims did. They committed suicide.

She struggled to slow down her heavy breathing. If she could stop all body movement, he would assume she was dead. She quieted her heartbeat. She had to talk herself silently into it. Not a croton shuddered. He was doing the same. She could outwait him. After all, she was prone while he had to be bent over or squatting. He could hold a living statue position for only so long.

The bellman almost stumbled over her. He had come upon her so quickly. He stopped as if he had slammed into a wall. He bent down. "What's wrong, madame?"

She could scarcely talk. "I've got this trick knee . . ."

He helped her up. She maneuvered to keep him between herself and the crotons. "It gives way and without warning I go down."

"May I help you to your room?"

She took a deep breath. "If you could get me to the doorman—and he could call a taxi . . ."

"Of course, madame." He noticed then the .22 on the floor, and picked it up as if finding weapons were quite ordinary. Nonchalantly she put it back in her purse. "It fell out," she said weakly.

"Of course." He had been trained to agree with the guests. "Can you make it?" He was young and concerned.

"I think so."

For the first time she noticed he was handsome. Thank God for concerned, handsome young men.

She was almost back to normal.

27

When Greg entered the Greeting Room from the customs check at Kai Tak Airport in Hong Kong, Lotus Tonkin was waiting for him. She was half French, half Chinese, from the Chinese city of Cholun in Vietnam. She had been on the Carson payroll in Hong Kong since the sea-mining project was first set up.

Smiling, she walked toward him. As befitted a proper Chinese woman, she had a certain dignity, a certain reserve. Her cheongsam, though, spoke otherwise. It was slit above her knees and molded every turn of a slender, graceful body. She had toenails painted Chinese red to match her fingernails. She wore no stockings, but her legs were well tanned and gave the appearance she did. A jade pendant of a fisherman hung on a thin leather rope about her neck.

She melded into his arms and said softly, "I wait. Wait much time to hold you."

He kissed her matter-of-factly. "It has been a long time."

"Me miss you. You miss me?" She clung to him, looking up out of innocent, sad brown eyes set in a face framed by coal-black hair. He had forgotten what a doll-like creature she was.

The time was April 1975, and the place, Saigon. The enemy was already filtering into the suburbs and the smoke of war lay heavy and acrid over the devastated city. The roar of big guns was incessant and explosions were blowing chunks out of buildings. Everywhere there was pandemonium as fleeing mobs churned about in the war-pocked streets. Both South Vietnamese and American Army units struggled with tanks and gun carriers to penetrate the mobs, to reach the last defense lines.

Only a few days before, Greg had arrived. He had been recruited by Powder River to attempt to rescue an orphanage a few miles outside of Saigon. He had been flabbergasted when Powder River asked him "to do this as a great favor to me." He had not known that Powder River had supported the orphanage for years.

Powder River said, "So what? So I'm a Jew helping a Catholic orphanage that rescues mostly Buddhist children. Hell, boy, we've all got the same God, and I figure we're put on this earth to help others, and it doesn't matter what faith they have as long as they have a faith of some kind."

Greg had arrived too late. The Viet Cong had cut off the orphanage. He was passing through the lobby of the Majestic Hotel hoping to God he could still get a plane out, when an army lieutenant, an old friend from his University of Arizona days, stopped him. "Greg," he said, his voice shaking. "I've got this girl, I've got to get her out."

That was his introduction to Lotus Tonkin. She was standing immediately behind the Lieutenant. She was in her late teens but poised even in this moment of raging emotions.

"She's been doing intelligence work for us. The gooks will kill her or worse if they get their hands on her. I've got to stay another day and that may be too late. For God's sake, Greg, take her with you. Try to get her out."

Greg found himself breathing hard. He would do well to get himself out. The rumor was circulating that all roads to Tan-Son-Nhut Airport had been cut. He took a moment thinking while his friend pleaded with him.

"Come on," Greg said, reaching out for the girl's hand. "Let's get going."

Outside they hitched a ride with an Air Force officer. A mile before reaching the airport, though, the mobs grew too dense. They deserted the car. Holding her arm in a tight vise, he pushed and pulled her through the packed, struggling, screaming bodies. He heard epithets being hurled from all sides. The Americans were deserting them. After all these terrible years, they were running out and leaving them to be butchered by the Viet Cong and the North Vietnamese.

And then suddenly the mob spread out and half disappeared, and ahead were South Vietnamese troops blocking a street leading to the airport entrance. They were demanding identification papers.

A hundred yards away, the girl spoke for the first time. "Put name," she said in a low voice. She pushed a paper at him.

"What is it?" The document was in Vietnamese.

"Here." She indicated where to sign. He scribbled his name, not knowing why, but the urgency of the moment was such that he had no time to consider.

"You, my husband now. I, your wife." He learned later she had bought the document from a print shop.

The soldiers stopped them. They took what seemed an eternity. One read the document and called another over. They asked her questions. She answered confidently but with humility. As the wife of an American, she had the right to leave the country. They let them pass.

In San Francisco he left her with a woman friend and loaned her a hundred dollars. On the faint chance she might repay, he gave her his address. A year later a letter came from Hong Kong with a check enclosed. She had added interest. She was in an executive position with Cathay Airlines and doing well. She signed the letter, *your wife*.

Barbara never let him forget the *wife* part. She told their friends, "He was in Vietnam only five days, but in those five days he lost the war, married this girl and then lost her."

Years passed and he had about forgotten her. Then when Carson bought the *Marco Polo* and they began assembling deep-sea equipment, he remembered. He needed to set up a clandestine office in Asia that would buy equipment unavailable at home for quick delivery, or if bought in the United States might reveal too much to Carson's competitors. He flew to Hong Kong to check her out and found beneath the soft voice and seductive femininity a young woman who knew her way around in the Asian business world.

Now in the Greeting Room he exchanged U.S. dollars for Hong Kong ones, then outside they saw the block-long queue for a taxi. He bought tickets for a hire car, a deluxe kind of taxi, and even then they had to stand in line.

She asked playfully, "I still your wife?"

He laughed and she continued, "I frame paper. Hang in bedroom. I never forget you, Grig." Greg always came out as Grig.

Idly his gaze roamed along the line behind them and stopped. A young, thin, hungry-looking Chinese averted his eyes more quickly than was normal. He was short and stooped, his trousers old and tired, and his shirt weary from too many washings. He carried a scarred, bulging briefcase, half unzipped.

In a few seconds the Chinese switched his eyes back to Greg, then away in an abrupt movement that Greg interpreted as a frightened one, a thief caught in the act. Greg memorized the squat, severe face.

Lotus continued, "I tell you something." Her pidgin English bothered him. She spoke Chinese and French fluently, and could speak fair English when she wanted to, but she had to think her way through, a slow process. So around him she lapsed into the broken English she had first picked up.

"I got what you wanted," she said.

His heartbeat quickened. He had talked by satellite phone with her before leaving Honolulu. "The guidance system?"

She nodded. "I can say if try. Guidance system."

"Don't keep me hanging . . ."

"I find it in Tokyo. I rang up last night. They no want sell. Twelve orders got before I ring up. They say take orders when come in. I offer bonus. They say no. Government think they take squeeze. I say you got many ships. Give Japanese all business. They say okay if many ships."

He questioned her to assure himself the system was identical to the IBM one destroyed. He had given her the IBM number and description. "Same," she said. "Japanese say IBM copied. I think Japanese copy."

"You're fabulous."

She smiled. "Yes, fabulous. I fly to Tokyo tomorrow. Make sure no hang-up. I fly on cargo plane to Honolulu. Make sure nothing happens. Japanese technicians fly also. They install it."

Leaving the airport, the hire car headed for the Walled City then turned sharply. Soon they were in the Hong Kong he loved, an adult fairytale setting. They were engulfed by double-decker buses and cars and the strangest people mixture. At a stop sign a girl crossed with a pole across her shoulders, with enormous baskets on each end, delivering noon lunches to modern offices. A woman hawking jade-ite sat on the sidewalk alongside a crowd of youngsters who had paid a few cents to borrow "Superman" books from a "library." A couple of Chinese youths were shadowboxing—108 routines with names that fascinated him, "Grasping the Bird's Tail," "Finding Needle at Bottom of Sea."

Then came a bamboo scaffold for a ten-story building. Construction workers would trust no other kind. Another corner and children sat on the curb eating rice out of plastic bowls. A baby peeped from a sling on the mother's back. A spoon seller clinked his porcelain spoons to attract attention. A store window displayed all kinds of paper objects from cutouts of cars and houses to television sets and beds, all for the dead to use in the next world.

And then there were more people: expensively suited financiers and merchants, stooped coolies in their black "fragrant" cloud linen, jeweled women as smartly dressed as any on New York's Fifth Avenue, *amahs* shrunken by hard work, old women gathered about a letter writer (a *shu shun* who used a brush), neatly dressed schoolchildren with the ubiquitous books, men in felt slippers and women in cotton pajamas, a fisherman in a conical straw hat, teenagers in jeans, a girl with a teapot nodding in a basket on her back, a tailor carrying a new suit, and despite the clamor, a cat curled up fast asleep in a cardboard box.

The sounds, too, belonged exclusively to Hong Kong: the shuffle of feet, the cries of hawkers, a gramophone playing somewhere, the click of clogs, the throbbing of engines on the ferryboats, a massage man's rattle, a coolie chanting, the sharp, loud clatter of Mah-Jongg tiles, the thunder and screech of trams, the moaning of a ship's siren, the snap of a firecracker.

Over all of this cacophony, bamboo poles jutted out from windows high up, festooned with laundry blowing in the breeze. A wit once had called the laundry Hong Kong's national flag.

The driver spoke in Cantonese to Lotus. He was agitated. They talked briefly, then she turned to Greg. "Man follow in car. We slow down, he slow down. You in trouble, Grig?"

"Nothing to worry about." He tried to sound casual. With a start, he realized that by coming to Hong Kong he had placed her in jeopardy.

"I think so. I think man make trouble. I stay with you. I watch him."

He was uneasy. He ordered himself to relax. He slouched and released his tight fists. "You're the prettiest bodyguard I'll ever have. But I'm more concerned about the ship than anyone following us."

She moved closer until their bodies touched. "Change subject. Good idea. Ship leaves three days. Maybe two, spirits willing."

She had leased for Carson Mining an old oil-drilling vessel that resembled the *Marco Polo*. It was anchored in the outer roadstead of Victoria Harbour. It was a decoy. Following Greg's instructions, she had spread the rumor that it would sail shortly for Saipan and engage in deep-sea mining operations in the Philippine Sea. After leaking this information, she refused to permit newspaper and television reporters to board the ship, or to talk with them, thus adding fuel to the rumor.

"We're already one week overdue."

She took the remark as a reprimand and was deeply hurt. "We need get burial place for Captain."

Greg looked at her in amazement. "He's dead?"

"No, no. He alive but wants burial place. No grave, no sail. We see *fung shui* man after I take you to bank. *Fung shui* man decide where bury him."

"What in heaven's name are you talking about?"

"You mad at me?"

"Of course not. But you lost me back there somewhere."

She crowded a little closer and let a hand rest on his knee. As a nuclear scientist might with a freshman student, she explained about the *fung shui* man. In English he would be called a geomancer. He was a learned person. He had studied I Ching, a book of philosophy and divining 3,000 years old. By consulting it and using a brass compass in the field, he could learn if the spirits might be disturbed by the construction of a home or building—or the choice of a burial site. He was a scholar in the way winds blew, water ran, the shaping of hills and mountains, the slope of flatlands, all of that and much more. Translated, *fung shui* was "wind and water." He gave each problem the same concentrated thought a stockbroker would to his charts. Once he had rendered a decision, no one would have to worry about the spirits. Moreover, to ignore the *fung shui* man might bring the spirits' curses down on a person's children and their children.

Greg shook his head in wonderment and amusement. "How much is this going to cost us?"

"Thousand Hong Kong. Maybe one hundred seventy dollars U.S. Very cheap. Big English company start big building five months ago. No talk with *fung shui* man. Workers quit, say spirits angry. Workers not come back. Only foundation there."

28

The hire car rolled along the curved driveway off Salisbury Road to the Peninsula Hotel, which dated to the years when Hong Kong was no more than a far outlying possession of the British empire. A doorman helped them out while the driver got their luggage. The driver nodded backward. The shadow cab had pulled within ten feet and the starved-looking Chinese was getting out. He reached back in for the briefcase. He had no other luggage.

Through glass doors flanked on one side by two enormous Chinese war lords out of a Chinese opera, they entered a lobby the size of a railroad station, vast but elegant. Great white columns held up a gilded, carved ceiling depicting scenes in bas relief from Greek mythology plus a few Chinese dragons the artist had sneaked in. A score or more of small tables were scattered about where guests could have morning coffee, noon snacks and cocktails. Here, according to legend, gathered the espionage agents of all Asia. It was a legend with some truth to it but greatly exaggerated. With a little imagination, however, one could look about at any time of day or night and swear he had spotted a spy.

A man in formal morning wear stood immediately behind Greg as he registered. The desk clerk noted Lotus and asked pointedly, "Room for only one, sir?"

Greg nodded and said to Lotus, "If you want to wait down here . . ."

Her eyes sparkled with devilment. "Remember I your wife," she whispered.

Once registered, the man stepped up. "I will show you to your room, sir." He led the way to the bank of elevators at the far right of the reception desk. With open disapproval, he glanced repeatedly at Lotus. Not too many years back he would have mentioned quietly that young ladies were not permitted in a gentleman's room, but this was another era and even the staid Peninsula had had to bow to a changing society.

Lotus busied herself unpacking the cases and hanging up his clothes. Afterward they left the Peninsula by a side door and walked quickly down people-packed Hankow Road. Greg stopped abruptly to glance back but found it impossible in the sea of bobbing, moving faces to locate the young Chinese. He regretted stopping. She sensed his fear, clung to his arm and said, "I have gun in purse. I never without gun. Police arrest me if find gun. I no have permit."

A permit cost $3,000 HK a year and the applicant had to convince the authorities that he/she had a specific need for a weapon.

"Get one," Greg said. "Carson will pay for it."

"No, no, too much. No run up bill." She accounted for every cent spent, including receipts for items that cost less than a dollar.

At 198 Hankow Road, they turned into a narrow entrance and passed an iron gate, locked at night. A bulky caretaker in rumpled pants and undershirt had a radio blaring Chinese singsong music. They passed an ancient lift that led to the Hong Kong Arts Tailor Company on the first floor (or the second by U.S. calculation). She unlocked the door to their office. It bore the sign: MIDDLE FORK, LTD.

Inside, she pulled on a traditional Chinese lantern with red tassels. It lighted up a rosewood desk which held a hand-painted jardiniere with a flourishing philodendron. In one corner was a tea table set with little black-lacquered cups and saucers. The table was flanked with three hardwood chairs with marble backs designed to test the resiliency of anyone's vertebrae.

There were the necessities, too: a phone, message recorder, electric typewriter and steel files.

On the wall was a motto in Chinese. "Old saying," she said and translated with an impish smile, "Lotus come from mud. Stay clean."

She added, "Stay clean mean live good. Honorable."

Greg placed a call to Lynne aboard the *Marco Polo* to tell her Lotus had located a guidance system in Tokyo, and Lynne in turn reported Colonel Montand had shaped up his mercenaries. They now wore Levi's and Hawaiian shirts. They still looked like pirates. Only cosmetic surgery could change their faces. They were maintaining a tight security.

Powder River, bless him, she said, had backed up her orders to the Captain and the crew. Janet had had no further threatening calls.

Did the date still hold, she asked, for their meeting in Beijing (Peking)? It did, he answered. "We've got a lot riding on it."

Next he talked with Laura who was ecstatic over a grade she had received in history class. "I told Mom and I feel sure she heard me."

He had scarcely hung up when the phone rang. Lotus answered and talked in rapid-fire Cantonese. Afterward she told Greg the call was from the South China *Morning Post*. A reporter wanted to confirm a rumor that the *Tai Peng* would sail the next day.

She laughed. "I tell nothing, but I tell so he know he right. He ask you here? I say yes but no know where. You big man, do not talk with little person. He laugh. He know not so. He feel good. He got story."

Greg nodded, pleased. If the story only warranted a couple of inches, Soviet agents would duly report it to Moscow.

From the office they went to the Far East Bank. She had arranged for a loan of HK $200,000, about U.S. $33,000, to finance the *Tai Peng*'s expenses. The banker, a Chinese in his early forties with a smooth, nicely rounded face, came from behind his desk to shake hands. Would Miss Tonkin and Mr. Wilson care for coffee? Tea? A soft drink? They settled for soft drinks.

Greg signed the necessary papers. At the time he opened the Hong Kong office, he had established Carson Mining's credit.

As they were leaving, the banker maneuvered Greg to one side. "Miss Tonkin is a very competent person. Very honorable, and we like to do business with her. I thought you would want to know."

"Thank you." When he first had proposed that she represent Carson Mining, she had been very frank. "Hong Kong men no like talk business with woman. Especially Eurasian. They say no ability make best wife. Talent mean girl want sell sex."

"One more subject to discuss, please," the banker continued. "I did not tell Miss Tonkin, but my assistant took a call yesterday from a party who said he represented you. He wanted to know the status of your account. My assistant did not give it to him because he thought Miss Tonkin alone represents you. The party asked, too, many questions about your ship and my assistant asked the party to come around and talk with us personally. No one has come."

"No one will," Greg said. "No one speaks for me but Miss Tonkin. Only Miss Tonkin."

Once they were out on the street, he reported the conversation and she was amused. It was the Chinese way, she said. "First he say good about me. He like me. Then tell about phone call. He tell you so you can say you got another agent. But you say no, I still only agent. He find out what he want to know, you happy to hear I good girl, me happy what he say. Chinese way."

They had lunch at Jimmy's Kitchen in Kowloon Centre on Ashley Road. For dessert she introduced him to Jimmy's fried ice cream, the specialty of the house. People from all over the world crowded into Jimmy's for fried ice cream.

Afterward they took a taxi out into the New Territories to visit the geomancer, who lived in a flat near the Chinese University, north of Shui. Greg had expected an Oriental copy of an American fortune teller. Instead he was distinguished looking in a blue silk gown and spoke cultured English. In his youth he had studied at Oxford. He ushered them into a small English parlor which was furnished with jade objects, costly Chinese carvings, an ancient Chinese screen, a Ming vase, a bird-feather picture and another of sea shells. He regretted that his wife was not home. It was her time of day to pray at the Shrine of the Bamboo Grove. He talked briefly about Buddhism, how it was a fading faith in Hong Kong. No, he said, the Christians did not number many. "Too many of our young people have faith only in themselves," he said. "It is sad. Even the tight family unit that has dominated Chinese life since history began is breaking down."

He advised he had about completed his study and would report tomorrow to Miss Tonkin. He could assure them he was highly pleased with the results. He had found an ideal burial site for the Captain. The spirits would never bother him or his sons or daughters.

Leaving the building, they both saw the young Chinese at the same time and halted abruptly. He was double parked behind the wheel of an old, dark Datsun. He was no longer making the slightest effort to conceal himself.

"What we do?" She clung nervously to Greg.

"Give me your purse."

She slipped it to him. "You no kill him here?" She tightened her hand about his arm.

"Not here." He was wearing no coat since the day was stifling hot. He bent to the ground, opened his briefcase, put the small purse in, and all the time watching the feet hurrying past him, dug into the purse. He found what felt to be a .22. He palmed it in his big right hand, and leaving the purse in the case, shut it. The maneuver had taken no more than a minute.

"The Peninsula," he told the driver.

They said little on the way back and neither did the driver. The gun was hot in Greg's sweaty hand.

At the Peninsula, Lotus, frightened, insisted on coming with Greg. She would be quiet while he worked. She would curl up with a magazine.

He spread his papers out on a carved teak table by the big window. Across the harbor a dark cloud mass brooded on Victoria Peak. He glanced down on the driveway and spotted a face looking up. He moved the table a few feet back into the room.

She said, "Hot. I take shower."

He turned frowning and she looked hurt. "You no want I take shower?"

He wiped off the frown. "Suit yourself."

She was perplexed. "What mean?"

"Go ahead." She smiled happily. It took so little to keep her happy.

He heard the shower running and she was singing a high-key Chinese song. He wished he understood the words.

He was getting nowhere with his work. He must concentrate. Then he heard the door opening and turned. She stood there naked.

"When go bed?" she asked in the most innocent way. "Now? Later?"

He shook his head and said quietly, "You know I'm married."

She took a step into the room. Her small, pointed breasts were firm with youth and his arousal instant. He glanced away. "What got to do with go bed in Hong Kong? I your wife in Hong Kong, no?"

He took a deep breath. "She's very ill. I wouldn't feel right."

"Oh." She thought that over. "Okay, no go bed. I do what you want, okay? Always do what you want. Maybe next trip?"

She picked up the cheongsam she had laid carefully on the bed and slipped into it. She wore nothing under it. He had suspected as much.

She would make some American a wonderful wife. *Always do what you want.* He was certain she would, all her life. She would make love in such an easy, natural, happy way. If he wanted to take a long time, she would go along. If he was too tired, she would laugh and say wait and maybe tomorrow night.

He could smooth out her English. That would be easy. She knew how to wear clothes and had poise and said the right thing. She could move easily in any world. She would be a tremendous asset.

She was highly intelligent and yet he didn't feel, as he did around Lynne, that he must match her brain output sentence by sentence. Lynne was so damn brilliant. Maybe Lotus was, too, but she cleverly masqueraded the fact. She never let her mind get in the way of being very much a female.

He remembered an uncle who went to Tahiti and wrote his wife he wasn't coming back. Later he told Greg that the Tahitian girl he was living with was "a mother, a companion, a friend, a cook and a mistress, all combined."

29

"I wish I first."

They sat in a floating restaurant in Aberdeen, the original Heung Kong, "the fragrant harbor." They looked across a tiny table at each other in a tiny private room that a costly Venetian glass chandelier overwhelmed. Long rows of beads on strings hung in the open doorway, swaying in the cooling breeze. She was in a dark blue cheongsam that outlined her thin figure. Her only jewelry was an exquisite white jade bracelet.

On the waterfront across the way girls of the night moved slowly, like so many hard-shelled beetles. Men yelled angrily at each other in a Mah-Jongg parlor as they threw their ivory markers down. The usual laundry flapped from bamboo poles jutting from windows, but the socks and shirts were interspersed with fish hung out to dry.

All about them were old, unpainted junks. At one time they had numbered 20,000, and the sight was one the old timers never forgot, but Aberdeen had changed. The Water-Borne People, the Shiu Sheung Yan, had yielded to the temptation of an easier life on land. They worked in labor-intensive industries and their children went to land schools. Big motorized junks had taken the place of the small ones.

"What do you mean first?" Greg asked.

"Before wife see you." She smiled. "I could love you, Grig. I say I your wife but I—I—"

"—just joke," Greg put in.

"Just joke," she repeated. "I never hurt wife. Chinese never steal husband. Americans do, no? I see cinema, read books. Americans play game, steal wife, steal husband, no?"

He smiled. For Lotus, making love did not count. That was not stealing. Making love was like a tennis date.

His answer was blotted out by the deafening booming of drums and the thunderous explosion of fireworks on the junk anchored a few feet away. He stared out the window but could see little in the gathering dusk.

"Important man die," she said. "Must let spirits know. Get him into heaven."

She was so serious. "You don't believe all that?" he asked.

The drumbeat ebbed into a monotonous chant and the fireworks cracked only intermittently. There were voices, but what they said could not be heard. Their tone was imploring, plaintive.

She said softly, "I believe much. Have much faith. I like Jesus. Taught beautiful things. Also like Buddha. Also taught beautiful things. I like Confucius. Taught how to live. I like bang-bang also. I die, I want fireworks and Jesus song and Buddha incense and somebody read Confucius. Not much, only little."

He couldn't help but smile. "What wrong?" she asked. "You no got faith?"

He shook his head. "I think that by hook or by crook, as we say in the States, you're going to make heaven."

"I think make heaven here. Now. I help sad people. Sad people help me. Make heaven now."

In one swift maneuver, he let go of her hand, said, "Keep talking," and stepped through the beads to seize the young Chinese who had shadowed them all that day. He pulled the twisting, wrenching figure into the room. The Chinese aimed a karate blow but before he could land it Greg delivered a crunching punch into his lower abdomen. Swinging him about, Greg clamped his hands behind his back and jammed him head first against the wall.

"Drown him!" she screamed. "Drown him!" She had a hammerlock about his head and was struggling to tug him toward the window.

Greg managed to draw the .22 from his right sidepocket.

"No kill him," she called out. "Leave mark. Drown him."

"Let go of him," Greg shouted.

A waiter pushed aside the beads to look in. "Get out of here," Greg yelled.

He turned the Chinese around and pushed the gun into his soft groin. He shoved it as hard as he could and the Chinese sobbed in agony.

"I'm going to kill you, you devil, unless you tell me who sent you."

The Chinese looked about to faint. Lotus said, "He no understand." She repeated the threat in Cantonese and horror fixed in his eyes. In desperation he glanced wildly about.

Greg rammed the weapon deeper into the groin. The Chinese went into spasm. The monotonous drumbeat continued and the chanting grew louder and more pleading.

The Chinese said something. The words came out as a death gasp.

"He talk," she reported. "He say he talk."

"Okay, who sent you? Who's paying you?"

She translated, "If talk, they kill him."

"How much they pay him?"

She translated, "Twenty dollars a day Hong Kong."

From a pocket, he pulled out a clump of U.S. bills. "Give him two twenties and tell him we won't squeal on him."

Again she translated. "He say get killed. We drown him, no?"

"Tell him he's got two ways to go. I'll kill him right now or he can gamble that his bosses will never know and he may live. Tell him I'm giving him another minute and that's it."

The Chinese nodded. His eyes spoke a universal language. He rattled in Cantonese.

"He work for Triad," she said. "Like your Mafia." The Triad, dating back centuries, was a loose aggregation of crime syndicates.

"He give me name. Man in Walled City." The Walled City was an enclave of a few blocks inside Hong Kong's New Territories. When China ceded the New Territories to Hong Kong, somehow the enclave was left out of the treaty. And now there was no police authority there. China could not reach it except by passing through the New Territories—and anyway was not interested. Hong Kong authorities were hesitant to enforce law and order since China could accuse them of violating its sovereignty.

She continued, "He gave me name man. I know name. He agent for Communists."

"Chinese or Russian?"

"Russian."

Greg backed off but held the .22 dead center on the man's heart. "Tell him if I ever see him again, I'll kill him."

The Chinese nodded repeatedly. "He say, you no see."

"Get out of here," Greg said.

Before she finished translating, the Chinese vanished.

She smoothed out her cheongsam and with a pert bob of her head shook her hair into place. "Mistake let go."

Beaten, he dropped his body into the chair. He was breathing hard. "I found out what I wanted to know. Anyway, we couldn't call the police. He hadn't broken any laws. And I wasn't going to kill him." He glanced questioningly at her. "You know that, don't you?"

She straightened the chopsticks. "You make good act. I convinced."

"You wanted to drown him."

"I also make good act."

He broke out laughing. She was puzzled. "Why laugh?"

"You."

"What I do?"

"Are you the same sweet, quiet young woman who was with me when we came in?"

She tightened her lips. "You no understand. Help good peoples. Punish bad peoples."

"I'm not arguing with you, Lotus. I'm with you all the way."

He raised his glass of chablis in toast to her. "To the gentlest, most caring, intelligent, dollar-smart, sexed-up little wildcat I've ever known."

Her eyes flashed angrily. "I very proper young Chinese lady."

"The hell you are."

30

Somewhat due north of the area known as West Point on Hong Kong Island lay the Main Harbour Anchorage where the *Tai Peng* was anchored. To reach it, Greg and Lotus engaged a speedboat. Although the time was only a few minutes after eight, they had to awaken the pilot. Many people worked most of every day and night to keep alive and slept whenever they could steal an hour or so.

Both discovered their nerves were shattered. Fear that had been more or less academic had taken body in the person of the young Chinese. "He wait," Lotus said. "Wait for right time. Knife move fast. No warning."

She reached up unexpectedly to kiss him on the cheek, and he was touched by her spontaneous affection. That was one reason he loved Barbara. She never pulled the window shade on her feelings. Lynne . . . he didn't know about her. She had the same precise control over her emotions that she had over her scientific probing. If moved to express her true self, she would analyze whether she should, and if in doubt, take her time.

While Lotus negotiated the price, Greg sized up the boatman. He was no more than eighteen, slender, wearing a T-shirt that read "Mickey Mouse" and vintage Levi's held up by a fraying rope. About his head he wore a faded red band with an insignia too washed out to read.

By nature the night was dark, but the mass of lights from skyscrapers crowded together for miles cast an ethereal glow on the world below. The heat of the day had been tempered slightly by the fall of the sun, and the breeze churned by the racing boat and the thin spray revived them. They passed a sampan where four men squatted around a goods box playing Mah-Jongg under a hurricane lamp, then a hydrofoil, a sightseeing vessel that looked like a pagoda, and a Mobil Oil boat making deliveries.

"You like Captain." She had her arm clutched about his that could have been an expression of fondness or fear. "He fine man."

About halfway they heard another speedboat bearing down on them. Both turned to look back. Her nails sank into his flesh. He suffered the quick, hot flash he invariably experienced when set upon by coyotes in his nightmares.

The boatman swung about every few seconds to check the oncoming craft. The sea was rougher and the boat thrust palsied at times. Overhead the stars were bright and a crescent moon hung crazily. They bore down and veered around an old junk, a walnut shell with drooping brown masts and the odd little lugsail up fore looking like a leaf that had attached itself.

The boat behind was gaining rapidly on them. Greg drew the .22 from his pocket and palmed it. Psychologically, it provided him with the same false courage an amphetamine would.

Then as the boat neared them, they came upon a Marine Police launch on patrol. They could see four officers aboard and the number 15 splashed big across the side. Only seconds after their speed had brought the launch into focus, the motorboat swung away sharply toward the Yaumati Typhoon Shelter off Kowloon Peninsula.

Together with seven or eight other ships, the *Tai Peng* was anchored well to the south of Stone Cutter's Island. It was no more than 20,000 tons, poorly lighted, and badly in need of paint. Large rusty splotches gave it a leprosy look.

They climbed a rocking, bouncing stairway to a teakwood deck where the Captain waited. Greg had expected someone old and gruff and was amazed when he shook the proffered hand. The Captain was about forty, much too young, Greg thought, to be looking for a burial site. He had a strong, squared-off face and the same style shoulders. He looked as smart as an Annapolis graduate in his sharply creased dark blue uniform with gold braiding at the cuffs.

"Good to have you aboard, sir," he said in English learned at the University of Washington.

"Thank you." Greg was conscious of the heavy drift of incense and eyes upon him. A pair stared from the stairway to the galley, only to vanish when he looked in that direction. Others popped up and disappeared around corners and rigging.

Lotus talked rapidly in Cantonese. "I tell him," she explained to Greg, "burial site okay."

"I thank you, sir," the Captain said. "I have two young sons and I did not want to place them in disfavor with our ancestors. I wished, too, to have the contentment of knowing I would find rest in the proper place. Come, I will show you the ship."

He led the way past three crewmen squatting by a clay brazier, heated by charcoal embers. With chop sticks, they were eating rice garnished with fish. "A late-night snack," the Captain said.

Then they passed two priests swinging cannisters of incense and chanting prayers. "They are cleansing the ship of evil influences. You Americans would call it evil spirits, but it is much more than that. The crew must believe that we will have good joss."

"Good luck," Lotus translated.

"A good trip," he translated. "The priests pray to Pak Tai. He is the sea god who protects everything on the waters. And to Tam Kung. He is the cargo man's god." He smiled. "Have you heard that when Tam Kung gets angry he throws a handful of peas in the air and we have a typhoon?"

He continued, "You may find this amusing until you think of Greek mythology. It is all the same. It is not Buddhism, of course. When Buddhism came to Hong Kong centuries ago the old ones added it to old faiths. You Christians did the same with Judaism. And there was Mohammed . . ."

Greg was growing restless. He had come aboard for business, not to discuss religion. "I want to cover several checkpoints before we look the ship over. First, the priests. When will they okay the vessel for sailing?"

"Tonight, sir."

"Is there any question they will hold us up?"

"None, sir. This is ritual. Once they have cleansed the ship, it is cleansed until the next sailing."

Greg continued, "Miss Tonkin informs me that you have barred the hold to everyone as instructed—"

"I will show you—"

"In a minute. What have you told the crew?"

"That we are on a secret scientific mission. However, they know from the way the ship rides that there is no weight in the hold and they are curious. I haven't given them shore leave since we signed them on—and I haven't permitted anyone aboard from land."

"What about supplies?"

"We haul them aboard from the lighters with ropes. There has been no contact between the crewmen and the land people."

"Miss Tonkin informs me a helicopter hovers over the ship every morning."

"Sometimes at night, too. A small bird. The pilot took pictures the first day. I don't know why. This ship looks the same as many plying between here and Singapore or Kuala Lumpur."

"Any other unusual occurrences?"

"None that I haven't told Miss Tonkin about. Two reporters took speedboats out, a telly man came out on a launch with a minicam, the police came once—"

"The police!"

"I referred them to Miss Tonkin." The Captain looked questioningly at her.

Greg turned to Lotus. "You didn't tell me."

"No need tell. The police nice, I nice. They go away."

"What'd you tell them?" Greg demanded.

"I ask why want look at boat? They say got report drugs on board. I say nobody board boat, nobody leave boat. How we smuggle drugs? They ask why can't go on board. I say we got American owner, he crazy. Afraid of germs. Nobody board boat. They understand. All Americans crazy. I say yes, it is so. I smile. They go away."

The Captain explained. "Here in Hong Kong we accept the word of honorable people. Miss Tonkin is most honorable. They know she would not bring shame on herself and her family and friends by deceiving the authorities."

They inspected the hold and walked briefly about the ship. Greg was conscious of bodies moving eerily in the dark as the crew members avoided them.

The speedboat was waiting at the foot of the ladder, but again the boatman was asleep. Greg had to shake him awake. He looked frantically about trying to determine where he was, then stood rubbing his eyes. He spun the motor and the boat thrust itself into waves higher than the hour before. The waves assaulted the boat, pounding the bottom with sledgehammer force.

Greg looked back at the *Tai Peng*. Its lights were dimming with the distance and a thin fog was settling in.

Lotus crowded as close as she could, body to body, her arm again inside his as if searching for security. *She is an honorable person.* It was a hard-earned designation that long ago had disappeared from the Western world. In America and other companion nations, the behavior of a person was controlled by a system of checks and counterchecks that were designed computerlike to force one to perform as the system demanded. No longer was there faith in the honorable man or woman. Even the word, *honorable*, was archaic.

They were rapidly approaching a launch that appeared anchored. When they were within a few hundred feet, though, the craft headed for them. The boatman turned about shouting, and Lotus withdrew her arm. "Police boat. They come, stop us."

A bullhorn was ordering them to heave to. Then a blue signal light was flashing the international code, K. Lotus shouted at the boatman in Cantonese. Immediately he brought the speed down to a purr. In easy stages he rode a couple of waves, veering toward the launch.

They were no more than fifty feet distant when Greg noted there was no number or insignia on the boat. He strained to bring the craft into better focus. He could locate no one in uniform, only two rough-looking characters with a grappling hook, waiting to sink it into the speedboat.

He yelled to Lotus, "Tell him to get out of here. Fast! Right now!"

Lotus stared, uncomprehending. "Police," she yelled back.

"No, not police," he screamed. "Tell him to get away. For God's sake, tell him."

They were within thirty feet, then twenty-five, then twenty. She understood and was screaming in Cantonese. The youth looked back, bewildered.

Greg took a step, then another. He rocked the boat until the water pouring into the hull threatened to capsize them. He grabbed the youth by an arm but his hold slipped and he lost balance. He floundered about a second, then righted himself.

Now they were within a few feet and the two characters were reaching out to bring the boat alongside. In a last desperate effort, Greg punched the youth in the midriff. He crumpled up and fell backward.

With no one at the wheel the boat went out of control, a piece of flotsam hoisted this way and that. Any second the sea was going to send them crashing into the launch. Greg seized the wheel. He was back in the rapids of the Middle Fork. He had to get control of the craft. He dared not swing it about too quickly or a wave would capsize them. He wasn't certain he could clear the launch. It was all happening too fast.

He heard the report of a bullet, no more than a slap on the wrist in the maelstrom he was riding, and then another and another. Lotus was screaming. He was upon the launch. He was going to tear into its aft. There was nothing he could do. He had the wheel turned as far as possible. He saw the characters a few feet away. They were shouting and a long muscular arm was extending the grappling hook. The possessor was jabbing it out as far as he could. He was trying to sink it into Greg.

Then by inches he cleared the launch. It was so close he thought they were going to scrape. He heard the angry shouts of the men, Lotus shrieking, then the bullhorn threatening them. The spotlight came dead center on him, and a bullet plowed noiselessly a few inches away into the hull, trailed by another.

An angry-looking wave rose up tall as a tall man and hesitated for a split second before crashing down. Once again he wrestled with the wheel. Don't panic. A slight turn here, a slight turn there. Don't overdo it. He didn't know the sea but he knew water. He knew the rapids of a raging river. There wasn't too much difference. Either way, a man had to be the master.

A moment later he had a clean sweep toward land. He relaxed a little. They were out of range of gunfire. Lotus was explaining to the stunned boatman what had happened. The launch had disappeared into the thickening fog.

She put a hand gently on Greg's shoulder. "You all right, Grig?"

He nodded. "You?"

"All right."

Back on land, they waved down a cab which took them to the Star Ferry, which in turn would take them to Kowloon. He dropped $.60 HK for each into the First Class turnstile. The sign was green and they hurried up the long approach, flanked by advertisements, and as the bell clanged in warning that the gate was about to close, boarded the ship. Almost immediately there was the groaning and clanking of the ramp being hauled up and the throbbing of the engines.

She led the way to a deserted corner at the far side. A chill breeze whispered past them and soon they were enveloped in a shrouded world of wavering, distant, yellowish lights. From far off fog horns sounded.

She put a hand on his and he felt the coldness. "Grig, I tell you something."

"Yes?"

She was nervous. "I read in America . . . workers, they get something . . . fringe benefits."

He nodded. "Pensions, medical coverage. Anything you want I'll get you."

She took a deep breath. "When you come next time . . ." She hesitated, then blurted out, "Grig, I want baby."

He was incredulous. "You want me to bring you a baby?"

"No, no. We go to bed, I get baby."

"Oh, my word!" he exclaimed without thinking.

She was hurt. "Why you excited? Like fringe benefit, no?"

He scrambled through his thinking for a quick answer. He found none.

He said slowly, "I'm touched you'd want my baby, Lotus, but we're of two different worlds. We think differently. I know it may be hard for you to understand, but please try. It isn't that I don't like you. I'm very fond of you. You're a beautiful person . . ."

"What has to do with baby?"

He was sweating. "Nothing, I guess. It's just that I think when you marry someone . . . make a commitment . . . if you love someone, it's more than a matter of morals. It's one human being promising another to be loyal, and when you're not, it's like selling out your mother or your country . . . it's like treason . . ."

She was quiet, trying to understand. "I think you little crazy, Grig. I ask nothing much. You think about it. We talk next time you come. Okay?"

They stopped by the office. A cablegram had been shoved through the mail slot. It was from Tokyo. With deep regrets and a thousand pardons, Tokyo advised that unforeseen difficulties made it impossible to deliver the computer guidance system earlier than three months hence.

Stunned, he walked about the room, hitting a fist into a palm. He felt the sting and it helped to calm him.

Someone had talked. Someone had passed the information along and in Tokyo someone had put the pressure on.

In time they quieted and thought of all the persons who knew about the deal. A part-time secretary Lotus employed had had knowledge. She had approached Hong Kong sources before making inquiries in Tokyo. He had informed Lynne. He had not asked her to hold the matter confidential. She probably had passed the news to Powder River, maybe Bill Madden, and very likely, Janet Stowe. They discussed the possibility that Lotus' phone had been tapped.

The next morning he left Kai Tak Airport for Guangzhou (Canton) en route to Beijing. "No worry, Grig, I fix. I say they lose entire United States Navy as customer if do this. No?"

"You're something," he said.

"What mean?"

"I still say you're the most intelligent, lovable, dollar-smart and sexed-up girl I've ever met."

She was indignant. "You little crazy, Grig."

An hour later she boarded a Japan Airlines plane bound for Tokyo.

31

The following coded message was routed at 9:40 A.M. to the State Department from the U.S. Embassy in Moscow:

> ATT: DEPUTY SECRETARY BROWNELL. SOVIET FOREIGN MINISTER PUSHKIN HAS REQUESTED AUDIENCE WITH SECRETARY OF STATE OR DESIGNATE BY SOVIET AMBASSADOR ALEXEI LITOVSK TO ARRANGE PLAN OF OPERATIONS FOR EXCHANGE OF INFORMATION AND VISITATIONS BY SCIENTISTS IN REGARD TO UNDERSEA MINING. PUSHKIN HAS ACCEPTED STATE'S OFFER AS SET FORTH MAY 10. HE HAS EXTENDED INVITATION TO AMERICAN SCIENTISTS OF ANY NUMBER TO INSPECT WITHOUT RESTRICTIONS THE U.S.S.R. MINING SHIP, THE VITIAZ, AT THE SAME TIME A LIKE SOVIET TEAM WOULD VISIT ON THE SAME UNRESTRICTED TERMS THE U.S. MINING SHIP, THE MARCO POLO. PUSHKIN REQUESTS STATE CONTACT AMBASSADOR LITOVSK DIRECTLY.
>
> BLAKISTON

32

Aboard the *Marco Polo*, Lynne packed for the trip to Mainland China. She traveled light; only one case. She had little interest in clothes and owned few.

She moved slowly, bone weary. Only the night before she had returned from Tucson where she had gone at Greg's request to check on Laura. Her grandmother was still with her and promised to stay until Greg found someone else.

With Laura, Lynne had sat briefly beside Barbara, and Laura had cried a little. "I don't know why God doesn't help Mom, but Daddy says God has reasons that we sometimes can't understand. I do a lot of praying . . ."

Lynne had put her arms about Laura. "We have to accept life as God gives it to us, hon. Take each day at a time. Do the best we can."

On her return from Tucson, she found Powder River waiting for her. "We've got a problem, girl. When you taking off?"

"Tomorrow morning at eight. Pan Am."

He nodded. "Tell the boy when you see him that I'm high-tailing it out for Washington. I'll ask Carlos to take over." He talked slowly, thinking his way through. "I think we've got some educating to do. The Secretary of State is too busy putting out fires around the world to know much about us. We're not a crisis. Not yet—but we may be soon."

"You know someone in Washington who can help us?"

He nodded. "Meg set me up a couple of times with this man who staked her in Boise. They was always fond of each other. I'm not naming names. Wouldn't be right. But he's a big shot today in Washington, and out of memory to Meg he might help us."

He put an arm about her. "You take good care of yourself, girl. And the boy."

33

The call from Washington, D.C., came at 10:37 A.M., the day after Lynne had flown out of Honolulu for Beijing. At the time Janet Stowe was walking the deck enjoying the soft, warm ocean breeze. At the first ring, she hurried and on the fourth picked up the phone. The call was from an unidentified party who spoke understandable English but with a heavy foreign accent, one she could not readily peg. She jotted the time by routine on the message pad before her.

He spoke slowly as if translating each word, "I can't give you my name but I'm a close friend of Mike McGraw and I was with him last night, but I can't find him today. I have something to tell him that you should know right away. Don't ask me questions, but they're going to murder Mr. Wilson and Dr. Kennedy in Mainland China today. The killers will be Chinese. Can you get hold of them?"

She was paralyzed by the shock. All she could hear was "they're going to murder . . . murder . . . murder . . ."

He spoke louder. "Did you hear me?"

"Yes." Her lips were so dry she could scarcely talk. "You scared me. I'll put in a call right away. I'll get hold of them. Thank you."

He hung up in the middle of the *thank you.*

Quickly she regained control of herself. She dialed the Hong Kong office direct and let the phone ring for minutes. She asked the Honolulu operator to get her the CAAC, the People's Republic Airline, in Guangzhou. A woman answered in Cantonese and there was a wait before another voice came over speaking English. She held for several minutes more while the woman checked. Yes, one Mr. Gregory Wilson was aboard the flight to Beijing yesterday afternoon. He was traveling with a deputy from the Foreign Ministry.

Next Janet phoned the Peking Hotel. This time there was considerable delay in reaching Beijing. The telephone system was set up for only a limited number of overseas calls. While she waited she opened the day's correspondence. Carlos came in on the fourth letter and she poured out the story. "What else can I do?"

He lost no time answering. His mind was honed sharp by gunplay on his ranch. "The Foreign Ministry. Put in a call right away. And the Peking police, too. Get the overseas operator busy on both. Tell her it's an emergency. Tell her someone's going to be killed if you don't get through. Ask her for priority and if she gives you an argument, we'll call the Honolulu police and get them on it."

The phone rang. The Peking Hotel was on the line, a woman who spoke British English. Yes, both Mr. Wilson and Miss Kennedy were registered. They had adjoining rooms on the eighth floor. Janet could hear her talking with the floor boy on the eighth. He reported both had left about an hour ago.

Carlos kept talking. "They hate the Russians over there. The Russians can't get anyone in there. The Chinese have got tight security. But if the guy who called you . . . God, if anything happens to them . . ."

He lapsed into Spanish. He was prone to do that when he was overwrought.

When Janet informed the overseas operator that the call was a matter of life and death and mentioned the Foreign Ministry, she was connected immediately. The secretary who answered spoke Mandarin. Again, there was a delay that seemed interminable, then a secretary said in American English, "This is the Foreign Minister's office, Miss Kim speaking."

Janet talked too rapidly. She had to slow down. She then explained the situation slowly and in detail. She put a hand over the phone and reported to Carlos. "She says not to worry. They'll handle it. Nothing will happen. She's left to take some kind of emergency action."

Then into the receiver: "Hello . . . yes . . . all right . . . I don't need to notify anyone else? . . . Thank you."

When she hung up, Janet said the woman—while Janet waited—had notified their "security people."

Carlos was a corraled cougar. "Dammit, I can't sit here hours waiting to hear something. They won't call back if nothing happens and they won't if it does. They clam up over there if there's a tragedy. Remember that big earthquake? The world didn't hear about it until weeks afterward. How long a trip is it there?"

Janet said about ten or twelve hours, depending upon the length of the stopover in either Hong Kong or Tokyo. "But it takes three days to get a visa."

"It'll be my fault if anything happens," Carlos said. "I was the one who kept egging Greg on. We should've stayed with gold and silver mining. Something we know about."

34

When Greg walked down the ramp at Guangzhou, a short, thin, pensive-looking Chinese of about thirty stepped up. "Mr. Wilson?" His English was soft and precise.

Greg nodded and he continued, "Welcome to the People's Republic of China, Mr. Wilson. I am Lun Shanh of the Foreign Ministry. The Minister asked that I meet you and escort you to Beijing."

Greg thanked him. "How very thoughtful of the Minister."

"Your passport, please."

Immigration stamped Greg's passport with a cordial nod. In the baggage-claim room, a porter waited with Greg's two cases. Customs waved them through. Next Greg exchanged American Express checks for *renminbi yuan.*

Lun Shanh said they had a wait of about two hours for the plane. Would Greg care to see some of Guangzhou? Greg would.

Outside a mob of people parted to make a corridor, then closed behind the two men. They stared at Greg in amazement. They had seen a few Americans but none in boots, tight jeans, Western shirt, bola tie and a silver belt buckle the size of a postcard. Here was a live cowpuncher right out of the Old West. They had seen Western movies. The younger ones knew he had a six gun packed away somewhere. They pulled back a little for fear he might whip it out.

They passed a billboard in English and Chinese which read: WE HAVE FRIENDS ALL OVER THE WORLD. The Communist regime welcomed visitors not only for the hard currency they brought but also as proof to their own people that China did have friends from all the Western nations. That was important to Beijing. China had cut itself off from the rest of the world for decades, and its people felt the isolation keenly. Now here came a flood of visitors. If Russia did attack their country, they had friends who would help them.

Greg was steered to a new Mercedes, a government-owned car. ("No one is permitted to own a car.") He reached into a pocket for *yuan* to give the porter. ("Please, no tip. You will insult him. Tipping is demeaning. Only for servants—and in China we have no servants, only workers.")

Greg scarcely heard. He was certain they were being followed. Two prizefighter types without luggage stayed a short distance behind. They moved only when he and Lun Shanh moved. One had prominent teeth, dark brown eyes that were slits, and over-developed ears; the other, a pinkish scar across the right cheek, smallpox marks and a low forehead.

Up until this dark moment Greg had been the teenager on that train to Chicago years ago, filled with delightful anticipation and wonderment. This day he had experienced the same feeling, warm and mica bright. China, remote, mysterious, unfathomable, like no other land on the globe.

One billion people, some said, although others docked the figure by fifty million. All eating—and that in itself was a miracle. No longer did people die before one's eyes on the streets of Shanghai or prostitutes descend like packs of starving wild dogs. No longer did thousands die every spring as rivers ran wild. China was on the mend. No doubt about that. But it was still an undernourished giant weak in the knees, badly in need of technology, free enterprise, money and other curses of capitalism. Men of vision and courage in Beijing knew it, and while they would violently reject the possibility, China in time might very well become a paradox, a Socialist-capitalistic system.

A weary, uncommunicative government man drove them about the city, which at this time of the year had a gray, graveyard cast. Tree skeletons rose against a murky sky. The people, including the women, were in dark Mao suits. It was a season when man moved slowly, awaiting the hypodermic needle thrust of spring.

The streets were clogged with bicycles. For the first time, Lun Shanh laughed. He was feeling comfortable with Greg. "We tell our visitors that Guangzhou has three million people and one million bicycles. No one has ever counted the bicycles, but I believe it. They are expensive. About a hundred dollars in your money. More than two months' wages. But I read your people may spend a year's wages for an automobile."

At four o'clock they boarded an ancient Boeing that should have been in a museum. An American behind him called it "a bucketful of bolts."

The luggage racks overhead were open and stuffed with cases, big parcels and other gear. Two slender, attractive stewardesses in dark Mao outfits passed out small candy bars. They spent most of their time keeping the children out of the aisles and picking up packages that fell out of the racks.

"If you think this is bad," said the American, "you should see the Illuysin the Russians sold them back in the sixties. I tell you, I boarded it one night in Beijing and we sat several hours waiting for takeoff, and so help me, I looked down and there were two men with a flashlight poring over a repair book in Russian they had spread out on the ground. They'd study it awhile and then one would climb a stepladder and tinker with the motor."

Well to the back, Greg saw their shadows. Both were waving to someone.

"You have quick eyes," Lun Shanh said. "They are from our security agency, like your Secret Service or FBI. They will stay with you until you leave us. We have little crime, but we cannot take chances. We know you have had problems in the United States and last night in Hong Kong. You will have no problems in the People's Republic, Mr. Wilson."

35

At 10:12 P.M. the ancient Boeing came into Beijing airport for a feather-tipped landing. The craft might be old and creaky but the captain was not. Only two other planes sat on the runways. The air age had not come yet to Mainland China.

Greg experienced the exhilaration of an adventurer putting foot down in a new land. Beijing's dim lights stretched for miles, encompassing by suggestion some 2,800 years of history, the heartbeat of one fourth of the world's population. Those lights might hold his future. It all depended on how the high-level conference went on the morrow.

It was a modern airport, beautiful in its clean-cut lines, vast open spaces, murals and ample escalators. It was virtually deserted and he had the eerie feeling of walking through an outer-space film set. He had expected Lynne to meet him, but she was nowhere about. Another Mercedes awaited him and Lun Shanh. The other passengers went by a Japanese-built Hino bus.

The streets were narrow, dark and faintly lighted. He was being sped through an alien world of shadowy dwarf homes. Now and then a lone, murky figure appeared and as quickly vanished. He felt a flutter of fear deep down. Quickly he dismissed it. McGraw had assured him that Chinese security was so tight it was highly doubtful if a Soviet agent could penetrate it.

Then they were in downtown Beijing. It, too, had been put to bed. Only a short distance from the Great Square, called Tienanmen, they came to the seventeen-floor Peking Hotel. It had the commanding but utilitarian look of a Hilton. Its modern design was sharply knifed. A Rotarian would have felt at home in this Communist showplace. Parked outside was a covey of expensive cars.

Greg entered one of three wide glass doors, electronically operated. He stepped into an enormous lobby of marble pillars and floors with runners of red carpeting. A large painting of Kweilin, that breathtaking mountain resort of south China, caught his eye.

Lynne was waiting. She had been reading a paperback. She rose quickly but not too gracefully. Her long legs swiftly closed the distance between them. He had an overwhelming desire to take her into his arms, but she extended a hand in the manner of one executive meeting another. Her eyes danced, though, and they confided she had missed him. She had wanted to meet him, she said, but could not find the deputy foreign minister assigned to her, and had no idea how to reach the airport. They went to her room to review the presentation they would make at 10 A.M. All this time the two shadows assigned to him were never far away. She had only one and he teased her. "You don't rate," he said.

In room 8028, which was large, well furnished and had luxurious blue, carved carpeting, she produced an enormous blue-enameled Thermos.

"Care for tea?" she asked. "The water's boiling hot." The floor boy had brought the Thermos and packets of tea.

They had barely started sipping when the phone rang. Absently she picked up the receiver, then came fully alert. "Dr. Kennedy?" The man's voice was heavily overlayed with an accent she could not peg.

"Yes?"

"Where Mr. Wilson?" The voice was curt, demanding.

She kept an even keel. "May I ask, please, who is calling?"

There was a quite perceptible pause, then she heard the receiver going down, not hard but quietly as though the other party did not want her to know.

She turned to Greg. "Strange. A man. He wanted to know where you were and when I asked who it was, he hung up."

Greg shrugged. With their three shadows stationed in the hall outside and the floor boy down by the elevators, there seemed little cause for alarm.

Greg told her about the cancellation of the computer guidance system and Lotus' trip to Tokyo in an effort to revive the deal. "If anybody can do it, she can."

"But in Japan? A Chinese?"

"She speaks Japanese. I'd say she was international when it comes to business."

"She's international in other ways, too."

He almost spilled the tea. "I hadn't noticed."

"Not much."

Playfully, he put a fist to her cheek. "All right—if you want the scam, I'll give it to you. She wants a baby."

"I didn't know she was married."

"She isn't."

"Oh—a boyfriend?"

"Not exactly."

She was amused. “Is there some other way I don’t know about?”

He laughed. “She wants Carson Mining to give her one as a fringe benefit.”

She looked up in amazement. “A fringe benefit! What’re you talking about? Oh!” And then a louder, “Oh!” And then, “I don’t believe it! I don’t . . . and I can see from the look on your face you were pleased to be asked . . .” She trailed off.

He turned sober. “I was not pleased,” he said slowly, “but I was touched. She was desperately serious. But don’t ever tell her I told you. She’s such a sensitive—”

“About as sensitive as an alligator . . .” She immediately had regrets. “Sorry, I didn’t mean to be bitchy, but don’t you see? She wants to marry you if Barbara . . . something were to happen . . . although it’s the strangest proposal I’ve ever heard of.”

“I rather liked it.”

She straightened. “I’m not going to comment. I’ll say something I’ll be sorry for.”

“No comment necessary. I told her I was very much in love with Barbara.”

“And she said, what’s that got to do with it?”

He stared in surprise. “You’re psychic.”

“Not at all. That’s the stock answer. Right out of the book, ‘How to Get a Guy.’ It’s in the chapter headed, ‘What to Say if He’s Married.’ ”

She quickly changed the subject. “Before we go over the presentation, I think we should reassess the situation.”

His expression took on the dark glower that came whenever he was challenged. He seldom showed his resentment around her. The subject, though, was one that triggered an angry built-in reaction; one that brooked no thinking.

“We’ve been all over it,” he said stubbornly. “I don’t want to hear anything more about it.”

She put a hand on his arm. “Please, Greg, hear me out. There’s a new element. And don’t you dare close your mind.”

He said stiffly, “I’m listening.”

“Give Powder River a chance. We desperately need Washington’s support.” She took a deep breath. “You can’t go it alone,

Greg, no matter how much you want to. You're a rugged individualist and—"

"That's a nice name for a loner. I know what people say."

"Whatever it is, I've admired you for it, for your courage, and yes, guts . . . there's no other word. But don't you see, Greg, that was all to the good when you could handle everything yourself, when Carson was just a mining company, but now you've got an enormous operation with unbelievable ramifications. We've got to—"

"He can't do anything in eight days. Not a chance."

"He can in one hour if he gets to the right person."

He struggled to rein in his anger. "The Secretary of State? The President? They don't know what's going on. How can any human being possibly know every corner of the globe, every corner of the nation? They get these summaries every day from their aides—what's likely to happen in Afghanistan, Poland, Syria, forty or fifty hot spots—and then summaries about all the problems at home, twenty or thirty of them. They don't even have time to read the summaries, much less digest them. Take the Law of the Sea. I've read the United Nations report a dozen times, the size of a book, and I don't know what they're talking about."

She was shaken. "True—but Powder River's been in finance all his life. He'll put it in a few words—in dollars-and-cents talk they understand."

He rose and paced about. He stood looking out the window at Beijing, at the Great Square straight ahead and The Forbidden City in the distance. He turned then. He was barely audible. "I'm not taking the chance he will. I'll put it to you once again in a few words—and this time listen."

She broke in angrily. "Don't talk to me that way, Greg. I don't like it."

He raised his voice. "I said to listen. So the *Marco Polo* sails and State says we're a threat to national security—they always drag that old chestnut out—or even worse, that we're pirates, and a destroyer meets us and that's the finish of all our dreams. The finish."

He avoided her eyes. He couldn't take the hurt he saw. "But if we're flying the flag of the People's Republic of China up there alongside the American one, nobody's going to stop us. State's not going to risk breaking relations with Mainland China over a cargo of nodules . . ."

Without thinking, she exclaimed, "Greg, for heaven's sake, it's a Communist country!"

"So what? I'd prefer the Japanese flag or the German, but they've got their own mining projects. As for China, they've got nothing going. They haven't the money or the technology—and this would give them the hard currency they need to buy all kinds of technology they've got to have if they're going to enter the twentieth century . . . and give us the minerals this country's got to have in the years ahead. It could save this nation—and take care of millions of starving people at the same time."

Unexpectedly she put a hand on his. "All right, Greg. I don't like it, but I'll go along with you—all the way—and I pray to God we make it."

He softened. "I know it goes against the grain. Let me say one more thing. When I was growing up, I used to dream I was with Washington and then Lincoln and Teddy Roosevelt and other heroes. Right alongside them. At Valley Forge and climbing San Juan hill. Now I've got a chance to be that boy. A part of history. I feel it—and nothing's going to stop me. Nothing, Lynne."

She whispered, "I know it, Greg. I know it. Nothing will ever stop you."

An hour passed and she still had not slept. She had angered Greg and regretted it. In the morning, though, he would have forgotten. He never held a grudge and never repeated words another said in the hostilities of the moment.

He liked Lotus and that depressed her. Maybe he loved Lotus. Whenever he mentioned her, he brightened. There was the primitive in Lotus that Lynne envied, a frank, spontaneous love that had not been conditioned by thought, planning or consideration of the future.

Lynne had missed Greg these last two days. Yet she could not bring herself to show how much when she had awkwardly shaken hands. However, she had reached a well-thought-out decision. If Greg passed up Lotus—because he decided he would never enter into a physical relationship with any woman as long as Barbara lived—then Lynne would be happy to work alongside him in a platonic love devoid of intimacy. For years, if necessary. She would give up children and all that living together meant. If that was what he ultimately wanted . . . and he would soon have to decide.

36

He awakened early, a little before six. He had slept fitfully. He wondered if the *Tai Peng* had sailed and how Lotus was faring. He felt isolated.

Thinking of Lotus was a happy moment. When he was with her the pressures vanished and he was his old self, as he had been with Barbara before the accident. While Lotus never hesitated to put forth her point of view, she never persisted if he differed. He didn't know what had come over Lynne. She had changed this last year.

He listened to the 6 A.M. Voice of America news. He had thought it would be blacked out the same as in Russia. An hour later the Far East Broadcasting program followed.

He pushed a button and the electrically operated draperies opened to reveal hovering, dark clouds which depressed him. His spirits soared and fell with the weather. Ridiculous, he thought, and he lifted his broad shoulders a notch and pushed them back. On the street down below men were going through their morning calisthenics. One was in slow motion as if acting out a ballet. Another was thrusting a make-believe sword as if dueling. Not a bad idea for Americans, he thought.

At eight he met Lynne in the restaurant. She was radiant and excited, and like a child at Disneyland. Would they have time in the afternoon to see the Great Wall or the Forbidden City? He felt guilt over ever having had the slightest doubt about her. Of course, she hadn't changed. He wanted her honest opinion, didn't he? She looked so appealing, the sparkle in her eyes, the clean, fresh look devoid of makeup, the studied way she tossed her hair, the polished words thought out with such care. Once she had said, "I inherited the love of words from my father. He taught me that we must use the one word that pinpoints what we want to say. He hated profanity—not so much because it was blasphemous but because it reflected a mind too lazy to hunt for the right word to express the feeling of the moment."

The waiter brought more food than they could consume in a week of breakfasting: very small eggs, not much bigger than pigeons', pork in a yellowish oil, Mandarin fish also in a heavy oil, and scallop soup. Lynne laughed. "I'd settle for a $1.39 breakfast at McDonald's."

Around them were visitors from most of the nations of the Western world. At the next table sat Americans. An older man said, "Great walk. Lousy temple." Another, "I'm just along on this trip as a pack mule." And another, "Didja notice all the women digging ditches? I tell you there's something to this ERA." A bejeweled woman said, "I'm out of Lysol. I've scrubbed every bath in China." A younger one, "They said it was bean curd, but I know it was Pablum." And another, "After that bathroom in Sian, I thanked God for Chanel No. 5."

At a little shop off the main lobby, Greg found a bat kite he thought Laura might like. It was beautiful in a frightening way. Its wings were Chinese red with white stripes. The head resembled a kangaroo rat's with big eyes as fearsome as the fake ones on the hind wings of the Io moth.

A woman shopping alongside him said, "Don't ask for aspirin. I did because my husband had a bad headache and the next we knew the desk had called in a woman doctor and she insisted on examining my husband from head to foot. Didn't cost us anything. All a part of socialized medicine. Said the people paid seventeen cents a year. But since we were Americans we got it for free. And all I wanted were two aspirins."

Lun Shanh appeared. He said there would be a slight delay. The Foreign Minister was running behind on his schedule. When Lynne and Greg started out the door to walk about, he stopped them. "Please, a few minutes. We wait here. We need to get the car ready."

The Mercedes sat outside with the driver behind the wheel. No one was working on it but there was an unusual flurry of soldiers and police officers moving about. Greg and Lynne exchanged glances. Both had the same forebodings. "Something happening we should know about?" Greg asked.

"No, no." Lun's voice betrayed him. He was a poor actor.

The police were permitting only one person at a time to leave the hotel. They asked no questions, offered no explanations and were most courteous. Obviously, they wanted to limit the number wandering around the hotel grounds.

The post and telegraph office was only a short distance away, down a corridor off the main lobby, and Greg suggested they buy stamps for Laura's collection. "Please do not leave," Lun Shanh said. "We will be ready in a minute."

Greg thought to test the situation. "Nothing can surely happen to us at the post office."

"No, no, nothing happen to you anywhere in China. All right now, we are ready. Please to hurry."

He had Lynne by the arm and was pushing her toward the car. Greg kept abreast of them. The driver said a pleasant, "Good morning." The three slid into the back seat with Lynne between them. Lun Shanh drew the shades, blocking their side view and also that of anyone looking in. "I hope you do not mind. The light bothers my eyes. They are very sensitive."

Not that sensitive, Greg thought. The day was still overcast.

Suddenly an army officer appeared and talked briefly to the driver who then left the car. The officer seated himself behind the wheel and another officer opened the opposite door and sat beside him. Immediately the electrically operated windows went up.

"It's hot," Lynne said. "I can scarcely breathe."

"A thousand pardons, Dr. Kennedy. It is only a short drive. A few blocks."

An army officer opened the door and spoke a few sentences. "We must make new arrangements," Lun Shanh said. "I will ride in the car behind." The officer took his place.

Greg said, "What seems to be the problem?" The officer shook his head. He spoke no English.

"I don't like this," Lynne whispered.

Greg bent his head to look through the windshield. "I don't either." Oh God, he prayed, don't let anything happen to her. What have I got her into? He knew now that no matter where they went—Asia, Hawaii, Arizona—someone would be waiting with a bullet, a neatly designed accident or other method of assassination. The enemy had unlimited manpower and funds. By the law of averages, if the enemy tried often enough, the enemy would come on target.

"What happened to our shadows?" she asked. "Were they out in the hall when you got up?"

"No." Then he reported, "They're clearing the parking area of everyone."

"Let's go back into the hotel and stay there until they tell us what's going on."

At that moment the limousine rolled forward. There was a lead car a few feet ahead. With the windows up, they sat in a silent world. The Mercedes was so airtight that there was no rumble of tires, no motor noise and no traffic sound. Lynne forced the panic down and said evenly, "You don't think we're being kidnapped and this isn't the army?"

He was staring straight ahead. He could see little. The army officer in front of him was sitting straighter, blocking a clear view through the windshield. Deliberately?

"I don't know. I do know where the Great Hall of the People is, and if we don't take a direct route . . . get yourself set . . . sit up straight . . . keep your feet awake . . . be prepared to move."

She responded. They were skirting the parking area on a driveway that led to Beijing's main thoroughfare, Chang'an, called "The Street of 10 Li." It was spacious, wide enough for six car lanes.

The lead car turned right and they followed. She looked back. Another car followed, presumably with Lun Shanh. All of the cars picked up speed. They shot through the next corner where other traffic had been stopped by an officer in a kiosk on the corner. He controlled traffic with a bullhorn. The support for the stop-and-go sign looked like a barber pole.

At the intersection where they would turn left to enter the Great Square, their car came to a sudden, screeching stop. Greg reacted faster than Lynne. He braced himself and grabbed her, keeping her from being thrown against the front seat. The officer beside her hit it with a resounding thud, shook himself and felt of his head. By inches their car had missed colliding with the lead one. The driver looked back to check on them. He said nothing.

The army was everywhere. They had brought all traffic to a stop. Four soldiers with hand weapons drawn cordoned off a school "bus" alongside them. About forty teenagers stood in a truck. A minute ago they had been laughing and chattering away like teenagers the world over. Now they stood silent, not moving. They were disciplined to obey police or army officers.

Up ahead were more soldiers. "Oh, no!" Greg had squirmed around until he had a view. "They're going to kill them. All of them."

A platform with eight persons standing on it had been jacked up from a large truck to a street light. Obviously they had been engaged in replacing a bulb. But surely not eight were needed, Greg thought. He learned later he was correct. That was one way of solving China's unemployment problem. Put eight to work to do a two-man job. There was no other alternative.

The soldiers were firing weapons and hand guns aimed upward. Slowly the platform was being lowered. It became apparent that the shots had been fired in the air, not at the workers. A young man appeared out of nowhere pulling a handmade wooden baby carriage with a chubby boy riding inside. A police officer rushed to him, grabbed the handle and pulled the cart out of the danger zone. Once out, the officer searched the man and the carriage with negative results.

When the platform was at its lowest point, the detail left one at a time. No one challenged them until the last stepped down. At once he was taken into custody and searched. The platform, too, was searched and a rifle found.

The door opened and Lun Shanh looked in. "A troublemaker.

Nothing to worry about." The door closed. Lun Shanh wanted to answer no questions.

Within minutes, the lead car turned left, followed by the other two. They entered the square which was so enormous that a party standing on the far side could not be seen distinctly. In the center rose the Monument to the Heroes of the Revolution. A squadron of girls, about twelve years of age, marched in unison to the monument. They were in blue skirts and white blouses. The lead one carried the flag of the People's Republic. Another bore a large wreath which she lay at the foot of the monument. They sang, but those inside the car saw only lips moving.

The car pulled up before the entrance to the Great Hall. A crowd had gathered, drawn by the draped windows, a sign that persons of importance were inside. No one monitored the hundreds who stood behind imaginary cordons. Greg and Lynne hesitated about leaving the car. A sniper could be waiting. It would be so easy. Lun Shanh said, "Please to come."

Greg said to Lynne, "Wait here."

He got out, stretched and took a few steps. He was an open target. Lun Shanh was puzzled. "Please, we must hurry."

Greg bent to look in at Lynne. "Okay."

As Lynne walked past the crowd, there was craning of necks and much whispering. The onlookers couldn't believe her earrings, hairdo, high heels, hosiery, and patent leather shoes which they thought were enameled. They had seen few American women. It was as if she were from outer space.

As she walked alongside Greg, she said in a low, angry voice, "Don't you ever dare play the hero again. I'll take my chances along with you."

Neither noted much about the architecture. Their eyes went to the enormous, billboard-size pictures of Mao, Lenin and Stalin hanging across the front of the building. No contemporary Russian leaders were up there. They were the hated enemy, denounced in the press and on television. Any day they might order the invasion of China. Several million Russians lined China's western boundary.

An intelligent-looking young woman with dark searching eyes crossed the high, vaulted lobby. She had her hair pulled back in a tight bun which left her round olive face without a setting. It seemed suspended in space. She was clutching a notebook.

"Dr. Kennedy, Mr. Wilson, welcome to the People's Republic of China and the Great Hall of the People. We are most honored to have you. I will be your interpreter. My name is Jiang Nanjing."

Lynne extended her hand. "We are most honored that you have invited us." Greg nodded.

Miss Jiang said, "Would you like me to translate literally word for word, or would you prefer me to use Chinese expressions and put it the way a Chinese would speak? I would be most careful to get your exact meaning across. I was the interpreter when your President, the Honorable Mr. Nixon, was here—and also the Honorable Mr. Kissinger."

"We'd like the Chinese way," Greg said.

They entered a long, vast room, two stories high, with more pictures of Mao, Lenin, Marx and Stalin. Miss Jiang led them to the only piece of furniture, a highly-polished, very wide conference table that ran perhaps thirty feet. At the far end eight men from the Foreign Ministry, including the Foreign Minister himself, were seated. They wore simple, high-necked Mao suits with no ornamentation or insignia designating rank. They could have come in from the fields, and this was the image they wished to project. Mao himself had been a peasant and constantly reminded the people and the Politburo that it had been a peasants' revolution and the government was there to serve the peasants.

Lun Shanh introduced them and there were nods, a few tentative smiles, and much scraping of the heavy, carved chairs as they rose, the sound echoing in the great chamber. Their glances dismissed Greg. He was one more trader come to China. They lingered on Lynne and studied her, but not because she was a woman. They had been briefed on her status as one of the world's foremost oceanographers, and they had the greatest respect for knowledge. Greg sensed the mood and questioned whether Lynne and he had made the right decision, for him to make the presentation.

Lun Shanh indicated chairs across from the eight and seated Lynne. Miss Jiang stood directly behind and between Lynne and

Greg. Greg opened the attaché case and took out a folder with a sizable sheaf of papers. The rustle sounded loud in the cavernous room.

Lun Shanh seated himself with the eight and said, "Please to proceed, Mr. Wilson."

Greg had his plan worked out. He would be businesslike; he would not attempt any of the familiarity he might with a U.S. Board; he would avoid the technical side; and he would stress the tremendous advantages to China.

He began by thanking them for the opportunity to set forth the facts about this breakthrough of a new frontier, possibly the last in the history of our planet. "You have before you the costs, the potential profits, the risks involved. So I don't need to repeat the information in the briefs. You will have questions, and the questions will be more important than any speech I might make. However, you won't find in the briefs our offer to the People's Republic."

He stated it in a very few words. Carson Mining Company would grant a 2 percent interest to the People's Republic in exchange for a $50-million investment. The People's Republic would put up no front money. The $50 million would be deducted from China's share of the royalties. The *Marco Polo* would have the right to fly the flag of the People's Republic alongside the U.S. one. "This is of paramount importance to Carson Mining. The flags of these two great nations will protect us from attacks by other powers. Frankly, we are in a race with the Soviets. We have every reason to expect to begin mining before they can move into the Pacific. If we do, they may attempt to delay or stop us by the threat or use of force."

This was the part the eight wanted to hear and they listened intently. The Soviets had the army and the technology to invade China successfully without the use of nuclear weapons—if they did not penetrate too far. If they attempted to take over all of China, then China might swallow them up as China had invaders throughout the centuries. But the Soviets probably would proceed slowly and cautiously. They would eat out a hunk of China, stay there, and in another century, gobble up another portion.

Personally, Greg was treading uneasy ground. He had called

Karl Neustadt about this potentially hazardous step he was taking. Karl had said, "I think it's brilliant, but you know as well as I do that if you put it up to the Mass. Board, they will turn it down flat. They'll think you have sold out to the Commies and are about to start another world war."

He had paused and Greg had thought he was about to pull out if Greg went ahead. Instead Karl said, "I've come to learn that if you're successful, no one's going to question any decisions you've made, but if you fail, that's when you're in big trouble. I'd say, go ahead. You and Lynne are going to bring it off." He added, "I think that's what Barbara would want. She had a lot of guts in a tight situation."

Greg asked if the eight had questions. He was prepared to spend several hours. The Foreign Minister looked at Lynne. "If we were to consider this, we would do so on your word alone. Am I correct in assuming that your presence here indicates you have no doubts about the success of this project?"

She straightened. "I am staking my reputation as an oceanographer who has been down on the ocean floor many times and as one who thoroughly knows the hardware. I haven't the slightest doubt."

The Foreign Minister rose. He had no further questions and neither did the others. Greg spoke up quickly, "I can't give you a definite date, but the *Marco Polo* will sail soon and I need your decision within two or three days."

The Foreign Minister looked startled. For a moment he mulled that over, then nodded and walked for the door, his deputies trailing him. Mr. Lun and Miss Jiang remained behind.

Lun Shanh asked if they would like to drive around Beijing that afternoon. He would be most happy to show them about.

Lynne brightened. "The Great Wall?" She glanced at Greg for affirmation. He hadn't heard. He was lost in thought.

Miss Jiang regretted she could not come with them. She thanked them and they thanked her, and it was all very polite and very Chinese.

37

They returned to the Peking Hotel for lunch. Greg shifted about constantly and toyed with the chopsticks. He considered the fact the Chinese had asked few questions indicated rejection. Lynne sought to reassure him. "They need time to study it."

"Time," he said flatly. "That's the trouble. We haven't got the time they'll want to take."

On his return for lunch he had fallen into conversation with an American hotel executive who was leaving Beijing for good. The Chinese Government had signed an agreement permitting his corporation to build a fourteen-story hotel with the proviso that the government would have final approval of the plans.

"So we start going over them and they're courteous and most willing to do whatever we wish because they want the hotel," said the American. "We spent eighteen months on preambles and thought we were all set and then discovered they wanted to discuss every little detail. The last straw was when we spent a week on the doorknobs. Would you believe it? At that point I threw in the towel."

Greg had a more immediate worry. "We're not going to the Great Wall," he told Lynne. "I'm not putting you into more jeopardy."

"Don't I have anything to say about it?" she asked sharply. What right did he think he had to be making decisions for her?

He put a hand over hers. "If anything happened to you . . ."

She softened. "I didn't mean . . ."

"I didn't either. Look, the guy with the rifle on that jacked-up platform, if he had waited until our car started to turn into the Great Square, he could have hit us through the rear window. He had a direct line, same as Lee Oswald when he took the same angle shot on President Kennedy."

She shook her head. "We don't know he was waiting for us. If someone would only tell us what was going on. . . . Anyway, we've got our three shadows back and Mr. Lun will get us an army detail if we think we need it. We can't quit life just because we've been threatened. They can take a shot at us right now —here—or at the airport when we leave tomorrow."

She dropped her voice. "I've wanted to walk the Great Wall since I was a little girl and first read about it. China's whole history has revolved around it."

He put forth more arguments and she countered them. They were still debating when Lun Shanh arrived to escort them. She gave Greg one last appealing look. As he rose to leave with her, he said in mock disgust, "Women have been giving me that look since I first started school."

She laughed. "You're a good sport."

"No, I'm not. I'm a dedicated male chauvinist."

"I'll try to remember."

Lun Shanh was puzzled. "What is male chauvinist?"

"A man who loves women but doesn't let them run over him."

Lun Shanh nodded vigorously. "I am male chauvinist, too."

As they exited, Greg brought himself to a sudden halt. The setup was the same as when they had left a few hours earlier. Three cars: a lead one, theirs and a tail car. The same army officers. The same policemen clearing the parking area. And as the door swung closed behind him, and he turned on hearing voices, there were the three army men of that morning sealing off the entrance.

He was shaken. The old fear that had mushroomed in Hong Kong now surged back. For a few seconds his thoughts threatened to fragment, but he held them by will power alone in a vise.

"Please to hurry," Lun Shanh said nervously.

The same dialogue.

He shot Lynne a questioning glance. She, too, had stopped, paralyzed. Then Lun Shanh had her by the arm and was pushing her along. Because she was expected to, she climbed in the back seat and slid over. The army officer of the morning gave her a quick, official nod. Greg followed. Later, he wondered why he hadn't called a halt and discussed the situation with her. However, their decision would doubtlessly have been the same. The government was taking routine precautions as they would with any distinguished foreign citizen. The government had no reason to anticipate trouble. China had little crime. Hadn't Lun Shanh mentioned that a man had held up a bank, been captured, tried and executed all within a week? In China justice was swifter than in the Western world.

Again they turned into Chang'an Street and rolled past the Great Square on their way to the Great Wall at Badaling. At each intersection traffic officers in kiosks stopped the bicycles and other vehicles with their bullhorns. The same as before, the windows were tightly sealed. They moved in a soundless, unreal world.

Outside, China passed by and Lynne would never forget the montage: two beast-of-burden women pulling a cart loaded with stones . . . a little boy with his basketball . . . three horses in tandem harnessed to a wagon loaded with produce . . . an old, tottering woman with the bound feet of ancient China . . . men crowding in to read newspapers posted behind glass on a long wall . . . a factory with a banner announcing the Peking Opera would play in a warehouse that night (the company took its productions to the outlying districts) . . . a woman with a lifetime of hard work written into her wrinkles carrying live ducks in pouchlike baskets . . . schoolgirls with hair parted in the center and braided, in colorful, padded, zippered jackets . . . boys with their hair cut medium, clean looking . . . a husband and wife struggling under heavy baskets swinging at the ends of long boards balanced over their shoulders . . . secretaries hurrying to work in dark, neat suits . . . young men in suits, too, and white shirts and ties . . . a billion people struggling to survive with a foot on the first rung and reaching for the second . . . under a Communist regime that was not above sneaking in here and there a little free enterprise.

As they approached Badaling, they saw the Great Wall rising and falling over the high, rugged mountains. It stretched for 1,500 miles, the only man-made structure on earth the astronauts saw from outer space. Back in 476 B.C., when China was many small kingdoms, several had started walls to protect themselves from marauding barbarians. In 228 B.C., when the Qin Dynasty united six nations, Emperor Shih Huang Ti connected the separate embattlements and extended them. Through the years the wall was expanded and restored. The Ming Dynasty, which took over in 1368, employed tens of thousands for the next hundred years to widen and strengthen it and construct scores of guard towers.

Lynne was all eyes. "There—that tower—I've stood there in my dreams many times with my father and watched the hordes come riding out of the north to storm the wall—and I still hear the thunder of the battle, men screaming, the pounding of horse hooves on the hard, dry ground . . . and don't look at me like that, Greg. I'm not crazy. Anyway, not very."

They passed a horde of tourist buses, scores of big yellow bugs waiting patiently by the roadside, and then eased into a mob of hundreds moving slowly toward the steep stairs that led up to the Great Wall. They had come from half the nations of the world. Most, however, were Chinese and most of them, too, had traveled far. This was their Mecca, more so than the Great Square or the Monument to the People's Heroes. Here was the history of China, of all the dynasties, a living history still.

Even the Communists took pride in it. In their literature they said "the workers" had built it, as if the workers had initiated it and thrown it up gladly and without a whip to their backs. Regardless, today's workers troop in by the hundreds of thousands every year, take inspiration from it, and find in it the embodiment of all the culture and the achievements of a great people.

Greg had been lulled by the ride, but as the car came to a slow stop his breathing quickened and his rawhide body tensed. He was prepared to move quickly if he had to, to duck, to fall flat, to pull Lynne with him. He had his quick mind programmed for all the hazards he could contemplate.

They stepped into a sluggish river of people. They pulled their coat collars up about their necks. A wind blew and howled carrying the bitter cold from mountain peaks ringed with snow.

Lun Shanh was at their sides as if a wish of theirs had conjured him up. "Please to come." He spoke quietly to the people and they opened up a little path. After Lynne and Greg passed by, they closed ranks. There was no shoving, no pushing, only heads rising on tiptoes to gain a better sight of the "white goddess." They knew from television and word-of-mouth that these were some of the friends from far places the government had told them about.

Then they were on the Wall itself, built in part of long, wide slabs of native stone and where restored, of concrete bricks. There was a stone walkway wide enough for an army of four to six men to march abreast. The sides were flanked with crenellated parapets where the archers and later the riflemen could kneel, take aim and fire on the enemy.

The walk ran almost solid with people and the sound was the babble of many languages, the universal cry of a baby or the universal chatter of teenagers. The two seemed surrounded by soldiers and yet the soldiers faded into the crowd. Lynne and Greg set their own pace with Lun Shanh sometimes alongside, sometimes ahead. They stopped to look out over the rolling, greening mountains or up to another long twist as the Wall snaked over one more high crest. It weaved its way over the terrain rather than followed a straight line. It was as graceful as a ballet dancer.

Only when they neared the guard tower, where sentries had stood duty and officers lived in other times, did the protective military net tighten about them. The Wall ran through the lookout tower ahead. "Please to wait," Lun Shanh said.

They moved to one side and stood shivering. The snow-chilled wind had turned into a sharp, freezing gale. The dark, brooding sky seemed about to settle on them. Greg shuddered. If it enveloped them . . . if the police officers and soldiers lost sight of them . . . both were panting. The ascent had been gradual but telling.

"How you doing, Greg?" Lynne asked.

"I'm damn cold."

She laughed. "But it's worth it—to think that we walk—"

"Oh, you and your romanticizing. Who knows how many tens of thousands died on this very stretch we've walked. Died horribly. And for what?"

"For what? For doing what we're doing, Greg. For struggling to open up new frontiers or protecting the ones they already had. For trying to find happiness in the security this wall offered them. Sure, we die by the thousands in every generation for what we be-

lieve in. It's an ongoing process, never ending. If it ends, we're finished."

Lun Shanh said, "Please to come."

They passed through the guard tower. It had been cleared to make way for them. Once they were through, they were swallowed up by another flow of humanity.

The climb was steeper and they were breathing harder. So was everyone else. There was a rail now and they pulled themselves along on it. "I've got to get in shape," Lynne said.

Greg never looked down. He continually scanned the people heading their way. He spotted one suspicious character after another. He was becoming paranoid. He had to quit that. There was no assassin lurking up ahead. If there were, how could the killer escape? The jump to the ground far below would be bone shattering.

The walkway spread out. Through the bobbing heads, they spotted horses festooned with red bow knots tied to their manes, warriors in bright blue uniforms sitting in primitive wooden saddles, silver foil reflectors, an old battered movie camera, and an assortment of film people. Lun Shanh said they were shooting a television movie that would re-create scenes from the Ming era, about A.D. 1400. The warriors carried Mongolian bows, about six feet in length and deeply curved in the center, made from one piece of supple wood.

They had watched for only a few minutes when the director came over to talk with Lun Shanh. He nodded in Lynne's direction.

Lun Shanh turned to her. "He asked if you were an American, and I said you were, and he said he would be most honored if you would play a scene. You would sit on the horse with bow and arrow and you would shout as if leading an army. I told him that you and Mr. Wilson were important guests of the government and you would not do that."

"But I would!" she exclaimed.

Greg broke in. "Just how would that fit in with the Ming Dynasty?"

"No, no," Lun Shanh said. "Not fit at all. It would be a . . . a . . . I do not know the word, but it would come before the film

starts. It would say an American watched the filming . . . a friend of China who had come to visit our country and see the Great Wall. It would be a—"

"—preview."

"I don't care what it is," Lynne said. "I want to do it."

The horse was of Mongolian stock, short, lean, neurotic and undoubtedly fast. She pulled up her skirt, put a foot in the stirrup, did a turn and sat sidesaddle. She had never ridden in that position and it was alien and uncomfortable. Once the word spread that the "white goddess" was acting in the film, the crowd grew. She rose up above the staring, curious mob. She was a perfect target. Greg wanted to shout at her to dismount.

Greg made a full sweep of the quiet, entranced audience. A short, male Caucasian in a black heavy topcoat with a fur collar hoisted up about his bull neck, caught Greg's attention. The man wore a cap, also of fur, with big earmuffs. The cap was positioned low on the forehead, almost to the heavy, shaggy eyebrows. It was as if the man sought to conceal his identity. He was threading his way skillfully through the dense crowd to the front. Greg moved quickly to cut him off but the going was slow.

The director handed Lynne the bow and arrow. With Lun Shanh translating, he instructed her. She had trouble lodging the arrow in the slot and once in, found the pressure of pulling the arrow back difficult. The horse paced about uneasily. A youth holding the reins tightened them. The director signaled the cameraman, and he, Lun Shanh and the youth moved swiftly out of the scene.

Greg was only a few feet from the bull-necked Caucasian when the man halted twelve feet or so from Lynne. He had his hands ensconced in topcoat pockets and his feet planted solidly a foot apart. The Chinese around him were too engrossed to notice him. Now Greg was alongside him. Greg had his hands free, ready to pounce if the man brought forth a weapon or moved on Lynne.

The camera was turning. Lynne raised the bow and with the arrow in place, pulled back on the string. The horse was pawing one foot. A murmur oozed up from the crowd. She leaned forward slightly and shouted, "Charge!" A roar of laughter went up. They

had no idea what the word meant literally but caught the meaning.

At that instant there was a swish through the air, a blurred cutting of air that only those very close heard. An arrow plowed deep into the neck of the horse. He reared in panic, pawing the air. Lynne made one desperate grab for his mane, missed, and was thrown backward. For a split second, it looked to Greg as though she were going over the parapet into the long drop below. She struck the stone rise and bounded back, rolled over a couple of times, and lay still. A few feet away the horse had crumpled with blood spurting from the neck. Stunned at first, the film company and the onlookers rushed forward to close a tight circle around Lynne and the animal.

Greg elbowed and pounded his way through and dropped to his knees by her. He fumbled for her pulse, found it. It was beating. He looked around wildly for help. A Chinese in peasant clothes, about thirty years of age, took over. Lun Shanh said he was a barefoot doctor. Not literally, but one who treated the workers in the fields and the factories. As he checked Lynne for broken bones or contusions, she slowly regained consciousness.

For long after it was necessary, Greg held her in his arms. He helped her to her feet and led her away from the dead horse. Repeatedly Lun Shanh apologized for the "accident." He said a curious onlooker had picked up a bow and was testing it. As he pulled the cord back, his hand slipped. Frightened, he disappeared. The arrow had missed her by only inches.

38

The General was putting away his gymnastic equipment when Rona Hale brought correspondence for him to sign.

"Please get me a reservation for lunch for two at Jean Pierre's." French restaurants were the "in" places this year.

"Right away." She headed for the door.

He continued in the same casual tone, "And please inform the FBI about my whereabouts."

She stopped as if yanked hard and turned. "I—I don't understand . . ."

"Just a little joke. They follow me all the time."

Her cheeks looked suddenly sunburned. "General, if you think I would ever, ever—"

"Nonsense. I ask your forgiveness. I make little joke—only not so good."

She protested further and offered to quit. He assured her he trusted her as much as he would his mother. His late mother. He could have added that he would not have trusted his late mother with his pocket change.

He left the office at 11:40 sharp, walked to the Jefferson Hotel, passed it and came to a phone booth. He spread his change before him and a scrap of paper with a number. At exactly twelve he dialed. On the third ring, Nataya answered in Honolulu.

Before she could inquire about his health or nonsense like that, he took the lead. "I hope you have some sad news to tell me about Mr. Wilson."

She met him head-on. "You know I don't."

He turned sarcastic. "I suppose you have a good excuse. You always do."

"How dare you talk to me like that! You know perfectly well I will handle the Wilson problem as soon as it can be done. What was I supposed to do? Follow him to China? You are being ridiculous and asinine. But I do have a sensational breakthrough . . ."

The General said quietly, "Before I forget, I want to ask a favor."

There was dead silence. The General continued, "As you know we have been having difficulties in getting Rashid's girl friend, Anya, into the United States. As a favor, would you find a pretty girl who would take care of Rashid until we get Anya in?"

She said in disbelief, "You mean a girl to sleep with him?"

He was caustic. "I didn't mean a cook."

She screamed, "You think I'm a pimp, a procurer!"

Mother of Rasputin, everyone in Honolulu would hear her. He

dropped to a whisper. "Forget it, Nataya. I did not mean . . . I ask your forgiveness . . . I never should have—"

"Don't you ever dare suggest anything like that again."

Who did she think she was? She had slept with half the French Generals in Paris at the start of World War II.

He continued, "What is the breakthrough?"

She waited a second to calm her breathing. But only a second. She could switch gears quickly. She was an actress. "I have enlisted a man in a key spot on the *Marco Polo*. He is in the confidence of Mr. Wilson and Dr. Kennedy. There's nothing that he doesn't know. He has been with them for years."

The General felt his adrenalin flowing.

"What's his name? What does he do?"

"I don't want to take a chance. I'm in a public place. I'll post it to you—in code."

"What've you got from him?"

"Nothing yet. I've had just one meeting. But I'm seeing him tomorrow."

"I've got to have his name, what he does, his address, all of that."

"You will. In the next mail. I've got to go. I've talked my time up."

She slammed the receiver down, to let him know she was still angry.

She proceeded by taxi to the Army Museum on Kalia Road. It was a low building that marked the site of fortifications long deserted.

Guns, personnel carriers and tanks, both U.S. and Japanese, were lined up across the building's front. Each bore a sign identifying it and gave the specifications. She found a U.S. M-381 half-track personnel carrier interesting. It could carry twelve infantrymen. She took notes, then proceeded to a light tank, the General Chaffee, an M-24. It was gray with a white star on the front. It weighed nineteen tons and had five wheels on each side for the moving tracks. A 77mm gun was mounted on the turret and there were also three machine guns. The sign said that it was powered by two V-8 Cadillac engines and held a crew of four. It had a speed of thirty-five miles per hour.

Finished with her notes, she crossed Kalia Road and walked a short distance to the Fort De Russy military reservation. During World War II and ever since it had entertained thousands of GIs as a Rest and Relaxation Center.

She prowled around for a half hour and satisfied herself that no one moving about either there or in the nearby vicinity would attract attention. She waved down a taxi and at the Oahu Bar, ordered a piña colada. She remembered a hand-painted Hawaiian-type dress she had seen that was too expensive for her. However, she could charge it off to a new informant, Mr. Piña Colada. What an inspiration! While she waited for the drink, she lit up a cigarillo.

Shortly she would be meeting Rashid at the Honolulu Stadium where the Hawaiian Islanders baseball team played. There a hawker of *saimin,* a noodle dish spotted with bits of meat, would hand her a note setting forth the exact location of the rendezvous. The *saimin* came with chopsticks and she would return one to the salesperson to let Rashid know she would be there. The Islanders was the only baseball team in the United States that had a budget for chopsticks.

When Rashid woke up, the clock showed it was a little after 11. He had overslept. He pulled the drapes and a flood of sunlight burst in blinding him and bringing alive a large picture of Anya. He had had it blown up from a snapshot. She was an exotic-looking girl with lustrous black hair cascading to her shoulders, framing a strong, angular face with full, sensuous lips and big, wide, inviting brown eyes.

Yesterday he had had a letter from her, postmarked Mexico City. The General said she was living there while the American Embassy processed her application to enter the United States. He had never had a letter from her before and remembered he had mentioned this to the General about a week ago. So he did not know her handwriting. The letter did not sound like Anya. She was effervescent and down-to-earth. The letter was written in cultured, proper English. But then, perhaps she had paid someone to write it for her. She might not know how to write.

All during breakfast at a nearby coffee shop, he was bothered, and afterward on the long taxi ride to the Welder's. He took the old, wooden, unpainted outside stairs two at a time, rapped, and when the Welder opened the groaning door, he forgot about the letter.

She stood there in surprise, clutching a box of chocolates in one hand and putting one in her mouth with the other.

"Well, as I live and breathe," she said. "Never figured to see you again. You lousy son-of-a-bitch, never told me you was heisting an armored car. You let me send my men—"

He broke in, smiling broadly. "Nobody got hurt. I warned them to clear out once they had the barricades in place."

"Coulda been killed, all of 'em. What the hell do ya want now?"

"Could I come in? I've got big money for you this time."

She held the screen door open. "Guess so. But I'll turn you in next time if you pull anything on me."

He took the same chair in the same dark, tiny living room. The cloying odor of chocolates lay heavy on the aging air. She sat three feet away in the other straight-backed chair.

She offered him chocolates. "Kron. Best made. I don't drink, smoke or lay up with men. I get a box a week. That's all the sinning I can pay for. Whatcha got?"

"About four grand, maybe five, and a box of chocolates every week for a year. How does that sound?"

"Whatcha want me to do? Kidnap the governor? I told ya I was legit."

"I know you're legit. I wouldn't come to you with anything that wasn't. That other, I didn't know—"

"Don't lie to me, you bastard. I've been around too long."

"For Allah's sake, give me a chance."

"Allah? You one of 'em cult guys who carves up women?"

He tightened his hold on the chair arms. He had to get the situation under control. He tried the quiet approach. "I'm sorry about the other. Yes, I lied. I did know something about it, but didn't know it would turn out the way it did."

She wiped the chocolate from her lips with a muumuu sleeve and put the box down. "I'm not one to hold no grudge. My mother, bless her soul, she told me to forget and forgive. Whatcha want for the five grand?"

"You know the barroom brawls you see in the movies."

"Go on."

"Well, I need about forty big, strong guys who know how to use their fists for a brawl like that. They may get bruised a little—"

"No guns. I wouldn't do it if there was shootin'."

"No, ma'am, no guns. I might hand out some baseball bats so they'd have an advantage over the guys they're fighting."

"Is this a bar over on Hotel Street? I got friends . . ."

"No, several miles away, and the other guys are all from the mainland. You don't know them."

"What's the brawl about? What's in it for ya? How come ya put out all that money?"

"I can't tell you. I'm sworn to secrecy. But it's legit. However, if you don't want to get in on it . . ."

"Hold on, buster. I didn't say I wouldn't, but a girl's got to be careful these days with all the psychos around."

"Do I look like a psycho?"

"Hell, no, but I almost got burned . . ."

"I apologized, didn't I? A guy can make a mistake, can't he? You've got my word this time."

For a long moment she stared at him. "If ya give me your word . . . when do ya want the men?"

"I'll let you know—and you'll never be sorry."

"I'd better not be—or I'll cut your manhood off. I don't mess around with lyin' sons-of-bitches."

39

The flight from Beijing to Saipan was a painful, arduous one for Lynne. She had suffered no broken bones and as far as could be determined, no internal injuries. However, she was severely bruised.

Greg had propped her up with pillows and kept her sedated. He would beat a pillow before he put it behind her, and this brought forth a smile. Even with the pain, she floated in a pleasant half world. His touching when he moved her with his massive, strong hands, his concern expressed in those clear, deep blue eyes, this business of having shared danger—all spread the warmth of an early spring day.

They put down in Tokyo for a brief stop and there the plane was inundated with flowers, smiles, soft voices and happy Japanese couples. There was an old Japanese superstition: If a couple were wed on foreign soil, they would be assured of a happy life. So in Saipan, the capital of the Commonwealth of the Northern Marianas, a U.S. Trust Territory, they would be taken by travel agents to a Buddhist temple for a marriage ceremony.

At the Hyatt Hotel in the town of Garapan, which had been totally destroyed during World War II, they checked in. A soft, warm trade wind was blowing and palm trees were silhouetted against a scarlet sunset. A bloody sunset, it could have been described, and he shuddered. It was a foreboding sprung from a mind that had been repeatedly bayoneted these last days.

He brought dinners from the Kili Terrace and they ate in her room behind a locked door. Afterward he left the door ajar to his adjoining room, in case she needed him in the night.

Alone with a night light burning, she heard the whispering of palm fronds and the more distant lapping of the waves. Her thoughts strayed to the quiet, shy Japanese couples on the plane whose love surfaced gently in the touch of hands and eyes that held the wonder of it all. This was a package tour with the wedding thrown in. Afterward they would honeymoon at a beach hotel and then take the yellow tourist buses to the Banzai and Suicide Cliffs where thousands of Japanese had leaped to their deaths. The couples would look over tanks rusting away, the skeletons of ships disintegrating on quiet beaches that once had been roaring infernos, and old cannons covered by time with green mold and tropical vegetation. They were young and these were historical sites where in defeat the Japanese had been heroic. Today, though, was another era and they would come away with no ill feeling toward their friends, the Americans. After all, what they saw was history. A long time ago.

One day she would like to come back to Saipan on her honeymoon. With Greg, of course. They would sit close together on the warm sands of Tanapag Reef and gaze out over the mystery-shrouded Philippine Sea. They would take a picnic along and talk excitedly about a glorious future. She would ask him about his boyhood and growing up. She knew so little about him. Then she would tell him about her father and all they did together and the first time she went down, trembling but confidently, to the ocean floor.

She would come back as a bride.

She turned in bed and a slashing pain in her shoulder ended the fantasies. Reality stomped back in, heavy footed.

She needed him. Despite the thrusts each time she moved slightly, she felt a wild, compulsive desire to lay her love before him. Yet tomorrow she would regret having done so. For a few ecstatic moments tonight, she might scatter to the winds a stack of dreams that some time might come true. The situation was so delicate; his feelings, she knew, so ephemeral. He could be suffering through a purgatory of wanting her or Lotus, but at this moment when his grief was only a thought away, of keeping Barbara alive forever.

Inside her stirred the competitiveness that had forced her to study and work long hours, and fired her with the ambition to research the oceans of the world. She would never turn against Barbara. However, she was not going to concede Greg to Lotus. She was going to come out with claws scratching. She was going to be a bitch. Every woman had vestiges of the primitive in her, and she was not going to let those nice, polite civilized ways submerge what was left of the Neolithic female.

First on Greg's agenda the next morning was a call on the Police Chief. Greg explained the situation and asked if an officer could stand guard outside Lynne's room. The Chief said he would do anything for "a fellow American from the mainland."

These Saipan people were Chamorros, seafarers of old like the New Englanders. They were intelligent, kindly and gracious. Proudly, they considered themselves Americans. They had hopes of becoming the fifty-first state. If not that, then possibly a part of California.

Greg tried to reach Lotus. The Hotel Japan in Tokyo advised that no one by that name had checked in. Next he placed a call to the *Marco Polo*. The Honolulu special operator informed him that the number was "temporarily out of service." He was worried and wished now he had stopped over in Tokyo. But time was closing in fast, and besides, there was nothing he could have done.

Frustrated, he drove in a rented car north to Tanapag Harbor. There he talked with the harbor master, presumably to verify that arrangements had been made for the arrival of the *Tai Peng*. He used the talk to establish that he was on the island. He asked questions about what kind of services one could expect on Ponape, a picturesque jungle island, with smiling people and bare-bosomed women, 900 miles southeast of Saipan. The harbor master was curious. What kind of cargo was the *Tai Peng* carrying? None, the ship was on a scientific voyage. What kind? Greg wished he could tell him but it was very hush-hush.

Next he drove to Susupe and received an effusive welcome at the Government House from the Governor of the Commonwealth of the Northern Mariana Islands. Greg confided in him the "true nature" of the *Tai Peng*'s mission. Each time he raised his voice slightly so that the secretaries would hear.

Later, he took a side road out of Chalan Kanoa to the Marianas Visitors' Bureau. There he made more inquiries about Ponape. The Visitors' Bureau asked if he would mind an interview with the *Sunday News*, a Gannett newspaper published in Guam? Well, there were certain aspects of the voyage he could not discuss, but he would enjoy talking in general about the trip. Off the record, he informed the Visitors' Bureau and everyone within hearing distance that the *Tai Peng* would begin sea-mining operations shortly off Ponape.

He took time to walk the beach at Susupe which had run red with blood on June 15, 1944, when the Americans invaded the island. Now every Sunday there was a cock fight where thousands of Americans and Japanese had fallen.

Afterward he returned to the Hyatt for lunch. Lynne gave him a hard time. She had dressed and wanted to sit on the beach. "I'm going to live as if nothing ever happened and nothing ever will," she said. "I can't live in fear. I won't live in fear."

Nonetheless she did promise to stay in her room until they boarded the Continental plane the next day for Honolulu.

Later in the afternoon, he got through to the *Marco Polo*. An excited Lotus came on the line. She had "made big deal" with the Japanese and had the computer guidance system aboard. She had accompanied two Japanese technicians who would need three to four days to "wire it up."

Janet followed and she was brief. "One of the seamen died this morning. I called a doctor in, but it was too late. They don't know the cause. Poor guy, he was only twenty-seven."

"He wasn't murdered?"

The question took her by surprise. "Murdered? Of course not. They are doing an autopsy. But it isn't anything to worry about."

He did worry, though, and far into the night.

40

Exhausted after fourteen hours in the air, Lynne and Greg deplaned in Honolulu. They took one of the little shuttle buses called wicki-wickis from the craft to the airport building where a very agitated Carlos Lopez met them.

"What's wrong?" Greg boasted he could smell trouble far off.

They edged their way through a mob and took two escalators down to baggage-claim areas 16 and 17. Greg ran tackle for Lynne, to protect her from possible collisions. Two husky Hawaiians were tossing bags back and forth and laughing heartily when they missed.

"Powder River wants you to call. Said we were about to be blown out of the water, whatever that meant."

In the taxi, Carlos continued, "Janet told you about the young crew guy who died?"

"Not much. Just that."

"Well, we've got a problem. The autopsy showed he died a natural death. Congenital heart trouble. But he also had hepatitis and looked a little yellow. No one knew he had it until the autopsy."

They passed the scene of the helicopter raid and Greg involuntarily shuddered. "So what's the problem?"

Carlos continued, "Well, seems Hawaii's got a deputy attorney general who wants to become governor, and he's out for all the publicity he can get. He's demanding an investigation. Says it's possible the fellow was suffering from a fatal tropical disease. Wants to quarantine the ship until the health authorities have looked into it. The crew's getting skittish. I called in the island's top authority on tropical diseases . . . not because there's anything to it . . . the medical examiner who handled the autopsy says it's ridiculous . . . but I thought we ought to have more ammunition . . ."

Greg breathed with relief. "That ought to wind it up."

The office was bedlam. He had no time to shave or shower. Janet hurried up with a sheaf of papers. Lotus kissed and hugged him. She wanted to show him the new computer. A few feet away FBI agent Manley nodded. In the back, unnoticed, stood Bill Madden. He raised a hand in greeting. Two men from the Honolulu Health Department got up hastily to make their way over.

He overheard Janet telling Lynne that the "fishbowl" had arrived the day before and per her instructions had been placed on a small ship Carson Mining had rented from the University of Hawaii. Any time Lynne wanted to take it down for a test run . . .

Manley was saying, "I came in to talk with Mr. McGraw." Greg reported McGraw was in Washington, D.C., and could he, Greg, fill in? No, Manley said, no, he would return. It was something concerning McGraw. The manner in which he said it led Greg to wonder what McGraw had done.

Janet said Laura had telephoned. Nothing important. She merely wanted to talk with her father. Greg instructed Janet to get Laura on the phone. While she dialed, she asked about China. Had he received the message she had forwarded from McGraw's informant? About the assassination plot? No, he hadn't, but the Chinese had had tight security and probably the Foreign Ministry had failed purposely to inform them, thinking the news would frighten them.

Laura came on the line bubbling as usual. In seconds she could raise him from the depths. "Am I bothering you, Daddy? I know you're busy."

"You're the most important call I'll make all day. How are you?"

She was fine and so was Rambunctious. "Do you want to talk to him?"

Rambunctious let out a bark that caused Greg to recoil.

"Did you hear him?" she asked.

"Did I hear him? They heard him in China."

"Daddy, school will be out in three weeks and I was thinking—"

"You get over here as fast as you can." By then the *Marco Polo* should be back in port.

Janet interrupted. "Dr. Randall's on the line."

"I've got to take a call, hon. I love you, darling."

He switched to the other line. "Hello, Emory. How are you?"

"Fine, thanks. I've got a development to report on Barbara. Nothing critical—at present. But her overall condition is deteriorating. Not rapidly but gradually."

Greg's voice trembled. "You mean—"

"I'm not God, Greg. I can't tell you how long. Maybe months. Maybe much longer."

Again, Janet broke in. "I've got Powder River holding, from Washington."

Greg nodded. "I'll call you in about ten days, Emory. Soon as we get back."

Hanging up, he said to Janet, "Give me a couple of minutes."

He leaned back and shut his eyes. *Barb. Barb.*

He squeezed the tears out, took a deep breath, and hit the desk hard. He asked Lynne to come on the line.

"Mike asked me to call, boy." Powder River sounded as if he were about to announce the death of a dear one. "He's off somewhere on something that had to be done. Said he was going to kill someone if he had to. I don't know what it was all about, but I didn't like it, boy. Not one whit."

Greg said, "Lynne's on the line."

They exchanged hellos, then Powder River said, "Before I tell you what Mike wants me to, I scouted around and learned that Tenneco filed a claim a few years ago on 20,000 square miles of the Golden Tide. Not acres, mind you, but miles."

Lynne broke in. "Did they work it?"

"Not as far as I can find out. Besides, they filed the claim with the State Department, and State rejected it on the grounds that State was not in the business of registering claims."

He coughed deeply. He sounded as if he had a bad cold. "Mike had two pieces of news—and they're bad, boy. I thought I ought to prepare you. The first is that we've got another spy on the *Marco Polo*. Mike didn't have a name yet but said it was someone who had known both of you for several years. Mike's informant said this party boasted he could get the sailing date and the exact destination. That makes three spies we got inside our tightly knit little organization. Three!"

"I don't believe it." Greg was adamant.

Lynne spoke up. "I don't, either. The informant's making it up —to get a bigger payout."

"I didn't believe it myself," Powder River said, "but Mike was positive. Said there was no mistake. Now about the second piece of news. It's worse yet. The *Kharkov* put to sea yesterday."

Greg reacted like a pitcher about to blow the game, then while Lynne asked questions, got hold of himself. "Lynne." He repeated her name several times before she heard him and quieted.

"Look, we're not pinned to the mat yet. If the *Kharkov*'s headed for Saipan, we've got nothing to worry about. If it's sailing for the Golden Tide, they've got a long way to go and we'll beat them there."

"If anybody can do it, you can," Powder River said. "I'm betting on you, boy. I have all through the years, and I've never lost a bet yet."

Greg cringed. He might this time. It would be close. If he gave orders this hour to prepare for setting to sea, they might possibly make it . . . if they got the breaks . . . if the weather was fair . . . if all of the complicated hardware performed as it should.

So the *Kharkov* had sailed. His worst fear had materialized.

Yet possibly, he might have a five-day advantage over the *Kharkov*. Lynne had come up with a technological breakthrough by which the vacuum could be placed on the ocean floor in a matter of hours. Previously, all sea-mining companies had needed about five days to get around 3,000 tons of pipe and an 80-ton-plus underwater pumping station in place. The *Kharkov*, of course, might have developed similar technology. Or stolen it.

With his air of superiority clearly showing, Captain Parker advised he could have the *Marco Polo* ready within three days. Colonel Montand said his mercenaries needed only an hour. He reminded Greg, though, that twelve frogmen flying in from Johannesburg, South Africa, would not arrive for four days. The underwater diver Lynne had chosen to man the submersible was scheduled to arrive in three days. He would come from Florida.

With Lynne at his side, Greg talked with the Tokyo technicians installing the computer guidance system. Lotus translated. They estimated they would have the system operational within seventy-two hours. At the same time they would install a detection system that would sound a warning if an attempt to use a laser beam was made again.

When Lynne learned that Greg was dispatching Lotus to Tucson to make certain everything was going well with Laura, she couldn't hide her feelings.

He said, "I would've asked you—but we can't spare you. Not even when we get back."

Her eyes searched his. "Are you being honest, Greg? With me? With yourself?"

He asked sharply, "What does that mean?"

She turned away. "It's none of my business really."

He was still troubled when Bill Madden came by. "How's everything?" Bill asked. "Anything you want to talk to me about?"

Greg shook his head. "Thanks for cooperating with them." He nodded toward Colonel Montand and the mercenaries.

"Glad to. Been wantin' to tell you how good you been to me.

Takin' me on and all and keepin' me when I know some folks wanted you to drop me. Sure do thank you."

Greg was embarrassed. Never before had Bill opened up.

Before Greg could answer, Carlos brought up two roughnecks borrowed from a Conoco oil-drilling team. When the pipe was put down through the "moon hole" into the ocean, they would join the sections, twenty-four and thirty-six feet long, by using hydraulic "tongs" that weighed several hundred pounds. Since the "tongs" dangled from cables and were constantly swinging around, it was a risky business that called for experience. Greg shook hands and welcomed them aboard.

Colonel Montand motioned to Greg and led him to the starboard side. "See that buoy out there, monsieur?"

About a hundred feet away, floating calmly, was a very ordinary-looking buoy.

"It was not there yesterday," Colonel Montand said. "Someone put it out during the night. It's the same as another that we fished up while you were in China. It's eavesdropping on us. It's picking up every word I say."

The buoy was a sound sensitive device, literally one big "bug." The Soviets had planted thousands around the world. Seldom did anyone notice them since buoys were common in all waters.

Obviously distraught, Janet hurried toward him. "Have you heard the radio?"

The authorities were probing into a report that there was a cholera epidemic aboard the *Marco Polo*. "It's all over the radio," she said. "They make it sound as if the seaman died of cholera."

A mercenary coming aboard the ship handed him a newspaper. The headline read: CHOLERA FEARED ABOARD SHIP. The story told of an ongoing investigation and then speculated that the feared disease could have been brought from India where there had been a recent outbreak. The story did carry a denial by the medical examiner.

The deputy attorney general had issued another statement. He would interview every crew member and all "mercenaries" on the *Marco Polo* to determine the ports from which they had sailed before signing on. For the first time, the fact the *Marco Polo* had soldiers-of-fortune aboard appeared in print, and this report was seized upon by various law enforcement agencies as calling for a thorough probe.

One story read: "Dr. Fleming pointed out that Asiatic cholera is very infectious and death can occur within the hour. If not treated, the mortality rate will go over 50 percent, and even when treated, 25 percent will die. Even if the patient recovers, he may suffer relapses, pneumonia and other infectious diseases that could result in death."

Greg found his heart pounding. "How can they do this?" he blurted out. If the campaign continued—and it had all the earmarks of a campaign—the *Marco Polo* might be quarantined for weeks.

"They're after publicity," Lynne said. "You can always find someone who will say anything you want him to if he's going to get a spread in a newspaper. You notice they talk about cholera as if we did have it on board, but at the same time they hedge. But who reads the hedging and the denials? You see the word, cholera, and it jumps out at you like a bulldog and that's all you remember."

Greg hunted up the two medics from the Honolulu Health Department who had been checking the water and food supplies, the galley and the latrines. They were prepared to give the ship a clean bill of health. They confirmed again that the autopsy definitely had established that the seaman had died of a heart condition and that he was suffering only from a mild case of hepatitis.

One explained, "He had epidemic infectious hepatitis, which sounds serious but isn't. It usually affects the young. The number of cases after age thirty is way down, and very seldom does anyone die of it. It's different with serum hepatitis. The fatalities from it will range from twenty to forty percent depending partly on age."

Greg showed him the newspaper article that set forth details about cholera. "I don't know why they slant it," the medic said. "Why don't they mention that the only way a person can contract cholera is if he consumes food or water contaminated by the stools of cholera patients."

He handed the newspaper back. "There's no way that hepatitis can be mistaken for cholera."

The Honolulu Health Department would issue another statement to the effect there was no cause for alarm, that the seaman had not died of cholera. The autopsy physician would reiterate his conclusions, and the expert on tropical diseases whom Carlos had employed would report his findings.

"We'll plant all three stories with the newspapers and radio and television stations," he told Lynne. "We should get good coverage tomorrow morning."

He didn't have until tomorrow morning.

That evening the crew of the *Marco Polo* walked off.

41

Mike McGraw was bushed but elated. He had gone thirty-six hours without sleep, working against time, going here and there, probing, asking questions, checking old records, talking, talking.

Now he sat in the back room of the Potomac Ferry bar chatting with the Swede. They both agreed that the Senators baseball team would have another year about like all the others.

McGraw was restless. It was 11:35 P.M. and his date with Nicolai Kazan had been for eleven. What was keeping his old friend? He asked to use the phone, to dial Abilene, Texas.

He got Sally out of bed and it was like old times, before they were married. They would call each other at any hour. He asked about the children and she said all they talked about was his homecoming. She hoped he could stay for months. Every time he left he sensed her apprehension, the old fear that this might be the last good-bye.

He was surprised when he turned and found Nicolai Kazan sitting quietly at the wrought-iron ice cream table. "I was getting worried about you, my friend."

"I couldn't get the car started. Dead battery. How's the family?"

"Good. I'm going home next week."

"Maybe not."

"What does that mean?"

"The crew walked off the ship tonight. There's been a big cholera scare. One of the girls in Disinformation set it up."

He recited in detail exactly what had transpired. Miss Maria Kaluga had posed as a correspondent out of New York for Universal News Service. As a courtesy to the Honolulu radio and television studios and the newspapers, she had dropped off copies of her "stories." She was a good investigative reporter and an excellent writer. She had dug up interviews with easily influenced persons and virtually "fed" them the quotes she wanted. She looked for politicians and others who would benefit by the exposure.

"Most of us don't think much of Disinformation," Kazan said. "It's like the Propaganda Section, a lot of wasted work. But she's changing some minds at the Embassy."

McGraw was thrown. "How long can she keep it going?"

"I'd say only a few days unless she comes up with a new development."

He shifted about. "I've got a lot to report and I'd better get with it. Got a big day coming tomorrow. What about a beer, you cheapskate?"

McGraw got a beer and a Pepsi from the bar. While waiting, he glanced idly about. No one seemed suspect. But that meant nothing.

Kazan took a long swig. "First," he said, "General Schepnov has asked the Wet Section—they're the assassination teams—to save day after tomorrow for him. He has a problem to take care of."

"Who?" McGraw asked.

"Could be his secretary. She peddles everything to the FBI, but they've known that since they hired her. Of course, that's why they hired her."

The General, Kazan continued, was disturbed because Rashid Jumeira had failed to find one Terri Kapiolani, the party Nataya had reported was her gopher. The General suspected that Nataya had given him a fictitious name.

Kazan finished the beer and refused an offer of another. "We've got a lot of movement based on the assumption the

Marco Polo was putting out to sea soon. Now that the crew's walked off . . . well, anyway, we've got terrorists flying in from Beirut, from a Libyan training camp, from the PLO and from a Sandinista hideout in Cuba, on the far side, near Santiago. Moscow has let the General know if he needs more, all he has to do is to ask. No limit."

McGraw looked up. "For exactly what?"

Kazan had no idea. No one had discussed assignments. "I do know that the submarine off Honolulu has been given orders to follow the *Marco Polo* and keep the listening post at Da Nang informed."

Da Nang was the former U.S. airfield in Vietnam, now occupied by the Soviets. Kazan reported further that TU-95 Bears, if needed, would be available to fly reconnaissance missions from carrier ships. At present they were spying on Hong Kong, Japan and the Philippines.

"The Soviet Pacific fleet has been put at the disposal of the General. Do you have any idea what that means? It's a matter of record. They've announced it—to scare the world. Fifty major ships, fifty amphibious ones, a hundred subs and I would guess, somewhere around ten thousand marines."

McGraw came up as if rocket propelled. "Don't tell me they're going to sink the *Marco Polo*?"

Kazan shook his head. "They can't—without starting a nuclear war. They're not going that far. But they can lead the United States into thinking they plan to. It's all a matter of which government can outbluff the other one."

"Washington isn't even supporting us."

Kazan opened his palms in a hopeless gesture, "I know. Well, as I said, we've got a lot of movement. The KGB is moving ten agents from the Silicon Valley to Honolulu. They fly out of San Francisco tomorrow morning. Oh, yes, did I mention that the *Kharkov* will dock at Cam Ranh and wait there for instructions?"

Cam Ranh also had been a U.S. base in Vietnam, an immense one.

"That's a relief," McGraw said. "We figured it was headed for a mine field."

"They had to get it out of Vladivostok, closer, so they can maneuver better. I figure the *Kharkov* will get refueled and outfitted at Cam Ranh—take possibly two or three days—and then begin actual mining."

McGraw turned quiet. "What about the new mole we got inside us? Does he have a name?"

Kazan rose. He had to get home. "I haven't heard one. If I do, I'll get in touch with you."

McGraw took from an inside coat pocket a legal-sized envelope which he handed Kazan. "I know you're doing this more for old times than money, but you might as well have it. Five thousand. That makes ten all told, but you should have a bonus and I'll see what can be worked out."

Kazan nodded. "Old times. Yes, for old times. They were great, weren't they, Mike? A good friend you've been all through the years. I don't have any left except you. They're all dead. When I go to Moscow I have to go out to the cemetery to see them."

McGraw put an arm about him. "Old times," he mumbled.

Kazan left the office as quietly as he had come. As he closed the door, he was still nodding his head, a broad smile sweeping his face.

That was the last McGraw ever saw of him. He vanished without a trace. His body was never found. The Embassy reported him missing, but it was only a routine report. The District of Columbia police filed it on the chance there might be a development.

Only the Wet Section knew.

42

McGraw remained in the back room of the bar. He slouched far down in the chair and closed his eyes. He had about thirty minutes to wait before he tightened the noose about Jonathan Switzer. He had never seen the man, not even a picture of him, but he had formed a definite image from what Greg had told him.

He could scarcely wait for the "kill." He felt exhilarated, as he invariably did after he had stalked a prey and brought him to bay.

He had phoned Jonathan Switzer that morning. Switzer had said, "Switzer here," as if God himself were speaking.

McGraw waited until Switzer repeated himself. It was good to get the adversary slightly off base. McGraw then said, "I'm a good friend of Bill Brockton." He let that sink in before continuing, "Just in town for the day, and Bill said to look you up . . . about that business matter. We're ready to ante up a lot more."

Switzer was wary. "Uh-huh. You work with Bill?"

"Yeah, we're old friends. Bill must've told you about me. Sam Baxter."

Switzer dropped his voice. "I was talking with him yesterday. He didn't say anything . . ."

McGraw decided to gamble. "Forget it, Mr. Switzer. I understand. It's just that Bill's leaving for Saipan . . . be gone a month . . . emergency, just came up. Well, it was good talking with you."

Switzer said quickly, "Wait a minute. I'm looking at my calendar . . . and I've got tonight free. What about the Mayflower around eight?"

McGraw took a tone that brooked no opposition. If he had guessed right, he held the upper hand. "There's a bar at the end of Wisconsin. The Potomac Ferry. Twelve-thirty. The back room."

"Midnight!" Switzer was taken aback.

"I'll explain when I see you. Okay?"

Switzer hesitated. "I guess it's all right. Rather unusual."

"I'd say all of it was unusual, wouldn't you?"

Switzer didn't know what to say to that. McGraw said, "I'll see you tonight then. The Potomac Ferry. Twelve-thirty. Back room."

Jonathan Switzer was not at all what McGraw had expected. They never were. The Swede took the drink orders. Switzer had a bourbon on the rocks and McGraw, a Pepsi.

"Thank you for coming," McGraw said pleasantly.

Switzer nodded. He was busy taking stock of the room—and McGraw. "How's Bill?" he asked idly.

McGraw answered slowly, "He seemed okay when you had lunch with him last week. Didn't you think so?"

Switzer stared at him and continued staring as the Swede brought the drinks. "I thought, from what you said on the phone . . ."

McGraw smiled. "I've never met the man."

Switzer knocked over the bourbon getting to his feet. "What're you trying to pull?"

McGraw brought his hand out from under the coat flap. The hand held a shiny .38. "Sit down. We're going to have a nice, quiet talk."

Switzer had frozen. McGraw raised his voice. "I'm a nervous person. Terribly jittery."

Switzer dropped his weight back into the straight chair. He was sweating. He pulled his tie loose. "Don't push me. Don't push me." His fear was overridden suddenly by a burst of anger. "You'll go to prison for this, Baxter. Threatening a government official with a gun. A high government official. Maybe you don't know I head up the State Department."

He looked around wildly for the door.

"Don't get ideas," McGraw said calmly.

Switzer continued, "I'm an old friend of the Attorney General and if he knew about this, he'd put you in prison so fast you wouldn't know what happened."

He got back on his feet. "We'll forget about tonight, Baxter. Right? I know how it is. I've been hungry, too."

McGraw fired a shot into the ceiling. Switzer's elevator cable snapped. He dropped into the chair so hard the blow rocked the room. The Swede looked in, wide-eyed. "Little accident," McGraw explained. "I was fooling around and it went off. Sorry about that."

The Swede looked relieved. "No problem." Hurriedly he retreated.

"Now where were we?" McGraw asked quietly. "Oh, yes, I'm going to state a few blunt facts. I don't want any denials, no arguments. I don't want you to break in until I finish."

He waited a few moments to give Switzer time for nervousness to set in.

McGraw continued, "You own a small office building in Indianapolis. I was there yesterday and saw it and I'd guess it's worth about a million. I asked myself how you could have saved enough money to buy it. I figure you make maybe forty, fifty thousand. Take a long time to save up a hundred thousand or two to put down."

He had the revolver lying loosely in his lap. He still had a finger, though, about the trigger. Switzer was casing it, his thoughts transparent.

"Maybe you'd like to find out how fast I can bring this weapon up and fire it?"

Switzer's body shook in spasms. McGraw smiled. "I'm not interested in how you got the building. But right now you're about to lose it, and good old Bill Brockton of W.W.W., he's been paying the interest. Twenty-two percent, $32,114 a month. Now there's the kind of friend to have."

Switzer came alive and shouted, "I gave him a note for every dime of it. It has nothing to do with W.W.W."

McGraw rose. "I think you'd have a hard time convincing your old friend, the Attorney General."

Switzer screamed, "You damn, rotten, sneaking, no good creep. You won't get away with this. I'll see you go to prison for life."

McGraw let him run down. "Nobody's going to prison, Switzer —not if you're willing to cooperate a little."

Switzer was instantly suspicious. "Like what? I'm not paying you a nickel. Not a nickel."

"I don't want your nickels. But I tell you what you're going to do. You're going to your office tomorrow and draw up a White Paper on the Law of the Sea. You're going to say you've been studying the situation in the light of recent developments—and this country's need for its own source of minerals—and you've decided this nation should encourage and assist American businesses to engage immediately in the mining of the seabeds. You got that, Switzer?"

"Why, you bastard!" Switzer was yelling. "You're nothing but a stooge for Carson Mining and that clown Wilson. You want me to free the *Marco Polo* for piracy on the high seas, that would start World War III."

McGraw looked at him a long moment. "Switzer," he began slowly, "I've been around Washington for more than twenty years and I love this city. Most of the people here are like those in any town in America. They work damn hard and there's nothing they wouldn't do for this country."

He took a deep breath. "But now and then a guy comes along who'd sell his mother and country out for a hunk of money. We saw it in Abscam.

"I've got a personal goal," McGraw continued. "It's to eliminate evil whenever I come across it—and I'm convinced the most effective way is to kill the bastards on the spot. No waiting a year, two years, three . . . no technicalities . . . no bleeding-heart judges. Don't worry. I'm not killing you here. I promised the Swede I'd take you at least a block away."

He laughed low. "Look, Switzer, if I don't read about your White Paper in the Washington *Post* morning after tomorrow, I'm coming for you. I haven't done my Boy Scout good deed yet this year, and I've been waiting for some bastard to come along."

Unexpectedly, Switzer relaxed. An evil, little smile crept into his pig eyes. "All right, Baxter—or whatever your name is—I'll give you your White Paper—and you keep any information you have to yourself. It's a deal, huh?"

McGraw nodded. There was a trick here somewhere.

Switzer continued, "It doesn't matter anymore. I guess you don't know that the directors of Massachusetts Diversified voted last evening to cut off all funds from Carson. I personally saw to it. I called everybody on the Board. The *Marco Polo* will never sail, Baxter. Gregory Wilson can't pay the bills. Carson will be in bankruptcy within a month."

43

Greg hung up the phone in shock. His body was trembling.

Karl had broken the news gently and sorrowfully. "Switzer put the fear of God into them, talked about World War III, disloyalty to one's country, flying in the face of government. I tried to reason with them, but they were running too scared. And this thing about cholera. It's been in the papers."

"I know you did your best." Greg was too stunned to think.

"They want you to know they haven't stopped the project. Just postponed it. Give everyone a chance to think it through. They're meeting in a couple of weeks and want you and Lynne here."

"Two weeks . . . too late. The *Kharkov*'s on its way."

"I know . . . I know. We could've made history, you and me . . . history. But it was a good try. We did all we could."

Long after he put the receiver down, Greg sat in a stupor. His mind was a shambles, his thinking wiped out, paralyzed.

"What do we do now?" Lynne asked.

He didn't hear. He didn't know she was sitting across the desk from him. The early morning sun laid down a swatch of brilliant light between them.

"Greg," she said gently and he looked up.

"Yes," he answered. "That was Karl . . . in Boston."

"I heard. How much do we need?"

Colonel Montand materialized in the doorway. "Excuse me, please," he said to Lynne and turned to Greg. "I must talk with you, monsieur."

"Come in," Greg said. He took a deep breath and straightened in the swivel. He hit the desk hard with a fist. The Colonel was as startled as Lynne.

Greg got to his feet, unbuttoned his shirt and took it off. His undershirt was soaked with perspiration although the day was not yet that hot. "The bastards want to stop us." His voice could be heard far out on deck. "But they're not going to. Nothing's going to stop us."

"Monsieur," the Colonel began tentatively, "my men read about it in the morning paper . . . your directors have cut off the money."

"I don't have to depend on the rat finks. I'll get the money."

The Colonel firmed up his voice. "My men are threatening to walk off . . . if there is no money. I tried to talk with them, but they're worked up. They want to get a lawyer and file a lien on the ship."

Greg stood a second transfixed. "You tell them that the first guy who walks off gets a bullet in his back."

"Please, Greg." Lynne shook her head ever so slightly, the way Barb would have.

He lowered his voice. "All right, get them together on deck right away and I'll talk with them."

The Colonel continued standing. "That might not be wise, monsieur. They lose their heads if they think they're being taken advantage of."

"Get them together."

The Colonel nodded. "Yes, monsieur."

When he had gone, Lynne asked, "What about the money?" He shrugged and sat down.

"Any word from China?" she asked.

"I'm expecting a card at Christmas." He fell serious. "Funny, I've been expecting this, but it's like a friend you know who's going to die. When it actually happens, it's a shock."

He saw her sadness. "Don't worry, we'll get the money somehow."

Janet called on the intercom. Mike McGraw was on the line.

He never began with pleasantries, not even a hello. "I had a little talk with your friend, Switzer, and he's changed his mind. He's getting up a White Paper today that'll urge the administration to give aid and assistance to companies engaged in sea mining. It'll be in the Washington *Post* tomorrow."

"What'd you do, threaten to kill him?"

McGraw was hurt. "I don't know why you think . . ."

"It's too late. The Board—"

"He told me, but at least we've got the go-ahead from the government if you can get the *Marco Polo* out to sea."

"Switzer is not the government. We've got to get the President . . . the Secretary of State . . . someone with authority. Anyway, he may not come through with the paper."

"He will."

"So you did threaten him? Look, McGraw, no gunplay. We've got enough problems."

McGraw reported on two developments. The *Kharkov* would put into Cam Ranh, Vietnam. He had no information about a sailing date from that port. He said the newspaper woman Greg had asked him to check on had been a Tass correspondent in Washington for seven years. What was more, the Universal News she said she worked for was the Hearst night wire service before the Hearst chain closed it out several years ago.

McGraw asked if Greg suspected anyone of being the third spy inside Carson Mining.

"I don't believe there is a third one," Greg said flatly. "I doubt if there is a second. I know there is one, and I know who it is."

He refused to yield to McGraw's pressure to divulge a name. "I'll let you know soon. In a day or two. Before we sail."

The moment he hung up, Lynne asked in surprise, "You know?"

"Look, I can't tell you now, but when I do you'll understand why I can't."

Colonel Montand came in to report the mercenaries were assembled on the main deck.

They were squatting and sprawling about. A few were dozing or pretending to. Others looked as if they would enjoy hanging him. He thought he had never seen such a scurrilous bunch. They would scare Dracula.

He gave them his best glower. "I understand you're threatening to walk off because you haven't been paid. Let me tell you something, your pay isn't due until Friday—and you'll get every dollar you've got coming. Every dollar. I don't like your attitude one damn bit. You're not being fair. We made a deal, and I expect you to live up to it the same as I will. You read something in a newspaper and believe it. I'm amazed at your stupidity. You fought in

Angola and Biafra and Zimbabwe and you know what was printed then. A bunch of lies. Any questions?"

One lean six-footer with a pink slash across a cheek spoke up. "You tellin' us your backers didn't vote to cut you off?"

"We've got a lot of backers. Germans, Japanese—and Carson Mining earned millions last year. I don't care what they did back in Boston. What else can you expect out of Boston?"

That got a laugh. A squat runt with a bull neck and head to match asked, "What's the lady got to say? You told us she was running the ship."

Lynne had been taking it all in from the deck rail. She walked over to stand beside Greg. "He's telling you the gospel truth. We've got plenty of money to meet payrolls, take care of suppliers and put to sea."

They took a vote by show of hands and agreed unanimously to stay aboard. They gathered around Lynne and Greg asking questions. The two had been "accepted."

Back in Greg's office they both sank into chairs, exhausted. "I've never lied before," Lynne said. "Not on anything important. How much have we got in the bank?"

"Not in the bank. In my pocket. About thirty thousand. I was afraid the account might be blocked. We need another fifty thousand."

Lotus appeared and as usual was in good spirits. She was a night person and slept until noon. They brought her up to date on events.

"How much got have?"

"Fifty thousand."

She thought that over. "I get twenty thousand, maybe little more. Hong Kong bank. Carson got credit."

"You're not there. You can't sign for it."

Lotus smiled. "You no think I honorable woman. Bank think am. I phone. Banker, he say no, no, no. I say yes, yes, yes. He cable money. Honorable person."

"You mean you can get twenty thousand dollars on a phone call?"

"Maybe little more, Grig. I see."

Lynne tensed. When Lotus said "Grig," the name came out as

an endearment. And why didn't she pull her cheongsam together?

Greg was excited. "We're getting there. Now if I can come up with thirty thousand."

"What about Powder River and Carlos? Would they advance it?"

He thought that was a possibility.

He decided first he had to get a crew together and that meant quashing the cholera story. He asked Lynne to come along. They took a taxi to the 700 block of Alakea where the Seafarers International Union, the Sailors Union of the Pacific, the Masters Mates and Pilots, the Marine Firemen's Union and others had offices.

At the first headquarters, a bulky girl receptionist tried to stop them. "There's a meeting going on in there."

Greg brushed by her. "They're expecting us. I'm the speaker."

The two barged in on fifteen men lined up on chairs around a small room painted a glistening white that under neon lights hit the eyes hard. They looked up curiously at first, then their expressions turned nasty over the interruption.

Before anyone could speak, Greg said, "We're from the *Marco Polo* and I want to tell you the facts about the cholera story you've been hearing."

Several protested but Greg talked over them. "We're going on a secret mission out into the Pacific, and the Russians are trying to stop us."

At the word, Russians, they fell quiet. Most of the unions were more American than the exclusive clubs of the wealthy.

They listened intently. "So what happens is this—the Russians send in a woman by the name of Maria Kaluga. She pretends she's with a news service out of New York. I'll tell you who she is. She was a correspondent in Washington for seven years with Tass, the Russian news service. She started these rumors about cholera. She went to the radio and television stations and the newspapers and acted as if she wanted to help, and planted these lies. Your own health department said there was nothing to them, and I invite you to hire a physician and tell him you want him to investigate. We'll cooperate with any doctor you name. Think it over.

We're not here to sell you a bill of goods. You do your own investigating. That's all we ask. Thank you."

He gave the same speech at a union hiring hall to about forty surprised members waiting for a work call. When he and Lynne had finished with the unions, they went to a newspaper office where again he got by the receptionist—this time a Donna Douglas beauty—and bearded a city editor.

"She says she's from Universal News Service, which, as you know, the Hearst newspapers closed down the same time they merged their International News Service with United Press. If you'll call the National Press Club in Washington, they'll tell you she was with Tass for seven years.

"Sure, she's a good writer and investigative reporter. The Soviets don't pick amateurs. I know the cholera rumor was a good story, but you've played it out and all I'm asking is that you give the same space to your own authorities. If you don't believe them, then get a doctor you know and start your own investigation. We want this cleared up. We can't sail until it is."

At each newspaper the city editor promised fair treatment. Each called the National Press Club and in the next editions, they carried a story about a former Tass correspondent who had masqueraded as a reporter for a deceased wire service.

In the meantime Greg and Lynne had talked by phone with Carlos and arranged to meet him for lunch at Patti's in the Ala Moana Mall. Patti's had Peking ducks hanging in the windows and Chinese lamps inside which cast a yellow, sinful glow. The place was mobbed.

While they waited, Lynne looked up at Greg with adoration that she made no attempt to conceal. "You're fabulous. Nothing daunts you, nothing stops you."

Memories of Barbara surged back. So many times she had said something like that.

At lunch over noodles, Carlos promised an advance of fifteen thousand dollars. Earlier over the phone from Washington, Powder River had come through with a matching fifteen thousand.

Rashid Jumeira roamed about outside Patti's. He estimated they would be there at least a half hour. He sauntered down to Mrs. Fields Chocolate Chippery and bought cookies, then went into Lyn's Delicatessen for a cup of coffee.

Ten minutes later he left and stopped outside briefly to enjoy the frenetic scene. The sidewalks were mobbed with teenagers. The Mall was their favorite hangout. They were in shorts, jeans and T-shirts. All were talking at the same time. Some had radios blasting forth the latest disco numbers. There was much laughter and shouting. They were of all cultures, Anglo and Japanese and Chinese and Portuguese and Hawaiian, but melded by geography and the same interests into one basic life-style.

He wandered on. By now he should have grown impatient and frustrated by the hours he had spent in stalking Wilson and Kennedy. Some agents would have been driven by desperation to take a pot shot. That was one reason why there were so many dead ones.

It was difficult to isolate a target in a crowded city such as Honolulu. One never pressed. One missed opportunities and accepted the fact that one would miss them. Then one day the perfect arrangement would shape up. Usually not more than two shots would be needed. More would attract attention and would be the mark of an amateur who was swept up in the thrill of the overkill. Two shots could be an automobile backfiring or merely the quick, low sounds that sped in and out of one's consciousness without that little signal popping up requesting an analysis.

He glanced in Patti's again. They were finishing. He moved to one side, to the adjoining storefront, and leaned casually against a wall. He sorted out his thoughts, which he did these days with effort. Anya had died of pneumonia in Mexico City. Only yesterday the General had broken the news. The General knew no details but would put through an urgent request for more to the Embassy in Mexico City. He would ask for a keepsake for Rashid.

Rashid had broken down. For the first time in his life, he had wept. He had loved Anya as he had no other woman. When he was finished with this mission, he would fly to Mexico City and learn what he could about her death.

Kennedy emerged first into the crowded street outside, then Wilson, then the Mexican. Kennedy was a good-looking woman, about Anya's age. Rashid experienced a sudden pang. He regretted he had to kill her. She even walked a little like Anya.

Rashid sauntered after them, weaving in and out of the milling throng, keeping a distance of fifty feet or so. He knew they were headed for a vast open area where they had left their car. A parking lot was ideal for a killing. There would be a few parties coming and going, yet not so many but what his quarry should be in the open any number of times. After firing his shots, he could easily escape by ducking low around the cars.

He noted then a man following them. He was tall and slender, in his twenties, with blond features. There could be no doubt that he, too, was running a surveillance, from the way he kept glancing about. He "hugged" them, staying only a few feet behind, and Rashid instinctively knew he was their own private guard.

Rashid stopped, took a deep breath in frustration, and then wandered off. He had no intention of engaging in a shoot-out.

Greg leaned against the bulwark looking out at the lights of the Coast Guard cutter splashing anchor off Sand Island. Nearby, great cranes that fed the hungry mouths of the freighters beneath them towered silhouetted against puffy-cheeked white clouds. A cool, soft breeze had come up and there was the gentle lapping of the water against the *Marco Polo*'s tired, old hull. He knew it was tired from the constant groaning.

Far out to sea lights twinkled, harbingers of ships passing in the night. Mysterious ships on a mysterious ocean, hiding secrets, and the *Marco Polo* would be one of them in a couple of days.

He had come from talking over the phone with Laura, and his thoughts moved in on her and Barbara. Once the *Marco Polo* had completed its mission and returned to port, he had hard decisions to make, and he was not up to them. He might command a historic voyage with Lynne's expertise, but no matter which way he turned in his own life, he would head into the eye of the hurricane . . . emotionally and physically.

He felt perfectly capable of rearing Laura alone. They had a deep love that bound them so closely that neither would ever do anything to destroy it. Laura would never yield in her adolescent years to a temptation that would hurt him—or the memory of a mother she had loved with such passion—any more than he would use drugs or alcohol or commit any act that would cause her grief.

Yet he couldn't take her to far-off places with him and would have to give up his work. Walk away not only from his dreams but Barbara's, too. Barbara wouldn't want him to do that. He was positive she wouldn't.

The most logical alternative would be to find a woman friend who would live with Laura.

Yet he was virile and with the passing of time realized it ever more. The buildup could be intense, compulsive. He wondered why human beings were constructed in such fashion, a throttle stuck at times on a floorboard, a car careening almost out of control.

He remembered the night they had lain side by side, and Barbara saying that without sex there would be no wine and candlelight, no lingering kisses, no great stirring of music, no pounding of surf, no waiting anxiously for one to return home, no tender, compassionate caring between man and woman, no growing old together with vintage memories. The song of birds would be heard but at a great distance, and the sunsets faded, and a new car only a means of getting from here to there. We would be eunuchs going about our jobs and doing them well but without ever knowing the happiness of soaring beyond one's self.

From out of the past he remembered Dr. Randall saying, "Why don't you sit down some evening when it's quiet and imagine you're talking this over with Barbara. After thirteen years of living and loving together you know what she would say if she were conscious."

He would do that, once he brought the *Marco Polo* back to port.

He must concentrate on the present. No crew member had returned. Lotus said she could arrange by phone to hire a crew in Hong Kong and Singapore, but there was no time to procure visas. Too, it would be non-union and there would be serious conflicts. Lotus was amazing. Seemingly, there was no problem she could not solve, and the odd part was that she was seldom serious and never appeared to give much thought to a baffling situation.

As if thinking could produce her, she glided silently up alongside him. He was startled and drew away. She laughed. Laughter was such a part of her. "I want tell, Grig, got money. Got twenty-five thousand dollars. Here in morning."

He was ecstatic. "Five thousand more than we need."

She was pleased that he was pleased. In the light from other ships, her eyes lit up. "Banker happy send to honorable woman."

She was teasing and he feinted a punch. "I'll get you a bonus for this."

They heard a heavy footfall behind them and turned to find Carlos approaching. He was breathing heavily. "Nobody's seen Bill Madden since last night, and his cabin looks like it has been ransacked. He said something yesterday to Colonel Montand about being threatened, but wandered off when the Colonel asked questions. I think we'd better get the FBI in."

44

In answer to Greg's phone call, FBI Agent Jim Manley arrived on the *Marco Polo* a little after 8 A.M. He had worked a case all night and was in need of sleep and a shave.

He refused breakfast but settled for several cups of black coffee. He joined Greg, Lynne, Janet and Colonel Montand at a table in a corridor that served as the ship's dining quarters.

Greg said to Manley, "Madden never left the ship except for Monday nights when he caught a bus out on Nimitz and went to a movie. He had no friends here in Honolulu since he couldn't get away from his work. He didn't drink and didn't use drugs. There's no explaining it."

"How much did he know about what was going on?" Manley asked.

Lynne answered, "He had access to the entire vessel, of course, the computers, the storage vaults, the equipment in the hold, all of that, but he didn't have the background to understand the technology and wasn't interested. He'd only laugh when I tried to explain something."

Manley persisted. "But he could've taken classified documents with him, couldn't he, without understanding them?"

Greg was incensed. "His character and integrity are beyond question."

Manley said softly, "I didn't mean to suggest he took anything on his own volition. But he could have with a gun in his back. He could be somewhere this minute in need of our help. For him as well as for you, I have to ask questions."

Janet spoke up. "I wasn't going to bring it up, but he had a phone call day before yesterday and he was terribly upset. I tried to talk to him, but he wandered out without saying anything."

Greg asked her to get each day's telephone tapes. When she brought them, he turned them over to Manley. "We've been taping all phone calls," he explained, "since Janet was threatened one night."

Greg spent the morning telephoning the crew members. They were noncommittal. They were waiting to hear the results of an investigation by three physicians employed by the unions.

Shortly after lunch, Mike McGraw arrived, brandishing a copy of the Washington *Post*. A headline on page three read:

STATE REVERSES SEA-MINING POLICY,
ASKS PRESIDENT TO SET UP CONTROLS

McGraw had a broad smile, an effect that occurred about as often as a moon eclipse. "I ought to have a bonus for this."

"You'll get it," Greg promised. "You've earned it, although the way you've earned it—"

McGraw interrupted. "Powder River's busting his ass trying to get to the President. If the President was to establish a firm policy and spell out the details . . ."

Greg's elation over McGraw's accomplishment was dashed an hour later when Karl called from Boston. There was a newspaper woman by the name of Maria Kaluga, from Universal News Service, New York, who was in Boston calling personally on the directors. She asked each his reaction to a report that the *Marco Polo* would sail despite the decision of Massachusetts Diversified to cut off funds.

"They're mad as hell that you'd defy them," Karl said. "They're talking to lawyers about getting out an injunction to stop the ship from sailing. I don't know whether they can, but I thought you ought to know."

Greg asked Janet to hold all calls, and shut himself up in his office. He placed one phone call after another. He had to locate someone of influence who would wave a red flag before the President. Powder River was getting nowhere in Washington.

He talked with Hawaii's governor and two senators. He cited a study by the State of Hawaii that indicated sea mining would open up six thousand new jobs in the state, and pointed out that Carson was presently employing six hundred on the construction of a metal-extracting refinery at Lahaina. Afterward, he tracked down Arizona's two senators and one in Idaho whom he knew from his river-running days.

Next he placed a call to Tokyo, to the multimillionaire financier who was the absentee owner of many of Waikiki's major hotels. Greg found him most receptive. He wanted to do anything he could for Hawaii, and in addition, he thought a presidential directive would be in Japan's best interests. He knew the Prime Minister and would request him to take up the matter with Japan's Ambassador in Washington.

Lynne stopped by to offer a suggestion. "Do you remember a very cordial but rather shy Board member back in Boston by the name of Bob McLean? Karl said he inherited fifty million."

Greg nodded and she continued, "Remember, Karl said he gets invited to the White House often. I got his number from the file."

"Why don't you call him?" Greg asked. "You're the Boston pinup."

She smiled and reached for the phone. McLean, his secretary said, was in an important meeting but she would see. He immediately came on the line and was as friendly as Lynne remembered. He regretted Mass. had cut off the funds. He had voted against the proposal. She explained in concise detail why she had called.

"So happens I'm having dinner tonight at the White House," he said, "but it wouldn't be proper for me to discuss business at a social gathering. I do hope you understand."

She agreed but persisted. Wouldn't it be proper if the President himself discussed politics or business?

"I'd like to help, Dr. Kennedy. I honestly would." He hesitated. "No, it wouldn't be right . . . as a guest in my host's home."

Greg had seldom seen her as crestfallen. "He'll be right there talking with the President, and all he'd have to do . . . You should've talked to him. Men do better talking with men."

"Talk about me being a male chauvinist!"

45

At FBI agent Manley's insistence, McGraw saw him in Greg's office. McGraw had no idea why Manley wanted to talk with him. He detested the man since he detested the FBI. In his career in the CIA he had had several run-ins with that agency. He had hoped Greg would stay, but Greg left to make phone calls.

Manley did nothing to banish McGraw's prejudices. Manley said abruptly, "I'll get right down to it. You're getting in our way and we can't have it. We won't have it. We can take legal action and have you arrested for obstructing justice."

McGraw came bolt upright. "What the hell are you talking about?"

"Don't give me that innocent act. I was there. I saw you try to kill Miss Fussen."

McGraw slouched back down. "Oh, that. I'm not admitting to anything. You understand that? I thought you had something important to talk about. What's one more Soviet bitch?"

Manley's lips tightened. "The Bureau is running several major espionage investigations that are vital to this nation's security. One of the key subjects, as you well know, is Nataya Fussen. When we have what we want, we will apprehend her—but not before we get the evidence we need to convict and the identification of everyone working with her. You could blow it. You almost did. I want your solemn promise, McGraw, you will not take matters into your own hands again."

McGraw shrugged. "If you had the goods on me, you would've hauled me into court. You just imagine you saw me. I was in Washington, D.C., that day, and I've got witnesses to prove it."

"How do you know what day it was if you weren't there?"

McGraw got to his feet. "Take any day you want. I can prove I was thousands of miles away."

He paused a moment, choosing his words. "Manley, let me give you something to think about. The FBI's okay and the courts are, too, but they move like dinosaurs. They've outlived their time. They let too many criminals slip by. So I figure we need to get back to the vigilantes of the Old West. String them up, shoot them down, and cut out the cancer wherever we find it. I wasn't there that day, but I wish whoever was had had better aim. The FBI should haul him up on the carpet for being such a poor marksman."

He walked slowly toward the door. "You don't get any promises out of me. If the government would see it my way, we'd get rid of every spy in this country quick. And most of the criminals."

"Hold it," Manley said. "How'd you know we were running a surveillance on Nataya Fussen?"

McGraw thought the question over. "I shouldn't say anything, but let's put it this way. It's possible that the man who took the shot—which was not me, you understand—figured if he ran a surveillance on you, you might possibly lead him to someone."

He slammed the door behind him.

Mike McGraw had a busy day. Late that afternoon, he wandered into Janet's office, shut the door and locked it. He was carrying a new, expensive attaché case.

"What're you doing?" She disliked the man and was brusque. Usually he acted as if she did not exist.

"I want to talk with you about a security matter—in confidence."

"Let me finish this letter." She resumed typing. She enjoyed keeping him waiting.

He dropped a tired body into a deep leather chair alongside the desk. He was so close he could touch her without moving. He slouched down and fixed on her. She was too lanky for his tastes. Women were all alike. They preferred the skeleton look. When Sally threatened to take off ten pounds, he told her if she did he would divorce her.

She pulled the page out of the typewriter with a flourish and placed it flat on the desk. "What can I do for you?"

He took his time. "You remember when my stoolie in Washington called you about an assassination plot against Lynne and Greg when they were in China?"

"What about it?"

"You put in several calls to inform the authorities. You phoned our office in Hong Kong and when no one answered, you called the China airlines in Guangzhou and got a woman who spoke Cantonese and you waited and a woman who spoke English came on."

He lit a cigarette. "Mind?"

"Not if you open the door."

He took a long haul, then stubbed the cigarette out. From his attaché case he brought forth a small Sony recorder and several tape cartridges. "These are that day's telephone tapes."

"Look, I've got a stack of letters to type up. Get to the point."

"I'm getting there. Okay, the airline said Mr. Wilson had left some time before for Beijing. Next you called the Peking Hotel and a receptionist checked with a floor boy and reported Mr. Wilson and Miss Kennedy had left shortly before. I can play the tape if you want me to."

Her hands were busy with each other. "I'm going to have to ask you to leave, Mr. McGraw. I can't sit here listening to this chatter about nothing."

"I'm getting there," he repeated caustically. "Now I think you should listen to this next tape." He dropped it into the recorder. "You called the Foreign Office . . ."

He turned the recording up. *"This is the Foreign Minister's Office, Miss Kim speaking."*

The tape continued turning but there was no further talk.

"You may remember that Carlos Lopez came in and heard you talking with Miss Kim. You reported to him what she allegedly said. But strangely the tape went dead. How do you explain that?"

She wet her lips. "I don't know anything about these gadgets. They're always breaking down."

He stopped the tape. "I know what happened, Miss Stowe. When Miss Kim came on, you pressed down on the button, breaking the phone connection, but you pretended you were still talking to her, telling her about the murder plot."

She was on her feet screaming. "Get out of here! You're framing me! That's what you're doing. I've been suspicious of you all along."

McGraw let a little wicked smile show. Damn, it was fun watching them squirm. The more they turned on the spit, the more he enjoyed it. "You're being very rude, Miss Stowe. I haven't finished."

"Leave me alone!" she shouted and fell back into the steno chair. She stared into a dark corner of the cabin, anywhere to escape his boring, merciless eyes. "You wiped off the tape. That's what you did. You wiped it off."

"No, I didn't," McGraw said. "I checked with the People's Republic in Washington and they phoned Beijing. Miss Kim remembered taking the call and the connection going dead. The only reason the assassination plot failed was because of the tight security."

He continued quietly, "Maybe you remember something else—the time you got the phone call at the hotel threatening you with rape if you didn't turn over our film footage and other research. Remember?"

She sat in silence, shaking. She was about to break. He recognized the signs: the dry throat, the glassy look, the trembling hands. "I checked, Miss Stowe, and the hotel has no record of an incoming call to your room. Not one single call."

She snapped, "Hotels don't keep track of calls to guests."

"This one did—because I asked it to." He was bluffing. "Don't you think it strange he never called back? Not once. And do you know why? Because the calls here on ship were being taped and you couldn't fake another one."

She rose swiftly and started for the door. He blocked her. "I've got a .38 in the case. Don't force me to get it out. It wouldn't look good."

Abjectly she returned to the desk. "I want to talk with Greg."

"Do you really? Because, you see, I haven't finished. I have more, lots more."

He stood across the desk from her, looking down. It was typical police procedure. Force the culprit to look up. Psychologically, he/she would feel intimidated.

"You've changed your habits, Miss Stowe, and I wondered why. In Tubac you got up at seven or seven-thirty and were at the office at nine. But since you've been here on the *Marco Polo* you've been getting up at five and five-thirty. Interesting, isn't it?"

She glared with all the hatred she could muster.

He continued, "You call a friend every morning, sometimes at five-thirty, sometimes at six or six-thirty, and in between. Odd, you always call her at a pay phone in Waikiki, a different one every morning. I've got the tapes here if you want me to play them. You see, Miss Stowe, I put on another bug in addition to the recording for the day's phone calls. Greg doesn't know about this bug or Lynne or Bill Madden. Nobody but me. What about it, do you want to hear them?"

She sat rigid. Now she had fire in her eyes. "You're framing me."

"The FBI will let you call a lawyer."

"The FBI!" It was a jackal cry.

"We'll take a taxi down there shortly. It's only a few blocks."

She mustered a different attack. "I'm going to talk with Greg and Lynne and you're not going to stop me. When they hear how this all came about . . . I didn't do it deliberately . . . it was something . . . something forced on me."

He broke in harshly. "Don't tell me. I'm not interested in why you did it. Save that for the psychiatrists your attorney will hire."

She rose. "I'm going out that door . . ."

He brought up the .38. "You could be dead awfully quick and nobody would ask many questions when I told them you were a Soviet spy and I thought you were drawing a gun on me. Fact is, I'd love to put a bullet through you. I'm fighting right now against doing it."

She sat down with a jolt that rocked the swivel chair. She was calculating what to do and he knew it. "I should kill you, but I'm going to give you a break. You're going to record this message"—he handed her a note sheet—"and I'll play it tomorrow morning for your friend, Nataya, and she'll think you're on the phone."

She simply stared at it. He said, "It says—you tell her that it's all set now definitely for the *Marco Polo* to sail within three days for Saipan to join the *Tai Peng*, and the two ships will mine the Mariana Plateau. Then at the end you say, 'I can't talk any longer. Someone's coming in,' and that will explain why you hang up suddenly."

She shook her head violently. She was breathing heavily. For a moment he thought she might suffer a heart attack.

He waited, then, "You have a choice, Miss Stowe. You can refuse to record this and be executed within twelve hours. I personally will sentence you to death, the usual sentence for treason, and I personally will carry it out. With pleasure.

"The alternative . . . you will tape this and we'll go together to the FBI. You'll get about twenty years and be out in seven. Not bad when you consider you sold out your country and in doing it didn't give a damn if Greg and Lynne were killed. So now, which is it?"

She thought about it a long moment and he waited patiently. She pulled the recorder over then, wiped the tears away with a tissue, read the message and began talking in a low tone. "Oh, hello, Nataya. I've only got a moment. I just found out the *Marco Polo* will be heading definitely for Saipan—"

She broke then. He said, "Let's start over." She cleared her throat, straightened, and with fists clenched kept a firm voice.

"Now I want to know," he said when she finished, "what time you're supposed to phone tomorrow morning and the phone number. If you try to pull a fast one, I'll get to you before the week's out even if you are in FBI custody."

She whispered the time and number. She covered her face and began sobbing.

"Let's go." He stared down at her, then lashed out. "The time you should've cried was when you broke the connection."

She walked unsteadily. Silently he followed her out on the deck. They were halfway across when Lynne came hurrying after them. "What's happening?"

He said solicitously, "Janet has had some disturbing news, and I'm going with her to take care of it."

"Can I help?"

"Later . . . yes, later. I'll be back shortly and tell you about it, but now we've got to hurry."

Bewildered, Lynne stood looking after them. Her gaze stayed with them until they disappeared down the landing stairs.

For three-and-a-half hours Special Agent Jim Manley and three other FBI agents questioned Janet Stowe. At the beginning and again at midway they informed her of her rights which included a call to an attorney. She said she didn't know a lawyer in Honolulu. They suggested she ask a friend for a recommendation. She refused. They pointed out that she could telephone a representative of the American Bar Association who would refer her to several attorneys. Again, she refused. Then it came out. She thought lawyers were "a lecherous, lying, double-crossing bunch of crooks."

She was grim faced, fighting back the tears but determined to keep control. She was straightforward in answering their questions and appeared honest. Throughout she maintained she was a victim of circumstances and more particularly, a victim of the United States Government.

At 7:30 P.M. the agents asked her to write out a statement that would incorporate her answers. She could take her time. She agreed and they brought paper and a fountain pen. Manley wrote the first paragraph setting forth the time and place, her name and address, the fact she had been advised of her rights, and that no coercion had been used.

She finished a little after nine. When they read it, they knew why she had readily acceded to penning the statement. She had wanted to set forth exactly why she had done what she had.

The statement read in part:

"First I want to say that I never intended to get into this. It just happened. It slipped up on me in the smallest way, and before I knew it I was into it, and then they wouldn't let me out. I wanted out and told them any number of times, but they always threatened to expose me if I didn't get what they wanted. I thought about going to Mr. Wilson and asking for his help, but I was afraid he wouldn't understand. By then I was so terrified I was paralyzed. I was in such a state of shock that I would push all of this business into the back of my mind and refuse to think about it.

"I know what triggered it. I remember it was the second week in January. That was when two things happened. I got the final settlement from the attorneys on my mother's estate and a small trust fund she set up for me. It showed about half of her estate and half the trust fund had been paid to the IRS for the inheritance tax and to California for the state tax and to the law firm and a bank for handling it. And to begin with, it wasn't very much. I couldn't even cover my bills with what was left.

"I was furious. Here was my mother who had worked so hard all of her life, and saved up a little nest egg, and the government and attorneys and bankers had stolen half from me. She had paid taxes all those years, but the bloodsuckers weren't satisfied. They had to have more. They send embezzlers and bank robbers to prison, but the government can rob you all it wants to.

"The second thing was my own tax payment, on which I'd got a postponement, was now due. The reason I had to get a postponement was that I was in the 43 percent bracket. I was single and had no deductions. Here I was working long hours and the government was taking 43 percent of what I made.

"I mention the tax matters so that others will know what I was thinking and how mad I was. They were ghouls. There is no other word for it.

"About this time a magazine writer came to interview me. I cleared the interview with Mr. Wilson. She was writing a piece about mines in the West and more particularly about a new generation as typified by what I was doing. I found her very likable as well as being knowledgeable. We had several sessions together and the last time I let my hair down. I guess I had to tell someone. I told her about the taxes and lawyers' fees and she was most sympathetic. In looking back I remember now I didn't bring up the subject. She did. She got me started. I don't know exactly how.

"I told her how desperate I was. I had a big car payment and one on the condo and MasterCard was hounding me, a collection agency threatening me, and the IRS was after me. I couldn't sleep nights, I was so worried. I didn't know what I was going to do. I was surprised when she offered to loan me a thousand dollars. She said she had received it for an article and was planning to put it into a savings account.

"A week later she brought the check and asked if I wouldn't rather help her with some research, and get paid for it, than to borrow the money. I jumped at the chance. I did think it odd that the check was made out on a Washington, D.C., bank and drawn on a magazine I'd never heard of. She said it was a new magazine.

"I was more surprised when she wanted a map of the best mining sites in the Pacific Ocean instead of more data on Carson's land mines. She repeated several times that I must not tell anyone since it would ruin the sale for her. Another magazine might go after the story. I thought I should ask Mr. Wilson, but I was even more desperate then for money—it looked as if the car would be repossessed and a guy from the collection place said he'd beat me up if I didn't pay—and I decided to go ahead. I told myself there wasn't any harm in it since there were many maps around of the 'best' mining sites. I did know that Dr. Kennedy had mapped them by television and that ours was the only map that was not a matter of speculation.

"A few days later she came back. The magazine would pay me $5,000 for film footage. I refused and that was the last I saw her. A man came to my condo the next night and identified himself as her friend. He was good looking and tall and dark and in his early thirties. He said if I didn't cooperate, he would reveal that I was a spy and that I would be arrested and go to prison. He said the thousand dollars I'd taken had been paid me by a KGB front, and everyone in Washington knew it was a front, and I did, too. He said the young woman had told me I was working for the KGB, which was not true. He asked what I wanted to do, get the footage or go to prison?

"He put $5,000 in cash on the cocktail table saying I was a fool if I didn't keep it. I decided that night I would go to Mr. Wilson, but the next morning I looked at the money. It would pay some bills and I told myself that it would make up some for what the government had stolen from my mother and me. If it hadn't been for the tax people and the lawyers stealing me blind, I wouldn't have had all those debts. I wanted to be honest about it so I bought a small ledger and put down on the debit side what I figured the government and lawyers had taken from us and on the credit side the $1,000 and the $5,000.

"When the man called I told him I would get the footage. He said a woman would phone me later, and the next evening a woman called who identified herself as Miss Nataya Fussen. I have never seen her in person, but she has been a good friend. She knew I was only recovering what the government had stolen. I told her about the ledger and that I would quit when I got my money back. She reminded me to charge 20 percent interest, and I have. She consoled me and was like my mother and it helped to have someone supportive. She said she had worked with many downtrodden people like me, and it was the only way a little person could fight back.

"I wish to state here that I never intended to hurt Carson Mining Company or my friends, Gregory Wilson and Barbara Wilson and Lynne Kennedy, and do not believe I have. I have sought only what was coming to me from the government, and I resent what one FBI agent said who accused me of committing treason. It was the other way around. The government committed treason against me and continues to commit high treason against thousands of good people."

At this point Janet Stowe set forth what she had taken from Carson Mining, detailed conversations with Nataya Fussen, and payments made. She had received to date a total of $42,765 from the KGB and was owed $5,768. For this she had phoned reports every day to Nataya Fussen, and had furnished copies of blueprints and documents, photographs of many mining sites in the Pacific, a breakdown of the ship showing its vital parts and where the dredge head was stored, a layout of the ship's security with a complete roster of the personnel, counterespionage measures taken, including the placing of the responders on the vessel's hull, and answered numerous requests submitted by Miss Fussen.

46

The General was in a foul mood. Too many worries had scurried in and out of his sleep, black cats darting here and there. The day's events were to add to them.

He was gruff with Rona Hale, but she appeared not to notice. She said the message desk had called.

He walked from the annex to the Embassy proper and picked up four confidential telephone memos addressed to the nonexistent Anatoli Ratoff. He headed briskly north on 16th and found a pay booth a block away. As he dialed Boston, he waved to the FBI agents. By now he felt he knew this pair. They ignored him.

When Maria Kaluga answered, he congratulated her again on her outstanding job in Honolulu and her work in progress with the directors of Massachusetts Diversified.

"Wait till you hear this." She was perennially exuberant. "At my suggestion the Board has retained a legal firm in Honolulu to seek an injunction to stop the ship from sailing pending a court hearing to determine ownership. The lawyers out there don't know whether they have a case, but at least it will hold up the ship for a few days and possibly a week."

She continued, "I got a good play in the Boston papers this morning and I'm flying out at 11:20 for Honolulu to follow up out there. I talked with the lawyers and they're writing into the filing a paragraph that suggests by innuendo that Gregory Wilson may be trying to steal the *Marco Polo*. Can you imagine what I can do with that in my news stories? This is better than the cholera caper."

Again he thanked her profusely. She was achieving more than Rashid and Nataya, and doing it openly and with a brazen flair. After all of these years, he wondered if he were cut out for espionage. He reveled in being center stage and playing life with a flourish.

He hurried another block before spotting another phone. He dialed the number Rashid had given. Rashid reported he had "everything in readiness" with the "troops." They numbered seventy, and he would plant two or three among the mercenaries aboard the *Marco Polo*.

His tone changed abruptly. "I wrote Anya's mother some time ago, General, and yesterday I had an answer."

His voice broke slightly. "Anya was executed. She was shot by the KGB. Like a common criminal. You lied to me, General. Why did you lie to me? Why didn't you tell me a mistake had been made? My Anya, dead—and by the people I've worked for all these years. My own people."

The General was stunned. Seconds passed before he could muster an answer. "I had no part in it, Rashid. You know I didn't. I was here in Washington."

"You didn't have to lie to me. You covered up for them. You covered—and after all I've done for you. I thought you were my friend. I've risked my life for you . . ."

The General was experienced at playing tragedy. "Rashid, my friend, please listen." He affected a stammer. "I didn't have the heart to tell you. You loved her so—and I did, too, because of my deep affection for you. You must understand. I made a terrible mistake. I shouldn't have done it. I know that now. But Rashid, I couldn't bring myself . . . I just couldn't . . ."

The pause was a long, pregnant one. Finally Rashid said tonelessly, "You deceived me, General. Twice I saved your life—but no more. The next time I'll let you die."

Before the General could start Act II, Rashid hung up. Still holding the receiver, the General stood minutes in shock. The disclosure had come so unexpectedly. Damn Anya's mother. The General remembered her vaguely, but had forgotten about her.

He walked slowly over to 14th Street. His next phone call would be to Nataya, but he couldn't put Rashid out of mind. The General needed him badly for the next twenty-four to forty-eight hours. He concluded that Rashid was too much the professional to desert. He would finish this mission and then turn in his resignation.

Nataya said sorrowfully, "I have some bad news. I might as well get it out of the way."

The General literally braced himself against the phone booth.

She continued, "Someone has 'made' my gopher."

"How do you know?" he asked nervously.

"She called me this morning at the time set, and the voice sounded like hers, and I think it was although I'm not certain. It's possible someone forced her to record the conversation. She ended abruptly and hung up before I could say a word.

"But if it were she—and I think it was—she tipped me off. When we first started communicating, I did what I always do to protect myself against a fake call. I told her never to mention names, and that included the *Marco Polo*. Always to refer to it as the ship. But this morning she called it the *Marco Polo*.

"Another reason I think she was tipping us off was the message. Today for the first time she said the ship would begin mining off an island called Ponape. Only yesterday she had repeated again that the mining site would be the Golden Tide. And now this sudden switch without explanation."

The General agreed with her conclusion. "You had better take extra caution if she calls again. The Carson people or the FBI may try using her as a double agent. What about the new mole? You promised to send me his name and all the data on him."

"I've lost contact with him. I'm trying now to reestablish contact."

"You've got to." The General spoke imperiously. He was exceedingly frustrated. Nothing was going as it should.

His next call was to MJ's representative. He was surprised that MJ's man had phoned. When he had hung up a few days ago, he was angry.

Now he was cordial. "I have the definite mining site. The *Marco Polo* will sail at ebb tide day after tomorrow for the

Mariana Plateau and then offshore near the little island of Ponape."

As he gave details, the General felt his gut muscles tightening. He had anticipated the glory of having discovered one of the most fantastic moles in years, and here MJ—if MJ existed—was a fraud. MJ's man was nothing more than a con artist. Looking back, the General saw how MJ's man had led him on step by step. He had given him film footage of ocean floors where no nodules existed, still pictures of sites difficult to reach, and pages and pages of maps that were misnamed.

The General asked, "You're absolutely certain that they will mine the Mariana Plateau?"

"I've told you before, MJ has access to every move of Carson Mining and to all meetings, all confidential memos, everything the *Kharkov* could use."

"Thank you very much," the General said. "I'll take up the payment with my superiors, but rest assured, it will please you."

"What did your other informant tell you?"

"The same. Incidentally, I've cleared the way for MJ to meet her. Could MJ get together with her late this afternoon?"

MJ's man thought that over, then said, "MJ would like to if MJ could meet your party in a remote place where it would be difficult for anyone to observe them."

"I know exactly the place," the General said. "On the other side of the island. It's a quiet neighborhood. Why doesn't my party telephone your Miss Punaluu with instructions on how to get there?"

"But not too late. Not after dark."

"How about an hour before sunset? My party can't come any sooner since she works."

MJ's man was agreeable and the General hung up with good vibes that cleansed Rashid out of mind.

47

Greg would always remember Lynne standing in the doorway to his office-cabin that morning. She rose tall, straight and lean, in dark blue shorts and an eggshell-blue T-shirt. She had dark glasses parked up on brown hair that fell straight down. Even with bony shoulders and bonier legs, she looked most desirable.

She was holding papers to show him, and when she found him on the phone, hesitated, wondering if it would be a long conversation and should she come back. As she listened, her face took on the contorted look of one suffering a stroke.

He knew she was overhearing his end of the conversation and wanted her to hear. The time had come for her to know.

He was saying, *"I've told you before, MJ has access to every move of Carson Mining and to all meetings, all confidential memos, everything the* Kharkov *could use."*

Then he set up the rendezvous and the last he said was, *"But not too late. Not after dark."*

Her nervous system shattered. She entered the cabin, fumbled for the door without looking at it, closed it, and with trembling hands, locked it. She turned toward him and her face had the look of sculptured marble.

When he hung up, her lips moved. Only her lips. "I don't understand . . ."

He smiled. "I'd suggest you sit down before you fall down."

As if a computerized robot, she took the straight chair by the desk. She repeated, "I don't understand . . ."

"Nothing to understand."

He talked so naturally and she thought, how could he?

He continued, "I'm the spy I told you about whose identity I refused to reveal. I was talking with my Control—I think that's what he's called—at the Russian Embassy in Washington, D.C. Don't look so horrified. It's not very becoming."

This wasn't real. It couldn't be happening. She couldn't be sitting here listening to what Greg couldn't be saying.

"Let me start at the beginning." He looked straight at her. "Please, Lynne, hear me out without looking . . . looking like you're having a heart attack."

He had never considered, he said, the possibility of espionage by the Soviets until his Papago friend, Al Nakya, brought it up at a Board meeting. Greg remembered then reading a newspaper story about an English spy who had broken a Nazi case during World War II by playing a double agent and pumping information out of the Nazis.

"At the start I only wanted to find out if the Russians were interested in Carson Mining. Interested enough, that was, to spy on us. So I wrote a letter offering just about everything Carson had that would interest them. I really never expected an answer and was surprised when I phoned a pay station and made the contact. I invented a character I called MJ, but I refused to say whether man or woman and that about drove them nuts."

In the days that followed, he sold his contact old maps, worthless documents ("I cleaned out the file of papers I'd been intending to throw out for ages"), several thousand feet of film footage labeled "The Golden Tide" but which was actually from the Atlantic Ocean, and complete blueprints of equipment, including a dredge head vacuum, all copies from *Popular Mechanics.*

"I threw in some good stuff occasionally. Usually outdated technology. Outdated for us but new for the Russians."

As he talked, her expression underwent a metamorphosis, from that of stark horror and disbelief to anger. "I'd kill you, Greg Wilson, if I had a gun. I'd kill you with the greatest of joy. How could you do this to me? How dare you!"

He was nonplussed. "Do what? What're you talking about?"

She gasped. "You mean you don't know? You sit there and pretend. Didn't it occur to you I might have had a stroke . . ."

He shook his head. "You didn't think I was—I was—"

"What else would I think?—and after Janet last night. I've had about all the shocks I can take . . ."

The arrest of Janet had paralyzed both. They still couldn't believe it. Last night they had refused to.

In a spurt of anger, Greg had fired McGraw for his "stupid, clumsy mistake." Even after McGraw had proven his case with hard evidence, they challenged him and offered all kinds of ridiculous excuses for her. This couldn't happen with a friend, a coworker, someone you had known every day for the last two years, whom you trusted and admired, who looked nothing more like a spy than a friendly collie. They probably would never accept McGraw's "version" that she had failed to report the assassination plot to the Chinese Foreign Ministry, a failure she knew might lead to their deaths. Something had happened to the tape. McGraw was mistaken, that was all there was to it.

Greg had wanted to post bond and take her back aboard the ship. At that point Colonel Montand had backed McGraw. The Colonel said, "If you do that, I'll pull out all my men. Only a madman would give haven to an enemy spy."

McGraw started to leave. "Where you going?" Greg demanded.

"You fired me."

Greg said angrily, "That's the trouble with you. You believe everything you hear."

Now Greg laughed uproariously. His contact had paid him a total of $30,500. "One of Meg's old friends—her name's Pearl Punaluu—she lives up on the Pali—has the money. She was the go-between. I've never even met her. I certainly wasn't going to go up there to collect the payments when I knew they would stake out her place and put a tail on me. That would've blown everything. I did take one chance. I got this unlisted phone put in and told my contact it was a pay booth. They never checked it out. Are you going to forgive me? I never thought . . . you know I'd never do it to you deliberately."

She bounced her hair. "In time—but it'll be a long time."

"I'm put out myself that you'd think I was—"

"I didn't. I didn't believe it anymore than with Janet. Why didn't you tell me? Didn't you think I could be trusted?"

He had asked himself that question and come up with no answer. "I was always going to—but it was something I wouldn't even admit to myself I was doing. I can't explain it."

"Don't try. I understand. I really do."

He turned deadly sober. "I thought all along the Russians would catch up with me—and they finally have. They plan to execute me one hour before sunset tonight in a lonely neighborhood."

"No, Greg, no!"

"My contact has consistently stalled my requests to get together with their woman—and now all of a sudden . . . I've got a feeling they know about Janet, even if it hasn't broken yet in the news."

They were lost in thought, then he said, "I should go. It's possible I might meet the new mole."

"McGraw thinks it's Bill Madden."

"McGraw would. But it isn't. I'd trust Bill with my life. There's nothing he wouldn't do for me."

The FBI and the police still had nothing to report about his disappearance. He had simply vanished.

"I beg you," Lynne said, "don't go. They're setting you up."

"I can take care of myself."

"For heaven's sake, Greg, you don't have to prove how brave you are. Look at Custer. He knew the odds were overwhelmingly against him, but just because they were, he had to prove he could win a victory at Big Horn."

Greg said soberly, "Look at it this way. They're going to send a key person in. We may learn a lot or it's possible we might eliminate one of their top people. We've got an opportunity here we haven't had before."

A short time later, McGraw joined them for a strategy session. McGraw was as surprised as Lynne had been to learn Greg was the second undercover agent.

McGraw was angry. "I thought we were being honest with each other. Wasn't that the garbage you gave me when I held back?"

Lynne raised her voice. "That's all in the past. The question now is what do we do. I've told Greg to forget the meeting and lie low."

McGraw said slowly, "I know the killer they'll send in. I've been trying to catch up with the bastard since Dubā."

"Who?" Greg asked.

"If you can be so damn secretive, I can, too. I've got to think about this. You two forget it. I'll handle it."

"We all will," Greg said flatly.

"You'd better let me. I've had more experience in dealing with these rats."

48

The General's temper was a wild horse racing across the range.

"I don't want to hear a word out of you," he told Nataya over long distance. "I'm furious with you and Rashid. By now Kennedy and Wilson should be dead. You don't wait. You walk right up and kill them at close range. That's how I've handled traitors."

He took a quick breath. "I'm coming out to take over. But about this matter tonight. You take charge of the setup. Rashid will handle the execution part. I want it to be a regular, standard execution. I want them to know that death is the penalty for a traitor the same as it has been in every war. I want MJ lined up—and MJ's man if he comes along—against a wall and Rashid can be the execution squad. But I want them lined up. Do you get that?"

"Yes, General." She was simmering, but this was no time for an angry battle over the phone.

He grew thoughtful. "It occurs to me that they might possibly bring in a substitute for MJ. I tell you what to do. I sent you a cassette of MJ's man talking in case you chanced on a man with the same voice. So when you make the setup, you insist that MJ's man come. In the meantime, Rashid can study the cassette and make certain the voice of MJ's man matches up.

Miss Pearl Punaluu dialed MJ's unlisted number as she had on numerous occasions in recent weeks. Only this time a stranger by the name of Nataya Fussen, who held a gun on her, sat nearby listening and watching intently.

Miss Punaluu was part Hawaiian and part Japanese. She was closing in on sixty-five and frail beyond her years. She had a pleasant smile and a soft voice, both befitting one who talked frequently with the God Pele and one's ancestors. She kept her hair in the same style as that day she marched up to collect her University of Hawaii diploma. She believed in the constants of life. She often said, "Man should emulate the moon, faithful, never changing, where you expect it to be." There were a few who thought she worshipped it.

The living room where they now sat had been constant for the last forty years. A dark brown sofa and covered chairs were well worn but clean, as were the pulled drapes. The three 40-watt bulbs in the colored-glass chandelier were the only objects that had been replaced. They and the macaw that viewed the scene from a relic of a well-dusted piano.

MJ answered on the first ring as if MJ had been waiting for her call. She knew who MJ was, of course, but was uncertain at this moment whether the stranger did. Miss Punaluu had parried Nataya's questions with the same deft skill she used with the skeptics who wanted to know precisely how Miss Punaluu found all those ancestors wandering around out in the galaxies.

She relayed the instructions to MJ that Miss Fussen had given her on how to reach the street that would provide the rendezvous. "Once you reach it, you will walk slowly down the street and keep looking between the homes. The houses overlook a small cove and down below them are other houses and a park on the beach. You will see a mountain range in the distance which is called the Sleeping Giant or more commonly, Alfred Hitchcock. You will see his head with the bulbous nose between one set of houses and then between the next houses his *opu* and later his shoes."

She added, "The older generation knows the Sleeping Giant as Guy Kibbee."

She listened and smiled. "Haven't you ever heard of *opu?* Why, the *opu* is a person's protruding tummy. At that point you will stop and will be met by the party you have come to see."

Nataya broke in. "Ask if MJ's man will be present. We insist that he must."

Miss Punaluu talked and then nodded. "He will be there with MJ."

"Very good," Nataya said. "You may hang up."

Miss Punaluu said good-bye and then to Nataya, "Would you care for tea?" She never forgot her manners.

"We will go now," Nataya said. "You will come with me."

Miss Punaluu continued sitting. "May I have permission to go into the next room? I must talk with my ancestors before starting on this perilous journey."

Nataya was curt. "No need to. It isn't going to be perilous. I assure you I will stay with you and will see that you are not harmed."

Miss Punaluu rested her head back against the chair and closed her eyes. "Oh, great grandfather, I must talk with you. A matter of grave concern has come up and I need your counsel." She fell to mumbling. In sympathy, the macaw scraped his vocal cords together.

Nataya stood helplessly by. In all of her years, nothing like this had arisen and she had no idea how to cope. She said sharply, "We must go." But Miss Punaluu continued in her hypnotized trance and Nataya's words sounded sacrilegious. Outside a high wind set tin to tin screeching on the roof.

Then without warning Miss Punaluu raised her voice until the volume was that of a television set turned far too high. "Oh, Pele, great God of all we worship who has given us the breath of life . . . oh, God Pele, I come beseeching you as I have so often . . . since I was a little girl . . . and you have guided me in the ways of harmony with nature . . . . I beseech you this day to cast down your molten lava and belching steam and smoke on mine enemies who would do me and the good people of my world grievous harm . . . oh, God Pele, I wait for you to incinerate mine enemies and bury them forever more in your volcanic ash . . . oh, God Pele . . ."

Rashid went house to house on Lihikai Drive in Kaneohe. He said he was taking a poll. Did the residents favor the President's policies on the Middle East? He slipped in questions about the neighborhood to determine who was usually home and who worked. He expressed interest in the Sleeping Giant and learned about the Sandbar, a speck of land not too far out that disappeared when the tide came in.

He felt his heartbeat quicken. What a bizarre way for disposing of a victim. Tie MJ up and leave MJ to drown on that Sandbar island. The idea fascinated him.

More questions, and he was renting a motorboat from one of the neighbors down below on the shoreline, an old codger who refused money. "Leave me a couple six packs when you pick up the boat. Miller Lite."

Late in the afternoon he phoned the residents, said he was with the FBI and they would be staging a raid shortly. Would everyone leave the neighborhood for an hour? "Hopefully, there will be no gunfire but just as a precaution . . ."

In a rented car, Greg climbed the Pali. It was capped in a swirling fog, but minutes after cresting he was again in brilliant sunlight and below him stretched a greensward dotted with settlements and towns dropping down to blue, foaming waters.

He turned left on Kahekili Highway and drove miles past banana palms, papayas, flamboyant trees and other tropical foliage. On the left rose the Valley of the Temples, a great mass of green sweeping up into the hills. These were burial grounds set aside for Protestants, Catholics and Jews, as if in death man still had to separate the three faiths and there could be no commingling for fear a tenet or two might be corrupted. Far away, in a Japanese garden setting, stood Byōdō-In Temple, a reproduction of the Temple of Uji, Japan. Here visitors could ring the great temple bell and view the Amida, an enormous wooden Buddha covered with gold and lacquer.

The directions stipulated he was to turn right at the next unmarked street, this side of a Texaco station. He was in open country and only an occasional car passed. Even at this late afternoon hour, the sun was fiercely hot.

As he made the turn, he discovered his hands clenching the steering wheel. Up to now this had been an exercise in precise planning, a study without emotion. Together with Lynne and McGraw he had worked out a script, exactly what he was to do, what he was to say. They had written it with care, revising a word here and a plot twist there. Even when they finished, Lynne begged him once more to give it up.

"We can plan for every eventuality we can think of," she said, "but they still may come up with the unexpected."

Shortly after the turn, he stopped on the left at the Pineapple Hut, marked by an enormous shell, to buy a fresh coconut and reconnoiter. As set forth in the instructions, there was a Latter-Day Saints church on the opposite corner and the street sign read Lihikai, and another, Laenani Beach Park—Have Fun—No Drinking.

While waiting to determine if he had been followed, he drank the juice and ate a hunk of the "meat." Satisfied he was not under surveillance, he drove a very short distance down Lihikai and parked close to the curb. He wondered how safe the car would be, and if it might get bullet riddled if a shoot-out ensued. Poor Avis, he thought, poor Avis. The humor broke the tension and he slid out with nerves under control. He left the car unlocked and the key in the ignition. Conceivably he might need to make a fast getaway.

He was in a neighborhood of modest homes with A-frames to handle the heavy runoffs, rusty screens, garbage cans lined up for collection, drunken mailboxes and cars jammed into driveways and yards. The latter were ablaze with wild orchids, anthuriums, cups of gold, pikake and jasmine, and pink, red and yellow hibiscuses. Alongside some of the houses were narrow dirt roads leading down to homes close to the ocean. The roads were rutted and potted. Slowly he began what would be one of the longest walks in his life. He was a standout, not only because he was the sole person about but because he wore slacks and a jacket. As hot as it was, he should have been in shorts and a Hawaiian or T-shirt. He wore the slacks to hold up the holster, and the jacket to hide it and the lightweight bulletproof vest.

A boy of about six popped out of nowhere and passed with a happy, "Hello." When Greg said hello back, the boy's face broke into a big smile.

Between the next two houses, there was a midget road. In the distance, far over the ocean swells, loomed Alfred Hitchcock's big nose, and then another two hundred apprehensive steps later, Greg clearly saw the *opu.*

Here he was to stop and he did so, nervously scanning the street, the parked cars, the immediate houses, and the windows. He had the sharpest feeling he was under scrutiny, but nothing within his vision moved. In the distance a cat cried out as if hurt, and nearer, a dog warned of an intruder. Over all was a cacophony of bird sounds, most of them strange to his ears. One stood out, a low, sobbing moan that set the fear within him pulsing even more.

They were playing a game. They knew that waiting alone could build the fright until even a calm man would break, and he was not a calm man.

About ten minutes later he heard bodies thrashing through undergrowth between the two houses. A young man of dark complexion and Arabic in look broke out of the thick, tangled brush. Behind him was a thin, anemic-looking woman of around sixty whom the man had firmly by the hand. Greg had never seen either but from McGraw's description, knew the man was Rashid Jumeira. Greg knew, too, that he was armed. He was wearing a cheap, shabby suit that bulged slightly over the navel.

In a monotone, the man said to the woman, "Is this MJ?"

She was breathing hard from the climb. "I told you I've never met him."

Greg spoke up. "She's never seen me. For your protection as well as mine, we talked only by phone. I'm glad to meet you, Miss Punaluu."

Her lips trembled. "Thank you."

Greg overlapped. "It's a pleasure, too, to meet you, Mr. Jumeira."

Rashid only stared. If he were surprised by being identified, he failed to show it. "You're MJ?"

"MJ and MJ's man. I thought I was going to meet your informant. Where is she?"

"You know damn well where she is." He shoved Miss Punaluu toward Greg. He was using her as a shield.

"Read it out loud," he said roughly.

She handed Greg a newspaper clipping. Greg read, " 'President Reagan announced today that Israel . . .' "

Puzzled, he looked up. Rashid turned on a cassette he had taken from his pocket. Satisfied, he nodded. "For your protection and mine," he said sarcastically.

He took a document from his inside coat pocket and slowly read, "I have been instructed by my Commander-in-Chief to read this to you. You have been charged with giving aid and comfort to the enemy by acting as a double agent and thereby endangering the best interests and the defense of a great nation that you swore allegiance to by accepting payments for services that proved to be fraudulent. You have been found guilty, and in accord with international law and the Geneva Convention you have been sentenced to death . . ."

Miss Punaluu let out a cry and stared skyward. "Oh, God Pele, where are you in this hour of my desperate need. Oh, Pele, speak out and burn these infidels who would kill—"

"Shut up!" Rashid yelled, and she went quiet. He glowered. "One more word out of you and I'll execute you first."

Greg was conscious of movement about him, soft footsteps and the brush of bodies disturbing the tepid air. Rough-looking men, mostly young and some with scars and half earlobes and other battle insignia, were encircling him with revolvers in hand. Other men were placing barricades across the street.

Rashid said, "One move out of you and you'll be blown to hell."

He continued, "Where was I? . . . You have been sentenced to death. I have been ordered to serve as an execution squad of one and my orders are to take you summarily to the nearest wall and execute you. You may request a blindfold."

"No blindfold," Greg said quietly, "although I should get one for you since you're going to need one before this is all over."

His brazenness shook Rashid for a moment, then recovering, Rashid said, "Give me your weapon."

When Greg's eyes narrowed in defiance, Rashid shouted, "Come on, come on!"

A voice boomed that instant over a loudspeaker. The voice was firm and sonorous and had authority. The loudspeaker was not to be seen. "We have you surrounded. Twenty men, two for every one here. Throw down your weapons and put up your hands or you'll be shot this minute."

For a second they stood paralyzed, stunned by the unexpected turn and the fear engendered by a voice coming out of nowhere. No one moved, no one spoke. Then, bullets tore up the ground perilously close to each man. One tossed his weapon, and another, and another.

Miss Punaluu was crying out again to the God Pele. Her screams could be heard over the continuing voice from the loudspeaker and the shocked babble of Rashid's terrorists.

Rashid yelled at her, and in the same moment drew a .357 Magnum, set it dead on Greg, and squeezed the trigger. It was all happening in the flick of an eyelash. Without losing a word in her outcry to Pele, Miss Punaluu struck Rashid's wrist a cracking blow and the .357 discharged into the ground. Greg's .38 answered and missed. The next he knew Rashid was fighting his way in desperate haste back down through the thick vegetation.

Greg stood rooted. He had an overwhelming compulsion to follow and shoot it out with Rashid. But that was not in the script. He was to stand where he was. He sagged and called out to Miss Punaluu, "Pele heard you." She quieted and looked around in a daze.

Colonel Montand roamed about directing his mercenaries as they took Rashid's terrorists prisoners and ushered them, sometimes with brute force, into a big, yellow bus. Now scarcely a voice was heard. The first outcries had been deadened by the stunned realization they were prisoners. It was a pantomime scene on a deserted street in a lonely neighborhood.

The beach was narrow but the sand fine-grained and soft to the bare foot. The sun was beginning its scheduled descent, and across the water the Sleeping Giant and the island known as Chinaman's Hat were only silhouette cutouts. Mr. Hitchcock's *opu* was more prominent than ever. The Sandbar was a small dark object.

McGraw had parked his shoes and socks by a child's tricycle, a marker he would remember. He crouched low behind a stand of crotons taller than those he had used as a shield when he waited for Nataya that morning at the Royal Hawaiian.

Soon he heard a thrashing up on the hill. The thrashing was descending rapidly. He strained to see but the undergrowth was too thick.

Within seconds, Rashid burst out of the tropical vegetation. He was only a few feet away. Hidden in the crotons, McGraw fired. Rashid fell and rolled over, and then scrambled for a wooden picnic table that he quickly overturned and hid behind. McGraw discharged two more shots which ricocheted off the table. It was too thick to penetrate with accuracy.

McGraw said in a monotone, "It's all over, Rashid. Where d'you want your body sent? You got a wife—parents?"

With this kind of talk pattern, he had caused others before Rashid to make a mismove. Words could prove a powerful force, the images they conjured up of dying and burial and the grief of dear ones.

McGraw continued, "Do you want a tombstone, Rashid, or do you Moslems go in for such things? You tell me and I'll see that you get a good Moslem burial with all your friends there. You do have friends, don't you, Rashid? Or better yet, give up. You haven't a chance. I've got dumdum bullets that tear you up something awful. I can see you suffering after you've been hit, and I don't like it. I don't want to do it to you."

In a swift, quick-as-a-glance movement, Rashid rose up and fired two shots into the crotons. One plowed into the soil only inches from McGraw's foot. McGraw had to move Rashid out fast.

McGraw lighted a cigarette, hoping Rashid might see the flame. With a forefinger drawn like an archer's bow, he flicked it in Rashid's direction. Rashid might think it was an explosive.

He did. He ran low and weaved like a drunk. McGraw squeezed off two shots that missed. By then Rashid had taken cover the other side of a concrete barbecue. It was like a World War II bunker and he could hunker down there for a long time.

McGraw stayed planted, debating how he could flush Rashid out. He said loudly, as if giving instructions over a two-way radio, "He's behind a barbecue under the brown house with the white trim. Come down from above and you can nail him."

Rashid was only twenty-some feet from the motorboat he had rented. Twenty feet. Each foot, though, could be his last. Should he make a run for it or slither through the sand? If he crawled, McGraw would have to stand up to get off a good shot, and then Rashid himself would have a fair target. If he ran . . . well, even a good marksman at that distance would have to get lucky.

Again McGraw pretended he had a walkie-talkie. "Move to your right ten feet. That's it. Come down a few yards and you've got yourself a corpse."

Rashid rose and dashed for the boat. McGraw fired once, twice, three times but Rashid was a blur. He was in the boat, he was pulling the starter rope, the motor was chugging.

Now McGraw had to make a sprint or lose his prey. Now he was the target. Rashid fired once, then decided a quick escape was better.

The motorboat roared away. It seemed to skim the water. McGraw rose to full stature. The cutting of the wind near his right ear signified a bullet had almost found its mark.

He sighted and took one well-calculated shot, and saw Rashid fall back into the boat.

McGraw waited. It seemed an hour. He watched as the boat plowed ahead, then swerved and came round in almost a circle before it struck a buoy, then headed straight back into the shoreline and ran a few feet up on the sand. Like a dying man, it shook in spasm.

Rashid was sprawled on his back, inert. A sandy beach at Kaneohe was a long way from the Street With No Name in Damascus. But no man could ever choose where he was to die.

McGraw spotted two police officers coming his way from the far end of the beach. He looked about frantically but there was no escape.

49

Shortly after Colonel Montand and his men had taken the nine terrorists prisoners, he reported to Greg, who already had been advised of the shoot-out between McGraw and Jumeira.

"My men are still holding the prisoners in the bus, out in a deserted area," the Colonel said, "but we can't keep them there, and what do I do with them? I can't turn them over to the authorities since they'd ask us questions that we shouldn't answer."

He walked about, thinking aloud. "We could scatter them around the city tonight, one to each motel, and in the morning put them on a plane bound for Johannesburg, my home town. I have friends in the government who would not like the idea of persons arriving without visas. They would be detained for a few days, and by that time we would be at sea."

Greg thought the idea brilliant. The Colonel had no idea how many terrorists were still at large in Honolulu or what their exact plans were. But at least nine would be eliminated.

As the Colonel was leaving, he half-collided with McGraw.

"I thought . . ." the Colonel began.

"Nothing to it." McGraw grinned. "The police and I are old friends."

The Colonel saluted. "You are most amazing."

Greg said, "I should congratulate you."

"You may."

McGraw explained that when he saw the police officers coming he had hurriedly wiped his fingerprints off the weapon with his jacket and dropped it in the boat. Half-jogging, he hurried to meet them. He identified himself as a tourist who had heard shots from up above and run down to the beach. He produced an old CIA identification card from his wallet. He was humble. He had worked so often with the police, he said, that he felt he was one of them.

He anticipated Greg's next question. "If they try to trace the .357 they'll have a hard time. I bought it in the market at Abu Dhabi in the United Arab Emirates."

He had no information about why the Russians had imported so many terrorists. "I've lost the only pipeline I had into the Embassy."

Lynne wanted to call in the authorities. "We can't fight this alone, if it comes to that. We need the police, sheriff's deputies, Coast Guard, everyone we can get."

The others opposed her. Greg was violently outspoken. "They'll ask questions, they'll want an investigation, they'll hold us up for days."

Carlos agreed. "Some politician will see a chance to get a splash in the newspapers and on television, and he'll call for a big investigation with hearings, witnesses, all of that. We could be sitting around here for weeks."

Lynne spread out her hands. "I capitulate. I guess I shouldn't have brought it up. I don't know the first principle about it." She smiled. "Anyway, I'm ready. I've even learned how to use a tommy gun."

At five the next morning Greg was awakened by unfamiliar noises on deck, men talking, going and coming. He shaved, showered and dressed hurriedly. Outside he discovered the crew returning. No one had advised him. They just appeared. The ones he met said good morning cordially and he answered that he was glad they were back. There was no residue of hard feeling.

He scanned the morning newspaper. There on page one was a picture, a shot with shadow effects, of a sinister-appearing Janet. He couldn't bear to read the story. If Barbara were here she would be devastated.

He turned to the inside and on page five read about a Honolulu law firm that would go into court this morning to seek an injunction to stop the *Marco Polo* from sailing. The grounds would be the moving of stolen property out of the jurisdiction of the federal courts, property allegedly owned by Massachusetts Diversified.

He set forth to find Lynne who was completing the last turn of jogging forty laps around the ship. He showed her the story. "We've got to move fast."

He would ask Powder River to return to Honolulu from Washington on the next plane.

"Are you all set?" he asked.

"All except the fishbowl, but the copter will put it on deck this morning. We don't have time to run a test. We'll have to gamble it's operational."

Next Greg looked up Carlos who said he would sit in on the court hearing as a spectator and later drop in on the U.S. Marshal. When he was in his thirties, Carlos had served as a federal marshal in Arizona.

"What about the *Kharkov?*" Lynne asked later.

No one knew. They prayed that it was still berthed at Cam Ranh.

That same morning the General checked in at the Royal Hawaiian. He produced a credit card with a name to match the alias he signed on the registration form.

He was in high spirits. He disliked masterminding an operation from a distance. It was too hard on one's mentality and butt. Today he would soak up the sunshine and exotic food and tomorrow would demonstrate to Nataya and Rashid exactly how a strategist handled these simple situations.

His spirits drooped considerably when Nataya called to report the killing of Rashid. The General experienced a slight heaviness of heart. At the same time Rashid's death did solve a serious situation. There was no telling what Rashid might have eventually done about Anya's death. It was truly amazing how problems, if given time, took care of themselves.

The General could scarcely contain his fury when Nataya informed him that MJ and MJ's man were the same, and that Greg Wilson had played both. The General would personally kill him in honor of Rashid Jumeira. "I wish it was fashionable to scalp a man. I'd like to hang his scalp up in my office."

When she hung up, he placed a call to Maria Kaluga who was now his favorite. She was easy-going and brilliant, two qualities he admired greatly.

She reported that the hearing to determine whether an injunction should be granted would be held this morning at ten o'clock in the United States District Court. The attorneys for Massachusetts Diversified had already filed a civil suit for 20 million dollars, a step required by law before they could seek an injunction.

"As I understand it," she continued, "injunctions are not easy to get but the attorneys believe in this case they have an excellent chance since it should be fairly evident to the court that the *Marco Polo*—the stolen property in this case—can never be recovered once it sails."

She paused a moment. "I'm checking my notes. The lawyers do have one hurdle and it's called 'diversity of citizenship,' which means the defense will argue over jurisdiction, whether the suit and injunction should have been filed in Arizona, where Carson has its corporate headquarters, or Massachusetts."

"What then?" the General asked impatiently.

"If we get the injunction, the U.S. Marshal will serve the papers. I had to do a lot of talking, but finally persuaded the attorney assigned to the case to follow through in person and expedite the paperwork. I'll stay with the attorney."

"How soon?"

"I think late afternoon."

"How about a night out on the town after we wind this up?"

"I'd love it. Especially if we keep the expenses down and share a hotel room."

If the General had been a collie, his tail would have thumped a tattoo on the floor.

A half hour later an emergency call came through from the Embassy in Washington. He took down a brief coded message, and needed only a few minutes to work it out. By way of the Havana antennae, Satellite 95 reported that conversations picked up from the *Marco Polo* established that the ship would sail at midnight.

That meant the General would have to move up his thinking and his plans by twenty-four hours.

Greg let out a yell that was heard over half the ship. He had taken a telephone call from Beijing, from a woman in the Foreign

Ministry whom he had never met, whose name he had trouble writing down, but whose message was clearly understandable.

The People's Republic of China had accepted his offer of joining in the sea-mining venture. Now Carson had a degree of respectability and perhaps even a legal basis for scooping up the nodules.

"Run up the flag!" he shouted to Lynne. He had bought a flag weeks before. It was a brilliant red with a large gold star in the upper left corner and four smaller ones in an arc to the right.

He couldn't resist the temptation to cable Jonathan Switzer. Never mind that Switzer had reversed course. Never mind that Switzer had recommended a presidential directive. All Greg could think of was the rude, brusque, arrogant Switzer who had done everything within his power to annihilate the Carson project.

Greg cabled:

> PLEASE BE ADVISED THAT THE PEOPLE'S REPUBLIC OF CHINA FLAG WILL BE FLYING ALONGSIDE THE U.S. ONE WHEN MARCO POLO PUTS TO SEA AND ANY ATTEMPT TO BLOCKADE SHIP OR HARM IT OR ANY ATTACK WILL BE AN ATTACK ON THE PEOPLE'S REPUBLIC AS WELL AS ON THE UNITED STATES.

Shortly after lunch, Powder River arrived from Washington. He had a broad grin. "You won't believe this, boy, but a fellow name of Bob McLean woke me up at two o'clock this morning. You may remember him. He's on the Board of Massachusetts Diversified."

Greg and Lynne exchanged glances but offered no comment.

He continued, "Well, seems this McLean was at a White House dinner last night and got to talking with the President about sea mining and Carson, and the President was highly knowledgeable about it. Seems he had had calls from a few senators, and State had passed along a memorandum from the Japanese ambassador. He said he had read summaries given him about the United Nations treaty, and he thought that treaty unfair to American interests.

"He said he was sending Congress a message within the next week about several matters and would include the situation in regard to mining the ocean floor. He asked McLean to talk with the administrative assistant who would draw up the mining part of the message. The President said he hoped the *Marco Polo* would put to sea since it would strengthen his message if the senators and representatives knew that an actual mining operation was underway."

Powder River leaned forward, his expression grim. "The President wanted a promise out of us. Would Carson and Massachusetts Diversified give a percentage of its profit to a fund for the underdeveloped nations? That was why McLean was calling at that hour. The President wanted something to offer the underprivileged countries. Especially those countries with starving people and thousands of refugees. He thought we should do something more about hunger in the world than we were, but with our economy the way it is we couldn't dish out billions as we once had. He said here was a way the private sector could help."

He hesitated. "I committed us up to a certain point. I said we would. I think it's only fair—"

Greg broke in. "We've talked about it, remember, at meetings of both Boards. I think we're in agreement."

"Hold on," Powder River interjected. "McLean told me he had to have something concrete and so I said how about twenty to thirty percent. Hell, boy, we can afford thirty percent, and I've always figured if I made a profit, let the other fellow make one, too. Don't be greedy. Anyhow, that's it, twenty to thirty percent, and for that we've got the President's backing, and McLean figures there'll be no trouble in Congress."

Greg couldn't contain himself. "So help me, you did it!"

That wasn't exactly the truth. Lynne had started the sequence of events when she suggested telephoning Bob McLean. It was an unlikely lead, but one never knew where a breakthrough would come from.

"Let's tell the Boards it's thirty percent," Greg said. "If this goes at all, we're going to make Carson and Mass. billions. It's just hit me for the first time. We've got enough nodules down there to feed the world for centuries to come."

Time speeded itself up that afternoon, the way it does when confronted by a deadline. They worked with a frenzy getting all the last-minute chores done. Even the mercenaries acted alive.

McGraw returned to report the nine terrorists had been put aboard a plane bound for Johannesburg. The newspapers carried stories about the murder of one Rashid Jumeira, a native of Syria. They told of mysterious calls by the "FBI" to the residents to evacuate and about armed confrontations between two small groups of men.

With the adrenalin flowing steadily, Greg nevertheless went about his work with burgeoning apprehensions. Any minute he expected an attempt to seize the ship or a United States Marshal to board the vessel and deliver the injunction papers. Carlos Lopez still had not returned.

Greg phoned Laura to say good-bye and inform her that Lotus would be coming to Tucson.

"It'll give you two a chance to get better acquainted," he said.

"You like her, don't you, Daddy? I can tell."

"She works for me."

"Uh-huh."

"What does that mean. Uh-huh?"

"It doesn't mean un-un."

"God help me, I've reared a Stone Age child. Can't talk. Can't read. Can't write."

"Haven't you heard, Daddy, it's the triumph of aboriginal man, as God made him, over civilization."

"It's going to be the triumph of something on your little behind if I catch you misspelling—"

"I'll take you to court for child abuse."

When he hung up, he found Lotus waiting to say good-bye. "I miss you, Grig."

"I'll miss you, Lotus." Her pixie smile had scattered a lot of despair these last few days.

"Want always be with you, Grig. Even if not wife. Work for you."

"You will—as long as I'm with Carson."

She kissed him good-bye full on the lips. Unknown to them, Lynne had come up, and when Lotus was gone, said, "She has such remarkable proficiency in the art of saying good-bye, but I'm sure that comes from years of experience."

The letter came from Bill Madden at four o'clock. A special delivery postwoman brought it.

Greg recognized Bill's big scrawling handwriting and opened it with his blood pounding. The letter could bring only grave news. Old Bill had been kidnapped, beaten, even tortured. At least Bill was alive or had been when he wrote the letter.

It read:

> Dear Greg:
>
> I've got something to tell you and it hurts awful. I wish to God I didn't have to write this. I thought I wouldn't, but I would have left you guessing and that wouldn't have been fair at all. You've been good to me and I've let you down. I didn't mean to, but I have.
>
> I should have told you a long time ago. I guess it was about twenty years ago and some of us was drinking and we got into an argument and a fellow who was my best friend lost his head and killed this other fellow and I got away and I was glad to go to work for you at the mine in Nevada because it was far from anybody and I was safe. I still knew there was a warrant out for me for murder although I didn't do it, but it was my gun my friend used. I don't know how they found out about it, but this woman called me up one day and said she knows and she is going to turn me in unless I give her dope about our mining project. I asked her what she wanted it for. I thought it had to be W.W.W., but she says she will meet me and we will talk about it, and we do, and right off I knew she was a spy and when I asked her if it was Russia she clammed up and said it was none of my business and she would pay me for the information she wanted and never call the police. I let her think I was going along because I had to get away and think out what I was going to do. I wasn't going to go back and go to prison the rest of my life and I wasn't going to sell her secrets. So what was I going to do? It didn't take me very long to know. I couldn't tell you when I left although I knew you would worry, but I got on a plane and came back here to Durango where I grew up. I took some flowers out to the cemetery and said good-bye to my ma and pa. They were awful good to me. I drove out about twenty miles to Dead Mule Canyon where me and my friends played when we was boys and dug me a grave near a trail that some Indian families use. I have wrote a

note that I will put on the dirt I dug out and ask them to cover me over since I don't want any vultures comin' for me. I'll leave a twenty-dollar bill to pay them for their time. I will go back to town now to put this in the mail and then go back to my grave, and I will be gone by the time you read this. Sometime if you come this way and feel like it, you might put up a little wooden marker with my name on it. Say good-bye to Miss Barbara and Miss Lynne and Powder River and all of them, but do not tell them what I did years ago. You can tell them I got tired and went back home and that is the truth. I hate it I let you down, but I hope you understand because you have been good to me.

Sincerely yours,
Bill Madden

Greg crumpled up the letter and stuffed it in a pocket. Lynne asked what was the matter. He turned so she wouldn't see the tears. "Old Bill's in Colorado. He had a breakdown. He won't be coming back."

50

8:25 P.M.

In the light of a full moon, Iolani Palace rose two stories tall, an imposing, nostalgic reminder of the long-gone days of the Hawaiian monarchy. It was a beautiful speciman of Italian Renaissance with deft touches of Hawaii spotted here and there.

The PLO man walked slowly taking it all in, including the charming bandstand that had served as a coronation site for King Kalākaua. His sister, Queen Liliuokalani, followed him and she was the last of a monarchy that had ruled for a thousand years. Her benevolent reign ended abruptly when wealthy American interests imprisoned her in a palace bedroom while they petitioned the United States for annexation. Washington grudgingly acceded in 1898, although what nation would want a cluster of little islands far out in the middle of the Pacific?

Tonight lights burned in big global glass bulbs before the entrance to the Palace; otherwise it was dark, the tourists gone. It was a museum faithfully re-created down to the red velvet, gold-leaf throne chairs that sat under a 24-carat gold-leaf canopy.

The PLO man was young, well built and friendly. Entering from Richards Street, he approached the guard, a white-haired gentlemanly sort who was augmenting his Social Security income.

"I see you're not open nights." The PLO man spoke with a distinct accent, even though he had attended the American University in Beirut.

The guard was in slacks and a Hawaiian shirt with a holster prominently displayed. "You'll have to call tomorrow morning for reservations."

The PLO man thanked him and walked away. Then he abruptly reversed himself, and the guard, who had turned away, was taken by surprise. In a matter of seconds, the PLO man had gagged him and tightened a leather band four inches wide about his chest and arms. While the guard struggled, the PLO man plunged a hypodermic needle into the guard's right arm. The shot, a tranquilizer, would render the guard unconscious for three hours.

The PLO man walked toward the Palace. Across a blocked-off street was the imposing State Capitol, partly blotted out by an enormous spreading monkey-pod tree. Beyond the monkey-pod was a fantastic banyan tree with branches dropping to the ground and taking root. They were so thick and extensive that a small army could be secreted there.

The PLO terrorist encountered another guard and again followed the same pattern as with the first. Then there was a third.

After ascertaining there was no one else about, he returned to the sidewalk, raised a hand, and within minutes a dark, rented limousine swung into the driveway and came to a stop directly before the Palace. Nataya Fussen walked up the steps with all the stateliness of royalty, a door swung open, and once inside, passed through ornate koa wood doors into the Throne Room, now brilliantly lighted. The throne chairs were on a dais at the far end.

Her staff following, she walked with regal step over thick, dark red carpeting to a small table. From an attaché case she took diagrams which showed where every soldier was and at what time he would move and where to. A swarthy but attractive Libyan began setting up the radio equipment.

Her gaze went to the feathered staffs, called *kahilis,* that lined the walls. In the days of the monarchy, royal attendants would wave them like fans as they accompanied the kings or queens on pilgrimages. They were the symbol of authority, the same as the mace had been in England.

Over objections from the General, she had chosen the Palace as her command post. It pleased her that she could be queen for a few hours, but there were more practical aspects. She needed a post where cars and men could come and go, one in the heart of the city, and one so conspicuous that nobody would ever dream anything nefarious could be taking place there.

She checked the small diamond studded, gold watch that an admirer had given her a quarter century ago. The time was 8:45. She would start the operation in exactly 45 minutes.

9 P.M.

Greg ran down the final checklist with Lynne. With customary efficiency she had prepared it, and now stood close, her body brushing his, as he penciled in O.K. before each point. Both were quietly exhilarated. They had worked long and hard, suffered through so much, met and conquered so many obstacles, and planned so intensely for this hour. Unbelievably, they would put to sea in three hours. The fishbowl had been lowered gently to the deck a few hours before by helicopter; they had personally checked over the dredge head and all of the other equipment; and IBM technicians and engineers had gone over the electronic equipment, including the computers, and everything was in excellent working order.

At six o'clock the twelve frogmen from South Africa had come aboard; and the mercenaries were at their posts, including the gunners who would man the antiaircraft and other big cannon.

Carlos Lopez had reported in to advise they need not worry about an injunction being served. The federal court judge had issued the injunction that morning but Carlos had taken the deputy marshal aside who was assigned to serve it. Carlos had identified as a former Tass correspondent the young woman who doggedly was insisting the papers be served immediately. The deputy promised to hold off until the next day.

9:20 P.M.

Aboard the *Marco Polo,* Captain Parker assigned two junior officers to keep watch on the radar screen. He posted another officer to make sure the lifeboats were properly attached to their davits and could be released within minutes. He pondered what to do if the ship should sink. The vessel was carrying about twice as many persons as the lifeboats could accommodate.

An uneasiness had settled over everyone. From Greg and Captain Parker to the mercenaries, they had expected an attack before now. Greg moved swiftly from one post to another, from the parking area and the dock which four mercenaries were watching, to the lone man at the foot of the landing stairway and the one at the top, to the lookouts along the bulwarks keeping watch below for small craft, to the frogmen who were patrolling the waters around the vessel, to the men manning the antiaircraft guns.

Part of the time Colonel Montand would join him and check out the ammunition supplies stacked at strategic spots over the deck. Overhead the copter would hang for minutes, then put out to sea to report on the Soviet submarine, then cover the beach for two miles in each direction.

9:30 P.M.

A quarter mile away, two enemy frogmen turned off the engine in the motorboat, put the oars in the water, and quietly moved toward the harbor entrance, an eighth of a mile of calm water between the main body of Oahu Island and little Sand Island.

By prearrangement, they would count silently five strokes, then quit and listen. It was a quiet, peaceful night with only a distant murmur of traffic and an occasional far-off muted roar of a plane taking off. No other craft was about. They were some distance away from favorite beaches.

Yet both kept the shoreline under surveillance. There was always someone about, sleeping on the sand or fishing for breakfast or a couple making love. No one, however, was likely to consider anything suspicious about a boat heading for the harbor. No one, that is, unless he was deliberately watching.

They floated into the entrance, truly a bottleneck. While one used the oars to stabilize the boat, the other worked as fast as he could. He lifted a heavy mine over the side and dropped an anchor hooked to it by a thick cable. The oarsman moved the boat about a hundred yards closer to Sand Island and the other repeated the process with another mine.

They were acutely aware that a Coast Guard cutter lay in dock a half mile away at Sand Island. They were fearful, too, that the copter patrolling the area might sight them. Once its powerful spot did cut a swatch across them. They both rowed at a leisurely pace, as fishermen might returning home, and the light that held on them a couple of minutes went searching elsewhere.

By radio they reported their mission completed. Nataya Fussen thanked them and ordered them to return the boat to the Ala Wai Small Boat Harbor. She warned them to take precautions when they tied it back up. To be caught returning the craft might be as much of a disaster as stealing it.

Once they were a short distance away from the channel entrance, they started the motor again and relaxed. They talked about the bottle of scotch they would buy and the girls they already had booked.

9:30 P.M.

Two middle-aged men in lightweight summer suits and subdued ties parked a Datsun outside the main gate to Pier 14-A, looked about casually, and entered. Under the steady scanning of mercenaries secreted here and there, they crossed the wide parking area heading for the landing stairs. Each carried an old-fashioned physician's black bag.

The guard at the foot of the stairs walked several steps forward to stop them. They identified themselves as medics with the Honolulu Health Department and showed credentials. The guard informed them he would call Gregory Wilson to escort them on deck. When the guard disappeared up the stairs, another mercenary joined the medics.

Descending slowly, Greg looked them over. They said they had been sent to conduct a last-minute check of the ship. Again, they showed their credentials which Greg studied. He nodded and they followed him.

At the foot of the stairs, he turned. "You may possibly know that we have been having some problems, and I hope you don't mind if I ask you to open the cases."

There was the slightest pause, then one swung a bag and struck him a hard blow in the face. They both ran. Greg pulled a .38 and fired. One man went down and the other put his hands high above his head and yelled words that were incoherent but had to mean surrender.

Still holding the .38 dead on them, Greg ran to the fallen man with four mercenaries close behind. He took one look and shouted at the nearest to call the paramedics. Two mercenaries took the second man prisoner. "What do we do with him?" they asked helplessly. It was a good question. No one had anticipated taking prisoners.

Greg said, "Turn him over to Colonel Montand."

The man on the ground was groaning and bleeding profusely. A quick examination disclosed he had suffered a flesh wound in the right leg, above the knee.

Within five minutes, the paramedics arrived and took him away. The two bags held identical contents, one dozen hand grenades. The men themselves were armed with .357 Magnums loaded with dumdum bullets, the kind that once embedded explode and blast a sizable hole in the body.

9:30 P.M.

General Schepnov strode back and forth at a good gait on Kalia Road. He was ten minutes early. He had intended it that way. He needed to whip himself into shape mentally. He had lived his life well ahead of time schedules.

He was in his captain's uniform. It was well creased and hung with medals he had bought from the widow of a fallen general. His boots were well polished, the result of an hour spent in working on them. He was corseted, stood tall and with shoulders thrown back.

This was his night of glory. He had dreamed of it ever since his arrival in the United States. He had been fearful that Nataya would interfere, but she had wanted to assume control of the command post and readily granted his right to lead the troops in battle.

At exactly 9:34 he walked head up, eyes straight ahead, the half block or so to the Army Museum, turned a sharp right along the narrow sidewalk that fronted it, and proceeded to the M-24, the General Chaffe tank. His three aides materialized at once from the shadows. One was a PLO tank expert imported from Lebanon who had openly worked over the tank with Rashid in daytime hours putting it into operable condition, including the 77mm gun mounted on the turret and the three machine guns. A U.S. Army officer had come out of the building the first day to inquire what they were doing and by whose order. They said they had been sent by the Pearl Harbor Army Command to rustproof it. The explanation had satisfied the officer and for three days they had worked without interruptions.

Without a word, General Schepnov climbed in first and was followed by the other three. He spoke into the microphone hidden beneath his jacket to inform Nataya that they were moving out at 9:45. She reported that one bus loaded with his troops would leave that minute from the parking area fronting Iolani Palace, and she would order the immediate departure from the other centers of his additional army.

The two V-8 Cadillac engines started on command. He gunned the 19-ton vehicle and quickly got it up to its maximum speed of 35 miles per hour. He swept it down to Ala Moana where he turned left. Even at this hour, traffic was running heavy and much to his frustration he had to slow his advance. People waiting on corners for stop lights to change gawked at the ancient vehicle, and drivers pulled cars up alongside to get a better look.

Although he passed several police officers, none stopped him. He had calculated that none would. They would think the tank was for use in some movie being shot. One officer saluted him and he responded.

He had informed his three fellow tank officers he would pilot the tank and would take full charge of the 77mm gun on the turret. He could scarcely wait to fire it.

9:45 P.M.

With their engines turned off, four motorboats holding four terrorists each glided within sight of the *Marco Polo*. A hand went up in the lead boat indicating for the others to hold back. Those in the lead noted the gun-toting mercenaries posted on the bulwarks scanning the waters below for just such a seaborne attack. They spotted, too, frogmen swimming on patrol about the vessel.

The boats were loaded with weapons and explosives as well as ladders with grappling hooks at one end. The master plan called for a silent infiltration of the ship's deck prior to a frontal attack. But now the men in the boats realized there could be no piratelike scaling of the ship's sides. That would be suicidal.

They turned the boats about. They would draw back into the dark and wait for the frontal attack to begin, then in the midst of it, attempt to sneak aboard.

They had pulled back only a few feet when the copter's brilliant spotlight caught them dead on and held on them. They were prepared. They had brought fishing poles and each man got busy with his. They realized the ploy might not work. Four men in each boat fishing at this time of night? And four boats?

10:15 P.M.

With a flourish, the General turned left from Nimitz and headed for the locked gate to the parking lot. Beyond it, the lights burned brightly on the *Marco Polo*. All the better, he thought, for target practice.

Thirty-two terrorists swarmed about him. They came out of storefronts across the way, dark shadows under trees, parked cars where they had been hiding, and as the police report later stated, "like termites coming out of the woodwork."

The General waited until they had all gathered. He was restless and impatient. It was possible that the mercenaries aboard the *Marco Polo* had spotted him and might attack. He wanted none of that. If he could maneuver into position first and take the initiative, he was positive victory would be his.

He was about to crash the gate when a police car startled him by pulling alongside. He had his script memorized. He rose up through the head and shouted, "We're filming a scene down here tonight. I've got a permit." He waved a piece of paper.

The older officer nodded. "I'd better get Traffic in here if you're going to block Nimitz."

The General was alarmed. "No, no. We're using this parking lot. We won't be working on the street."

The younger officer said, "It's a World War II film, is it?" He was inspecting the tank with great interest. "I was a tank man myself. In Vietnam."

"What's the title?" asked the older officer. "I go see all of them shot in Hawaii."

"'The Last Tank.'" The General was about to blow a gasket. They would all be under gunfire soon if he didn't get rid of the officers—and it wouldn't be movie bullets.

"Pardon me," the General continued, "we've got to get started. Costing us a lot of money—all of these extras."

"They sure look like the real thing," said the younger officer.

"If we can do anything," said the older, "let us know. We'll be cruising along on Ala Moana and drop back from time to time."

For them, this was just one more film. For years Hollywood had been riddling the islands with gunfire from the likes of *Magnum*, *Hawaii Five-O* and numerous films. Moviegoers and television viewers liked excitement set among palm trees, along exotic beaches with blue, blue waters, and amid girls in hula skirts and less.

10:15 P.M.

Shortly after receiving word from an unidentified helicopter pilot about four men in each of four boats in a tight "formation," the Coast Guard sent its lightest cutter out toward the channel entrance. The cutter's broad swathe of brilliant light located two boats with four men in each and by bullhorn ordered them to proceed immediately to the Coast Guard station. The boats tagged along without protest. Surreptitiously, the boatmen slipped overboard the weapons, explosives and grappling hooks.

At the station, Guardsmen searched the boats and men for drugs and found none. The boatmen said they had been out fishing and were late in returning. They had the fishing poles to back up their statements.

The Guardsmen, however, were skeptical. For one thing, they found no bait. The fishermen said they had used it all and thrown the cans out. For another, these were men with strange accents. Still, what could they have been doing out there other than fishing? They were not running contraband, they had no weapons.

The Coast Guard advised the Harbor Police that they would release the eight men unless the Harbor Police had reason to hold them.

10:20 P.M.

With the police officers gone, the General, sweating heavily from the nerve strain, lifted a hand in signal to proceed. The tank smashed down the gate with ease and its tracks lumbered loudly over the concrete until it came to a sudden stop at the nose of the *Marco Polo*. The General said into the radio mike, "Zero One. Zero One." The answer came back immediately, "Proceed Zero One. Proceed Zero One. Copter coming over. Copter coming over."

The guard at the foot of the landing stair was seized the moment he walked forward. The guard at the top sounded the alarm. His yell could be heard a block away.

The General trained the 77mm on the *Marco Polo*'s hull, just above the water mark. He spoke into the loudspeaker system. "Hear this. Hear this. The first one who fires a shot will blow up the ship. We have a helicopter coming over which will drop a bomb in dead center. We've got heavy fire power on this tank and we will blast a hole that will sink this vessel. We have one hundred men ready to storm it when I give the signal. You have no choice but to surrender. Once you have surrendered, we will take command for a few days and return the ship to you in good condition. We don't want to sink the ship or hurt any of you."

He raised both hands to silence his own men. He heard from

the deck loud talking, the running of feet, swearing and yelling, and then the loud rumble of machinery. They were planning to sail.

He shouted, "Fire!" to the three manning the machine guns. Simultaneously, he let go with the 77mm which gorged a hole the size of a big tray. He let out an old Sioux war cry.

Before the first "Hear this" was out, Greg was shouting orders. To the Captain, to take off at once, to notify the control tower, to request the pilot boat to assist. If the pilot boat couldn't report at once, then the Captain was to move the *Marco Polo* without it through the narrow bottleneck.

To the radio room, to get the latest weather forecast. To the antiaircraft gunner on the foredeck, to target in on the tank and hold until ordered to fire. To the antiaircraft gunner on the stern, to target in on the enemy copter when it came over. To the Carson whirlybird pilot, to bring the craft over for aerial cover, to zero in on the enemy copter but hold his fire until ordered. To the mercenaries without assignments, to gather near the bridge and prepare for attack.

To the lookouts along the bulwarks, to fire without orders on any parties attempting to scale the ship. To the frogmen just going over, to knife any enemy frogmen found close to the vessel, to keep a constant check on the hull for explosive sandwiches. To the guard at the ladder top, to pull it up.

He took up position on the bow. He heard the explosion when the 77mm hit. He called out to the gunner on the antiaircraft weapon to open fire. The first ejectile struck the tank dead center and knocked it several feet. For a second it looked as if it might roll over but then it straightened. There followed a series of explosions from the 77mm and bursts of fire from the three machine guns. They were chewing up the hull. The deck gunner hit again with deadly accuracy and the tank careened wildly, but still was in action.

Greg didn't know how long Lynne had been standing by him. She had a tommy submachine gun in hand and was firing volley after volley at the terrorists who were advancing on the ship. They retreated and took cover.

Colonel Montand, followed by McGraw, was hurrying from post to post, checking his men and the ammunition supplies. Powder River had taken a spot on the stern with his .30-.30 to guard against a sneak attack from the waters below.

While the others were depending on a ferocity of fire to stem the onslaught, Carlos Lopez calmly stood at a forward position and took careful sighting before firing. He brought down one terrorist and then another before he was hit in the shoulder. He screamed for a second, then stifled the outcry and dropped to the deck where he sat struggling stoically to contain the pain.

Then the whole ship seemed to blow up. The concussion was beyond belief and great flames were leaping skyward. A bomb from the enemy copter had struck midship. Men were screaming and others shouting orders.

Greg took command of the fire fighting as the soldiers dropped their weapons and wrestled with hoses emitting powerful streams of chemicals. Lynne stayed at her post, continuing to stymie an assault that could come any minute. Carlos saw her predicament and though wounded, joined her. While one dropped behind the bulwark to load, the other kept up the fire.

Within minutes, the blaze was brought under control and all except a few were back at their positions. The Captain surveyed the damage and reported that it was heavy but would not prevent sailing. The control tower, which had given permission to leave, now rescinded the decision.

"Let's get going," Greg shouted. "We're sailing with or without their okay."

The Captain had to yell to be heard. "No! I absolutely refuse. I could be—"

"The hell you won't! We'll see about that soon as—"

His words were blotted out. A vast sheet of flame lit up the sky. The Carson copter had shot down the enemy one and what was left after the explosion plunged to hit the water a few feet distant. The hulk shook in spasm and then the dark waters engulfed it. Shortly afterward, the frogmen reported they were unharmed.

During the excitement of the conflagration—it was now discovered—eight terrorists had landed on deck from a ladder they had thrown up. They were firing wildly. A mercenary went down on Greg's left and another on his right. Before the terrorist could get off another shot, Lynne felled him. Powder River took two at gunpoint and turned them over to Montand.

For several minutes, sporadic fighting continued with the terrorists firing from behind a bulkhead. But the mercenaries were closing in and they surrendered. They were taken to a cabin McGraw had set up as a center to hold prisoners. Even while gunfire and explosions sounded outside, he began grilling them. He threatened to kill them if they didn't talk and fired several shots within inches of their bodies to convince them they should.

Out on the dock it was quiet except for the tank that continued to pound the hull. The antiaircraft gunner had hit it repeatedly, but it refused to die. The General, standing straight in the cockpit, seemed impervious to all the gunfire directed at him. The tank's three machine guns had been silenced.

"Protect me," Greg shouted to Lynne as he went down a ladder that the terrorists had thrown up. She drew fire away from him with repeated outbursts from the tommy gun. She ran out of shells and had to reload. As she did, she said a little prayer for him. When she resumed firing, she saw Greg running fast and close to the ground. She saw bullets ripping up the concrete by his feet. Then he threw a grenade straight for the General. It exploded a few feet away and the tank rocked back and forth. The General rocked with it and when it stabilized itself, he turned the 77mm dead on Greg.

He never fired. The tommy gun riddled his shoulder. For a moment, he doubled up, then biting his lips, straightened. With the agility of a twenty-year-old, he hoisted himself in one swift movement from the tank, drew his revolver, and advanced on Greg. The daring move took Greg by surprise. Crouched behind a rubbish can, Greg took slow aim. The bullet caught the General in his right side. He barely paused and again straightened, and still walking, though ever so slowly, fired. The clatter was earsplitting as the shell ripped into the can and sent it spinning, leaving Greg exposed.

The General was bleeding heavily. Greg waited a long moment until he was closer. Greg thought he had only two shells left. This time he had to bring him down.

The General, too, was nursing his ammunition. He was suffering horribly. His twisted face showed that, though through grit alone he kept a smile pasted over the pain. This was his moment of glory. Singlehandedly, by willpower alone if not by bullet, he would stop the *Marco Polo*. All the others had been too cautious, too concerned for their mercenary hides. He had walked over many a mine field, never wavering, straight ahead, always straight ahead, and there would be no turning back tonight, no surrender.

He fired his last shot. Greg was weaving deliberately at the moment, as if he could sidestep a bullet, and he almost did. The shell caught him in the fleshy part of the right arm and a collapsing muscle relaxed the hand. His .38 dropped noisily on the pavement.

The General laughed and pulled the trigger, but there was no answer and he knew there would be none. Slowly he sagged to the pavement, ever so slowly, and crumpled up. He still had the faint smile.

Andropov would be there and Fedorchuk and all the Politburo . . . to walk in the shadow of a fallen hero.

10:45 P.M.

A teacher phoned in a complaint to the downtown headquarters of the Honolulu Police. From a high-rise condominium she had been watching an extremely violent scene being filmed at the harbor. She thought that by permitting Hollywood to photograph such scenes, Hawaii was condoning violence in movies and television.

She was very wrought up. "We've got to put a stop to it."

The officer on duty agreed. He said he would forward her comments to the department head who issued permits.

The Harbor Police, too, received complaints, but these were from parties who objected to the noise. Harbor was downright incensed. Downtown had failed to notify them about the filming.

10:45 P.M.

From the door, Nataya took one last look at the throne room, then turned out the lights. Ten minutes ago, when she knew the battle had been lost, she had dismissed her aides.

She walked out the front door, closed it firmly, and at the limousine, looked up at the Palace that had known so much history. Is this how Queen Liliuokalani felt when deposed by the American imperialists, when she had left for the last time, realizing there would never be another tomorrow for the old Hawaii?

Yet tonight, to quotc an old hackneyed saying, the battle had been lost but not the war. She wondered if this far away she could hear the explosion when the *Marco Polo* blew up.

She had the driver let her off in the heart of Waikiki. She paid him in cash and thanked him. He was curious about this old woman and her stay in the Palace, and all of the swarthy-looking men running around. He watched as she walked, with dignity, down the street and disappeared into the International Market.

No one who knew her ever saw her again. She simply vanished. The FBI searched for her, and after the FBI came the KGB.

She was a survivor.

51

Eventually curious passersby from Nimitz wandered down toward the docks and discovered that the drama was not make-believe. Within a few minutes, a score of police cars roared into the parking area with sirens wailing and lights flashing. The Coast Guard was alerted and a cutter quickly came alongside. Soon after, ambulances began arriving.

Greg, with a shirt wrapped around his arm to stem the bleeding, stood spread-eagled on deck. From below, the Police Captain who had crossed swords with him before yelled up, "We're coming aboard. Get the landing stairs down."

"Go to hell," Greg shouted back.

Lynne, with eyes bloodshot and face taut with strain, was at his side. "We've got to get the wounded off—and the dead."

"The police will seize the ship," Greg retorted, "and we'll never get out."

"Please, Greg, we can't let someone die. We've got wounded."

"We'll take care of them at sea."

The Police Captain used a bullhorn. "I'll have to put you under arrest, Wilson, for obstructing police officers if you don't let us board."

Captain Parker was approaching. Greg said, "Let's go. What's keeping you?"

Parker's tone was tough. "The harbor master says absolutely no."

"Who cares what he says? Come on, move it."

Below him, the police prepared to storm the ship. Then, moving with authority, came FBI Agent Jim Manley. He pushed officers aside until he reached the Police Captain. "This is a matter of national security, Captain. Give me a few minutes alone with Wilson."

He called up, "I want to see you alone, Mr. Wilson."

"Talk with him, Greg," Lynne said. "For me."

Powder River materialized by Greg's side. "Go on, boy, see him—but stall him until I get back. Keep talking, kill time. Don't let anything happen until I come back."

"Okay, Manley," Greg yelled. "Do I have your promise? You and no one else?"

"You've got it," Manley answered.

Greg turned. "Somebody get the landing stairs—and get the wounded and dead off while we talk."

"Let me take care of your arm." He pulled away, but Lynne took it firmly in hand and proceeded to dress it.

Colonel Montand came up. He had been inspecting the damage. "We can sail, monsieur. The blast on mid-deck blew through to the hold but spent itself before it did much damage. The tank shot up the bow pretty badly . . . a couple of gaping holes . . . but they're both above the waterline and we'll cover them with mattresses like that ship did returning to England from the Falklands. We'll be all right unless we run into a big blow."

"What then?" Greg asked. The Colonel shrugged.

"How many dead?"

"Three," the Colonel answered, "and six wounded, including you."

"I don't count. How many seriously wounded?"

"Two."

"Hey," Greg shouted down. "We got any paramedics down there?"

Five hands went up. "Come on up, all of you," Greg said.

Manley took the stairs two at a time. "Would you care to tell me exactly what happened and the order in which it happened?"

Greg shook his head to clear the shell shock. "They tried to seize the ship and didn't know we were ready for them. That's all there was to it."

Powder River locked the office door and dropped his weight behind the desk. He told the phone operator he wanted the White House. When the White House switchboard answered, he explained carefully who he was, what had happened, and asked for the presidential aide who had prepared the President's message. The operator said she could not put the call through.

"Not even in case of war?" Powder River asked.

There was a long moment of silence. "I'll tell him what you have told me, and if he wishes he can call you back."

Five minutes passed, then another five. Powder River paced around the room. Greg could stall only so long.

Then the phone rang and the aide came on. He said the President should know about the situation and make any decisions. He would try to get through to the President.

Another five minutes, and another, and a tapping on the door. Lynne reported that Greg could not stave off the police much longer. Manley had pointed out that he had no authority over local peace officers, that a sizable battle had been fought, and they were certainly entitled to an investigation.

Again, Powder River was saved by the bell. A secretary's voice said that the FBI Director, on behalf of the President, wanted to speak with any FBI agent aboard the *Marco Polo*. Lynne left to inform Manley.

When Manley hung up, he was shaking his head in amazement. "The President wants me to advise the authorities to permit the *Marco Polo* to put to sea immediately. I am to tell them that this is a personal request in the interests of national security."

"Thank God," Powder River said reverently. "Thank God."

Manley continued, "I'm to stay aboard the ship and keep in touch with the White House and the FBI Director."

Powder River was going out the door while Manley was still talking. "Boy," he shouted to Greg. "We're sailing. The President is backing us all the way."

He turned to Captain Parker. "Like the boy said, get it moving, Captain. Get this old boat moving."

Not more than a half hour later, the Captain eased the *Marco Polo* away from the dock, without benefit of the pilot boat. The Captain was confident he could handle the ship through the narrow channel at Sand Island. By now, the news of what had transpired this night had spread through the police ranks, and as the ship ever so slowly moved out, a cheer went up from the parking area.

On the demand of the Police Captain, McGraw had turned over his prisoners. All except two. He had them handcuffed and locked in a cabin. He told Greg he wanted to grill them. "They know more than they're telling. They may know about the *Kharkov*."

Now with the vessel moving, there was kicking and pounding on the inside of their cabin door and the shouting of desperate men. McGraw unholstered a .45, unlocked the door, stood back, and pushed it sharply open with a foot.

Both stood there screaming but not moving. He couldn't understand what the trouble was. They were obviously terrified, as if about to be killed.

At last one fell quiet. The other could scarcely control his words. McGraw pieced a few together, and without taking time to lock the terrorists back in, went scurrying for the bridge.

He shouted up to Captain Parker, "The harbor's mined! We're going to be blown up!"

The next minute the ship shuddered and shook in violent spasm as it was put in reverse. People spun around and were thrown and objects hurled off shelves.

Once more the President's name was invoked and Pearl Harbor sent a mine sweeper to clear the channel. But the sun was rising before the *Marco Polo* again throbbed with life.

52

Late that same afternoon, after ten hours of sleep, Lynne and Greg stood at the bow, pleasantly damp from the cool ocean spray. As if it were an old-fashioned rocker, the ship rose and fell gently. It glided through waters that were breathing without exertion. As far as the eye could see, the Pacific spread darkly. A ruby-red sun was about to call it a day.

"That's your world out there, isn't it?" Greg said. "The same as the desert and mountains are mine."

She looked up longingly. These last twenty-four hours, they had been through so much together. They had been so close. Yet she wondered if he felt what she had. They had shared danger; they had heard the whisper of death; and out of the melee, when it was all over, had surged a love she had never known before.

"I'm going to take you down there one of these days," she said, "and show you great plains—Kansas wheat country—and mountains of sheer cliffs and peaks higher than any on earth. You can fly between the mountains and reach out and touch a peak and float through a canyon."

He smiled. "I think I'll do my mountain climbing in the Rockies."

"That's the hard way."

They talked to ease the shock they had suffered and the dangers closing in with every league the ship traveled. Ahead was the unknown, man's first attempt to mine the ocean at great depth and with far-out technology that had not yet been fully tried. Ahead, too, were terrors that man as a political animal might create to thwart those of a different political persuasion. As a constant reminder, the periscope of the submarine bounced less than a mile behind. For reassurance, the flags of the United States and the People's Republic of China flew side by side above them.

FBI Agent Manley summoned them to a meeting with Powder River and Carlos, who struggled to conceal the excruciating pain he suffered from the shoulder wound. Manley had in hand a radio message from Bob McLean, the Massachusetts Diversified director. It was addressed to: DR. LYNNE KENNEDY, ABOARD THE MARCO POLO.

It read:

> DEAR DR. KENNEDY: THE WHITE HOUSE HAS ASKED ME TO INFORM YOU THAT THE PRESIDENT WILL SEND HIS DEEP-SEA-MINING MESSAGE TO CONGRESS TOMORROW WHICH WILL CONTAIN PROVISIONS HE RESPECTFULLY REQUESTS THAT YOU APPROVE OF ON BEHALF OF CARSON MINING COMPANY. THE SALIENT POINTS ARE: (ONE) CONGRESS WILL SET UP OR DESIGNATE AN AGENCY TO GRANT MINING PERMITS TO AMERICAN AND FOREIGN CORPORATIONS WHICH ARE FINANCED FOR SUCH OPERATIONS AND HAVE THE REQUIRED TECHNOLOGY. (TWO) THE UNITED STATES WILL NOT CLAIM OWNERSHIP OR SOVEREIGNTY OVER SUCH MINING SITES. (THREE) THE MINING COMPANIES WILL CONTRIBUTE THIRTY PERCENT OF THEIR NET PROFITS TO AN AGENCY THAT CONGRESS DESIGNATES THAT WILL DIVIDE THESE FUNDS AMONG THOSE NATIONS THAT OFFER PROOF THEIR CITIZENS ARE LIVING AT A SUB-SUBSISTENCE LEVEL AND/OR ARE CARING FOR SIZABLE NUMBERS OF REFUGEES. (FOUR) IF THAT AGENCY SHOULD BE THE UNITED NATIONS, THEN THE UN MUST AGREE TO CONSIDER THE FUNDS AS CONTRIBUTIONS AND IN NO SENSE AS TAXES AND SHALL NOT SET ITSELF UP IN ANY MANNER AS A SUPER SOVEREIGN STATE. (FIVE) CONGRESS WILL NOT RECOGNIZE THE UNITED NATIONS RIGHT TO SET UP ITS OWN MINING CORPORATION. (SIX) CONGRESS WILL NOT AGREE TO ANY UNITED NATIONS REQUIREMENT THAT CORPORATIONS SHALL BE FORCED TO DIVULGE THEIR TECHNOLOGY. END SALIENT POINTS. PRESIDENT MUST HAVE ANSWER SOONEST IN ORDER TO OFFER FULLEST COOPERATION TO CARSON PROJECT.
>
> BOB MCLEAN

Each waited for the other to speak up. Greg finally did.

"I don't see how any mining company could take exception. It gives us a legal base, lays down some rules, and states unequivocally the profit contributions."

Carlos tried to stand up. He always stood when talking. This time, though, the pain was too intense. "But we can't vote for the Board. It wouldn't be legal."

"Come off it, Carlos," Lynne said. "Since when have you been so legal?"

Manley had another message, forwarded through a Washington, D.C., agency from an American "ferret spy" satellite. It read in part:

> TWO SOVIET DESTROYERS, FOUR GUNBOATS AND ONE AIRCRAFT CARRIER HAVE LEFT CAM RANH. DESTINATION UNKNOWN. HEADING DUE EAST. SOVIET FLAG FLYING ON ALL VESSELS.

Carlos cleared his throat. "What're they going to do, blow us out of the water? But they don't need all of those battle wagons for that."

"When dealing with the Russians," Powder River said, "we have to think as they do. They're going as far as they can without starting a nuclear war. They're going to the brink of the precipice, but mark my word, they won't go over. They're masters of control."

"What the hell are you talking about?" Carlos asked. "Do they or don't they open fire on us?"

Lynne spoke up. "They wouldn't dare fire on us on the surface. That would call for an American response. But they can do anything they want to under water. Nobody sees them and nobody can prove it."

That night Greg couldn't sleep. His right arm throbbed until he could take the hurt no longer. He rose and stood on the stern, staring down in a trance at the foamy cleavage left by the ship. An anchor chain clanked, men on the deck coughed or muttered in their sleep, the engines rumbled, and there was a torrential gush as the ocean parted. He took a deep breath. The smell of fresh-air and salt water was biting and enlivening.

Lynne joined him and they talked for an hour. Not out of spontaneous desire but because talking was a cathartic.

"I never thought I'd kill, that I'd have to . . ." Her words pleaded for understanding and forgiveness, her own and God's. "It's something I'll pray over and have to live with . . . somehow . . ."

He put an arm about her and pulled her close. Not as a lover might but as one human being reaching out to comfort another, and finding comfort for himself.

"I used to read books about the gunfighters of the Old West and wonder why they were gunfighters. What did they get out of it? I understand now. Some killed to be killing, but many, I'm sure, were sucked into it as we were. I guess there comes a time for some of us when we have to fight. I know how you feel . . . I feel the same, Lynne."

He seldom used her name, and now it was like a caress. "Why, Greg, why? We started off so innocently . . . and tomorrow when we get there . . ."

Both knew the killing might not have ended.

53

With clanking of chains and rumble of the engines, the *Marco Polo* dropped anchor in a spot marked on a map with a dot. Greg could no more understand how the Captain found it than how a pilot could locate a city 5,000 miles away he had never seen.

No other ship appeared on the horizon. They were alone—except for the submarine—and he could have shouted for the joy of knowing they had beaten out the *Kharkov*. Lynne hugged him and Powder River slapped him on the back and Carlos lapsed into Spanish.

They swung into action. The huge doors to the hold opened with the push of a button and when another button was activated the dredge head itself rolled on tracks through the door. Still on rails, it glided over the "moon pool" far below and came to a halt.

High overhead the two roughnecks pulled up on the hose curled about the vacuum, pushed more buttons, the tracks disappeared, and the dredge head slowly descended on an elevatorlike cable until it touched water. They kept playing out the hose, as the vacuum sank out of sight, until there was no more. They grabbed for sections of pipe and locked them together and dropped the dredge head more feet. They worked fast. Behind them heavy hydraulic "tongs" that could have dealt them a horrible blow swung on cables. They seemed, though, to know exactly where the "tongs" were. More pipe and more pipe. It took a lot to string it out three miles to the ocean floor.

Up on deck, a crane was holding the fishbowl out over the water. Lynne inspected it and then with Greg went directly to the Operations Room where on a small television screen they saw the dredge head settling as easily as a bird into a nest. It carried two television cameras, one that scanned with a 250-watt light the area immediately ahead that it would be working, and another on a rod that extended twelve feet out, with the camera shooting in reverse on the vacuum itself. The technician monitoring the screen could watch the vacuum's performance, and if there were trouble, would know instantly. This camera, too, had a 250-watt lamp. The light seemed brighter than it was since down there the ocean was pitch black.

Colonel Montand reported that the frogmen were suited, armed and ready. He advised, too, that the mercenaries had taken the same battle stations that they had been assigned in Honolulu.

McGraw entered hurriedly. Tireless interrogation of the two prisoners had produced results. One revealed that the *Kharkov* had set sail the day of the battle for this exact location. The prisoner thought it would be arriving the next day.

A crewman called out there was a ship on the horizon to the west. It looked like a freighter, but until it drew closer it would be impossible to tell. A moment later Captain Parker discovered four ships, all eastward bound. They were widely separated. Everyone reacted to the news by working faster. All except Lynne. What had to be done, had to be done right.

With Greg trailing, she went from one computer to another. The stabilization system was working well. It was modeled after the Honeywell one used in the Boeing 767s and 757s. Three laser gyros, mounted at 90-degree angles, sensed the motion in the pitch, roll and yaw, and the high-speed, digital computer forwarded this data to the navigation system which held the ship steady over the area that was being mined.

Next she studied a film printout that showed the density of the earth that was being washed away from the nodules. The earth's "toughness," if too compacted, could stop the operation and conceivably damage the dredge head.

A few feet away three sonic scans were turning on cylinders. Here the printout resembled an EKG. The scans were reporting what the sensors, submerged under water at the bow, the stern and the dredge head, "heard." The sensors picked up all sound. Hence, a whale passing by or a submarine could excite the scan as well as an enemy frogman.

From the bridge came the news that two of the ships sighted were freighters flying the Liberian flag, one was a low-slung oil tanker bearing the American flag, and the fourth was a gunboat with a flag that no one immediately identified. It was flaming red with a gold star in dead center. Colonel Montand was summoned and readily recognized it as belonging to the Socialist Republic of Vietnam. He was immediately concerned. He couldn't fathom why a Vietnamese gunboat would be 3,500 miles from home base. He went up on the bridge to keep watch. The submarine had not surfaced. Its periscope looked like a sea monster's eye.

As Lynne was about to step into the fishbowl, Greg notified her the dredge head had quit working. Everyone in the Operations Room was near panic. Calmly, she checked out the various recording devices, then studied the television screen.

"Let's move the vacuum back a few feet." She programmed the computer and on the TV screen the dredge head pulled back to reveal a sizable rock. She maneuvered the vacuum around it and the equipment began sucking up nodules again.

Back at the fishbowl, she stepped inside and checked the "life line." A cable tethered to the *Marco Polo* brought into the submersible one line of proper breathing mix, another of voice communication, and a third that measured the depth. She would descend fifty feet along the pipeline to the dredge head, to "ride shotgun" as Greg put it.

She had added to the bowl, which was modeled after the Navy's NEMO (Naval Experimental Manned Observatory), a television camera, which sat on top, and a strobe light, which penetrated 300 feet. She had three machine guns mounted which could be fired by pushing buttons inside. She also had had installed an inside television camera that held on her. In case the voice communication line failed or she was knocked out (fainted because of bad air mix, wounded in an attack, etc.), those above would know.

"Mademoiselle." Startled, she turned quickly. Colonel Montand stood there. "The gunboat is heading directly for us."

She called a conference for the Operations Room. Present were herself and Greg, Powder River, Carlos, McGraw, the Colonel and Jim Manley.

Powder River summed up the situation. "The Russians are dumping five million dollars a day into Vietnam and they figure they're going to collect interest on it. That gunboat can do anything it wants to, wreck our mining equipment or sink us, and there's nothing Washington can do. After what happened back in the seventies, we're not going to declare war—and of course, Russia will play innocent. They had no idea Hanoi was planning to blow us out of the ocean."

Lynne announced that the mining would continue; the Colonel would order the mercenaries to prepare for an attack; and Jim Manley would notify the FBI Director and the White House.

By now the gunboat had taken up position a few hundred yards to the west. The radio operator came dashing in. "They're asking us to surrender." He could scarcely talk. "They've given us five minutes before they open fire."

Powder River said matter-of-factly, "Let's do what my grandpa did the time he was surrounded by a hundred Sioux."

"What?" Carlos asked.

"He talked them out of it."

Greg turned to the radio operator. "Let's tell them they've made a mistake. They've got the wrong ship. If that doesn't work, insist that they've got to give us a little time to prepare for evacuating the ship."

Powder River said, "If you trust me, I'll handle it." Everyone spoke up at once agreeing.

Without a word, Lynne left with Greg following. As he suspected, she headed for the fishbowl. He blocked her. "Don't be a fool. You're not going down. We've got a man for that."

Carlos, who had followed them, shouted, "Look at that!" They looked in the direction he had pointed, to the stern of the gunboat. "My God! The whole Russian Navy." They counted an aircraft carrier, two destroyers and four smaller warships.

Powder River said, "Let's cool it. So they're closing in on the wagon train."

Carlos shouted again and pointed at the Vietnamese gunboat. "They're coming for us."

Enemy frogmen were dropping down a ladder.

The Colonel's voice could be heard over the entire ship. He ordered his frogmen to assemble at the battle station. He posted one man on the bridge to keep watch over the submarine which remained immobile.

At the fishbowl, Lynne pushed Greg gently aside. "Get your male chauvinism out of my way!"

From inside she closed the door so quickly he had no chance. She signaled to the crane operator to lower the bowl. Greg was talking with him. The operator shook his head and eased the bowl down. Soon it splashed gently and disappeared.

This was her world. Ten feet, twenty feet. Through the eerie glow of filtered sunlight passed a well-disciplined squadron of brightly colored fish. Thirty feet: luminous green eyes stared curiously at her. Forty feet: more eyes, a score of them. Like school children they pressed their stub noses against the acryllic, staring in disbelief at this new sea creature.

Fifty feet: She asked the operator to put Mr. Wilson on the communication line. She turned on the strobes. Their light reached to the ship's hull.

She was satisfied. She could sit here, and turn about, and see in all directions. She discovered she needed a sonic scan. If a frogman slipped up on her, she would have only scant seconds to react, to decide which gun to fire.

Greg came on. "How are you down there?"

She had feared he would be angry. "I'm sorry. I shouldn't've said what I did."

The Vietnamese frogmen were getting closer. The Colonel still held his men back. He signaled to a gunner who fired the big cannon on the stern. Obviously, the Vietnamese had not expected gunfire, especially not after Powder River, as a part of the delay tactic, had indicated surrender was imminent. At least two frogmen were hit. The others scattered. A minute passed and another. On the *Marco Polo*, they literally held their breath. They anticipated the Vietnamese might sink them with a single torpedo.

More minutes passed. By now it was apparent that the Vietnamese were consulting with the Russians. The decision came through to resume the attack. The frogmen spread far out and swam once more for the *Marco Polo*. The Colonel ordered his men into the water at mid-deck but to hold back until the enemy swimmers were actually attempting to board the ship.

When they did, the mercenaries fired on them with small arms from the bulwarks. Then the Colonel's frogmen swam far out on the flanks and began picking off the enemy one by one. Soon, the Vietnamese ordered a pullback. As fast as they could, the enemy frogmen retreated with the gunner on the *Marco Polo* lobbing shells far out from the big cannon.

As they watched in amazement, Carlos said, "Why don't they sink us? We're sitting ducks."

Powder River had a theory. "They want our technology. They sink us, they lose it. The Russians are giving the orders."

The Soviet battleships were drawn up in a semicircle around the Vietnamese gunboat. As far as the Colonel could make out, the Russians had no men in battle readiness on the decks and the guns were not manned. They simply sat there protecting the gunboat. They were biding their time until they could board the *Marco Polo*. The sub's periscope continued to ogle them from the same spot.

There was still no sighting of the *Kharkov* and Greg and the others were puzzled. The presence of the Soviet warships indicated, surely, that the *Kharkov* would be along.

The submersible operator kept Lynne informed. She had caught only distant flashes of frogmen, so distant she could not make out their identity. Still she maintained a careful watch in all directions. An enemy might slip through and come directly for her.

When the last enemy frogman was back aboard ship, the Vietnamese swung out derricks along both the starboard and port sides. From the derricks hung small, dark blue submersibles that were known in oil drilling circles as "flying eyeballs." Usually they weighed less than two hundred pounds and were seldom more than three feet in diameter. They were operated by a tether line that carried power and computer orders to four electrical thrusters that controlled the craft. Usually, too, they bore small television cameras that used halogen lights. The sphere was filled with foam and glass bubbles. The oil companies used them to inspect offshore installations where divers could not go. One had prowled around at the blowout of the Ixtoc I oil well in Mexico, and after sending pictures back had been consumed in the flames.

Through binoculars, the Colonel studied these "free swimmers." He had encountered them previously during the Angolan civil war. Instead of foam and glass bubbles, they carried explosives. By means of the television camera, the "gunner" back aboard the mother ship could pick out the exact spot he wanted to hit and the extent of the havoc he desired. The robots were good for damaging ships when the attackers wanted the cargo or perhaps the ship itself rather than to send it to the bottom. The Viet arsenal could not possibly have possessed these "flying eyeballs." The Soviets had provided them.

The *Marco Polo* had no defense other than sharpshooters who hopefully would explode them in the water before they hit the hull. He called on his best marksmen to man the outer bulwarks. The trouble was: the robots might come in too deeply to be seen.

While he was giving orders, a shout went up from the crew and mercenaries. In the distance, six destroyers, five gunboats and an aircraft carrier hove on the horizon. They were flying the American flag.

By now, the "flying eyeballs" had been released and disappeared under the sea. Since they were tethered, it was possible to guess where they were. The lines that were being played out indicated their rapid advance. While they waited, the tension was almost beyond endurance for each marksman. The Colonel called out to Greg to bring Lynne up at once.

Lynne put her fingers lightly on the buttons that triggered the machine guns. She knew about the "flying eyeballs." She had used a RCV-225 once when employed by an oil company. She had never known them to be used in war, but then war was not her business. Not until now, and her heart beat faster. Slowly the cables pulled the fishbowl higher. Forty feet, then thirty.

Then it was coming, a dark blue sphere heading straight for her. To aim it with such accuracy, the enemy had to know her whereabouts. Perhaps through a sonic device or a frogman. The halogen light sought her out. In the dark waters, it seemed weak. But not too weak for the "gunner" back aboard the mother ship to watch her on his television screen.

With manual control she pointed one machine gun in the direction of the sphere and pressed a button. The fire missed. She turned the control slightly to target the weapon in better on the onrushing eyeball.

She pressed another button which provided the power needed to open the exit door against the tremendous pressure of the water. She was scrambling out when the eyeball struck, the fishbowl shattered, and the explosion was like a hurricane renting the waters.

From on deck, Greg recoiled as the water shot into the air, an explosion that rocked the ship. The next second, he was in the water, diving deep, ever deeper, his body lambasted viciously by the after shocks. The wreckage of the bowl was all about him. Some bits had been hurled high out of the water.

On his right, he saw another ball hurling toward him but before he could react, a shot from the deck had exploded it. Again, the water was a whirling vortex, tossing him unmercifully about, whipping and pounding him. The pain in his right arm was excruciating.

A few feet farther down, he found Lynne. Miraculously, she was not only conscious but struggling desperately against the fury to fight her way up. He sought to help her but she was doing better on her own than he was. She was the first to surface.

On deck, she stood shivering with cold and water streaming from her. She simply stood, stunned, not quite grasping where she was or what had happened.

Greg was saying something. She couldn't make it out. Then he was pointing and slowly the American ships came into fuzzy view. She remembered to breathe deeply and discovered she was leaning on Greg's arm and he was walking her about. She could walk.

Slowly, words, thoughts and sights fell into logical place. She recognized the confusion of mind and struggled to penetrate it, and rearrange it, and then it was no longer there.

A technician from the Operations Room hurried up to her. He was agitated. "You must take a look. We've got little creatures crawling all over the ocean floor near the dredge head."

"I'll go," Greg said. She staggered along, gaining strength with each step.

At the television screen, with pictures emanating from the camera mounted on the vacuum and shooting into the blackness, were four dark-colored, bulky, eyeless forms crawling slowly toward the dredge head. They were sea creatures she had never seen before, ugly ones with no apparent mouths. She might be viewing a form of life no man knew existed. At this depth of three miles, not all of the sea animals and fishes had been catalogued.

Still, they were reminiscent of something from out of her past. And then she knew. These were camouflaged "mud crawlers." They, too, belonged to the oil business. These had been painted a dirty black and their shapes altered to give them the look of weird creatures in a horror film.

In offshore oil work, they crawled over the ocean bottom laying pipe. They could climb over obstacles two feet high and put down 2,000 feet of pipe an hour. Usually, they had "umbilicals"; that is, they, too, were controlled by power that came through a "line" from a mother ship.

Once again she was her old self, and the adrenalin was flowing.

She even smiled when Greg asked, "What are they going to do, swallow up the dredge head like in Pac-Man?"

She ordered a little robot brought on deck called NOMAN 100. It was an adaptation of the PAP-104 used by the French Navy. It was eight feet in length and battery-powered with side-mounted thrusters. It was controlled by an umbilical. The French used it to explode sunken mines.

The technicians worked fast. It was a race to see who or which won, Lynne and Greg or the mud crawlers. Minute by minute the latter shortened the space.

They dropped NOMAN into the water from a derrick. The workers played out the tether cable until the robot was in the general area above the mud crawlers. As she watched the television screen, Lynne gave orders. Three times the computer had to change the position of NOMAN. Finally it was fifty feet directly over the mud crawlers.

Lynne said, "Okay. Drop it."

NOMAN let go of a 250-pound charge. When it struck between the first two mud crawlers, it set off the explosives they carried. Any one of the crawlers, if it had made contact with the dredge head would have blown it up. While the charge was dropping, NOMAN escalated on its own power, rising sufficiently high to avoid being trapped in the explosion.

Lynne ordered another charge dropped and this one wiped out the other two crawlers.

Jim Manley was waiting to report to Lynne and Greg on "the diplomatic front."

"I'll begin with the U.S. Navy. We've got an Admiral with us." He indicated the American ships. "To give us status. He sent a message advising the Navy was offering us protection on the direct orders of the White House and would we keep them informed about our movements and plans. He asked about damage suffered to date and a report on exactly what had transpired. Here is the answer I sent back."

Manley handed it over and continued, "When the Viets sent the frogmen in, I advised Washington, and Washington in turn consulted with the People's Republic in Beijing. The result was that the People's Republic informed Hanoi that if they fired on the *Marco Polo,* Beijing would consider it an act of war and invade Vietnam."

Powder River spoke up. "I think that blocks the Vietnamese ship from taking further action. The way I figure it, the Soviet ships will not fire on the U.S. Navy or the *Marco Polo* since that might be the tinder box that sets off World War III. The same with our Navy, except they could sink the Vietnamese gunboat without serious repercussions. The Russians would protest but wouldn't really care, and what could Hanoi do?"

They all felt better. They thought they were out of immediate danger. They could keep the dredge head gobbling up the nodules.

54

As it does in the tropics, the sun took its time turning itself off. Slowly, the *Marco Polo* advanced eastward. Four times Lynne ordered the dredge head pulled up. She would then skip twenty to twenty-five miles to stake out another claim and work it. Each time the U.S. Navy pulled back to give them room, and the Soviets would advance, always keeping the same distance between their warships and the *Marco Polo*. The gunboat, too, kept its position during the moves.

Each side was stalemated, waiting for the other to make a move. Powder River was certain that Politburo members were engaged in long conversations in the Kremlin attempting to come up with a maneuver that would make it possible to seize the *Marco Polo* for its technology or to wreck it partially. The Soviets wanted no "Welcome Home" that would broadcast to the world that the Americans had been the first to work the ocean floor.

Aboard the *Marco Polo,* the roar was incessant as the air pressure shot the nodules out of the pipe into the hold which was rapidly filling. On the next trip, Greg would bring along an ore carrier. Already he had one en route from Chile to Lahaina on the island of Maui where the refinery was under construction.

Powder River, Carlos and McGraw agreed to stand watch every two hours. Lynne, Greg and the Colonel refused to sleep. They feared an unexpected chess move. They feared, too, that an enemy frogman might still sabotage the pipeline, or more mud crawlers might ooze their way through to blow up the vacuum.

The Colonel kept his own frogmen in the waters about the ship, changing every fifteen minutes. He assigned the best ones to depth dive along the pipeline. Without special equipment, their limit was a hundred feet. At sea level, man was subjected to 14.7 pounds of pressure per square inch. With every thirty-three feet he dropped in the ocean, he added the same pressure. If he could live one mile down—which no human could without a submersible—the pressure would build to one ton.

Their best protection was the video screens in the Operations Room. They could watch the vacuum at work, the area about it, and also the NOMAN robot as it climbed and descended along the hose and pipes leading up from the vacuum.

It was a little after 4 A.M., and Greg and Lynne were munching a sandwich when a dark hulk showed up in the far distance, to the north. It was an eerie ghost ship out of nowhere. Gradually it took shape. With its open derrick on deck, silhouetted by starlight, they realized that it had to be the *Kharkov*. Its few lights grew brighter and as it neared, it slowed. It ignored the Soviet fleet. It was headed straight for them, and alarmed, they summoned Colonel Montand and Captain Parker. "We'll keep mining," Lynne said. "What else can we do?"

When the *Kharkov* was only a short distance away, Powder River said, "You don't think they're planning to ram us and put men aboard?"

Each had the same thought.

The Colonel sounded an alarm and his soldiers took up their positions, armed and ready for another attack. There was much scurrying about as more supplies of ammunition were brought out of caches and stacked on deck. The men were abnormally quiet, numbed by sleep. Lynne hurried to the galley to see about coffee. She rudely awakened two cooks who were dozing.

Back on deck she overheard McGraw haranguing the Colonel. McGraw wanted to sink the *Kharkov*. "We've got to hit them first, take them by surprise."

"No!" Lynne cried out. "We're a mining ship. Not a gunboat. We can't do it unless the White House orders us to."

Greg backed her up. McGraw had had a stomach full of their views. "You're nothing but a couple of weak-kneed pacifists. After what happened back in Honolulu—and here today . . ."

The Colonel said quietly, "May I point out, monsieur, that if any Soviet ship fires one single bullet—only one bullet—the American Navy will blow them out of the ocean?"

The *Kharkov* came dangerously close. They could see the Russian sailors aboard and soldiers armed to the hilt and in smart uniforms. The *Kharkov*, too, had big guns fore and aft and they were manned. The gunners sat under spotlights.

"They're not planning an attack," Colonel Montand said. "Not with all that light. They just want us to see what they have and could do if they decided to."

Their anger grew as the *Kharkov*'s captain maneuvered the ship into position only a few yards from them and on the side that blocked them from continuing their mining. The *Kharkov* shut off its engines and prepared to bed down for what was left of the night.

Greg said, "We'll pull up the dredge head and go around."

Captain Parker readily agreed. He considered that his equal on the *Kharkov* had violated the ethics of the sea. He took to the bridge, gave the orders, and the *Marco Polo* came alive. The Captain's instructions were to keep five ship's lengths distant at all times from the *Kharkov*. There must be no accident.

The operation had barely started when the radio officer hurried forward with a message from one Dr. Georgi Kerensky aboard the *Kharkov*. It was addressed to Lynne who recognized the name. "He's one of the great oceanographers of our time. I worked with him once briefly."

The message read:

> DEAR DR. KENNEDY: YOU MAY REMEMBER ME. I WORKED WITH YOU ON THE SOVIET-AMERICAN TEAM IN 1978 IN THE RED SEA. MIGHT I INVITE YOU OVER FOR COCKTAILS ABOARD THE KHARKOV OR IF YOU PREFER I WILL VISIT YOU ON YOUR SHIP. I AM APPALLED BY OUR WARLIKE SURROUNDINGS AND THOUGHT IF WE SAT DOWN AS TWO SCIENTISTS WORKING TOWARD THE GOOD OF ALL MANKIND WE MIGHT REACH A SOLUTION THAT BOTH OUR NATIONS WOULD ACCEPT. EVEN IF WE DO NOT FIND A COMMON SOLUTION A MEETING MIGHT PROVE BENEFICIAL FOR THE FUTURE. I WOULD BE MOST PLEASED IF YOU WOULD ACCEPT. BE ASSURED OF MY GREAT ADMIRATION FOR YOU IN WHAT YOU HAVE ACHIEVED AS ONE OF OUR FOREMOST OCEANOGRAPHERS.
>
> GEORGI KERENSKY

Greg and the others were waiting with the greatest curiosity. She hesitated to show the message to them. She knew what their reactions would be.

Greg read it hastily. "I think you'll be walking into a dangerous situation, for you, personally, and what have you to gain? No matter how he may feel as a scientist, he can't go against his government."

McGraw was terse. "If you want to commit suicide, go ahead. You'll never come back here alive. They'll tell us you drowned accidentally or fell down stairs or something."

Colonel Montand said, "I believe we should have assurances that he represents something Soviet besides himself. Does he represent that armada out there? If you reach a solution, will they withdraw?"

Carlos believed it was a trick. "What if they hold you hostage and sweat a deal out of us?"

Jim Manley wanted to inform the White House, and to this, Lynne agreed.

Powder River's massive, old face was a study. "Well, girl, you've got yourself a situation, haven't you? I've always figured it was good talking with the other fellow. Sometimes something comes out of it and sometimes nothing does. The way I figure, you've got nothing to lose. Fact is, we hold the ace hand. We're the first to mine the ocean floor and we've staked out claims that Washington will back up for us."

Greg asked, "What kind of a man is this Kerensky?"

She chose her words carefully. "He's no dissident. He goes along with the Communist line. If I remember right, he is a member of the Communist Party."

"That does it!" McGraw said.

"It could be an advantage. You must remember that he is working in a field the Kremlin leaders know nothing about, and since he is a Communist in good standing, he has clout. He's a practical man, and I don't believe he'd let Communist ideology interfere with working out a solution."

"It's a trick," Carlos repeated. "While you're talking with him, they'll blow up the dredge head."

Lynne shook her head. "Dr. Kerensky has a global reputation, and as I remember, quite an ego, and he isn't going to front for any kind of dirty work. He's bound to know he's up against a bad situation. We've beaten them soundly at every turn. In a sense, he's surrendering for the Russians—and he's got to put the best face on it he can."

She had talked herself into a decision. "I want to talk this out with him. Here, on the *Marco Polo*. Will you sit in on it with me, Greg? And you, Powder River, as the oldest Board member?"

She drafted an answer:

DEAR DR. KERENSKY: THANK YOU FOR YOUR KIND INVITATION. COULD YOU MEET ME TOMORROW MORNING AT NINE O'CLOCK ABOARD MY SHIP? I DO REMEMBER YOU WITH GREAT PLEASURE AND OUR WORK TOGETHER.

LYNNE KENNEDY

55

Since the *Kharkov* did not carry a tender, four muscular crew members rowed Dr. Kerensky and two others over in a lifeboat to the *Marco Polo*. The morning was bright with sunshine and the clouds billowy and white.

As the three climbed out, Lynne lifted a hand in greeting from the deck. The gesture was not as confident as it appeared. Inwardly, she was trembling down to her calves. She had changed to loose jeans and a work shirt.

McGraw and Carlos had insisted the three Russians should be searched, and she had reacted violently. Finally they reached an agreement. The Colonel's men would discreetly keep the three and the four crew members who remained in the lifeboat under armed watch.

Dr. Kerensky took the stairs with a firm step. He had a lean and hardened body of seventy years. His hair was wispy and white, his eyebrows bushy, and his face old parchment. She had remembered him as more physical. But the years whittle all of us down.

She offered a hand. "Thank you for asking me over," he said in a raspy voice, the result of a throat operation. "If you hadn't, I would have understood. These are difficult times for all of us, no?"

Agreeing, she introduced Greg and Powder River. In turn, he presented his two "associates." "This is our political commissar." A clean-cut, studious-looking individual of about thirty stared belligerently through thick glasses. "I hope you don't mind? He speaks no English and I've asked our first mate to translate."

The first mate was built like a stevedore, but he knew his English and often put the Russian into American idiom.

Seated in the ship's office, Dr. Kerensky said, "I congratulate you on being the first to mine the ocean bottom. I am happy for you, Dr. Kennedy"—he ignored Greg, which disturbed her—"but extremely disappointed for myself. We had . . . we had"—he glanced fleetingly at the Commissar—"problems."

She was certain he had been about to explain.

Greg wished to be polite. "Yes, we all have problems."

The Commissar interrupted with a torrent of Russian.

Dr. Kerensky nodded. "The Commissar has been kind enough to tell me that we have no problems. No problems of any kind."

Powder River smiled. "That's what my ranch foreman said the night before we lost forty head of cattle to a rustler."

Lynne said, "May I please give you some background on what has happened to us in the last forty-eight hours so that you may know . . . well, our emotional state."

She described the attack at Honolulu and again by the Vietnamese gunboat. He appeared surprised and appalled. Either he was a good actor or had no knowledge.

He chose his words carefully. "As a friend, I am glad you have not been harmed. These political matters . . . as a scientist . . ."

"I understand, Dr. Kerensky," Lynne assured him.

"Thank you. I knew you would. Now to the present. I have the *Kharkov* ready to mine . . . and the Pacific, it is a big ocean, no?"

She nodded and he continued, "Our Captain found it necessary to position our ship very close to yours and . . . these political matters . . ."

Again, she said, "I understand." She did, and she wanted him to get to the point.

"You have done considerable mining and staked out many claims and achieved what you came to do, no?"

"In part. We still have claims to stake out."

The Commissar frowned. She thought: *He knows at least a little English.*

"Yes. As an oceanographer the same as you, Dr. Kennedy, I have responsibilities . . . My ship is beautiful, is it not?" He indicated the *Kharkov*. "Up above?"

Up above! Was he telling her it was not *down below? Down below* where the technology should have been.

He continued, "We have situations, the same as all scientists. At times more than other times."

They have insurmountable problems. Is that what he was telling her?

"May I interrupt?" Greg asked. "If you would tell us specifically what the Soviets want, I will get on the satellite to Washington . . ."

Powder River added, "Yes, let's round up the cattle and be done with it."

"They believe . . . I mean, we believe, the Soviets, that we, I mean, Moscow does, that we have as much right to the Golden Tide as the Americans."

Lynne said, "I agree."

He was floored. "You mean . . ."

"The United States is not interested in a monopoly. The ocean floors are for all the nations of the world to use—but as a practical matter, only those with the money and the technology can. Let me go over the points in the President's message about this that he is sending Congress this morning."

The Commissar stopped her at mention of the 30 percent of the net profit the mining companies would pay. "This money, it is only for the capitalist nations?"

"Of course not!" She was miffed. "It is for any country—whether communist, democratic, a dictatorship or whatever—where there are hungry or homeless people."

Powder River spoke up. "If someone's starving, you don't ask him his politics." He had to tell his favorite story. "Hell, I had this orphanage outside Saigon. The nuns were Catholics and the kids Buddhists, and here I am a Jew, and some friends who helped me were Methodists."

The Commissar asked to be excused. Colonel Montand, who had positioned himself outside the office, accompanied him to the lifeboat which returned him to the *Kharkov*. Lynne was certain he was bound for the satellite room.

She said, "What would you think, Dr. Kerensky, if we continued mining and staking out claims—and the *Kharkov* did the same? The Golden Tide stretches for 2,500 miles. Is there any reason why you shouldn't work the other end"—the other end was a long way for the Russians to go and the nodules scarcer—"and recognize that we have a right to our own technology that we have developed over the years and at tremendous expense?

"In other words, leave us alone and we'll leave you alone? What have either of us got to gain by killing and lying and stealing?"

Greg couldn't take his eyes off her. He hadn't expected she would be so blunt.

Dr. Kerensky said slowly, knowing the Russian interpreter was mentally recording every word, "I wish I could tell you . . ."

"I understand." She smiled. "I guess by now you know I'm a very understanding person."

"We speak the same language. We would, of course, since we're scientists and have the same hopes and goals, no?"

"Definitely."

The Commissar returned and a long conversation followed between him and Dr. Kerensky. Again, the Commissar left.

Dr. Kerensky took a deep breath of relief. "A scientist can only do so much and then . . ." He gestured surrender with his hands. "You have been most gracious, as I knew you would be."

Gracious in accepting the Russians' surrender?

That afternoon the *Kharkov* disappeared to the east, and the Vietnamese gunboat to the west. Sometime during the night, the Soviet armada, including the submarine, vanished as did the American ships. The next morning only the *Marco Polo* remained.

The dredge head went about its business of vacuuming nodules, and the roar on board was deafening. Then would come long lulls as the ship skipped miles of nodules to stake another claim. At last the hold was filled and the *Marco Polo*, wallowing low under the great weight, turned about with the Hawaiian Islands in mind. On board they worried about the mattresses still stuffed in the gaping holes. The mattresses were getting soaked.

56

Everyone was bone-weary and still suffering from shock but so exhilarated that no one could rest, much less sleep. Greg pretended to inspect the damage, but all the while he was wishing with a great emptiness of heart that Barbara was walking beside him. Desperately he longed for her to be with him in this moment of victory. She had been such a part of the beginning and the middle, of the planning, the long hours, the times when it seemed they would bog down. More than the work and the thought she had put into it was the inspiration. During the worst days she had kept them fired up. She was the motivating, driving force.

And now, what to do about Laura? She would spend the summer aboard the *Marco Polo*, and they would have good times together. But come fall? He could keep her with him and hire a tutor, which is what he yearned to do. He could employ a regular housekeeper. And then, she might spend the winter in Hong Kong with Lotus and go to a British school.

Her eyes bright and her step quick, Lynne brought a satellite message. "The President," she said breathlessly. "He's congratulating us and wants us at the White House as soon as possible. He wants us to let him know when we can be there. Can you imagine? When *we* can be there."

Powder River said he would rather be shot than return to Washington, and Carlos echoed the sentiment. Greg told her he would send his regrets and for her to go ahead.

Lynne said firmly, "You'll be there in a regular shirt and tie and wearing a suit."

"You sound like a wife."

"And you'll get a haircut."

He pretended to cringe. "Don't forget you promised all the Mass. directors they'd get invited to the Rose Garden."

She thought that could be worked out. She had doubts, though, about another promise, the one about the directors sitting on a flattop out in the Pacific being photographed.

"You can tell them," Greg said, "that all the flattops are in use."

He couldn't get his mind away from the conference with Dr. Kerensky. He said again for the tenth time, "You were great. You handled it better than even a top diplomat would have. It all goes to show what ordinary people can do just by sitting down—people who aren't influenced by recent history or a strict interpretation of a government's foreign policy or world or domestic politics. Two people who want to do what is right and simply talk it out. Maybe we need the diplomats and ambassadors, although at times I doubt it."

She thanked him. "You're kind to say that." She hesitated.

"You've got something on your mind?"

She nodded. "Maybe I shouldn't say it, but when the State Department woman asked to bring the Russian scientists on board—I know how it was at the time, with all the spying in the Silicon Valley—but I think it's important that we have the cultural missions, including the scientists. For the most part, it's ordinary people meeting ordinary people. We may get a spy or two now and then, but overall, it helps us to know that most Russians, and for them, most Americans, are pretty much the same—people struggling to make a living, hoping for a better world. All through history, it's usually been governments and not people who have made the wars."

He shook his head. "I don't know, Lynne. I don't know."

They came back to the same pier where five days before only a miracle of God had saved them. They came back to bands playing, and banners fluttering in the soft Hawaiian breeze, and thousands shouting and waving. He stood on the deck with his arm through Lynne's, a gulp in his throat and a hard pounding of his heart. He wanted to cry out, "By heavens, we did it! We did it!"

The television, radio and newspaper crews moved in. Then they were being shoved toward a microphone where the mayor stood ready to welcome them. On the periphery he saw Laura struggling to get through, and he stopped and called out to her. The crowd parted and she was headed for his arms when she saw the bandaged one. She started to cry, but he assured her he was all right.

She had a package beautifully wrapped and tied with a big, red bow. "It's from Rambunctious," she said excitedly. "He sent you his most precious possession."

He was being pushed toward the microphone and at the same time, was tearing into the paper. He opened the box and there was a much-jawed bone. He broke into a boisterous laugh and when it came time to speak he held the bone up in his left hand to show what "the best friend I have in the world" had sent him. The crowd roared.

He never knew what else he said. He remembered Lotus kissing him. And all of a sudden he knew Barbara was there, somewhere.

That night there was a ball up north of Diamond Head at the Kahala Hilton, a luxury hotel so difficult to find that the management should furnish Seeing Eye dogs or radar. All of the directors from Carson Mining were there and about half from Massachusetts Diversified, including big, rough, old Karl Neustadt, without whom none of this would have happened.

J. M. Radcliffe was there, too, reminding Greg that he, Radcliffe, had been right that only by the grace of God had World War III been averted. "I knew it, I knew it," he said. "You almost started it." Still, he was not above accepting plaudits as if he alone had made one of the last great breakthroughs in history. Nor was he above accepting an invitation to the White House.

Bob McLean showed up, too, shy as always, and despite his wealth, a humble, ordinary guy. He renounced all credit. He just happened to be at the White House that night; he just happened to mention the problem to the President. Greg thought: *The people who accomplish things in this world are often the quiet ones.*

Not one of the Mass. directors mentioned that they had stopped all financing of the project. When asked about it by a newspaperwoman, Radcliffe said there had been a "slight misunderstanding" one time, but it hadn't amounted to anything.

To Greg's great joy, Laura claimed him for the first dance. He was in a rented tuxedo that Lynne had come up with at the last moment. The right sleeve dangled. He couldn't get the bandaged arm through it. It was surprising how in the excitement of the evening the hurt had vanished.

Laura rattled away about her grades—all A's—and about Rambunctious who missed Greg and, according to her, checked his bed every night.

About Lotus: "She's nice. I like her so much . . . like I do Lynne, but they're sure different, aren't they? Lotus is exotic. I've never known anyone like her."

Once he had accused her of having the fastest mouth in the West, and she was demonstrating as much tonight.

A couple of dances later, he discovered Lotus in his arms. She was wearing a subdued red cheongsam set off with black touches, silver Buddhist temple earrings from Thailand and a temple pin on the mandarin collar.

She called up her sad voice, "You no need Lotus? No more Hong Kong office?"

"Always need Lotus." He laughed. "Now you've got me talking pidgin English. I want you to find a site for a refinery in Asia—and build it."

"Okay, I build it. You come Hong Kong? See me?"

"Every chance I get."

"Maybe wife get well. You come, we go to bed."

He shook his head over the logic of that.

She continued, "You give fringe benefit?"

"Sorry, no fringe benefit."

"Because I Eurasian lady?"

"I've told you so many times, we're not married."

"Okay, if insist, I marry you again. Got one marriage paper already. Remember? How many times I got marry you?"

Why was it he felt so damn good when he was around Lotus?

As the night wore on, he kept glancing in Lynne's direction. She was the center of attention; the "heroine" of the adventure. Every director had danced with her and half of Oahu's luminaries.

Finally he cut in. "Remember me?"

She looked up with dancing, bright eyes. They were adoring eyes, and tonight she let it all show. She was in a long, black skirt and a ruffled white blouse. Black obsidian earrings from Mexico bobbed about playfully. Her hair was beautifully cut and styled and for the first time she wore delicately applied makeup.

She asked, "What were you and Lotus talking about so merrily?"

Greg acted nonchalant. "Oh, just business. About fringe benefits."

She put on a deep frown. "I might've known. You men are all the same. You like to brag about your conquests—especially to other women."

"She's the one negotiating. Not I."

"But you were loving every minute of it. I could tell."

"Strictly business. It's hot in here. Let's get some fresh air."

Outside, they drifted past the porpoise youngsters still frolicking about in their pool and the giant turtles fast asleep. They laughed over two penguins standing as rigid as plaster-of-paris figures. To make sure they were real, she bent down to touch one and was told off in vile language.

Crossing a grassy area, they came to a sandy beach where flaming luau torches cast playful shadows that hinted of tropical nights in tales long ago told. Within swimming distance was a toy island dotted with small palms softly backlighted by the glow of a moon up on the distant horizon.

For minutes they stood staring in wonderment at the thundering, billowing waves that crested high and fell so suddenly. As millions before them for untold centuries, they were held spellbound by the tremendous force and power, and the mysticism of it all that no one could explain.

She looked up at him longingly. "I wish things were different for us."

He continued in his bantering tone, "If you think I'd ever fall for you . . ."

She was shocked. "I didn't mean—"

He added quickly, "I'd like to think that was a proposal."

"Greg!"

"To brag a little, my second for the night. How about that?"

She was furious. "You're nothing but a—"

"—male chauvinist."

He slipped his hand into hers. "I can't ask you to wait, Lynne."

She couldn't believe what she was hearing.

He continued, "It wouldn't be fair." He had trouble getting the words out. "I don't know how to tell this to a woman I can't love now . . . but some day . . ."

It took her a moment to organize her thoughts. "Let me then," she said softly. "I know you and Barbara have had a marriage few couples ever have, and you can't walk away and leave her after all you've meant to each other for all these years."

She hesitated. "I don't expect you to, Greg. I wouldn't want you to. It wouldn't be right."

She glanced up. "Don't look like that. It worries me. I'm not exactly a dream woman, you know. I can do some things well, but when it comes to being female, let's face it, I don't have it. Lotus does—and she's going to make a wonderful wife . . ."

"Not for me." He was blunt and positive. "A man may think he wants a beautiful body and all those great nights in bed with a sex kitten—but life's more than that. You love for many reasons besides sex—not that it doesn't mean a lot to me—but any man who thinks about it at all would want . . . well, a woman like you."

She looked up at him through misty eyes. The roar of surf almost drowned her out. "I'll be waiting, Greg."

He nodded and pressed her hand tightly.